PAST RECALL

Jack Nevin has had a successful and adventurous career which, most recently, has taken him to the trouble spots of Eastern Europe and the Middle East. He is now a full-time writer and lives with his family near Exmoor.

'A white-hot storyteller' CLIVE CUSSLER

'Not only is this book utterly compulsive, but also topical – a real winner' *Maxim*

'Nevin takes you through the hell of a loving father dragged before the courts, and the damning effect on family relationships ... there's a superb twist at the end of a nail biting read'
Peterborough Evening Telegraph

JACK NEVIN

PAST RECALL

HarperCollins*Publishers*

HarperCollins*Publishers*
77–85 Fulham Palace Road,
Hammersmith, London W6 8JB

This paperback edition 1998

1 3 5 7 9 8 6 4 2

First published in Great Britain by
HarperCollins*Publishers* 1997

Copyright © Jack Nevin 1997

The Author asserts the moral right to
be identified as the author of this work

ISBN 0 00 649834 5

Set in Sabon and Photina by
Rowland Phototypesetting Ltd,
Bury St Edmunds, Suffolk

Printed and bound in Great Britain by
Clays Ltd, St Ives plc

I am deeply grateful to Richard Rains, for his invaluable help and unflagging good humour in the face of my totally unreasonable demands, and to Heather Morgan for her warmth and tolerance. Both of you responded to the demands of an unscrupulous stranger with a generosity far beyond the call of duty!

Thanks also to the following, whose patience in the face of my interrogations made such an important contribution to this book: Mark Wagner, Philip Drinkwater, Richard Powell, John Wood, Jon Weall, Julianne O'Leary, Rachel Mounsey, David Martin.

My gratitude, too, to David Woolf, Richard Burgess, Margaret Mylett and Clare Trevelyan Thomas for the introductions.

One

Matthew Stenner paused, anxious, his big square hand resting on the glossy mahogany of the banister rail. Another flurry of sleet slapped wetly at the window. Grimacing, he turned and strode across the wide landing. A sofa stood beneath the window, barring his way. Irritation flickered in his face as he leaned forward, one knee sinking into the silk fabric. Even now, he could not suppress a tight little memory of the brief argument about the sofa. He had been unable to see the point of a sofa halfway up the stairs, however grand the staircase. Liz, and the decorator, had insisted. The space cried out for it. Liz had won. The space had got the sofa, and for the last dozen years he had not been able to look out of the window without a threatening twinge in his back. He leaned closer, his face almost touching the glass in the effort to see through the crust of slush.

The cobbled courtyard, with its border of perfectly tailored shrubs, was bathed in the glow of the floodlights set along the parapet of the house. A ring of cars stood with their noses clustered around the circular flowerbed that was the centrepiece of the courtyard. Matt smiled wryly to himself. Their friends were a more predictable bunch than any of them would have liked to think. The cars, already cloaked with a half-inch layer of slushy ice, were the expensive but resolutely practical transport of rural money – Volvos, Range Rovers, a four-wheel-drive Audi. The Ford Escort he was looking for was not there. He glanced quickly at his watch. Camilla would never be this late without phoning. Frowning, his mouth twisting in disappointment, he straightened and continued down the stairs towards the hum of voices.

He paused on the bottom stair, surveying the wide hall. The only light was the muted glow from the dozens of tiny red lanterns draped on the ten-foot Christmas tree. Swags of evergreen and red ribbons hung over the pictures on the walls. It was pure Charles Dickens.

Matt's fingers were on the drawing-room door handle when he spun and strode out into the vestibule to stand staring through the bevelled panes of the front door. The sleet was worse, almost snow now. He could barely see as far as the parked cars. He stood for several seconds, staring anxiously into the murk. Then, with another glance at his watch he turned away and walked quickly back inside.

A ragged, laughing cheer greeted him. A few people clapped. Grinning, he raised a hand in acknowledgement. 'Don't,' he said. 'It'll go to my head.'

'It went to your head *years* ago,' a woman responded with jaunty reasonableness, from near the hearth.

Matt gave her a theatrical scowl. 'You could always read me like a book, Annie,' he said, smiling broadly. She was still looking at him as he turned to let his eyes sweep the room.

'Sorry I'm late, everybody. Bloody phone. Does everybody have a drink?' As he spoke he caught the eye of a plump woman in a makeshift uniform of black skirt and cardigan. 'Celia, are you leaving me to die of thirst?'

The woman threaded her way through the crowd, beaming happily, and proffered the tray she carried. Smiling, Matt plucked a glass of champagne from it. 'Thanks, Celia.' He drank off half the glass, sighed

2

appreciatively, and turned to move into the knot of people nearest to him.

One of the men, a big-name London libel lawyer married to one of Liz's obscurely aristocratic circle of charity activists, thrust out a hand. 'Congratulations, Matt. Great news.'

The rest of the group, mostly in their forties and fifties, the women in cocktail dresses, the men expensively casual in sports jackets and slacks, echoed the words.

'Thanks, David. Thanks, all of you,' Matt said, surprised to find himself a little embarrassed by their warmth. He shrugged. 'It is sort of nice.'

One of the women laughed. 'Oh, Matt! Sort of *nice*!' She shook her head. 'A book sells ten million copies, and the best he can do is "nice". It's absolutely bloody brilliant.'

He shrugged again. 'The thing is, it was written so long ago it's difficult to feel any ... *connection* with it.' He laughed, swallowing more champagne. 'Although the cheques do help!'

Matt remained with the group for a few more jokes, before detaching himself with practised grace to begin drifting among the shifting clusters of people. But every few moments, he glanced at his watch. His smiles grew quicker. Unease began to play around his eyes. For goodness' sake, where was the girl?

Over the heads of the crowd, he sought Liz, catching sight of her back as she disappeared, moving with restrained haste, through the double doors connecting with the dining room.

Even in his anxiety Matt could not contain a smile as he watched her body move under the material of her dress. He could hardly complain if she were too busy to talk to him. He had made her late. An hour earlier they had been getting dressed for the party. He had emerged, towelling himself, from the bathroom to find her pulling on the dress, her head hidden among the folds of dark purple crêpe de Chine. Even after more than twenty years of marriage there were still moments when the sight of Liz made his throat constrict. He had watched spellbound as she struggled into the dress, unaware of him looking on. At forty-five and after two children, her figure had the same compact, athletic quality that had so attracted him when they first met, seated side by side on a flight to Toronto. With her narrow hips and her raised arms pulling her small breasts taut, she could have been seventeen years old. She dragged the dress down over her shoulders, her face lighting up at the sight of him, enjoying the thought that he had been watching her. He looked on as she smoothed the dress over her hips, the soft cling of the silk subtly emphasising the shape of her body. Before either of them really knew it the dress lay in a soft heap at the foot of the bed. Now, Liz was twenty minutes late with her preparations, but at least they could both concentrate on the party.

He worked the room systematically, returning the eager handshakes, presenting his cheek for the craning women to plant congratulatory kisses. Only a few guests, the two or three men who joined him for twice-weekly work-outs on the weight machines by the pool, and the hard core of charity wives who made up Liz's regular Wednesday gatherings, did not seem to need to touch him, as though his success made him some sort of talisman.

Although he knew the congratulations and the guests' pleasure in his achievement were genuine, the initial glow soon wore off. For Matt, who preferred listening to others to talking about himself, reliving the high points in his career soon began to grow tedious. With a laugh, he disengaged himself from yet another kiss and drifted clear of the group. Taking another glass from Celia's tray, he raised his head, again seeking Liz. She had not reappeared. He looked down at his watch and then at the door to the hall. He was standing, undecided, his eyes on the door, wondering whether to go and check the courtyard again, when he felt a hand on his arm. He turned to find Annie Trevellyn smiling up at him, with his own son, Mark, at her shoulder. Mark was hand in hand with a slender young woman of his own age. Her pretty but rather long, horsy face was framed by straight, shoulder-length hair, almost the same dark blonde as Mark's own.

Annie spoke, her expressive, intelligent face clouded. 'Something wrong, Matt? You've been on edge since you walked in.'

He did not answer immediately, instead smiling lopsidedly, and stooping to kiss the air an inch from the other young woman's cheek. 'Hello, Jane. Glad you could make it,' he said warmly. He straightened and looked Annie in the eye, shrugging. 'It's Camilla,' he said quietly. 'She was supposed to be here hours ago.' He swept a hand at the window. 'I hate to think of her broken down in this filth.'

Mark looked at Jane and laughed. 'Come on, Dad. She's a big girl. She would have phoned if she had a problem.'

Matt's smile was brief. 'That's part of what's worrying me. She knows she's expected. Surely she could have called us.'

Mark smiled knowingly at Annie. 'Meet the mother hen. It's the end of term. She's probably gone for a drink and forgotten the time.'

'Thanks,' Matt answered sourly. 'That's a very reassuring thought. My only daughter's late driving home on an evening when visibility's down to twenty

5

feet, on freezing roads, because she spent the afternoon in a *pub*!'

Annie touched his arm. 'Come on, Matt! You know what Mark means. Nobody's suggesting she's plastered. And this weather will have slowed her down.' Her mobile, intelligent features exploded into sudden laughter. 'You were only upstairs, but you still managed to keep us all waiting for forty minutes!'

Her eyes were on Matt's face as she spoke. For just a fleeting instant, amid her laughter, they were still. Laughing himself, Matt glanced at Mark and Jane. They were looking at each other. 'I was on the phone,' he said softly.

'You weren't trying to get Camilla all that time?' Mark protested.

Matt shook his head. 'No. Harry called. My American agent,' he added, in response to Jane's quizzical expression.

Mark was looking expectantly at him. 'And?'

Matt beckoned them half a step closer. Despite his efforts, his face split in a grin. 'It looks as if it's on.'

Mark's mouth opened to mime a cheer. He clenched both fists and shook them in the air in front of him.

'Can I share the secret?' Annie looked from one to the other.

Matt glanced around him and shuffled closer, so that their heads were almost touching. 'Does the name Stan Kowalski mean anything to you?'

Annie and Jane exchanged blank looks. 'Kowalski?' Annie repeated, grimacing with concentration. 'Oh, of course. Ko*wal*ski! The animation man?'

Matt nodded, leaning so close that he felt her hair against his forehead. 'That's the man. The one who did *The Last Eagle*.'

'I remember now. There was a big legal furore a

6

couple of years ago, wasn't there? About whether he'd stolen their techniques, when he walked out on, or was fired by, Disney?'

Matt smiled. 'That's the lawyer in you talking! To most people he's just the man who made the biggest grossing animated film in history. That's what *really* pissed Disney off.'

Annie opened her mouth to answer. Before she could do so, a voice boomed in Matt's ear. 'Disney? Did I hear the magic word?'

A glint of irritation flashed in Matt's face. In Annie's eyes something moved far, far below the surface. A plea, perhaps, or an apology. Then, Roger Trevellyn, her husband, the same height as Matt but with twenty pounds more flesh around his belt, was bellying his way, drink first, among them.

'Is that what the conspiracy's about?' he asked, at the same time gulping down half a glass of champagne, dabbing away the drop that dribbled on his chin with the back of a beefy paw. 'You finally flogged something to Disney? There's no stopping you tonight. Congratulations again.'

Matt's lips formed a smile. His tone was even. 'It *was* sort of confidential, Roger. And the deal's not done yet. My agent's discussing it, that's all. And one thing I've learned with these big deals, especially where the film world's concerned, is that the only thing you can count on is money in the bank. Until then, it's all hot air. And, by the way, it's not Disney Harry's talking to. It's Stan Kowalski.'

Roger gave a pitying bray. 'Stan who? Surely it's Disney you want for your stuff?' He grabbed another glass of champagne from Celia's tray, his empty one toppling as he put it down. He spoke with the fresh glass already tilted to his lips. 'If I were you I'd go straight to the people with the clout.'

7

Matt nodded, looking into his own glass. 'Thanks for the advice, Roger. I'll pass it on to Harry. He might not have thought of it. By the way, Kowalski made *The Last Eagle* after he left Disney. Do you know how much it has taken, worldwide?'

Roger shrugged, grinning round his glass as he drank off another gulp of champagne. 'Ask me something about corporate finance. I think the last time we went to the pictures must have been before we were married. Couldn't stand all the proles eating Maltesers. Could we?' He made a motion with his arm which fell just short of a jab in Annie's ribs.

'No, we couldn't, could we?' she said, her lips barely moving.

Matt took a mouthful of champagne and let it roll around his teeth. 'It's taken somewhere over four hundred million dollars. So far.'

'Really?' Roger threw back the last of his drink and waggled the empty glass in a peremptory summons to Celia. 'I still say if I were you I'd go for Disney,' he grunted sulkily. 'They've got the track record.'

'Merchandising probably brings in twice that figure again. They sold four million copies of the book in America alone. Do you have any idea what that amounts to in royalties?' The moment he had spoken, Matt was angry with himself. Annie stood with her eyes lowered, the muscles of her jaw taut. The last thing in the world Annie needed was to be reminded of what an easy target her husband was. Taking advantage of the moment of silence while Roger pressed a handful of nuts into his mouth, Matt leaned close to Mark. 'Mark, do you want to try Camilla's numbers again?' His voice was low, conversational, but with an unmistakable note of anxiety in it that even Roger caught.

'I tried fifteen minutes ago. Still no answer.'

'Did you try her mobile?'

'Sure. Same thing. Come *on*, Dad. She'll be here.'

Matt looked again at his watch. It was past nine o'clock. 'Yeah? You'd think she would have called, though, if she knew she was going to be this late, wouldn't you? She'd promised to help Mum.'

Mark's rangy shoulders rose and fell. 'Her mobile might not be working. Or she's let the battery go flat.'

Matt chewed his lip. 'She's never done it before.'

Mark laughed. 'God, Dad, what does that prove? She might have just left it in the flat.'

'I suppose so.' A sudden surge in the noise level in the room made him look up sharply. Individual voices were becoming more strident. People were starting to get drunk. He took a step back, withdrawing from the tight circle. 'I'd better go and see if we're going to get anything to eat.'

The dining room was an illustration from *Homes and Gardens*. Candles flickered in iron sconces, their light licking softly at the polished mahogany of the furniture, glinting on the crystal and silver set on the huge refectory table. Heavy-framed oil paintings lined the walls, many of them Liz's work, including the portrait of Matt that smiled down from the chimney breast. Matt strode past it all without even seeing it and burst into the kitchen.

Liz was stooped at an open oven, the cords of an apron loosely knotted over the crêpe de Chine dress. As she worked she was talking quickly to the two women who shared the kitchen with her. One of them, in an improvised uniform like Celia's, was spooning sauce over plates loaded with intricate arrangements of shellfish and shredded vegetables.

The other woman wore an ankle-length black dress protected by Matt's own butcher-stripe apron. As Matt entered Liz turned to speak to her. 'Rachel, the meat's going to be ready in twenty minutes. Would you like to get everybody seated?'

Nodding, Rachel turned away from commentating over the other woman's shoulder and reached to unfasten her apron. Matt watched her back as she lifted the apron over her head, taking care not to disarrange her hair. Twenty years ago he had thought of his sister-in-law as an attractive, though already sharp-tongued, woman. Now, eleven years after his brother's death, her body had grown bulky and her face had hardened, the years of self-pity sculpting the muscles into taut planes. Although only two years older than Matt she had already begun to look as she would as an old lady.

'Hold it, Rachel.' He held up a restraining hand, turning to address Liz's back. 'Can't it wait another few minutes? Camilla's still not here.'

Liz straightened. Her face was filmed with sweat. 'No. Matt, it can't. Really,' she added, catching his look. 'It'll be a terrible mess if we wait any longer.'

'But we can't start without her. She'll be so disappointed.'

'For heaven's sake, Matt,' said Rachel, 'she's old enough to be here on time. Liz may have sprung this evening on *you* but Camilla's known about it for months. She was supposed to help. I don't know what Liz would have done if I hadn't been here.'

She was drawing breath to go on when Matt broke in, speaking to Liz. 'She's not answering her phones. I'm worried shitless.'

Liz moved to him and took his hand. 'Come on, Matt,' she said with gentle, affectionate mockery in her eyes. 'Camilla's not your darling little Shirley Temple any more. She's a full-grown woman. It's the end of term. She's probably gone for a drink and completely forgotten the time. Didn't it ever happen to you, you abstinent creature?'

He looked at his watch, and dropped his voice to a murmur. 'Seriously, Liz, I'm worried. The people here tonight are her friends, too. She wouldn't deliberately be late. Supposing she's had an accident?'

Liz shivered. 'Don't! We would have heard about it.'

'Well, what if the car's broken down? It's filthy out there.'

Liz sighed. 'We would have heard about that, too. She's coming from Oxford, not Murmansk. She could find *some* way to get to a phone.' She indicated the oven. 'Please, darling, it's all going to be a disaster if we wait any longer. Apart from anything else there are one or two people out there beginning to be the worse for wear.' She kissed him on the cheek as he grimaced assent. 'I've put a lot of work into tonight. I want people to know how proud of you I am. And not even Camilla should be allowed to spoil it. Please, we *have* to start.'

'Okay, I guess you're right.'

It took Celia and a helper to carry in the main course, an awesome roast of wild boar, its crackling craggy in the candlelight.

Matt accepted the plate Celia put in front of him and looked up to catch Liz's eye. He shook his head in affectionate disbelief. Once again, she had excelled herself. Guests were already making swooning noises as they began to eat. He cut a tiny piece and, with a conscious effort, put it into his mouth.

He had eaten the first two courses in virtual silence, hardly tasting the subtle and exotic flavours of the food, or of his best wines that had so delighted the guests. Every few seconds, he had stolen surreptitious glances, first at his watch, and then at the empty chair halfway down the table.

He was still chewing listlessly on the first bite of the boar when Roger, putting down his glass with a thump that sent a couple of pounds' worth of fifteen-year-old Bordeaux splashing onto the tablecloth, jerked his chin at the empty seat. 'Doesn't look as if the prodigal's going to make it, after all. Bit ... *légère* ... of her, isn't it, for such an auspicious occasion as this?' He gave auspicious an extra syllable.

Matt gave an unconvincing shrug. 'Today's the start of the Christmas vacation. Maybe something held her up. An end-of-term crack-smoking party, for instance. You read the *Telegraph*, Roger. You know how it is with today's youth.' Roger snorted happily at the response, impervious to the edge of irritation.

Liz and Annie caught it, flicking quick glances at each other. Annie placed a hand on Matt's sleeve and said softly, 'Why don't you go and give her numbers another try?'

'What's the point? We tried half a dozen times. They aren't answering.'

'They *weren't*. That was an hour ago. Is the phone at her digs in her room?'

He shook his head. 'Downstairs. In the entry.'

'Give it another try, then. Maybe somebody else will be there who can put your mind at rest.' Matt hesitated, glancing at the woman who sat at his other side. Annie smiled across at her. 'Just do it. Believe me, it's not going to be much fun for either Alice or me sitting through the rest of the meal with you in this state.'

He hesitated a moment longer before wiping his napkin across his lips and, with a muttered apology, pushed himself to his feet.

*　　*　　*

Matt shoved open the door. Liz was leaning back in her chair, giving Celia room to clear her plate from in front of her. The words she had been addressing to Roger withered instantly on her lips. Her eyes searched Matt's face. Total silence had fallen on the room. Every eye was on him. It came to him with a sudden shock how stricken he must look. With a self-deprecating laugh, he shook his head. 'No, no. That's just my anxious father face. There's no disaster.' His gaze focused down to Liz. The smile had not spread to his eyes. 'I finally got one of the house-sharers. Luckily, she'd just come back to collect something. Otherwise the place seems to be deserted.'

Liz frowned. 'So Camilla *is* on her way?'

'I asked the girl to try her door, to see if Camilla might be in her room.' He moved his hands in an apologetic gesture. 'I don't know . . . if she might have been taken ill or something.'

Liz shuddered. 'Matt! She *wasn't* in there, was she? Was the girl sure?'

'Absolutely. She went inside and looked around.' Seeing Liz's brow knit, he nodded. 'Right. Her door was standing *open*. You know the lock. All she has to do is slam it behind her.'

Liz was sitting forward, her hands at her mouth. 'What was it? Burglary?'

'The girl didn't think so. She said it just looked as though Camilla had gone out to the shops or something. The computer was still on. There were glasses on the floor. And two bottles.'

'Perhaps she *did* see a friend for a drink, then.'

'And got too plastered to remember to shut the door?' He was speaking only to Liz now, as though the other people in the room had ceased to exist.

Liz shuddered. 'If she did, then I hope to God she's *not* driving home.' She gnawed at her lower lip.

'Unless . . . unless she really *has* had an accident.'

'Mmm.' Matt pulled back his lips in a grimace. 'I tried the police. They don't have any report. What bothers me is that she doesn't have her phone with her. The girl saw it lying in her room. So, if she *is* stuck in a ditch somewhere she wouldn't have any way of letting us know.'

Roger's voice came jarringly loud in the hush. 'Don't want to seem to be teaching Grandmother, Matt, but if you ask me the best thing you can do is sit down and carry on eating. Camilla's a free-spirited young woman. She'll turn up when she's ready. Nobody could be lying undiscovered in their car without anyone finding them. Not between Oxford and the *Cotswolds*, for Christ's sake! No sense spoiling the party.' He waved a paw clumsily at Matt's empty chair, grinning around him. 'Camilla's probably in the pub waiting till we've all gone home. Who could blame her, not wanting to eat with a bunch of old farts like us?'

Annie, in a flash of irritation, opened her mouth to reproach her husband. Matt laid a finger gently on her shoulder. 'You're right, Roger,' he said good-naturedly. 'I guess there's not a thing we can do.' Inclining his head first at Liz, then at the company, he lowered himself slowly back into his seat. Celia eyed the plate of congealed food in front of him. Ruefully waving it away, he poured himself some more wine. 'Sorry, everybody.' He made an effortful smile. 'Liz, how about the dessert? Are we allowed to see it now?' He looked around. 'It's been a better-kept secret than the Manhattan project. I haven't been allowed in the kitchen for a week.'

Smiling, but with the worry still tugging at the flesh around her eyes, Liz rose and followed Celia towards the kitchen. 'Can somebody blow out the candles, then?'

They sat in the darkness for a full minute, the fidgety silence broken by one or two tentative attempts at jokes. Then, the door flew wide and Liz swept in, behind her Celia and the other helper, holding between them a huge platter. On it, a reproduction of Matt's most successful book, four times its actual size. The cover of the book was an exact reproduction, colour for colour, of the original. Half open, it revealed a fan of wafer-thin chocolate pages. Both sides of each page were covered in tiny script in hair-thin white icing. He didn't need to look closer to know that it was a verbatim extract from the book. The perfectionist in Liz would have permitted nothing less. He sought her face and laughed aloud, his first genuine laugh of the evening, then sprang to his feet and strode towards her. Liz, too, was on her feet, running eagerly to meet him. Sobbing with happiness, she threw herself against his chest. A lump rose in his own throat as he folded her tight in his arms. Swallowing, he looked down into her radiant face, the tears that she could not keep back glinting in the candlelight. His chest tightening, he bent to kiss her.

The insistent clamour of the doorbell brought his head snapping up again. For a moment they were quite still, staring into each other's faces as the laughter in them died. An instant later, the door was slamming wildly on its hinges as Matt charged from the room.

In a few strides he was through the hall and into the vestibule, straining to make out the figure on the porch, no more than a blur through the heavily misted glass. His heart pounding, Matt snatched at the tarnished copper doorknob, as big as his fist. In his haste he fumbled the awkward lock, his hand slipping. Through the streaming glass, he saw the silhouette reach out once again to the bellpush. The harsh dringing splashed like acid on his raw nerves. Disappointment and fear flooded his throat, stifling him. Camilla would have let herself in, using her key. Gripping the knob so hard his knuckles blanched, he tore the door open.

'Good God!' His mouth half open, he stepped out onto the porch. 'What happened? Camilla, sweetheart, what in God's name has happened to you?'

Two

Behind him, the jangle of the doorbell continued to echo through the house as Camilla went on leaning on the bell. With an exclamation, Matt darted forward and gripped her by the arms, forcing her hand from the button as he dragged her into the warmth of the house. 'Camilla! Darling! Please! What's happened to you?' She stared dumbly ahead, her eyes on a level with his chest but blank, unseeing. He flexed his knees, bringing his face level with hers. Still she looked through him, her eyes staring, unfocused. Gripping her arms tight, he gave her a sharp shake. Her head rocked, unresisting. 'Camilla! Please talk to me! What is it?' As he spoke he raised his eyes to look over her shoulder. The parked cars were under two inches of fast-freezing slush. There was no sign of the Escort, only footprints stretching towards the gates. 'Where's the car? Did you have an accident?'

His eyes went back to her. For the first time he fully took in the picture she presented. Her hair was plastered to her head, a web of icy slush woven into the crown. Water streamed down her face. Thin crusts of slush lay on each shoulder. Her clothes, a thin T-shirt and a skirt of flowered cotton, clung to her, saturated, outlining her body in indecent detail. With a groan, Matt dragged off his jacket and swung it around her, pulling her deeper into the vestibule.

He kicked the door shut, hugging Camilla to him, shuddering as he flicked at her hair and shoulders, sending the ice slithering onto the coir matting. 'You're frozen stiff. Let me get that shirt off you.'

Silent and indifferent, she allowed him to peel the T-shirt over her head, her arms falling lifelessly back to her sides. She gave no sign of knowing he was there, neither responding nor recoiling as, his face etched with anxiety, he kneaded her body through the jacket, trying to rub some warmth into the slender, quivering frame. His voice was tender but hoarse with urgency. 'Please, Camilla, tell me, has anybody . . . has anything happened to you?'

Very slowly, her head moved from side to side. At the same time a great shudder racked her body. It could have been returning warmth or it could have been something else.

Matt held her closer to him, letting out a long breath of relief. 'Thank God for that, at least. But what *did* happen? Did the car break down? Where is it?'

She shook her head, again the slow, trancelike movement, her face still blank. 'Oxford,' she murmured in a textureless voice.

Matt frowned. 'Oxford? Is there something wrong with it?' He tried to smile. 'I'll murder that damned dealer.' The attempted smile withered before her vacant look. 'Why didn't you call? I would have driven over and collected you.' He looked her up and down. 'How on earth *did* you get here?'

'I hitched,' she answered in a hollow, bored voice.

He dragged his eyes from her face with an effort and looked her up and down, seeking the scratches, the torn clothing, that would confirm the fear that surged back to him. 'But . . . did somebody . . . did they try to hurt you?'

Again, the slow swing of her head. 'It was a woman driver.'

'But how . . . I mean . . .' He made a sweeping back-

18

hand gesture. 'Did *she* . . . I mean, how did you get in this state?'

'She dropped me outside Ashworth.'

'However did you get from there?'

'How do you think?'

'You walked?' His voice was hoarse, his eyes flicking past her to the door and the freezing night. 'In this? It's five miles. More.'

He was still speaking as she stepped suddenly out of his grip. Walking with a strange, stiff-legged stride, her arms hanging almost still at her sides, she moved into the hall, her drained face taking on a sudden ruddy glow from the light of the Christmas tree.

Recovering his poise, Matt followed, almost cannoning into the back of her as she halted abruptly. Across the hall Liz and Mark stood side by side in the open doorway to the drawing room. Mark's smile of relief and welcome mingled with a deep, shifting frown. Liz's face was filled with pure alarm. Then it was swept away by a smile that appeared to well irresistibly from deep inside her, bringing her whole face alight with love. She took a step forward, her arms outstretched, the smile seeming to bathe her daughter in its glow. 'Darling! This is lovely. At last, you're here. Everybody's been missing you.'

Nothing in her face undermined the gladness of the smile, nothing indicated that she even noticed her daughter's dripping hair, or Matt's jacket hanging open over her bare breasts. Nobody but he would have sensed the tinge of wariness in her step, as though she were approaching an injured animal that might suddenly show its teeth. Matt allowed himself the beginning of a smile that glowed stronger as Liz threw open her arms to clasp her daughter to her.

With an ugly, gnawing sound in her throat, Camilla spun away and ran, stumbling, up the wide curve of the stairs. As she turned, icy droplets flew from her hair across Matt's face, making him flinch.

They watched in dumb shock as Camilla raced wildly away, her sodden shoes making soft sucking noises as she ran. Mark moved first. With a sharp cry, he sprinted from where he had been standing, rooted, in the doorway.

'Come on,' Matt rasped, snatching Liz by the hand and dragging her in pursuit.

The three of them gained the top landing just in time to see the pale flash of Camilla's back at the far end of the corridor as she reached the door of her room. She hurled herself inside, and the door shut with a slam that shook the air around them, shocking them to a standstill.

Matt's eyes closed. 'Oh fuck!' he said in a dull, emphatic voice. He repeated the words three or four times before slowly opening his eyes and turning to the others. Liz was chewing at her lip, the flesh around her eyes puckering. 'No,' he whispered, placing his arm over her shoulders. 'Don't cry, Liz. Please.' He began herding them along the corridor towards the door. 'Not yet.'

The three of them stood grouped outside Camilla's room, their eyes searching each other's faces as they listened. No sound came to them. Matt leaned closer, his lips almost touching the wood. 'Camilla.' He waited and then repeated the name, louder and more forcefully. 'Camilla! Can we come in? Please.'

They waited. The only sound, drifting up the back stairs, was that of crockery being shifted. 'Camilla.' Matt's knuckles cracked against the door. 'Camilla, please. Open the door.' From inside the room there came a sound that might have been the mattress creaking and then again silence.

Matt dropped his hand to grasp the doorknob. He

looked questioningly at Liz. She nodded, tight-lipped. 'Camilla, we're going to come in.' He waited a moment and then turned the knob. The door resisted. Matt sighed. 'It's bolted.' He spoke low, tapping a finger at the door at the level where they knew the bolt to be. He had installed it himself, years earlier, at Camilla's request, one of the first harbingers of adolescence. With its tiny screws it was designed for privacy, not for security. There was an immense, weary sadness in the movement as his shoulders rose and fell. 'Shall I break it?' He sounded unbearably tired. Liz nodded, blinking back tears.

With another sigh, Matt drew back a few inches from the door, gathering himself. His face sombre, he set his feet, rounded his shoulder against the impact, and slammed his rangy frame forward, aiming his weight at a point a foot beyond the door. It opened with a screech of tearing wood.

Liz and Mark hurried past him, making for the bed, where Camilla lay face down. She still wore her soaked skirt and shoes. Water from her hair had spread into the quilt cover, forming a darker cusp in the crisp white linen. As Matt came up to stand at her shoulder, Liz bent and stroked the drenched hair. 'Camilla?' Apart from the slow rise and fall of her back Camilla might have been dead. Liz leaned closer. 'Camilla,' she murmured, fiddling with the wet hair, lifting it off Camilla's shoulder, squeezing it gently so that drops ran between her knuckles onto the quilt. 'Please, darling, you must speak to us. Has something horrible happened? To you? To somebody you care about, perhaps?'

Camilla lay motionless, her face buried deep in the duvet. Liz looked up at Matt, her eyes pleading. Matt stepped closer, a hand extended to caress Camilla's back. 'Camilla?' The touch of his fingers sent a shiver wrenching through her like an electric charge, making her outstretched arms leap and twitch. Matt withdrew his hand, a wounded look on his face. 'The poor girl's freezing.' He turned to Mark. 'Can you find her some pyjamas? And a towel?'

As Mark ran to comply, Matt took Camilla by the shoulders. Another seismic shiver ran through her. Very gently, murmuring reassurance, he lifted her, trying to turn her onto her back. He reared back in surprise as Camilla gave a moan and, in a convulsive movement, shook herself free, bringing her knees and arms together into a foetal crouch.

'Please, darling. You're like ice. You must get those clothes off and get dry.'

As he spoke, his hand found the fastening of her skirt. He slipped the button. Feeling the movement, Camilla gave a shrill cry and clawed at his hand, ripping it away from her. Matt let her do it, looking helplessly at Liz.

She shouldered him aside. Very tentatively, she leaned over her daughter, her face close to Camilla's ear. 'Dad's right, my love. You must get dry, and warm.' Mark came to her side, a heap of towels and pyjamas in his arms. Without taking her eyes from her daughter Liz took a towel and, with infinite gentleness, began blotting Camilla's hair, talking the whole time in a low, repetitive croon of reassurance.

In slow stages, Camilla unfurled, sinking back among the billows of the duvet. As she straightened, her arms remained folded across her breasts, her fingers clutching at her upper arms. Her head lolled back on the bedclothes, her gaze not meeting theirs. Instead, her blank, deep blue eyes stared unblinking at the ceiling, and into the void beyond it.

With the same careful slowness, as though Camilla had been flayed, Liz dabbed at her neck and shoulders. All the while, her eyes remained locked on her daughter's face. Lifting each elbow in turn, she rolled the wadded towel in the armpits. Taking Camilla's wrist in her fingertips, she tried to raise her hand in order to dry her breast. With a fresh tremor, Camilla pulled away, her fingers tightening on her own biceps. Liz did not insist. With no more than a rueful glance at Matt, she went on with her task until Camilla was dry to the waist. Still speaking constantly, Liz flicked a look at Matt. Catching her meaning, he kneeled and, his touch as light as Liz's, reached for the zipper of the sodden skirt. Instantly, Camilla gave another throaty screech of protest. Her knees came up to her chest as a hand flew to her waist. Her fingers clenched around the zipper, folds of cloth protruding between whitened knuckles. Matt retreated as though scalded.

Liz's lips tightened as a flash of anger mingled with her sympathy for Camilla. 'Mark,' she said, 'do you think you could go down and get her a hot drink? Milk, or cocoa or something?'

With a troubled, lingering look at his sister he nodded and loped from the room.

They listened in silence to the noise of Mark taking the back stairs in a couple of leaps and then the sound of the kitchen door protesting as he thrust it open. With one hand mechanically smoothing Camilla's hair, Liz spoke very softly, her voice carrying no more than the two or three feet to where Matt had dropped to a crouch close beside her. 'What do you think?'

Matt's cheek muscles twitched. 'God, I don't know. She sounded fine yesterday. Maybe we've caught it in time. Perhaps if she gets a good night's rest she'll get away with it.' He shook his head, his eyes going to Camilla's face, the cheeks hollowed by distress, the eyes staring at some spot beyond the ceiling, as though intent on some film being projected inside her head. 'I wonder what the hell's set it off. Especially if there was nobody special on the scene.' Then when Liz didn't answer: 'Oh no! Don't tell me . . . ?'

She let her gaze slide over his shoulder for a moment before fixing him again with a candid stare. 'I wouldn't be sure. She certainly hasn't mentioned anybody. But . . . I don't know, Matt. I've just had this feeling lately, that she's had that sort of *distance* about her again. Wrapped up in something that she wasn't sharing.'

'Oh, shit!' Matt turned to Camilla, reached out a hand and then let it drop awkwardly to his side. 'Please, darling,' he breathed. '*Please* not again.' They heard the kitchen door protest as it was slammed back on its hinges once more. He stood up, dropping his voice to the barest murmur. 'Shall we leave you to get her into bed?'

Liz rose, moved a pace away from Camilla and took Matt by the hands. 'It's probably best. Perhaps I can get her to talk. With luck we might nip it in the bud.'

Mark hurried into the room carrying a steaming mug. He made to offer it to Camilla. Gently, Liz prised it from his grasp. Matt laid a hand on his shoulder. 'Come on, Mark. Men aren't wanted.'

Mark hesitated. Liz stepped forward, smiling wanly, and kissed him on the cheek. 'Go with Dad, Mark. It'll be best, believe me.' She turned back to Matt as though to speak further. The next instant they were locked together in a tight embrace. She kissed him as they pulled apart, then turned back to Camilla, flicking at a tear.

Matt walked from the room, his arm round his son's shoulders, his chest constricted. In the corridor Mark stopped and turned to face him. 'Dad, is this how it started last time?'

'Yes,' Matt said softly. 'Pretty much.'

'Last time was because a boyfriend threw her over?'

'That's how it looked. Who knows if that was the whole story?'

'How long did she take – to get over it, I mean?'

'She was off school for three months. Another six before she was really herself again.' His voice fell to a musing whisper. 'I guess that's always been Camilla's trouble. She just never learned to hold back. She's too anxious to please. It's great when it works. The problems start when she trusts the wrong people.' His mouth twisted in wry distaste. 'Unfortunately, there seem to be an awful lot of *those* around.' He took Mark's elbow. 'Let's go down. I don't suppose Camilla's entrance has exactly set the party alight.'

The guests had already moved into the library where Annie had taken over and was pouring coffee while Rachel busied herself setting out trays of liqueurs and glasses. Drawn by Annie's enquiring look, Matt moved to her side. 'Thanks,' he said, indicating the tray of cups.

'Just trying to keep the show on the road.' Without forming the question, she flicked a glance at the ceiling.

'It doesn't look that great,' he murmured. Then, raising his voice, he addressed the company. 'Sorry, everybody. I'm afraid Camilla's very under the weather. She had a problem with the car and decided to hitchhike. The daft girl ended up walking all the way from Ashworth. In this!' He paused to let the murmur of sympathy ripple round the room. 'Liz thought she ought to stay up with her for a while, just to be sure she's okay.' He waved a hand at the tray of drinks. 'Meanwhile, please don't let it spoil your fun. The one without a label's Armagnac. My French publisher's personal stock. It's twenty-five years old.' As he spoke he stepped forward and poured himself a big measure and gulped at it. 'And it's pure velvet.' As a few men,

25

headed by Roger Trevellyn, jostled for the bottle, Matt began to circulate, accepting expressions of concern for Camilla lightly, trying to change the subject, to breathe life back into the party. It was hard going. Within minutes the first couple put down their coffee cups with unnecessary clatter. Matt turned and almost moaned out loud at the predictability of it: Jane's parents.

Only five years older than Matt, they seemed to be from a different generation. Major West, still clinging to his rank fifteen years after being let go by the army, was a man of narrow experience but sweeping opinions. A laughable snob with a couple of collapsed business ventures behind him, he now played gentleman farmer while living off his inheritance from a property developer father and milking his spindly wife's tenuously aristocratic background. All his army career seemed to have done for him was leave him with the habit of talking to everybody as though they were subordinates. He thrust a hand into Matt's. 'Delightful evening, Matthew. Enjoyed ourselves. Thank Liz for us. Oh, and well done on the literary front, old boy. Keep it up.'

Matt nodded, returning the Major's self-consciously firm grip. 'I'll try,' he said, with restrained satire.

'Yes. Good. Hope Camilla's all right. Funny idea, though, wasn't it, *walking* in this? Believe me, I've done some of that kind of thing. Need to be dressed for it.'

'I'll buy her an anorak for Christmas.' Matt kissed Mrs West on both cheeks, dismayed at his own hypocrisy. 'Thanks for coming.' He stood watching them make their way out of the room, Mrs West simpering her farewells as they went. In three days Camilla's problem would be all over the county.

The trickle of departures started by the Wests

quickly became a stream. Matt drifted to the front door to take leave of the last guests, shaking the men's hands and kissing the women, warding off their parting congratulations with a self-deprecating laugh, and fielding their hushed concerns for Camilla with a twist of his mouth and some brief, optimistic platitudes. An insistent hand on his arm made him look up. The crumpled, affable face of Dick Field was smiling as he tugged Matt inside. 'No need for you to get pleurisy, too.' Dick and his wife were an intelligent, sociable couple who had spent the last five years restoring a crumbling farmhouse in a nearby village, sweet-temperedly treating the discovery of each new form of decay as a fresh challenge. Both of them were doctors. 'Thanks for the dinner, Matt. We'll die remembering that wine.' Dick's smile was muddied by the concern that stirred deep in his eyes. His hand still held Matt's sleeve. 'Matt, I know Peter Monroe's her GP but do you want me, or Jenny, to have a look at Camilla?'

'Thanks, Dick. She doesn't have a temperature, or anything. Although God knows how,' he added, jerking his chin at the open door and trying to smile. The smile faded. 'Liz is probably the only person she needs. For the moment anyway.'

Dick exchanged looks with his wife. His hand fell from Matt's sleeve. 'Well, just call if you need us. We're a lot closer than Peter.'

'Thanks for the offer. Good night.'

With a last expansive wave he closed the door, cutting out the sound of husbands hacking at icy windscreens, puffing thick gobs of mist as they called laughingly to each other.

He had a foot on the bottom stair when he heard Roger's laugh boom through the open door of the library. Letting out a sharp hiss of irritation, Matt turned and re-entered the room. Roger was clutching a newly filled glass. His head was thrown back in laughter at something he had just said. Rachel wore the guilty smirk she used when somebody had made a risqué joke she did not quite want to be seen finding funny. Several feet away, her back to Roger, Annie was piling the last of the coffee cups and glasses onto a tray, while Mark and Jane pulled furniture back into place. Matt glanced at his watch. 'Sorry. I didn't realise you were still here. I thought I must have missed you in the crowd.'

Roger grinned and brandished the glass. 'Couldn't resist another snort of this. And Annie wouldn't let me go anyway. She's anxious to talk to you.'

His eyes flickering to Annie, Matt caught the almost imperceptible hardening of her face at the belligerent note that had crept into Roger's banter. For the briefest instant she dipped her head. When she looked up again, her face was expressionless.

'Shouldn't you be getting back . . . to William?' Matt asked.

She nodded. 'We're going.' She stepped closer to him. 'Matt, I just wanted to say . . . Look, it *is* happening again, isn't it?'

Roger and Rachel had moved closer. Roger's face carried a sheen of sweat. 'It looks like it,' Matt said, almost inaudibly. Louder, he added, 'I hope to God it's not, though.'

'Oh shit,' Annie said distinctly, slashing at the air with a hand. 'What an absolute bastard.'

'Mmm. I hope this time'll be different. Then, we were working like hell in the period leading up to it. She was pretty far gone before we even knew there was a problem. At least this time we're all on the spot. When Mark spoke to her yesterday she apparently sounded in great shape.' He tried to smile and failed. 'With luck we've caught it before it's gone too far.' He kneaded a hand over his eyes. 'I *hope* so, for Camilla's sake. Anyway,' he added, 'if anyone doesn't need to be saddled with *our* problems, it's you.'

Annie shook her head. 'That doesn't enter into it. If there's *anything*, anything at all I can do, day or night –'

'God, there she goes. The Good Samaritan,' blurted Roger. 'As if she didn't have enough on her plate already with William.'

Annie's nostrils flared, her eyes still on Matt's. She stepped forward and kissed him. As she did so, the length of her body touched momentarily against his. 'Anything, Matt. Tell Liz to call me, day or night.'

Her eyes held his. He blinked, forcing himself to look at Roger. 'Thanks, you're great. Both of you.'

Matt watched the two of them cross the courtyard to their car, then turned back inside and hit the stairs at a run, taking them three at a time. He was at the half-landing when Liz emerged at the top of the stairs, bringing him up short. Relief leaped in him as he saw that much of the tenseness had gone from around her eyes. 'How is she? Is she talking to you?'

Liz nodded, descending towards him. She carried a towelling robe over one arm. Drawn, but smiling, she took his hand and led him down to where Mark, hearing their voices, waited at the foot of the stairs. 'She's in the bath. And I need a cup of coffee. Badly.'

It took Liz several minutes to herd Celia and the other helper gently out of the house. By the time she returned, Matt had managed to perform the same trick on a reluctant Rachel and the smell of fresh coffee filled the room. Mark was seated at the breakfast counter with a cup in front of him. Matt stood at his shoulder, pouring cream into his cup with one hand and holding the Armagnac bottle in the other. He splashed two inches of the liqueur into a glass and waved the bottle at Liz. 'Want one?'

She shook her head. Worry once again filled her face. 'No. It's too late for me.'

Matt drank off a good part of the Armagnac, then sat at the cluttered counter next to Mark. 'Where's Jane?'

'She went to bed. She thought we'd prefer to be alone.'

Matt smiled, half to himself. 'The more I see of Jane and her parents, the more I doubt the validity of genetic science.' His smile faded as he turned to Liz. She sat hunched on her stool, her hands clasped around her cup, staring into the coffee.

Mark spoke up first. 'How is she? *Have* we caught it in time?' His gaze shifted from one to the other, studying their faces, anxious for any nuance he could find there.

Liz reached out for Matt's glass and drank, closing her eyes as the old liqueur warmed her throat. 'I'm hoping so, Mark. Oh God, how I'm hoping so.' She began crying silently.

The young man worried at the edge of the worktop with a thumbnail. 'This is heavy shit, isn't it?' he said softly. 'Really heavy shit. Poor Camilla.' He, too, had tears in his eyes.

Matt gripped his son's arm. 'None of us should let it get to us yet. Believe us, Mark. You were young last time. There are a lot of reasons why it shouldn't hit her so hard this time. You spoke to her yesterday and she was fine, wasn't she? Well, last time she was on the school skiing trip when it happened. She was practically left on her own for a fortnight. The teachers thought she was faking it to skive off skiing. Christ, she *loves* skiing! You know that. They just weren't about to let it keep *them* off the slopes! They gave her

30

an aspirin in the morning and disappeared. This time she's right here with us. With a bit of luck, and your mother's touch with her, she'll be on the mend again by tomorrow evening.' He looked at Liz, who forced a smile and dipped her head in a barely perceptible nod. He reached out and covered her hand with his.

Mark ground away his tears with his knuckles. 'What *exactly* set it off? The first time, I mean.'

'A boyfriend, as I told you. As far as we were ever able to judge, anyway.'

'Who was he?'

'You never knew him. Neither did we, really. It was someone she had met at a school function.'

'What did he *do* to her?' Mark asked, anger welling at the very thought of somebody having hurt his sister.

Matt sighed. 'Nothing, Mark. He was eighteen, a couple of years older than Camilla. He went off to university, went his own way, that's all.'

'You mean he dropped Camilla?'

Matt shot Liz a patient smile. 'Mark, he was eighteen years old. University was another world. Camilla just wasn't part of it. That kind of thing happens all the time. In fact, the boy was a lot more decent about it than most kids that age would be. He took the trouble to write and *tell* Camilla he didn't want to see her any more, instead of just leaving her to figure it out.'

'Was that what started her . . . problem?'

Matt's face clouded at the memory. Liz spoke for him, her voice low. 'She got the letter the morning they were leaving on the skiing trip. Apparently she didn't actually read it until they got there, waiting for some privacy. She went into her shell that evening. And didn't come out again for a year.'

'But wasn't there any warning? Wasn't she depressed or anything, before that, I mean?'

Liz glanced at Matt, her teeth digging into her lip,

biting back the old taste of self-reproach. 'Yes, she was. With hindsight. At least, we wouldn't have, anyway, we *didn't*, see it as depression. Moping would have been the word. Fretting because he hadn't phoned.' Her voice had fallen to a whisper, hardly carrying across the space between them. 'Dad was working to meet a deadline. I was spending a lot of time in New York . . .' Her voice broke up as she choked back a sob.

'But still, you must have noticed *something*? Not eating? The way she spoke?'

Matt flinched at the edge in his son's voice. He spoke very gently. 'Mark, you spoke to her yesterday. Was there anything then?'

Mark stared at him for a moment and then looked down into his lap. 'No,' he whispered, 'nothing. In fact, she sounded over the moon. She has done for weeks. *You* must have seen it.'

Liz swallowed a gulp of coffee. 'Mmm, you're right. Now I look back, it started some time early this term. Also, the weekend she was here she was biting everyone's head off. She couldn't wait to get back to Oxford.'

Matt grimaced. 'Which spells new boyfriend?' He looked questioningly at the two of them. 'And now *he's* thrown her over?'

'It certainly looks like it,' Liz responded glumly. 'I phoned her after that weekend, just to see if anything *was* wrong. She was on top of the world again. So either she suddenly couldn't stand us, or there was something, some*one*, she couldn't bear to be away from.'

Matt drew himself up, sliding the unfinished glass of Armagnac away from him. 'I'm going to call some of her friends, to see if they can tell us what's been going on.'

Liz looked at her watch. 'Now? You can't. It's nearly midnight.'

Matt reached for the electronic organiser that lay by the phone. 'We let time slip away before, Liz. I don't care if we have to disturb a few people, I'm not going to let it happen *again*.'

'Hello? Mr Rowley? Esther's father? This is Matthew Stenner. Mr Rowley, I apologise for waking the household at this hour but I wonder, could Esther possibly come to the phone?' He paused, his eyes now on Mark's as his son hung on every word. 'Well, yes, I do realise. But it's about my daughter, Camilla. She's had a . . . a bit of an accident, to tell you the truth. No, no, nothing *too* drastic, but I wondered if Esther might be able to give me some information that would help.' He paused again, his face blank. 'Thank you. You're very kind.'

Liz collected the robe that lay on the Aga and draped it over her arm, folding it to keep in the warmth. 'I'll take this up to Camilla and get her to bed.' She bent and gave Mark a lingering kiss high on the side of the head. She straightened. 'In fact, I'll be glad to get to bed myself.' She gave Matt a wry, faintly ambiguous smile. 'It's been an unusually eventful day.'

Matt returned her smile, his fingers curling in a minuscule wave as he abruptly resumed speaking. 'Esther? This is Matthew Stenner. How are you?' He was silent for an instant. 'Yes, fine. I'm terribly sorry to disturb you. It's just that Camilla isn't terribly well. No, there's nothing physical. It's more . . . well, an *emotional* thing. I . . . we . . . look, Esther, we, Camilla's mother and I, we need to know. Has Camilla been . . . has she been *well* recently? I don't mean sick. I mean . . . normal. Herself. Has she seemed *happy*?'

Mark had risen from his seat and now pressed close

to Matt's shoulder, trying to make sense of the soft, tinny blur.

'Really?' Matt's cheek twitched. 'Look, please don't think I'm just prying into Camilla's affairs, I have a good reason for asking, but can you tell me his name? Or, better still, where I could get hold of him?' Matt's eyes closed and slowly opened again as he listened to the young woman's answer. 'But you and Camilla are pretty close friends, aren't you? Surely she can't have kept him a secret all this time, not if it's been going on for months.'

He chewed at a thumbnail as he listened to the answer. 'You mean *nobody* at all?' He laughed resignedly. 'I see,' he muttered. 'I was afraid it might be something like that.' He paused as the girl interjected. 'Okay. Thanks very much, Esther. I really do apologise for dragging you out of bed.' He hung up. '*She's* convinced Camilla's in love,' he said wearily to Mark. 'According to Esther, she's been walking on air for weeks.'

'But Camilla's never told her who the man is?' He gripped Matt's arm, the strength of the grip surprising Matt, another of those tiny, jolting reminders that his son had some time in the recent past ceased to be an angular youth and was now a man, an inch taller than himself, at six feet two, and with the same wide-shouldered swimmer's physique. 'And now the bastard has thrown her over?' His fingers tightened further on his father's arm. '*He's* responsible for . . .' he waved a hand in a gesture of helpless fury, '. . . this?'

Matt rested a soothing hand on his son's forearm. 'Perhaps, Mark. I don't know yet.' He turned for the door, drawing Mark after him. 'Let's see how Camilla's doing. The bath will have thawed her out. Mum might even have started coaxing something out of her.'

34

The impotent anger not yet fully drained from his face, Mark fell into step beside his father. Before they reached the door Liz's scream brought them to a run.

Three

They burst through the bathroom door and, in unison, let out sharp cries of distress. Liz was bent low over the bath, up to her shoulders in the scarlet-streaked foam, supporting Camilla. Her face was a hand's length from her daughter's. The first, blind panic already under control, she was talking to her, asking questions in a low, carefully articulated voice.

Matt dropped to his knees at her side and plunged his own arm into the water, groping for Camilla's hand.

'Oh shit!' For a frozen instant, he stared, his face utterly drained of colour, at the blood that oozed from the damaged wrist. Then, without taking his eyes from the wound, he rasped, 'Towels, Mark! Quick.'

He clamped a fold of the thick white bath sheet that Mark thrust at him against her inner wrist and raised the arm high. 'Another one. Hold that there.' He delved again into the water and scrambled to his feet, lifting the other arm clear. He pressed the second towel hard to the wrist for a few seconds and then slowly peeled it back, examining the wound. There were several puncture wounds. Blood came from only one of them, snaking down her arm, tracing a vivid red vein on her skin. With a half-articulated sound of relief, he clamped the towel tightly back over the cut.

The other wrist bore the same cluster of marks. The bleeding was worse but still no more than a trickle. Matt closed his hand over hers, taking the pressure. He spoke softly, trying to keep the panic out of his voice. 'Mark, go and call Dick. Tell him he's needed here. Fast.'

Without breaking off from her soft, insistent questions, Liz manoeuvred past Matt and clambered into the tub, sending water sloshing over the side to make a startling pink stain on the pale rug. She kneeled astride Camilla, cradling her head, their faces almost touching. Her eyes were moist now, her lips colourless. 'Camilla!' she said again, a growing urgency in her tone. 'Darling, come on, now, please. How long ago did you . . . do this? Dick's coming. He'll need to know?' Camilla stared at her, giving no sign of having heard. A tremor entered Liz's voice. 'Please, darling. You must tell us. So we can help you.' Camilla's eyes drooped shut as her mouth gaped in the huge, unself-conscious yawn of the totally depleted. When her eyes slowly reopened they were empty of all expression except the glazed look of bone-deep boredom. Liz shot Matt a quick glance. Deep in her eyes he caught the first, unmistakable glint of panic.

Holding both of Camilla's wrists in one big fist, he reached and stroked Liz's blood-spattered hair. 'Take it easy, darling,' he breathed, his eyes on Camilla's face. 'The actual bleeding doesn't look that bad.' Before she could respond, Mark erupted, panting, back into the room.

'Dick's on his way.'

Matt nodded. 'Great. Give me a hand to get Camilla into bed.'

He carried her, dripping blood and water, the few steps to her bed where Liz, moving with quick, fear-driven efficiency, had already spread a thick layer of towels. He was stooping to let Camilla slither from his loosening grip as the bell rang. Leaving Liz and Mark to dry and cover Camilla, he ran for the stairs.

*　　*　　*

Dick Field lowered Camilla's bandaged wrist carefully onto the duvet and straightened, turning to look down into the pale, still face. A shadow of pain lay behind the kindness in his smile. 'There you are, Camilla. Not too much harm done, really.' He dropped abruptly to a crouch, leaning his head close to hers. 'Except that you gave us all a nasty few minutes. Now, will you promise me you won't do it again?' He looked deep into the vacant eyes, willing her to answer, making it personal. At length, Camilla's head moved, a vague movement that might have been assent. He squeezed her fingers. 'Good.' He glanced pointedly across the room, reminding her that Matt, Liz and Mark were on the sofa where he had confined them, out of earshot. He bent closer. 'Do you want to tell me what it's all about?' Another three seconds passed before her head shook, almost imperceptibly, from side to side. Dick reached into his bag and produced a small vial of tablets which he held in front of her face. 'I'll leave these with your mother, in case you need anything to help you sleep. You need total rest for a few days. Good night, Camilla.' The ghost of an acknowledgement wafted across her face. Her eyelids were already drooping again.

They sprang up to meet him. With an out-turned palm, he suppressed their questions. 'She's all right. As far as those wounds are concerned, anyway,' he added, after a pause. 'They're quite small punctures. She didn't actually lose much blood, although I expect it looked as though there'd been a pig-sticking when you found her. What did she do it with?'

'These.' Matt held out a pair of nail scissors.

Dick studied them briefly and then handed them back to Matt with a grimace. 'I guess you had better keep these out of the way for a while. Any other sharp instrument, too.'

38

Matt slowly pocketed the scissors. 'You think she'll try again?'

Dick sighed. 'I have no idea. I'm a GP, not a psychiatrist. Shall we talk about it downstairs?'

Matt glanced at his watch. 'If you have time.'

Dick laughed softly. 'Come on.' They were making for the door when Dick turned, bringing them all to a stop. He looked mostly at Liz. 'Look, it isn't up to me. I'm not even Camilla's doctor, but I don't think it would be a bad idea if she were not left alone, at least for a day or two, until you see how she's reacting to all this.'

Before Liz could respond, Mark intervened. 'Let me.' He was already running for the door. 'Wait here while I just get my sleeping bag.'

As he went, Liz looked at Matt, disquiet in her eyes. 'Should we let him? It seems like a terrible responsibility.'

'If he wants to. He's a mature boy. And he worships Camilla. And who knows, she might even talk to Mark. More likely than to me, anyway.'

Dick hitched himself onto a stool, facing Liz and Matt across the tiled counter top.

'So. What do you make of it, Dick? Where the hell do we go from here?' Matt asked.

Dick let out a slow breath. 'Has Camilla done anything like this before?'

'Not exactly. Nothing this serious.'

Dick's eyebrows rose. 'But *something*?'

'Mmm. A few years ago. She had a bout of . . . I don't know what to call it really. A breakdown, I suppose. It was before you arrived, but I kind of assumed you knew about it.'

Dick's shoulders twitched. 'A lot of things get said. I try not to listen. What were the symptoms?'

Liz spoke up. 'Anorexia.'

Dick raised his eyebrows. 'That was the diagnosis?'

'It was mine. Ours.'

'What was the professional opinion?'

'Alex Lawton agreed with us.'

'Of course. Peter's only been your GP since Alex retired, hasn't he?'

Liz nodded. 'Yes, although we knew Peter for years before Alex went off to New Zealand.'

'Didn't Alex suggest any, er, specialist help?'

'Yes, he did. Some woman in Gloucester.'

The edge of bitterness in Matt's voice made Dick draw back in surprise. 'And Camilla saw her?'

'Mmm. Heather Biss was the lady's name.'

Dick's mouth twisted into a lop-sided smile. 'Obviously, you weren't impressed.'

Matt spread his hands, laughing apologetically. 'I'm sorry, Dick, I know she's a doctor, too, so you don't have to comment, but she was worse than useless.'

'In what way?'

'In every way. Camilla was off her food but she didn't become anorexic until she started seeing that bloody woman. She managed to turn a particularly acute case of adolescent sulks into something with a name.'

'And you really think the treatment was responsible?'

Liz spoke, her voice quiet and distinct. 'We were absolutely sure of it, Dick. The woman was trying to lead Camilla into some very dark places. The poor girl was coming out of the sessions shell-shocked.'

Matt joined in. 'Her story was, she was trying to unearth the root causes of Camilla's problem. To us, she seemed to be working out her own hang-ups. Shit, Dick, even *Camilla* knew what the problem was. Her boyfriend had thrown her over! She was taking it very hard. Christ, if every teenage girl that went through that called in a psychiatrist . . .'

Dick nodded. 'And tonight's events? More boyfriend trouble?'

Below the counter Matt sought Liz's hand, his fingers entwining with hers. 'We think so. I spoke to one of her friends. It seems Camilla's been acting strangely for weeks. The girl is convinced she's been head over heels in love.'

'Did she tell you who with? It might be a good idea to speak to him.'

Matt shook his head. 'He's a close-kept secret. None of her friends has been allowed to see him. In fact, from what the girl said, since this has been going on, Camilla's virtually let her friends drop altogether. Her work's gone to hell, too.'

Dick made a sour face. 'I don't like the sound of that.' He looked steadily into their faces, weighing his words. 'Not in someone with a history of . . . obsessiveness.' On the last word his voice rose in a delicate, questioning inflection. He watched their faces, waiting to see how they reacted. Sure they had not taken offence, he went on. 'I guess it might feel like prying but I definitely think it would be a good idea if you *could* talk to the man, find out as much as you can about the circumstances.'

Matt nodded. 'I already intended to.'

The vehemence behind Matt's words made Dick's eyes narrow. 'You won't forget she's a big girl, though, will you?' he said, half smiling.

Matt laughed. 'Don't worry. I'll be a model of discretion.' He turned his eyes upwards, in the direction of Camilla's bedroom. 'It's just that tonight she's . . . well, you can understand it, she's our baby girl again.'

Dick nodded slowly. 'Of course she is. But, and I say this more as a friend than as a doctor, you all probably need to be very careful about letting anger cloud your judgement.'

Matt sighed. 'I know.'

'Good. So, tomorrow, I suggest you see Peter, tell him all that's happened. I think he'll probably suggest . . . help.'

Matt gave a short bark of laughter. 'Come on, Dick! Not more psychiatrists. Not after what we just told you.'

He looked steadily at them. 'Peter's Camilla's doctor, not me. He *may* take a different view. And there are other kinds of therapy besides psychiatry, you know.'

'You mean some kind of *counselling*!' The word was thick with contempt. The sharp pressure of Liz's fingers made him change tack. 'Dick, do you really *believe* in all that?' he asked, straining hard to be reasonable.

'Not all, no. But some. I don't think you should dismiss it out of hand. Tonight's episode might just have been a cry for help, to use the cliché. Failed suicides usually are. But there was only a quarter of an inch in it. Those scissors could easily have killed Camilla.' A sudden yawn gripped him, making him clap a hand to his mouth. He pushed himself off the stool. 'Look, if you don't mind, I'd better get to bed.'

Matt and Liz stood, too, and moved with him towards the front door.

'Talk to Peter. And to the boyfriend, if you can.' Dick gave Matt's hand a squeeze and leaned to kiss Liz.

She put her arms around him and hugged him hard. 'Thanks for coming . . .' A sob obliterated his name.

Dick rested his head against her hair. 'Don't be silly.' He extricated himself gently from her embrace. 'If you need me again, just grab the phone. Probably best not to speak to Peter until tomorrow, when you've had more time to think.'

Hearing the door close behind Dick Field and her family, Camilla's eyes flickered open, panic in them as she stared around the room. Then, certain she was alone, she let her head fall back to the pillow, her eyes closing once again. A single, aching sob escaped her as the memory of that afternoon came rushing back.

Seated at her desk, trying to finish her long-overdue, final essay of term, every passing car would shatter her concentration, bringing her head up. Each time a car passed, its tyres hissing on the soaking asphalt, her glance flicked to her watch before dropping reluctantly back to the work that lay spread in front of her.

The abrupt clamour of the doorbell had brought her instantly to her feet, almost sobbing with relief, to throw open the door.

Martin Bohill staggered back, laughing, almost losing his footing on the top stair, as Camilla crashed against his chest, her mouth already locking onto his. Laughing through their kisses, they moved awkwardly along the dingy landing and stumbled inside, Martin half carrying Camilla in the crook of one arm, clinging with the other to a scuffed briefcase, a bottle of wine clutched in his fist. Kicking the door closed behind them, his mouth still grinding against Camilla's, he let the briefcase fall to the floor, disgorging papers over the worn carpet. He dropped the bottle into an armchair, its stained and threadbare fabric camouflaged with a brightly coloured throw, and enfolded Camilla in his arms.

It was a long time before she drew back her head and looked up into his face. 'Oh God, Martin,' she whispered. 'I've been frantic. I thought you weren't coming.'

He grinned and gave a little shrug. 'A tutorial.' He leaned to kiss her again. 'Bloody girl,' he muttered. As he spoke he shucked off his leather jacket and bowed his head, fiddling to free the cuff where it had snagged on his watch. 'Turned up forty bloody minutes late.'

A shadow of surprise flitted across Camilla's face as he spoke. The smell of strong mints on his breath was not enough to mask fully the scent of alcohol. Her lips moved, forming a question. Then, as he lifted his head, she changed her mind. By the time his eyes met hers again the look was gone, the question banished.

'I thought I'd never get rid of her.'

'Is she pretty?'

He laughed aloud, throwing back his head. Then, he frowned in a parody of deep thought. 'I suppose she is.' He grinned. 'Bit heavy for my tastes, though. Not terrifically bright either. And does she *talk*. On and on and on. Drives you completely nuts!' He sighed extravagantly. 'Thank *God* for the vacation.'

The emphasis with which he disparaged the girl stabbed at Camilla's senses. She felt a plunging sensation in her stomach, as though she were plummeting from a great height. She clasped her arms tight around him, squeezing herself hard against his body. 'But, Martin, I'm not going to see you for a month! I don't think I can stand it.'

He bent and kissed the top of her head. Again she caught the sour smell of stale wine. 'Don't remind me,' he murmured. 'I don't know how I'm going to get through it without you here.'

'Don't, then.'

He drew back, looking at her. 'Huh? Don't *what*?'

'I told you. I could stay here until Christmas Eve – just go home for a couple of days.'

He shook his head, letting his hands slide down her arms until he was holding just her fingertips in his.

'Oh Christ, don't even talk about it. I wish we could just go away somewhere. France, maybe. Rent a house, get in some wine, make a fire, and just forget about everything, except loving you.'

Her eyes shone. 'Let's do it!' She stepped closer to him, her hips against his. 'Please! Tell her. You promised you would. Weeks ago, months! Tell her now.' She reached up and twined her fingers around his neck. 'Oh God, Martin, let's just *go*.'

Lifting her hands from his neck he half turned away from her.

'I can't, darling. Not just now. Not at Christmas.' He swallowed, the sound audible. 'It would break the kids' hearts.' He placed his hands on her shoulders. 'Please, don't let's talk about *her* any more. Let me get us a drink.' He moved towards the tiny kitchenette, catching his foot in the folds of the leather jacket that lay on the floor. Camilla's eyes widened as he swore and kicked out, sending the jacket sailing across the room. By the time he turned back to face her, already twisting the corkscrew into the neck of the bottle, the vexation had gone from his face again, leaving only his broad, boyish smile.

The words of protest Camilla had been forming died in her throat, her impatience melting in the glow of the smile. He drew the cork from the bottle with a soft plop. 'And, please, let's not argue.'

They drank the wine with the gas fire scorching their faces, sitting side by side on the Chinese rug Camilla had brought from home to relieve the drabness of the landlady's cheap, salmon-coloured carpet. In less than twenty minutes Martin was draining the last dregs into his glass and tossing them back. He put the glass down heavily on the rug and scrambled laboriously to his feet. Camilla reached up and grabbed his hand. 'Where are you going?' There was a hint of alarm in her voice.

He grinned down at her, and his expression had a strange, smudged quality. He jerked a thumb. 'To get another bottle.'

Camilla frowned and shook her head, putting down her own glass on the hearth. 'I don't want any more.' She was still holding his hand. She squeezed it. 'I want to go to bed.'

His grin widening, he slipped his hand from hers. 'Me, too.' He waggled a finger in mock reproof. 'But just remember, I've spent the day trying vainly to pound knowledge into the heads of impervious youths. I need another drink.' Touching a hand to the mantelpiece to trim his balance, he stepped over her legs and crossed to the kitchen.

Sitting heavily beside her again he sloshed two inches into his glass and wafted it under his nose, his eyes on the label. He swilled a mouthful around his palate before swallowing it noisily. 'Mmm.' He smacked his lips. 'Another of Daddy's finds?'

Camilla nodded. Her expression as she watched him was clouded, tentative. 'That's right. His last trip to Bordeaux. One of those "little" producers he likes to think he's discovered.' She gave a private, affectionate little laugh.

Snuffling into the glass, he took a copious mouthful, sieving it noisily between his teeth before tossing it back. 'Mmm. I must admit, your old man certainly knows how to pick them. Must be nice to be stinking rich.'

Camilla's face clouded. 'Please. I've asked you so many times not to talk about Daddy like that.'

He shrugged and made to refill her glass. She shook her head and took the bottle by the neck. Reluctantly, he let her draw it from his hand and set it down. Then she prised his glass from his fingers and reached to stand it with the bottle. As she did so, her face came

46

within inches of his. Her breasts flattened against his chest. The boyish smile spread slowly across his face. She leaned and kissed it. 'Just make love to me, Martin, please.'

She kissed him again, harder. A fancied coolness in his response sent a shudder of panic through her. With a soft whimpering sound, she began fumbling at his shirt.

He lay on his back, naked, watching as Camilla scrabbled at her own clothes, breaking a nail on the zipper of her jeans in her haste. She kicked away the jeans and pants to stand naked herself now, looking down hesitantly at him, as though seeking his approval. With a faintly ambiguous smile, he reached up and took her hand, pulling her down.

They rolled and slid among the discarded clothes, their bodies entwined, biting and clawing at each other's flesh. All the jealousy, all the anxiety that had been eating at Camilla since Martin's arrival, flooded out of her, transformed by relief into a blind, groaning frenzy. An elbow sent the wine bottle tumbling. The wine chugged noisily into the deep wool of the Chinese rug. They rolled and grappled in the wetness, unaware of anything but each other's bodies. They wrestled off the rug and crashed against the leg of the work table. Pages covered with Camilla's neat, close handwriting fluttered unnoticed among them, getting crushed and torn, turning to blood-coloured mush in the puddle of wine.

Camilla was aware of Martin's hand sliding beneath her, readying her. She arched, moulding herself to the pressure of his hand. His mouth was at her shoulders, her neck, his teeth teasing at her flesh, more than kissing, not quite biting. His body shifted on hers. She whispered assent. Her senses were spinning. She knew nothing of the heat of the fire on her skin, nothing of

47

the greasy carpet or the spilled wine. She was aware only of the man who over the last few months had become the absolute focus of her being, whose presence filled her mind to bursting, robbed her of her ability to think. And somewhere, deep in her being, the chill tendrils of fear that she might, even at this moment, be losing him.

Tears ran back through her hair. She clung fiercely to him, her arms and legs working as she sought more purchase, wanting him never to leave, wanting to *become* him, to lose herself in him.

Spurred by Camilla's wildness, he drove himself into her, making her gasp in involuntary protest. The unfamiliar, almost vengeful force of it was overwhelmed by the consoling, consuming knowledge that he *wanted* her.

His breath scorched her cheek as he muttered a stream of barely coherent obscenities. His fingers gouged deep into the flesh of her hips, touching bone. Flecks of detritus from the carpet stuck to their sweat-slickened skin. Camilla's head jarred hard against the foot of the armchair, making her moan.

Without warning, Martin reared back, breaking from her grip, withdrawing. Instantly, panic rose in her, a rank, intolerable fear that her protests had gone too far, that he was about to abandon her. To return perhaps to the student who had made him late, with whom he had drunk enough wine for him to have arrived already half drunk at her door. Blindly, she reached out for him, trying to draw him back inside her.

'Don't stop! Don't stop, please.' Her voice was breaking with need.

Instead of replying he reached down and took her by the hips, dragging at her. She went on for some seconds struggling to pull him back down into her

48

before she understood what he was trying clumsily, almost brutishly, to do. With a throaty sound of agreement, she stopped reaching for him and rolled over. Guided by the painful bite of his fingers she let him raise her hips until she was on all fours. With another brusque movement that was almost a blow, he put a hand between her shoulder blades and drove her face down into the cushion of the chair. She felt him settle himself, his knees between hers, easing her thighs wider. She moved herself, eager, offering herself to him, oblivious to his unaccustomed roughness, knowing only how much she wanted him. A soft, rising moan of assent escaped her as she felt him once more against her, probing. Then, abruptly, the full weight of him bore upon her, bringing her hips back and down. One hand went to her head, pressing her cheek into the musty fabric of the chair. His other hand was still at her hip, the fingers biting, harder than ever. Amid her pain, she felt a fleeting surprise at his strength. 'Martin, darling! You're hurting me. Please!' She tried to straighten. The pressure on her head increased, pinioning her.

'Stay still. Relax.' He repeated the words several times, a hoarse, barely coherent litany.

She felt him probing, not entering her, just moving on her, slick with her own juices. 'Please! Martin! Darling! You're *hurting* me!' For the first time there was a thread of fear in her voice.

'No! It won't hurt. Not if you can just relax. Just let me . . .' His voice tailed off, his breath sawing.

His hand moved from her hip to seize the flesh of her buttock, his fingers digging cruelly into the muscles, prising her apart.

The realisation of what he was about to do came like a blow, forcing a gasp from her. 'No! You mustn't! You *mustn't*!'

With a throaty, inarticulate sound, he thrust at her, testing his own hardness against the tight ring of muscle.

Pain, fear, betrayal, all mixed in her cry. Even as she screamed, she knew nobody was there to hear her. She was the only person in the building who had not yet left for the vacation. The street outside was deserted. Then, her cry was cut short, the breath driven from her by the weight of him. His wine-rank breath mingled with the choking, ingrained dust of the worn brocade of the armchair, his grunts merging with her own stifled protests as he chewed clumsily at her face and hair.

Revulsion pulsed through her in great, engulfing waves. The sweet, considerate man who had first made love to her with such generous, tender passion only three months earlier no longer existed. He had become a foul-breathed, sweating, vindictive *creature*, oblivious to her pleas as he tried clumsily to force his way into the forbidden part of her, intent only on his own pleasure.

He thrust again, a sharp jabbing of his hips. Camilla's head came up off the chair. Her face was contorted into a look of sheer horror. Her scream filled the room.

Martin reared back, a shifting look of panic in his eyes. 'Don't! Be quiet! You'll have the whole . . .' His words ended in a groan. The moment his weight was lifted from her back Camilla had jerked upright. Her head struck him across the bridge of the nose. As he fell back onto his haunches, she scrambled to her feet, a choking cry escaping her as she pulled free.

Wild-eyed, her breath coming in whooping gasps, she snatched the throw from the chair and clutched it to her.

Martin crouched at her feet, a hand to his nose. Watery-eyed and aggrieved, he reached out, apparently wanting to pull her down again. With a whimper, she lashed out a foot. The blow, though ill-aimed and clumsy, was enough to send him sprawling on his back.

As Martin watched, stupefied, her eyes widened into a look of sheer terror. The throw slid from her lifeless fingers. Her chest began to heave, slowly at first, then faster, her breath a harsh rasp. Panic was beginning to flood into Martin's eyes when she wheeled around and ran blindly across the room where she crumpled to the floor against the wall. As Martin moved tentatively towards her, hurriedly pulling on his clothes, she drew her knees up, hugging them to her chest.

Martin must have left. Her next memory was of the overwhelming sense of loneliness and then the recollection of wildly running, fleeing the room and the house.

The sound of the door softly opening brought her abruptly back to the present. In the horror of remembering, she had once again brought her knees up into a foetal position. Raising her head she saw Mark standing in the doorway, a sleeping bag trailing at his side. His smile was hesitant.

'Hi. You, er, okay?' He gestured awkwardly at the sofa. 'I thought I could sleep there. If you . . .'

She stared at him for a moment, as though hardly knowing who he was. Then with a mute nod, she buried her face in her pillow and, hugging her knees, began crying soundlessly.

Matt turned from staring vacantly from the window at the slate-coloured sky. As he had been doing every few minutes since he had entered his study at eight o'clock, he looked mechanically at his watch. It was almost eleven. In a few minutes, according to the routine he had followed so strictly, six days a week, for years, it would be time to stroll along to the kitchen to join Liz for a cup of coffee, smug in the knowledge that he had written a thousand words. He glanced at the screen of the word processor. There was not a single word on it. Twenty times he had sat down to begin. Each time he had got to his feet again to roam the room, totally unable to concentrate on the final redraft of the book.

Half a dozen times, he had gone up to Camilla's room, tiptoeing to the door to listen in silence before entering, hoping for the sound of her voice. Each time he had found either Liz or Mark taking a turn seated at her bedside, sometimes just watching her, sometimes carrying on one-sided conversations, talking in the faintly desperate way in which people speak to stroke victims, unsure if they are being understood.

Camilla's position hardly changed. She lay immobile, staring at the ceiling, her pale and hollowed face bereft of expression. When he sat on the edge of the bed and took her hand in his she neither withdrew it nor returned his grip, but simply ignored him. They talked across her, a steady flow of self-consciously upbeat conversation, their Christmas plans, the guests they expected. None of it brought even a flicker of life to Camilla's face. Only once did she display any sign whatever of animation, reaching out to drink from the glass of water and to eat a fragment of the cold toast that stood congealing on the bedside table.

After a few minutes, when his own words began to feel clumsy, as though he were speaking through a mouthful of cloth, Matt left to return to work, keeping to the arrangement Liz had insisted on as they lay awake through the early hours; she would take responsibility for nursing Camilla back to health while Matt continued working to meet his publisher's deadline.

He sat down in the worn swivel chair and stared at

the empty screen, trying to force his mind to the task. He was still sitting, almost half an hour later and still without a single word on the screen, when the doorbell brought him leaping to his feet.

He reached the hall to find Peter Monroe already inside, being directed upstairs by Celia, wax-soaked duster in hand. The two men shook hands on the hoof and Matt began giving the doctor a terse account of the events of the previous evening. They had got as far as the landing when Liz appeared above them. Although the sleepless night had drained the sparkle from her eyes, her step retained its usual energy as she moved purposefully down to meet them. In response to Peter's greeting she flashed a brief, tight-lipped smile. 'She won't see you.'

Matt frowned. 'Huh?'

Liz spread her hands. 'At least she's talking. Although still not to me. She heard the car. Mark mentioned it was you, Peter. She told him to tell you to go away. At least it's progress. They're the first words we've had out of her since yesterday evening.'

Matt shook his head. 'But that's plain silly. At least she should let Peter check her cuts.'

Peter Monroe laid his fingertips on Matt's arm. 'Perhaps I should let her be for a while. Have *you* checked the cuts, Liz?'

'I changed the dressings this morning. They look all right.'

Peter nodded and turned, beckoning them back down the stairs.

'Fine,' he said brightly. 'If the cuts are healing, and she's started to communicate again, perhaps we should leave well alone. Is there somewhere we can talk?'

Matt shut the door of the study and ushered Peter Monroe into his own chair while Liz installed herself

53

across the desk. Peter knew the room well. He and Matt, like their wives, were plugged into the same social group, occasionally playing tennis or going on holiday together, often finding themselves at the same parties. He waited until Matt had made himself comfortable, hitching his rump onto the old-fashioned safe that stood close by the desk, its door permanently open, revealing a jumble of dilapidated buff envelopes, documents, and paper wallets of photographs, and then spoke. 'I had a look back over Camilla's notes before I came over. Do you want to tell me about that, and then go on to last night?'

Peter sat listening with silent attention, his head bowed. The only time he showed any reaction was at Matt's description of the encounter with the psychiatrist, grimacing and tugging at his lip. When Matt had finished speaking he sat in silence for many seconds before asking, 'Did Dick give an opinion?'

Liz glanced at Matt before answering. 'He feels we should consider "counselling".'

'And that I should try to talk to the mystery boy-friend,' Matt added.

'Mmm.' Peter nodded several times, musingly. 'It might give us some insight. You'd need to tread very carefully, though. In her present state Camilla might not take kindly to you probing her love life, especially talking to the very person who rejected her.'

Matt pushed himself off from the safe and paced to the window. 'But if he *did* something, something specific, that precipitated this, then . . .'

'As long as you confine yourself to some gentle conversation, Matt. Camilla isn't a child any more. She's a consenting adult. The solution to Camilla's problem is in her, not him.'

'All I want to do is *talk* to the man.'

Peter laughed outright, looking at Matt's bunched

54

fists. 'Sure you do!' He sat back in his chair, the laugh dying. 'If you and Dick think it might serve a purpose, go ahead. Just be careful. Hitting him might help *you*, it won't be any good to Camilla. As for the matter of some sort of counselling ... I would go along with Dick, up to a point. Last time, it was Liz's tender, loving care that pulled her through. Of course the wrist-slashing this time puts a different light on it. But Camilla's problem seems to be handling rejection. Psychiatry *might* help that. It would claim to. Frankly, my approach would be for you two to give it a try on your own. If Camilla improves, then maybe we should look at some counselling to try and ensure it doesn't happen again. And, of course, if she gets worse, I would have no option but to refer her.'

Matt woke in pitch darkness. The first sensation he registered was the sound of rain drumming on the windows, the same cold, relentless rain that had hardly let up since the morning after Camilla's breakdown, making it almost impossible to set foot outdoors. Then, came the dull shock of realisation that it was Christmas Eve. He turned to look at the illuminated panel on the clock. Six twenty. He eased himself out of bed and stood for a moment, naked, listening to Liz's steady breathing, then walked soundlessly into the bathroom to wrap a towel around his waist. He was halfway down the back stairs when he hesitated, then turned and padded back up the stairs and along the corridor to Camilla's room.

For some seconds he stood with his head close to her door, listening. He heard nothing. Without a sound, he eased open the door. Pain flooded his face. Three days earlier they had decided that the most immediate danger had passed and that Mark and Liz, drained by broken nights, could safely abandon their night vigils.

55

Now, Camilla lay sprawled on the sofa. In front of her the television set flickered, the screen blank. Treading softly, he dragged the quilt from the undisturbed bed and crossed to where she lay, her mouth open, a tiny trickle of saliva at one corner. He stood looking down into her face. Her hair hung in lank, lifeless clumps. The flesh of her face seemed to have been pared away, leaving the cheekbones jutting hard against the skin. Purplish shadows had spread beneath the eyes, made darker by her unaccustomed indoor pallor.

His face creased in concern, he stooped and carefully covered her with the quilt, then went across to switch off the television. As he turned from the set her eyes were wide open, staring at him. Hesitantly, he stepped towards her.

'Camilla?' he said, tentatively. 'I was afraid you'd be cold. Do you need anything, sweetheart?'

She continued staring at him, her eyes taking in his bare torso, the powerful legs beneath the towel. Then, abruptly, she wrenched away from him, turning to bury her face in the folds of the duvet. For a moment more Matt stood, a hand half outstretched. Then he strode from the room.

He paced through the darkened kitchen into the utility room, and through the door into the converted barn. He flipped a switch and in the same movement, tossed the towel aside, took two swift strides and dived. The fluorescent lights were still stuttering to life as he cleaved the stillness of the forty-foot pool, making hardly a splash.

He swam hard into the first of his eighty lengths, a smooth, coordinated crawl, relishing the renewed sensations. It was the first morning since Camilla's return that he had followed his routine. It was the first night he had not lain awake through the early hours, tortured by thoughts of Camilla. It was not that he had stopped worrying, only that exhaustion had finally let him sleep through. Many nights, he had awoken to find Liz already sitting in the blackness, staring at the paler rectangle of the window. The two of them would hold hands in the darkness, sometimes talking, sometimes just sitting in silence until fatigue overwhelmed them.

Camilla had not once left her room. The little she ate or drank she requested through Mark. He was the only one with whom she seemed prepared to have any contact at all. Each day, after the cup of weak black tea that was all Liz could now stomach for breakfast, she mounted to Camilla's room hoping to cajole some communication from her. As the days had passed without progress she was now at her wits' end. Camilla spoke to her only flatly to refuse to see the doctor again. Apart from that she simply acted as though Liz did not exist, either lying on her bed or slumping in front of the television, rarely bothering even to change the channel, often staring as though in a trance at a blankly flickering screen, hours after transmissions had ended.

His eighty lengths completed, Matt pulled himself from the pool and towelled himself off. He was breathing hard, his pulse pounding. For the first time since the incident, he felt his head might be clear enough to do some work, and he headed for the kitchen with a new vigour in his stride.

Matt sat hunched in the deep leather chair, toying absently with the keyboard, erasing much of what he had spent the last hour writing. The sight of Liz sitting opposite him at the kitchen counter, nursing her cup of weak tea, hollow-eyed and discouraged, had dissipated most of the invigorating effects of the swim. Even scanning the mail – mainly the usual tedious, and no longer even gratifying, crop of invitations to attend charity functions, the copies of book reviews from around the world, the last-gasp Christmas cards – had required a determined marshalling of his will. The image of Camilla's pale, wasted face once again dominated his thoughts, crowding out all other concerns.

The sound of a car in the lane brought him out of his reverie and to his feet with an exclamation of pleasure. He reached the kitchen in time to see Jane duck inside, laughing, her blonde hair spotted with rain, Mark at her heels carrying her travel bag and a brightly coloured carrier stuffed with impressively wrapped presents. She hurried to kiss Liz and then Matt, a grave expression driving the laughter from her face. 'How is she?'

Mark glanced at Matt before answering. 'Pretty bad,' he murmured.

Jane's face clouded. 'She hasn't . . . ?'

Matt shook his head, smiling ruefully. 'No. She hasn't done anything silly. She's just very low, not responding. Not to me or to Liz, anyway,' he added sombrely. Unthinking, he touched Mark's arm. 'Mark's the only one she's spoken to since it happened, and that doesn't amount to a dozen words.'

Jane's frown deepened. 'Poor Camilla. I wanted to come over earlier. Except that . . . Daddy . . . he thought you would probably prefer to be alone.' Matt flicked a glance at Mark. The young man consciously did not return it, his eyes fixed on Jane's face as she went on speaking. 'He didn't even think I should come now, really. He was afraid I'd be in the way.'

'That was thoughtful of him,' Matt murmured. The hint of irony buried deep beneath his matter-of-fact tone brought a quick warning look from Mark. 'Your dad was wrong, though. It will do us all good to have you here for a few days. I think Liz and I have been looking forward to it as much as Mark. I just hope being among our problems won't get you down too much.'

'Oh, no! I really *wanted* to come. To see if I could be of any help. How is she? Could I see her now?'

Mark nodded vigorously, ignoring Matt and Liz's hesitation. 'That would be great. I'll take your stuff upstairs.' He indicated the coffee jug. 'I was just about to take that up, to see if Camilla might be interested. Why don't you do it?'

Matt shrugged, and reached for a tray. 'I guess you're right, Mark. Jane's the girl she's always been happiest to share her secrets with. It might be just what she needs.' As he handed her the loaded tray his grin faded. 'Camilla thinks the world of you, Jane,' he said, suddenly hoarse. 'Try and get her to talk to you. Just a word, an acknowledgement that you're there, would be something.' He blinked and ground the heel of his hand quickly at the corner of his eye. 'Please do what you can, Jane,' he whispered, moving with her to the door. 'I don't think Liz can take much more.'

The phone and the doorbell sounded almost simultaneously. Matt turned towards the phone, a frosted champagne bottle still in one hand as he worked at the cork with the other. 'Mark, do you want to get some glasses while I take this?' He raised his voice in the direction of the open door. 'Rachel, please can you let them in?' He raised the phone to his ear.

'Matt? Harry.'

Matt felt the excitement surge in him. 'Harry! That's your good news voice! God knows I need some. Do I go ahead and open this bottle I happen to have in my hand?'

'Open it, Matt. And drink one for me, too. I just

came out of my meeting with Stan Kowalski. It's a done deal, Matt.'

Matt gave a whooping laugh. 'Harry, you're a genius! Tell me about it.' As he spoke, Annie Trevellyn pushed the door wide and stood back to allow her son's wheelchair to glide into the room, followed by Roger, a faintly sulky look on his face. Matt waved the bottle in distracted greeting. 'Just give me the numbers, Harry,' he said, smiling at William as he rolled, beaming, towards him. 'I've got guests.'

Listening intently, he put down the bottle and laid his arm around William's wasted shoulders as the boy, crumpled and deformed by spina bifida, nestled at his side. When Matt finally put the phone down, he was grinning from ear to ear. 'Liz!' he bellowed at the ceiling. 'Can you come down here? We're finally in the film business!'

Opening a fourth bottle of champagne, Matt was surprised by a sudden upsurge of anger. The dinner had turned into a wake. It was Christmas Eve, he had just found out he was about to sign a deal with Kowalski which, even by Hollywood's inflated standards, was a monster, practically guaranteeing an income from additional book sales and merchandising that would make the fortune he had earned over the past dozen years look like small change. The dinner should have been a celebration of the culmination of his career. Instead of which, it was on the way to becoming a total disaster! Liz was trying hard but was simply too exhausted to be happy. What energy she could muster was spent trying to console Jane, still in tearful shock at Camilla's murmured invitation to 'fuck off'.

Rachel sat mute and immobile, the harsh planes of her face radiating disapproval as Roger worked his way through successive bottles. Matt took relief in William, sharing jokes and secret laughter as he helped him load his fork, and in Annie, who slipped seamlessly into the role of hostess, managing to keep up a conversation designed to take Liz's mind off Camilla while also deftly deflecting Roger's stubborn efforts to provide Matt with more gratuitous career advice. The ringing of the phone brought Matt instantly out of his chair, grateful for the relief.

'Matt Stenner.' There was still a residue of anger in his voice.

'Oh, yes. Hello.'

Matt frowned, not recognising the voice, not liking the drawling hint of vanity.

'I'd like to speak to Camilla, please.'

'Sorry. Camilla isn't well.' He was about to hang up when, on a sudden afterthought, he asked, 'Who's speaking?'

'Martin.' The man stretched out the sound, as though he expected its significance to be understood.

Matt took a long, hissing breath. 'Hold on. I'll see if she wants to take it.' He laid the phone down with a clatter and sprinted for the stairs.

'Camilla?' He opened the door fully and advanced into the room. She had been emerging from the bathroom. As he entered she froze, staring at him, her lips tight together. 'Camilla,' he said, stepping tentatively towards her, 'there's a call for you. Martin?'

Camilla's shriek made him fall back. The noise filled the room, a continuous, high-pitched wailing. As he stood there, dismayed and uncertain, the wail gradually coalesced, though without dropping in pitch, into words. 'No!' she shrieked. 'No!' She fell to her knees. 'Keep him away from me. He hurts me! Don't let him . . .' Her words trailed off, back into the formless keening.

Matt stepped forward, shocked and afraid. At his

61

approach she reared back, throwing herself into the angle of the wall and floor, drawing up her knees. Matt stood for a moment staring helplessly down at her. Then, anger flooding his face, he turned and ran from the room.

Liz was starting up the stairs with Annie at her heels. 'Help her,' he called, in answer to Liz's frightened look. Pushing past them, he ran for the phone, Camilla's shrieks carrying loud to his ears. He grabbed the handset. 'Hey, look, who are you? Where can I . . . ?' He broke off, breathless. He stared for several seconds at the dead phone before slamming it back onto the receiver. 'You don't want to talk to me, you bastard, but I'm sure going to talk to you.'

Four

Liz fought her way slowly out of sleep. Her mouth was parched, her lips dry and cracked. A tingling sensation below her nose announced the onset of a cold sore, a sure sign that she was run down. She squinted at the clock and fell back onto the pillow, groaning. Seven fifteen. Almost ten hours of sleep. She had ended the worst Christmas Day of her life by going to bed at nine thirty. Since they had finally managed to calm Camilla down after the Christmas Eve phone call, she had stayed holed up in her room, refusing to see or speak to anyone, not even allowing Mark to enter. Matt had dialled the recording informing him of the number of the last incoming call. It had turned out to be a payphone in a pub.

Christmas lunch, and the exchange of presents, had been miserable, heart-sinking affairs, with Jane still on the edge of tears from Camilla's rebuff, while Rachel mixed barbed innuendo about their skills as parents with lachrymose recollections of Patrick's deft touch with children.

With a sigh that became a sob, Liz turned to reach for Matt. In the same moment the door opened and he entered, clasping a tray in each hand. He set one down beside her and sat on the edge of the bed, the second tray on his knees. He put a hand on her brow, stroking her hair, sculpted into whorls and spikes by her deep sleep. 'You okay?'

She reached for the coffee, grimacing. 'I will be when I've had this. I feel disgusting.'

Matt smiled. 'It's the sleeping pill. I told you it would make you feel shitty.'

'Didn't she eat anything?'

Matt looked down at the waxy roast potatoes, the cold, greasy slices of goose on the tray in front of him. 'She hasn't touched a thing since that call.'

'Hence the clothes?'

He wore outdoor clothes – a leather jacket, corduroys, thick-soled shoes. He took her hand in his. 'I have to talk to him, Liz.'

'But you don't even know who he is!'

'Camilla does! Surely there'll be something in the flat, a phone number, letters.'

Her eyes narrowed. 'How are you going to get in?' He shrugged, saying nothing. Her eyes widened. 'But you can't do that!' He looked at her levelly, still silent. 'You *can't* just go prying in Camilla's papers. You know we've *never* done that, not since they were tiny . . .' Her voice tailed off in the face of his steady gaze. She nodded ruefully. 'Okay. But at least promise me that if you *do* find him you won't beat him up. Whatever her problems, she's not your little baby any more, Matt.'

He kissed her and stood up, laughing drily. 'I promise. I'll just ask him, nicely, what *he* did that drove Camilla to attempt suicide.'

The house was part of a four-storey Victorian terrace that had once been imposing. Now, the front gardens had been concreted to provide parking spaces for dead-beat cars, and the woodwork decayed undisturbed under the peeling paint. The house where Camilla lodged was masked by a neglected privet hedge. Matt slotted the grey Mercedes under a dripping plane tree and hurried through the gap in the hedge where a gate had once hung, his shoulders hunched against the rain.

He ran his thumb down the row of a dozen bell-pushes. A minute later he was still standing in the porch, cursing softly. Everyone had gone home for the Christmas vacation. After a few moments' thought, he looked around him. The overgrown hedge hid the porch from the houses opposite. He put a palm against the door and pushed. There was a quarter of an inch of play before the latch caught. He stood listening for the sound of footsteps. Nothing moved. Bracing himself against the front wall of the porch, he raised a foot waist high, took a deep breath, and kicked out. The screws holding the latch pulled from their holes with no more than a squeak. Inside, he picked up one of the letters strewn on a side table and tore off two corners. He twisted the scraps of paper around the screws and drove them into their holes, using his car key for leverage. It held, with less play than before. It was probably the first repair that had been done on the house in a decade. Purposefully, he mounted the stairs to Camilla's rooms.

'Anybody home?' He looked around him, listening to his words echoing off the grimy woodchip walls. He called once more, counted to ten, and barged the door.

As he stood contemplating the day-to-day disarray of the room, unease seized him for the first time. For several seconds he stood rooted, fighting down the overwhelming sense that he was invading Camilla's life in a strange and despicable way. Finally, with an effort of will, he moved into the room.

He made straight for the work table, stepping gingerly in an instinct to avoid damaging the papers strewn on the floor around it. Among the papers lay a bottle and two glasses. He picked them up, looking pensively at the glasses for a moment before putting them on the kitchen bar and returning to the table. After another moment of hesitation, he stooped and yanked open the drawer.

He searched through the wads of papers, taking care to leave no sign of disturbance. Not that he thought Camilla would remember in what order they had lain. Rather, he could not bear the idea that he was grubbing around in her life. At the back of the drawer he found a bundle of letters, held together with a rubber band. He riffled through them. All were addressed in the same hand, postmarked locally. He slipped the top one from under the rubber band and opened it. His fingers were on the letter inside, sliding it from the envelope, when he paused. With a sharp shake of his head, he reinserted the envelope into the bundle and replaced it in the drawer. Slamming the drawer, he crossed to the wardrobe.

Camilla's leather shoulder bag was slung from a hook inside. With a shudder of self-loathing, he lifted it down and upended it onto the bed. Among the junk that tumbled out was her address book with its familiar marbled cardboard covers.

Seated in the worn armchair, Matt thumbed page by page through the tiny book. He found no Martin. There were, however, three numbers which stood alone, which he copied onto a piece of paper. He crossed to the work table and again took the bundle of letters from the drawer. Taking a long breath, he removed the top envelope and drew out the letter. The letterhead was blurred, cheaply printed. Although he was expecting it, it still gave him a jolt. Martin and Eve Bohill. Naturally, the bastard was married! The phone number beneath the address was one of those he had noted.

'Hello?' The woman's voice was polite but guarded. A child wailed in the background.

'Good morning,' Matt said briskly, 'I wonder if I could speak to Martin, please?'

'Mmm. Are you one of his students?' she asked warily.

Matt closed his eyes, weary at the sudden sense of the paltriness of it, the man a lecturer, using his position to seduce his students. 'No, I'm not,' he said, trying not to let her hear his despondency. 'My name's Stenner. Matthew Stenner.'

'Oh. Really? *The* Matthew Stenner?' He smiled sourly at the new brightness in her voice. 'Just a moment.'

She had spoken his name unnecessarily loudly, letting someone in the room with her hear it. Matt heard muffled voices. He thought he heard suppressed anger in one of them. It was not surprising. Boxing Day was no time to have a stranger phone you to pick at your emotional scabs. It was several seconds before another extension was lifted. The woman mumbled something and put down her phone.

'I'm Martin Bohill. What can I do for you?' The voice was truculent, sulky.

'I'm Matt Stenner. We spoke on Christmas Eve.'

There was a brief silence. 'Yes, I believe we might have,' he said cagily. He paused, waiting for Matt to take the initiative.

'I want to talk to you.'

'Oh? Is that so?' Matt grimaced at the man's sudden change of tone. It was the voice of a weak man trying to sound in control. 'What about?'

'My daughter. And you.'

Another pause. Matt imagined he could hear the man moistening his lips. 'Well, as you realise, this is the vacation. I'm afraid I only discuss student affairs during term. You could call –'

'Today, Mr Bohill. It can't wait.'

'Really?' The drawling attempt at disdain could not hide the queasiness in the voice. 'Well, I'm sorry, Mr Stenner –'

'Do you know the Trust House hotel, on the Bicester Road?' As he spoke, Matt tossed the bundle of letters lightly in his hand. He glanced at his watch and then, without waiting for an answer, added, 'I'll see you in the bar. At eleven thirty.' Bohill began to protest. Matt cut him short. 'Be there. Or I'll be around to read your letters to your wife.'

Matt studied the man as he stood hesitantly looking around the lounge. He was squinting hard. Short-sighted, perhaps, but too vain to wear glasses. He was good-looking, in his mid-thirties, with healthy brown hair that trailed over the collar of his scuffed leather jacket. His jeans rumpled just so over yellow suede boots. Matt raised a hand, beckoning him to the isolated corner where he sat.

Bohill perched on the edge of his chair and glanced around the lounge, licking his lips, as though afraid he might be photographed. He cleared his throat and shrugged. 'Okay, you won. I'm here. What do you want to talk about?'

'What made Camilla ill?'

Bohill frowned, leaning forward. 'Ill? What's wrong with her?' Beneath the cocky manner his concern might have been real.

'She seems to be having a nervous breakdown. Any idea why?' Matt asked flatly, his eyes on Bohill's face.

A furtive look flitted momentarily across the man's features. He pushed out his lower lip. 'Not really. Should I have?'

'You've been having an affair with her for the last few months. I'd expect you to know something about

68

her emotional state. Or is Camilla just another of the female students you like to fuck?'

Anxiety flickered briefly in Bohill's eyes at Matt's rough tone. Then he leaned towards Matt. 'Look, Mr Stenner,' he said in a confidential, man-to-man voice, 'can I ask you to understand one thing? It was Camilla that started it. I know I shouldn't have let myself be tempted. It was wrong of me. But your daughter's a very pretty girl. And determined,' he added, smirking. 'She looked up to me.' For a moment he seemed about to wink. 'You're a public figure yourself. You know how it is.'

'Do I?' Matt asked coolly. 'Camilla was besotted with you. You could have put her off. Or is that what makes you feel a man, letting girls nearly young enough to be your daughter fall in love with you?'

Bohill drew back, stung by the lacerating contempt in Matt's voice. 'Look, it was ... an episode. I'm a married man. I've got children. Camilla knew that.'

'Sure.' Matt spoke through clenched teeth, his anger rising in his throat. 'And you never told her you were going to leave them? You never gave her the idea that there was something to hope for?' He had leaned forward so that their faces were inches apart.

Bohill swallowed. His eyes slid guiltily away from Matt's gaze. The man was so transparent Matt could almost see him thinking, wondering what Matt had heard, what tack to take. Bohill dropped his voice to a whisper. 'Look, I hate to say this, but are you sure Camilla's not, well, I'm not sure how to put this ... a bit ... flaky?'

For the first time in his life Matt knew what it meant to see red. An explosion of blinding red light behind his eyes blotted out his vision. Before it had cleared, his open hand hit Bohill on the side of the head. The force of the blow jolted him off the smooth synthetic upholstery to land on his knees. Without knowing how he got there, Matt was on his feet, standing over the man, his fists clenched. Bohill cowered, making no effort to get up, one hand clamped to his cheek, where the white outline of Matt's fingers was only slowly fading. Pouting, he looked around him in a vague plea for rescue. The few customers, middle-aged couples, stared but showed no interest in intervening. The barman, an unhealthy-looking youth whose tight uniform jacket emphasised his slight build, eyed Matt's height and went on stacking shelves.

Letting out his breath between his teeth, Matt reached down to take a handful of Bohill's jacket front and heave him back into the chair. Bohill pressed himself against the back. His cheek had gone from white to an angry red. Matt sat down opposite him, his chest heaving. He spoke softly, forcing the words through gritted teeth. 'You had better have a good explanation for that, pal.'

It was mid-afternoon when Matt wearily returned home. Liz was in the kitchen drinking tea with Jane. Both looked pale and bereft. Without waiting to be asked, Jane finished her tea and slipped out of the room.

'Did you find him?'

Matt poured himself some tea. 'Mmm. He's just a preening little prick.'

'A student?'

'Lecturer,' he answered, grimacing.

Liz covered her eyes with a hand. 'Oh God. Her damned dependent streak again. Don't tell me. Married. Four children.'

'Two.'

She looked at him, shaking her head. 'Was he any help, at least?'

'Maybe. He was with her that afternoon. He told her he was breaking it off.'

'Oh shit. That fits, doesn't it?'

'I'm afraid it might. He claims he had been trying to cool it off for weeks.' He laughed, despite his anger. 'By the time he'd finished he was quite carried away with his heroic behaviour, the selfless hero, sacrificing true love for the sake of his wife and children.'

'Clearing the decks for next term, more likely. Another young woman to play God to. Don't those bastards realise the damage they do?'

'Probably,' Matt said drily. 'Anyway, now we're a bit clearer about the problem, let's go up and see if it's any help.'

Camilla and Mark sat at opposite ends of the sofa in front of the television. Camilla sprawled, her eyes glazed, looking at something far beyond the garish glow of the screen. Mark had been watching Camilla. As they entered, he rose and crossed to meet them. He pointed to a tray of sandwiches on the floor by Camilla's feet. 'She hasn't touched it.'

Matt laid a hand around his shoulders. 'Mark, we think we may have found out what set all this off,' he murmured. 'A boyfriend *did* throw her over again.' Feeling Mark's body harden with anger, he said, 'Don't bother, Mark. The man's a prick. She's much better off without him. Mum's going to try to talk to Camilla about it, though, to see if it helps. Why don't you take Jane out for a while? The poor girl's going through the Christmas from hell.'

As the door closed behind Mark, Liz lowered herself gently onto the sofa, leaving only a few inches between herself and the impassive Camilla. Matt strolled across to the television and switched it off before dropping to a crouch next to the sofa, on the other side of

71

Camilla from Liz. His face puckered involuntarily at the sour smell of unwashed skin. He looked at Liz in renewed dismay. All her life Camilla had been scrupulous about personal hygiene. To the point of obsession, he told himself, grimly.

Liz laid her fingers on her daughter's arm. 'Camilla?' Camilla continued staring into space. 'Camilla, darling, we know what the problem is. We know it must have been very upsetting for you, but you must try to accept that it was for the best.'

Gradually, Camilla's eyes lost their blank, unfocused look. Painfully slowly, she turned her head until she was looking directly into her mother's eyes, their faces a hand's span apart. Still she said nothing.

Liz flicked a momentary, excited glance at Matt. 'Really, darling, you do understand that, don't you? Martin has his family. There are the children. He really had no choice but to end it.' Camilla's eyes widened again. Crimson spots appeared on the point of each cheekbone, giving her a feverish look. Apprehension entered Liz's face as she went on, 'Daddy went to see him, my love.'

Camilla looked at Matt. He groped for her hand. It was icy cold. He met her gaze. Her eyes had a wild new glint in them. 'That's right, sweetheart. I talked it over with him. It's not that he didn't, doesn't love you . . . I'm sure he does.' The words felt lumpy and awkward in his mouth as his mind played on the cowed, evasive Bohill, with his vain, self-regarding smirk. 'But in the end he couldn't go through with it. He couldn't just walk out on his commitments. You have to understand, he knew that calling it off . . . it was his way of being kind to you.'

Camilla's nails flashed across his vision, slashing the skin of his nose. As he recoiled, she brought her other hand raking downwards, catching the flesh just below

72

the eye. Leaning away from her, he grabbed her wrist as her hooked fingers came at him again. Whimpering in horror, Liz threw herself onto Camilla, smothering her other arm. 'Camilla!' she screamed. 'Stop it! That's your *father*, for God's sake!'

Her face contorted, Camilla twisted and fought. 'You've been prying, haven't you? Nosing in my life.' She snatched an arm from Liz's grip and brought her talons arcing at Matt's face again. He parried the blow, clamping his fingers around her wrist, pinioning it hard against his chest.

'Camilla! Stop it, for God's sake. Listen!' His fingers bit into her wrists as she struggled, kicking and writhing. 'We weren't prying. I just *talked* to him, that's all.'

'You went to my room!' The words were a screech through tightly gritted teeth.

'But don't you see? We just wanted to *understand* what was happening to you.'

She bucked away from Liz, managing to get to her feet, her hands still in Matt's grasp. 'You were interfering! Playing God with *my* life.' She dug her heels into the carpet, dragging at Matt. He allowed himself to be steered towards the door. 'Why can't you just go away? All of you! Just leave me alone!' She bumped against the door and Liz stepped forward to open it. Matt released Camilla's wrists, allowing her to shove him into the corridor, followed by Liz. 'Why didn't you just let me die?' The floor shook under their feet as the door slammed shut.

They remained in the passage, clinging to each other. It was some seconds before Liz pulled back, her cheeks glistening with tears. She looked up into Matt's face. 'We have to get help, don't we?'

He nodded, the movement sending blood from the parallel slashes down his cheek flicking onto his shirt.

73

'Yes,' he said, his voice cracking. 'I guess we do.'

At four o'clock the following afternoon, Matt was on his way downstairs with yet another untouched tray of food when he saw headlights slice through the thickening dusk as a car turned into the courtyard. He dropped the tray onto the sofa, the first time it had been useful since it was put there, and hurried down to the front door.

The car was a late-model Jaguar with an unblemished metallic sheen. The occupant eased himself out and headed towards the door with an easy, unhurried stride. Two inches taller than Matt, but narrower in the shoulders, his clothes and haircut obviously expensive, the man exuded confidence and prosperity. At six paces, he started smiling. At three, he was already extending a manicured hand. Matt took it, returning just enough of the unnecessary pressure to make his own point without turning it into a contest.

'David Everett,' the man said, still working Matt's hand. 'You must be Matthew Stenner. My children *love* your books.'

Matt responded with a taut little smile, the force of his antipathy at the suggestion of condescension in the man's tone taking him by surprise. Forcing the smile wider, he ushered him into the dishevelled study and went off in search of Liz.

He found her on the phone in the drawing room. She curtailed her call and rose, closing the book. 'Just checking the guests for the Save the Children breakfast,' she said.

'New Year's Day? Are you sure?' He jerked his chin at the ceiling and shrugged. 'I just thought, in the circumstances, you would have called it off.'

'We have to go on living, Matt.' He shook his head, half laughing. 'I don't know how you can stand seeing

74

most of those old bats at the best of times, let alone with what you're going through at the moment.'

She reached an arm around his waist. 'It helps keep my mind off it,' she said, deep weariness in her voice.

Stepping through the door of the study, Liz rekindled her smile and offered her hand. 'Delighted to meet you, Dr Everett. Peter Monroe has a very high opinion of you. *Do* I call psychiatrists "Doctor", by the way?'

He gave a self-deprecating laugh. 'Mister. David, in fact, please. I haven't actually worked directly with Dr Monroe, but I suppose I have been lucky enough to have acquired a certain reputation. I, er, I write a little, too, you know.' He glanced at Matt and gave a small shrug. 'Eating disorders, of course, not fiction.'

Matt looked at his feet. 'Congratulations. Peter explained our problem, I think.'

Everett pursed his lips. 'Mmm, but I'd like to hear it from you, in your own words, from the very beginning.'

It was almost six before Everett closed up his notepad and slid it and his gold pen into an inside pocket.

'So, now you've had Camilla's life story, and ours, what next?' Matt asked.

Everett smiled, oblivious to the impatience in Matt's voice. 'I think I should talk to Camilla, don't you?'

Matt choked back his renewed irritation at the superciliousness in the man's manner. 'Right. No sense wasting time. I'll show you the way.'

Everett was looking at Liz, ignoring him. 'Or perhaps Liz, if Camilla's responding better to her.'

Matt caught Liz's eye, giving her a wry smile. 'Fine. Why don't you take some food up with you? Maybe David's persuasive powers will induce her to eat something.'

*   *   *

75

Matt paced restlessly, circling the kitchen like a caged animal. Liz stood at the counter, slicing food. Fifteen minutes had passed since, at Everett's request, she had left him alone with Camilla, glancing back to see him draw up a chair to the bed where Camilla lay staring at the ceiling, the plate of buttered toast cooling on the bedside table. Mark sat in the battered sofa with an arm around Jane, both of them quiet and grave, their eyes on the door.

A sound made Matt whirl towards the back stairs. He listened, head cocked. This time they all heard it, a piercing shriek of rage. Matt leaped up the stairs, Mark racing across the kitchen in his wake.

They reached Camilla's closed door to see Everett at the end of the corridor, striding towards the main stairs. At the sound of their running footsteps he spun to face them. His face was congested with indignation. He held his left hand clutched to his brow. With the other he dabbed a handkerchief angrily at the greasy streak on his lapel. Matt reached out and took him by the shoulders, as though he were about to shake him. 'What happened?'

There was a flurry as Liz ran to join them, Jane at her heels.

Everett was breathing heavily. With an angry flourish, he drew his hand away from his brow, revealing a livid red weal. Above it, toast crumbs clung in the dishevelled hair. 'Your daughter hit me!' A white spot formed beneath the taut skin across the bridge of his nose. 'I interrupted my Christmas break because Dr Monroe begged me to treat your daughter.' He tapped a finger to his brow. 'And this is what I get for it!'

'What did *you* do to her?' Matt asked softly, still holding Everett.

'*Do* to her? I tried to befriend her, of course. I tried

76

to convince her that she should eat. I managed to get her to take the tray. She seemed as though she was listening. And then she threw it at me.'

'On *purpose*? Are you sure?'

'She practically threw it. I just placed it on the bed next to her. And before I could even stand up, she lashed out, like that.' He flicked his wrist, as though launching a Frisbee.

'But surely she didn't mean to hit you?' Liz insisted.

He shook out the perfectly ironed handkerchief, pressed it to the wound, and then pulled it away, staring at a minute bloodstain. 'I could easily have lost an eye!' he said surlily.

Matt let his arms fall to his sides. 'You could have,' he said, sighing. 'We're sorry.' He glanced at Liz, speaking more to her than to Everett. 'Now what do we do?'

Everett sniffed, dabbed again at the cut. 'Well, if you want me to treat her, I would insist she be taken into –'

'Into what?' Matt moved a step closer to him, his eyes narrowing. 'A hospital? A mental hospital?'

Everett nodded. 'That would be my advice. If you want –'

'Thanks for coming,' Matt interjected, cutting him off. As he spoke, he took Everett by the elbow and led him towards the stairs. 'We appreciate your taking the time, what with Christmas, and all.'

'It's the only sensible solution, you know. Supposing she had grabbed scissors, or a knife? You can't expect a doctor to risk –'

They were already at the foot of the stairs. 'We appreciate the advice. We'll just have to find *someone*, though, David. Because Camilla's definitely not going to some mental institution.'

They watched from behind the glass of the front

door as Everett swung himself into the Jaguar and gunned the car out of the courtyard.

Matt's arm was around Liz's shoulders. He looked down into her face. 'So, what *do* we do now?'

She moved closer against him. 'I think you should let me do as I wanted to in the first place, and ask around among the London crowd.'

'Do you still think so? After that?' He grimaced and jerked his head in the direction of the departed Jaguar. 'According to Peter, Everett's supposed to be the best in the country. As he didn't omit to tell us, he's the man who writes the books. He's the source. And you saw what a prick *he* turned out to be!'

'Of course, he's a conceited, vain little nobody, and his reputation has gone to his head. He's more of a politician than a doctor. That doesn't make *all* of them useless, though. I still say you should let me ask around to see if we can find someone whose approach would be more ... well, gentler, more understanding, less *conventional*.'

Matt frowned. 'What do you have in mind? Putting Camilla in the hands of some new age charlatan who wants to read her aura, or massage her feet with mandrake root to realign her psychic matrix, or some crap like that?'

'I know only too well how you feel about the whole area of counselling, therapy and the rest. And you know I agree with you, up to a point. But Camilla, and we too, need *some* sort of help. If there's somebody out there who really *can* do it, somebody who has some references, don't you think we owe it to Camilla to at least try them?'

He turned to look her full in the face, smiling. 'Liz, you're trying to tell me something. Do you have someone in mind?'

She laughed. 'Well, I did speak to Janet.'

Janet Goad was a fashion journalist. She and Liz had shared a flat long before Matt had come on the scene. She and her husband were down-to-earth, smart and sceptical, unlikely candidates for a realignment of their psychic meridians.

'You told her about Camilla?'

'Not directly. Although she guessed the broad picture.'

'And she suggested someone?'

'Someone who knows someone. Trish Campbell. She used to work on *Harpers*. I've met her and she always came over as very sensible.'

'How does she fit in?'

'Her daughter. When Trish got divorced the girl just broke up. Lost thirty pounds, took to her room. They tried everything; doctors, analysts, pharmaceuticals. The girl just got worse and worse. According to Janet she was dying, starving to death. Then somebody told Trish about this person. From what Janet said, she charges a fortune, and only takes on a very carefully selected clientele. She seems to be successful and eating disorders are her big thing. She's published work on the subject.'

He snorted. 'Just like Everett!'

'Matt, it *worked*. Where everything else failed. It took nearly a year, but it seems she pulled her through it fantastically. The girl's never been so well.'

'Then let's get the woman's phone number.'

It was three days since they had left a message on the woman's answering machine. In that time Camilla had visibly lost more weight. Her T-shirts and leggings hung in slack folds. The flesh of her face was being pared away beneath the greyish, lifeless skin. Her one sign of any reaction to events around her was occasionally to speak to Mark, usually to refuse food. The only time he had extracted anything like conversation out of her was a few muttered references to the incident with Everett. It was his own fault. He had come too close, invading her space. Ignoring her protest, he had sat on her bed. She had lashed out with the first thing that came to hand. She told it with a bored, detached air, as though it belonged to some distant past in which she could not be expected to have any interest.

Liz, too, had lost weight. A slight tic under her left eye, barely noticeable when she was really well, had grown more pronounced, causing the tightened skin to leap and twitch. Lack of sleep had chiselled the lines of her triangular face into a look of permanent exhaustion.

Sighing deeply, Matt turned from the study window to his word processor. The screen was almost blank. Next to it lay the note from his agent reminding him of the deadline for the completed redraft. He cupped his hands over his face and kneaded the flesh, as though trying to massage some life into his brain. For years he had prided himself on his disciplined ability to focus clearly on the project in hand, on having never lost the executive skills acquired in his years in the chemical industry, clearing his desk each day. Now, several days' accumulation of mail, letters and Christmas cards lay scattered on the desk, some unopened, some still among the ripped ruins of their envelopes. He had not even read any of it, let alone replied to it. Dropping heavily into his chair, he had just swept a random handful towards him when the phone rang.

'Matt?'

'Harriet?' he responded, surprised at hearing the voice, the girl Friday at the office of his London agent. 'Merry Christmas. Happy New Year. Are you working? I thought it was the Big Sleep until after New Year.'

'Somebody's got to hold the fort, Matt. Not *every* country in the world goofs off for the entire period.' She paused. 'Are you okay?'

He raised his eyebrows. He had not thought he was letting it show. 'Sure. I'm fine. Why?'

'Matt, you do realise you've missed the recording this morning?'

For a moment he faltered, groping. Then, abruptly, it hit him. 'Oh shit!' He clapped a hand to his head. 'The interview!' He scrambled futilely among the junk on the desk, looking for his diary. He gave up before he found it. 'I'm supposed to be there now!'

'The BBC just called. They're very unhappy. They have the crew set up, everything. Tom Reiner broke off a family holiday to do the interview. Apparently he's *seething*. I faxed you a reminder yesterday. Didn't you get it?'

Matt looked desolately across at the fax machine. Paper snaked from it, gathering in an unruly swirl on the floor. He groaned audibly. He had not glanced at it for days. 'Sorry, Harriet. The fact is, I haven't been well. Would they set it up for another day?'

'I already tried. The woman bit my head off. They aren't used to being treated like that, Matt. Most people they want to interview get their dates right!'

He let out a long breath. 'Sorry, Harriet. Really.'

'Okay. The damage is done. As long as you're all right. Happy New Year, Matt.'

He stood for several seconds, staring blankly at the dishevelled desk. Harriet was right, of course. Reiner's programme was the most prestigious arts broadcast on television. Writers would kill for two minutes on the show. They had planned to devote an entire forty-five minutes to him. The thing had been set up for months. And he had totally forgotten it. He was still leaning on the phone, shocked at the evidence of how far he had unravelled, when it rang again under his hand.

'Mr Stenner?' The American accented voice was deep and unhurried. 'This is Naomi Butler.' For a moment Matt was so intent on the voice, with its extraordinary, enfolding warmth that the name did not register. 'You left a message. You want to talk to me. About your daughter.'

Five

'Doorbell!' Emma Trafford cried, superfluously, from the hall. 'Shall I answer it, dear?'

Liz and Annie, grappling with a trestle table, could not suppress smiles, as, without waiting for Liz's response, Emma sailed past the drawing-room doorway, already on her way. In her rubber gloves, stained sweatshirt and drooping leggings, it was only her tinkling porcelain vowels that gave a clue to the fact that the Honourable Emma Trafford's father had inherited a substantial part of Suffolk.

'If it's for my bring and buy, put it with the things in the cloakroom,' Annie called after her.

A few moments later Emma thrust her head into the room. 'Sorry, Annie,' she called, loud enough to be heard at the far end of the house, 'no luck!' She looked at Liz. 'An American lady, dear.'

Liz looked apprehensively at Annie. 'It's her!'

'The counsellor woman?'

'Mmm. She's early. Could you take over here for me?'

Annie straightened, shaking back the layered brown hair that hung over her brow. She laid a hand gently over Liz's. 'You go ahead,' she said softly. Lifting the cloth from Liz's hand, she turned to where her son sat in his wheelchair, watching the busy women, some in working clothes like Emma's, others in the charity circuit uniform of ruff-necked blouses, Liberty skirts and dark tights. 'Hey, William,' she called, smiling, 'come

83

and make yourself useful. Wipe these tables over for Liz.'

The woman was standing at the library window. At the sound of Liz's approach she turned slowly, already smiling as she stepped forward to offer her hand. 'Good morning. I'm Naomi Butler. And you must be Liz?' The voice was thrilling, low and rich, the slow vowels unmistakably American, though without any giveaway regional twang. 'I hope I'm not sowing havoc by arriving early.'

The woman was three inches taller than Liz. Her clothes, of beautiful woollen fabrics in deep, rich colours, did not quite conceal the thickness of her body, deep-breasted and wide-hipped. Her hair, nearly black, but marbled with grey, was pulled back from her wide, smooth face and coiled in a thick braid at the nape of her neck. Her bulk might have made her awkward. In fact, there was a deep stillness about the woman, a placidity in her movements that made Liz feel faintly ungainly and overwrought.

Liz brushed her palm on her jeans before taking the offered hand. 'Annie doesn't need me. It's kind of you to come at all, on New Year's Eve. My husband's working. He's struggling with a deadline. I'll get him.'

Matt ushered the two women into the study and closed the door firmly behind them. Naomi Butler sat, straight-backed and perfectly still, radiating physical and spiritual ease as she waited for him to speak. He smiled to himself at the contrast with Everett's blustering vanity. He splayed his fingers. 'So, Naomi, tell us where we start?'

It was late afternoon when Matt went to the kitchen to make tea. He was filling the kettle when Annie entered, buttoning her coat, a scarf wound around her neck. She held two empty Chardonnay bottles in her free hand. 'Tell Liz everything's ready for the morning.' She deposited the bottles on the worktop. 'I even managed to keep dear old Emma more or less sober.' Her laughing expression faded. 'God. What's the woman been doing to you? You look washed out.'

'I am. I feel as if I've been flayed alive. She's dug up things about us I'd forgotten years ago.'

Annie looked down. 'There are still some secrets, though?'

Matt gave her a long look. 'There always will be,' he said softly.

Her smile was wistful. 'Anyway, I thought she was supposed to be treating *Camilla*.'

He laughed, relieved. 'She needs the background. If she *is* going to treat Camilla, I guess she'd want to know if there were skeletons in *our* cupboard, first.'

Once again, Annie averted her eyes. Then, abruptly, she flicked a glance behind her and moved tight up against him. 'Happy New Year, Matt,' she whispered hoarsely, and kissed him.

He moved too late, taking the kiss half on the mouth. He was conscious of her body pressing against him through the coat. Her hand was behind him, grasping his sweater. It was a second or two before he pulled away. 'Yeah. Thanks,' he breathed, as her fingers reluctantly unfurled from his sweater. 'And to you, Annie.' He stood quite still, listening to her receding footsteps.

It was another hour after they'd drunk the tea before Naomi stood up and walked to the window. She stood for some moments, staring out into the gathering darkness. 'Liz,' she said, without turning around, 'one thing has been bothering me. The period of insomnia you mentioned, was there any *particular* reason for it? An emotional upset, for example?' She turned slowly to face them. 'Any problem between you two that might have transmitted itself to Camilla?'

Liz shook her head. 'You're barking up the wrong tree. I was just working too hard, that's all. And travelling too much. I'd been asked to do a series of pieces on the New York scene, fashions, faces. I didn't know what I was letting myself in for! I was back and forwards to New York so often my body didn't know *what* time it was. I was up wandering around the house all night, then I'd fall asleep in the middle of a meal. It was a bad time, but there was no problem with us.' She sought Matt's hand, grasping it tightly. 'Matt was incredibly supportive. He never complained about me being away, even though it meant he had the children to take care of, on top of his own work. He could have put me under pressure to travel less, but he never did. He was great.' She leaned closer to him, so that their shoulders touched.

Naomi nodded, smiling broadly, and threw up her hands. 'Well. I guess that's about all I need to know. Sorry if you feel I've given you a grilling, but I warned you I would be direct.'

'Direct to the jugular,' Matt responded.

She laughed, a lovely, deep-throated sound. 'It's the only way I can work. I can't help people who hold out on me. It wouldn't be fair on Camilla for me to try. Now, before I try to talk to Camilla, is there anything you want to ask *me*? After all, if you're going to put your daughter in my hands . . .'

Matt nodded, smiling wryly. 'After the grilling you've given *us*, the least you can do is give us a run-down of your sexual fantasies!'

She laughed again, her eyes shining. 'Better not. But I'll tell you why I think I'm qualified to try and help Camilla.' She sat opposite them again. 'My background is conventional psychiatry. I worked for several years in hospitals and a couple of prisons around America. I ended up heading the psychiatric unit in a major hospital, but I eventually had to quit.'

'Why?' Liz asked.

Naomi smiled. 'Basically, I couldn't stand the nut-cases!' She laughed briefly. 'It's true. It became very heavy. In the end I just couldn't deal any more with people so far beyond reach. Spending your life with psychopaths and schizoids, always wondering if one of them is going to come at you with a blade, can be very wearing, believe me. Also, my interests were lead-ing me elsewhere.'

'Where was that?' Matt asked.

'There was some research I wanted to do that I was never going to have time for. The connection between diet and health, mental *and* physical. That led me into looking at eating disorders, and before I knew it, that had pretty well taken me over. It had the attraction of being an area where there was a chance of *curing* people. So, after a couple of years as a dropout, that's what I started doing, in New York.'

Matt nodded. 'What brought you to the UK?'

'I'd been to London and liked it. Also, frankly, the field seemed less crowded here. Or should I be saintly and say the need was greater?'

They all laughed. 'Let's stick with the bald truth,' Matt said. 'When do you want to start talking to Camilla?'

Naomi rose with a fluid, effortless grace. 'How about right now?'

Camilla held the curtains open a crack and stared down into the courtyard, cast in the yellow light of the secur-ity lamps. The black Volkswagen Golf was still there, gleaming wetly in the lamplight. Expressionless, she let the curtains fall back and turned into the room where the light from the television screen threw her eyes and eroded cheeks into deep shadow. She was about to curl up among the dishevelled cushions of the sofa when a soft tap at the door stopped her. With a muted cry, she ran barefoot to the door and checked the flimsy bolt which Mark had repaired, unasked, when he and Liz gave up their vigil. Her chest heaving with relief, she stood immobile, listening. The tapping came once more, still barely audible.

'Camilla?'

Camilla stepped back a pace, startled by the proximity of the voice.

'Camilla? My name's Naomi. May I speak to you. Please? There's no need to let me in. I'll just sit here and talk to you. As long as you don't mind. If you want me to go away, just say so. I promise I'll leave you alone immediately.'

Camilla bit her lip. The velvety texture of the voice was seductive, completely unthreatening. The warmth in it seemed to trigger a strange, thrilling sensation, like something half remembered from childhood. As the woman spoke, her voice changed position, coming from lower down, as if the speaker had indeed sat down. After a short pause, in which Camilla made no protest, the voice came again.

For some time she stood quite still, making no effort to take in the words, only finding a pleasant, unnameable comfort in the deep timbre of the voice and its relaxed, uninsistent tone. After perhaps two minutes, she lowered herself into a crouch. With her back to the wall for support, her arms clasped tight around her knees, she remained motionless, letting the reassuring warmth of the voice flow around her.

Gradually, some of the sullen, pinched look ebbed from Camilla's face. Without any effort of will, she found herself attending to the woman's words. They were not about much, vague reflections on misplaced anger, misdirected energy, personal identity, relationships awry. Even as she listened part of her mind scorned it as new age nonsense. And yet, there was some quality in this voice, a seductive, gentle logic in the words, that somehow stilled her objections. At length, there was a soft swishing of fabrics, and then the voice came from above her. 'Thanks for your time, Camilla. I enjoyed talking to you. Would you mind if I came back tomorrow?'

Camilla remained in a crouch, blinking, as though emerging from a pleasant daydream. She made no response to the question.

'Good.' The woman sounded genuinely delighted at not being rebuffed. 'Same time? Bye then, Camilla. Take care.'

Only when the muffled footsteps had died away did the girl clamber stiffly upright and throw herself, face down, onto the crumpled bed.

Naomi swung the Golf into the courtyard, glancing at the dashboard clock. Over the preceding days she had fallen into the habit of arriving at one o'clock, to coincide with Matt's ritual lunch break. Today she was almost an hour early. She parked next to the green Rover that was already drawn up on the mossy cobbles. For a moment, she sat contemplating the other car, and then, gathering a leather document case from the passenger seat, she climbed out and walked quickly to the back door of the house.

'Good morning.' She smiled at the back of the tall woman at the sink. 'You must be Rachel.'

Rachel broke off from peeling carrots and offered Naomi the back of her wrist in lieu of a handshake. 'Yes. And you are Naomi?'

89

Naomi nodded. 'Matt and Liz mentioned me, then? I'm a little earlier than usual. Has Liz got you preparing lunch?'

Rachel tossed her head. 'Liz had to go up to London today. Didn't she tell you? So I said I'd come by and make some lunch for Matt. You might have noticed, my brother-in-law likes his routine respected.'

Naomi registered the faint edge in Rachel's voice. She clapped her fingertips to her temple. 'Of course! I clean forgot! I'm afraid thoughts of Camilla take precedence over everything else. It had gone right out of my mind.'

'Shall I make us some coffee?' asked Rachel.

The coffee prepared, Rachel sat down opposite Naomi, her bony, stiff-necked manner contrasting with Naomi's dancer's grace.

Naomi smiled. 'You live in the village, don't you? It must be wonderful, especially for the children, having their aunt nearby. Do you have children of your own?'

Rachel looked down at her cup. 'We meant to. I had a . . . some problems. And then Patrick had his accident.'

Naomi sipped at her coffee. Without speaking, her face creased into the hint of an interrogation.

'A car accident,' Rachel murmured. 'He died.'

'I'm sorry, Rachel. I didn't . . . Nobody told me.'

'It doesn't matter.' Rachel swallowed. 'Patrick was a lovely man. He had so much wanted to be a father.'

'I bet you would have been a great mom, too.' Naomi rested her hand lightly over Rachel's.

Rachel looked down for some while. 'At least any child of mine wouldn't have been spoiled.'

A hint of emphasis on the last word left it hanging heavily between them. Naomi glanced around her. 'Do you *really* think Mark and Camilla are spoiled?' she asked, surprised.

Rachel, too, flicked a glance at the door. She made as though to speak and then clamped her lips shut, shaking her head.

Naomi leaned closer, her hand still over Rachel's. 'Please, Rachel, it's important. Anything that helps me get into Camilla's mind . . .'

Rachel threw another swift glance at the door, listening, then abruptly shook her head. 'I mustn't talk about it. People will always think I'm being bitter, losing my own child. But you see the way they live. Those children have *everything*.'

Naomi spread her hands. 'But that's normal. Matt's books must have made him a lot of money.'

Rachel laughed, a short, dry bark. 'Money?' She waved a hand in a gesture that took in the house and their whole life. 'God, yes. There's money, all right. More than they had any right –' She broke off short, biting her lip. 'Well, let's just say I don't think it's necessarily good for children to have too much, too easily . . . If you ask me, that was a lot to do with that business of Camilla's at school!' she added, in a sudden change of tack, vehement enough to make the other woman blink.

'Trouble?' Naomi murmured.

Rachel pulled back, taking her hand away. 'I shouldn't mention it. It's none of my business.'

Naomi reached and touched her hand again. 'Rachel, if there's anything that even *might* help me gain an insight into Camilla, I'd be grateful . . .'

When Rachel spoke her voice was confidential, almost a whisper. 'We all act as though it had never happened but, in fact, it was a nasty little episode. It was really when I first started worrying about the way Liz and Matt were bringing up the children. Liz was hardly ever here. Matthew was never out of his study. It was all left to that little Norwegian au pair. Obviously, the girl wasn't up to it.'

'And the actual *trouble*?'

'Camilla had turned from a delightful, friendly girl into a sulky, withdrawn little madam. She was doing nothing at school, just sitting in the corner, sulking.'

'Was that all?'

'No. She stabbed a teacher!'

'Fu –' Naomi bit off the curse. 'My God! What with?'

'A pencil.'

'Oh!' Naomi half laughed. 'I thought you were going to tell me she had gone at her with a bread knife.'

'Him,' Rachel corrected spikily, nettled by Naomi's laugh. 'The man needed seven stitches! It tore his hand open.'

Naomi's laugh faded. 'What happened to Camilla?'

'Well, she had to change schools, of course.'

'Was she all right at the new school?'

'Eventually. At least she didn't attack any of the staff.'

Before Naomi had time to respond to the surprising flash of sardonic humour, Matt's footsteps sounded in the corridor. With a warning murmur Rachel got to her feet and moved quickly towards the Aga.

Matt put down the phone and looked at his watch. He was astonished to find that it was nearly seven o'clock. It was the first occasion in weeks that he had been able to lose himself in his work. Leaving the study to get himself some tea in the late afternoon, he had found Naomi in the kitchen, jubilant. Camilla had allowed her into her room for the first time, letting her stay for over an hour before losing interest and climbing into bed. Buoyed by the news, he had been able to attack his rewrite with more vigour than he had done for weeks. When he had finally run out of steam, he had spent time on the phone, finalising arrangements for an impending promotional tour of Japan. The last hour had been spent taking a call from Harry Gregory in Los Angeles, thrashing out details of the contract with Stan Kowalski's studio. Humming to himself, he prowled from the office in search of a drink.

He found Mark alone in the kitchen, eating cereal. 'On your own? Isn't Mum back?'

'In the library. With *Naomi*,' he added, through a mouthful of food.

Matt stopped smiling. 'Naomi's only here to help Camilla, Mark.'

Mark let his spoon clatter onto his plate. 'Yeah, I know,' he said, not looking at Matt. 'And I know she's terrific, and the sun shines out of her ... I just don't see why she has to hang around all the time. She never seems to go home any more. Every time I walk into a room she's in there, nosing through the photo albums, making herself at home.'

Matt sighed. 'I know. It can get oppressive, having someone in the house. Try and live with it, though. For Camilla. Naomi needs to get to know us. Mum's contacts swear by what she did for them.'

'I *am* trying. But why, every time she gets me on my own, does she have to go on about the past? *I* didn't cause Camilla's problems. Why doesn't she talk to the boyfriends who let Camilla down?'

'Everybody has broken romances, Mark. Not everyone gets suicidal over them. At least she's making progress with Camilla.'

Two days later, after another good day's work, Matt walked through to the kitchen, smiling in anticipation at the sound of Liz and Naomi's laughing voices. Liz was crying through her laughter. He took her by the shoulders. 'What is it? What's happened?'

'Matt, she's eating! Naomi's got her eating again.'

He looked jubilantly at Naomi. 'That true?'

She nodded, her face grave, though her eyes, too, were moist. 'We shouldn't lose our heads. She ate a banana, that's all. And a couple of bites of an apple.'

Matt punched the air, yelling, 'Naomi, you're great.' Dragging Liz with him, he moved to kiss Naomi.

Naomi took his kiss on the cheek, beaming. 'There's more.' The two of them stared expectantly at her. 'She's been talking, too.'

Matt gave another yell, and whirled Liz around. 'What? What did she say?'

Naomi shrugged. Despite her effort to appear measured, her eyes shone with barely suppressed excitement. 'Nothing much. Yes, and no. But it's a start.'

Matt was already opening the refrigerator, yanking out a bottle of champagne. 'A start!' He flipped the cork, laughing as the foam spurted, drenching his shirtfront. 'Shit, Naomi, it's the best news this family has had in weeks.'

As the days passed, Naomi's sessions with Camilla grew longer. Gradually, with each day, she ate more of the fruits and salads which Liz painstakingly prepared, and which Naomi carried up at the start of each session.

Each day, coming downstairs at dusk, Naomi would be totally drained, her smooth face pale and waxy. Despite her own exhaustion, she smilingly sidestepped Matt and Liz's eager questions, impressively refusing to be drawn into betraying Camilla's confidence, telling them nothing beyond the hugely encouraging fact that their conversations were growing daily more coherent.

94

By the Sunday, seeing Naomi so spent she could hardly keep awake, they suggested she should sleep over, rather than drive home. She shook her head, sighing. 'I can't do that. I've got other clients to see.'

Matt waved a hand. 'Drive back early. Or, better still, call them and rearrange their appointments.' He grinned. 'At least then you could have the drink you look as though you badly need.'

She got to her feet, her dancer's grace unaffected by her fatigue. 'Damn! You just found my Achilles' heel,' she said, laughing. A few drinks and dinner revived Naomi, and the three of them sat up until two, talking and drinking.

The next morning Matt walked into the kitchen to find the aroma of coffee already filling the room. Naomi turned to greet him. Her hair, unbraided, hung in a dark mass over her shoulders, giving her an appealing, faintly unmanageable look. The robe Liz had lent her was barely big enough, obliging her to cling to the hem, holding it closed over her thighs as she moved. She laughed at his surprise. 'I'm one of those lucky people that can get by on five or six hours' sleep. Here.'

She put two cups of coffee on the table and sat down, clutching now at the robe at the top of her bosom as he lowered himself into the seat opposite her, pulling his own robe tighter around him. She was looking at him with an odd, musing expression on her face.

'Matt, may I ask you a question?'

He laughed. 'You never *stop* asking questions.'

She smiled. 'Matt, why didn't you tell me about Camilla's trouble at school?'

He paused with the coffee cup halfway to his lips. 'Rachel,' he said, almost to himself.

She nodded. 'That's right. She mentioned it the day she was here preparing lunch. I was hoping you were going to tell me about it yourself. Why didn't you?'

95

He let air hiss out between his teeth. 'Because there was nothing to it. What version did Rachel give you?'

'Camilla stabbed a teacher. She had to change schools.'

He took a long sip of coffee. 'Poor Rachel. She still can't let it alone.' He looked up to find her dark green eyes on his face. Tiny golden glints shone in them. 'You have to know something about Rachel, Naomi. She had a hard time herself, back then. First, her miscarriage, which *was* pretty awful, even if it wasn't quite the piece of medical history she likes to believe, and then Patrick being killed. It was a terrible year for anybody. But Rachel didn't take it well. It left her very . . . resentful. It colours the way she looks at some things.' Her eyes were still on his, unblinking. He licked his lips. 'The school incident was an accident. The teacher himself acknowledged it. They were in a stockroom, getting some stuff out. He somehow got a sharpened pencil through his hand. Rachel usually tells it as though she went for the man with a meat cleaver.' Naomi returned his smile. 'We changed schools because Camilla simply wasn't making progress. Period. There was nothing more to it, believe me.'

Naomi was silent for some seconds. Then, smiling ruefully, she briefly laid her hand on the back of his. 'Okay, Matt. Sorry.' Matt moved his hand away. They both drank in silence. 'Matt,' she said, at length, looking into her cup, 'how wealthy is Camilla?'

He frowned. 'Rachel again?'

Naomi shrugged. 'Is she, well, a wealthy girl?'

Matt laughed. 'You've seen how we live. The books have made us a lot of money. They'll make a lot more, too, especially with a little help from Stan Kowalski. If I croak tomorrow the children won't exactly be left destitute.'

Naomi hesitated, then said, with another touch to

his hand, 'But I . . . I got the impression that she was rich, in her own *right*.'

A shadow of anger passed across Matt's face. 'Forget it. I told you, Rachel has a few problems.'

She nodded, her teeth over her lower lip. 'Because, you know, it could affect the way Camilla sees herself. Her relationships.'

Matt's eyes flashed. 'Let it drop, Naomi. There's nothing in it. Camilla's been used to the idea of being rich all her life. Her uncle's money's not the cause of her problem.'

'Okay, Matt. Sorry. I didn't mean to pry.'

'That's all right.' He reached out to touch her arm lightly with his fingers. He hesitated, his hand in mid-air as the back door was thrown open. Annie stopped, framed in the doorway, the smile on her face fading. 'Sorry, Matt, I didn't . . .' She broke off as Naomi turned to look at her. 'Oh, Naomi. It's you.' She stepped deeper into the room. She was wearing her courtroom uniform of dark grey suit and high-necked white blouse. Her eyes flickered for an instant to where Naomi's robe had worked loose, revealing a swell of breast, and then settled on Matt's face. 'I was on my way into town. I just thought I'd drop by and see how Camilla was doing.'

Matt smiled, nodding appreciatively at Naomi. 'Great. She's eating, she's talking. Though still not to *us*,' he added, ruefully. 'Coffee?'

'No, thanks. William's waiting in the car. It's his swimming.' She made as though to say something else, and then changed her mind. She swallowed. 'Well, that's good, about Camilla.' She looked directly at Naomi. 'Keep up the good work. I'd better be going.' She spun round and hurried from the room.

Matt's eyes went to Naomi. She was drinking coffee, the cup clasped in both hands, masking all but her eyes. For just an instant he thought he caught a knowing glint in them. But, as she lowered her cup to call goodbye to Annie, he saw that she was simply smiling, pleased at Annie's words.

The following week they had been able to reassure anxious friends who called with the news that Camilla was eating enough to stabilise her weight. Buoyed by the improvement, Matt and Liz had settled back into something like their regular routine. Matt was catching up on his work schedule, closeting himself in the office from seven thirty each morning until late afternoon. He was even managing to take an interest in the promotional tour his Japanese publisher was setting up. Liz was juggling her time between the charity circuit and working on a piece she was writing for a Sunday newspaper supplement. Only Mark, back at school now, and out of the house from seven thirty until after five, seemed immune to the general optimism. His resentment smouldered until, by the Friday evening, it had hardened to a black, silent rage. Matt took his drink and sat on the sofa, close to his son. 'Do you want to talk about it?'

Mark stayed silent, biting his lip. When he finally looked up there were tears of anger in his eyes. 'I hate that woman.'

Matt shot Liz a startled look. 'Why? What's wrong? You can see what a difference she's made to Camilla.'

'Can I?' His voice was breaking with anger. 'Camilla used to talk to me. Since that fat cow practically moved in here, she won't even let me in her room.'

'You and us alike, Mark. On the other hand Camilla *is* eating. And yesterday Naomi managed to coax her into taking a shower, the first since she cut herself. That's a big step.' He dropped his voice. 'Mum and I have been here before, remember.'

98

'I'm not saying she's not doing *any* good. I just don't like the way she's here all the time.' He jumped to his feet. 'And she's been nosing in my room!'

'That isn't true, you know, Mark.' Naomi's soft voice made them jerk around to where she stood, framed in the doorway. Her smile was pained and gentle. 'Really it isn't.'

Mark shook his head, blond hair flying. 'That's a bloody lie!'

'Mark!' Liz called sharply. 'Why would *Naomi* do that?'

'How would I know? But I'm sure *someone*'s been poking in my stuff.'

Matt tried to put an arm around his son. 'Mark, Celia's in your room every day. She –' He broke off as Mark rushed from the room.

'He's right, in a way,' Naomi murmured, moving into the room. 'About me being around too much, I mean. It must seem to him as if I've moved in. I try not to intrude, but with the pressure you're all under . . .' She tailed off, looking around at them both, reading the strain in their faces. 'I needed to get close. Perhaps I'm getting *too* close. Also, I must say I've been neglecting my other clients. In fact, I was just about to make a suggestion. I think we ought to move Camilla for a while.'

'What? Out of the house?' Matt asked incredulously. 'Why?'

Naomi drew a long breath. 'Well, she was doing very well. But she seems to have reached a plateau. It often happens. My professional advice is that a change of scene, away from the associations of the house, would do her the world of good.'

The flesh around Liz's eyes was pinched. 'Where are you thinking of? Some kind of mental institution?'

Naomi laughed aloud, reaching out to take Liz's

hand in both hers. 'God, no! A place I've used for other young clients. It's more like a country hotel. They only take three or four guests at a time. And it's run by a man I respect immensely.'

'A psychiatrist?'

She gave another good-natured laugh at the open hostility in Matt's voice. 'No. Stephen Letzer is a psycho-therapist. He specialises, like me, in the problems of young people. And, anyway, I would still be treating her.' Still holding Liz's hand, she took Matt's, too, drawing the three of them into a tight knot. Her voice fell to a murmur. 'Look, Camilla and Mark are very close, aren't they? He's terribly afflicted by what his sister's going through, more than he can possibly express. His anger at me is a classic symptom. As long as Camilla doesn't pick up on it, it doesn't matter. I can take a few insults and it's probably good for him to have an outlet. But if Camilla *did* pick up on it, and took Mark's part, we could be looking at a disaster. I have to say clearly, to both of you, I think it could destroy all we've achieved so far.'

Six

Matt eased the Mercedes over the potholes of the neglected drive and onto the loop of gravel around the
circular lawn. Beyond the rectangular outline of the
imposing Georgian house the Stenners caught a distant
flash of sunlight on the sea at Shoreham. He slotted
the car next to the familiar black Volkswagen.

Before they were out of the car the door of the house
flew open and Naomi ran down the steps to meet them.
She hugged Liz and planted kisses on each of Matt's
cheeks. She made to do the same to Mark, the gesture
changing to an awkward compromise between a wave
and a shrug as he shrank from her. She looped her
arms through Matt's and Liz's and began walking them
towards the house, beaming excitedly around at them.

'Isn't this *great*? She's only been with Stephen a
week, and already she's agreed to see you. I never dared
hope things would go this well.'

Liz's response was hardly more than a grunt. The
tic beneath her eye twitched furiously. Like Mark, she
had hardly spoken on the journey down, too preoccupied with the memory of her feelings a week earlier,
watching Naomi drive out of the courtyard with
Camilla, rigid and blank-eyed, at her side.

Naomi led them through the shabby hall, with the
unopened circulars still strewn on the table and the
Chinese vase, veined with cracks, into Stephen Letzer's
office. 'Stephen's with Camilla now. He'll be down in
a minute.'

The slender figure of Stephen Letzer appeared almost
immediately in the doorway. His white nylon coat was

open over a cashmere roll-neck sweater and woollen slacks. After a momentary hesitation, he stepped into the room and perfunctorily shook hands. 'Good morning. Naomi mentioned that you wanted to come.' He showed his teeth in a quick, unhappy smile.

Matt had wandered behind the man's desk to study the framed diplomas. Without moving, he said, 'Naomi said Camilla was *ready* to see us. She is, isn't she?'

Letzer shrugged, moving towards his desk. He made to draw out his chair, checking the movement almost imperceptibly in a tacit invitation to Matt to move away. The two men stood for an instant toe to toe before Matt slowly withdrew to sit down opposite him.

Letzer ran splayed fingers through his short, blue-black hair, taking his time about smoothing it at the nape. 'Prepared to see you, certainly. Ready?' he said, coolly meeting their anxious gaze. He sighed. 'I don't know.'

Matt's eyes narrowed. 'What's that supposed to mean?'

'No more than it says, Mr Stenner. At Naomi's insistence, I asked Camilla, and she agreed to see you. But please remember it wasn't her initiative.'

A shifting of Matt's feet made Liz look sharply at him, willing him to silence. She, too, had caught the faint, fleeting glint of something in the voice. Disdain, perhaps, or a distant spark of hostility. A quick, reproving contraction around Naomi's eyes indicated that she had also noticed it.

'But she hasn't changed her mind?' Liz asked in a conciliatory tone.

'No. I'll take you up in a moment.' As he spoke, he reached down and lifted a briefcase from the kneehole of the desk. Holding it on his knees, he flipped it open. Matt caught a quick sight of the Gucci logo embossed in the dark red suede panel of the lid. He shot Liz a dry smile. There was more money in the psychotherapy industry than the functional desk and the tubular chairs were designed to make them believe. Letzer closed the case and slid it back out of sight. He smiled noncommittally, holding out an unsealed envelope. 'I was going to mail this to you, but since you're here . . . We do ask clients to settle their accounts weekly.'

Matt took the envelope and shoved it inside his jacket without examining it. 'I'll send you a cheque. Can't we see her alone?'

'I'm sorry, no. It's Camilla's condition, not mine.'

Once more, for a fleeting moment, the two men's eyes locked.

'Whatever Camilla wants,' Matt said.

Half an hour later Matt herded his family out into the cold drizzle, bringing the front door crashing shut behind him. He was tight-lipped and pale. Naomi fell in beside him as he strode down the steps. 'I'm sorry, Matt. It's my fault. I raised your hopes too much. You were expecting to see her jumping about. We aren't *at* that stage yet.'

Matt's jaw tightened. 'That's not the problem. I don't care if she's in bed. I just don't want that bastard climbing in with her!'

Naomi stepped into his path, a hand on his chest, stopping him. 'No! Matt, you mustn't jump to those kinds of conclusions. It's not fair. Believe me! I *know* Stephen Letzer.'

Matt punched a fist into his palm. 'But, for Christ's sake, Naomi, you saw them! She won't say a word without looking at him first to see if it's all right.'

'Matt, a week ago she wouldn't have let you into her room at all! Please trust me. Be patient.'

'Patient! While some weasel of a psycho-gabbler screws my daughter!'

Naomi put a hand to her eyes, sighing. 'Look, there's a nice pub in the village. Can we go there and talk about it, please? I'm famished.'

Settled opposite the still simmering Matt, Naomi fumbled the wrapping from a pack of cigarettes. The surprise in their faces drew an embarrassed laugh. 'Do you mind? There are still times when I need it.' She lit up and blew a mouthful of smoke over her shoulder. 'Look, there are some things I should explain to you. I understand why you're so upset, Matt. And you, Mark. Camilla *is* feeling a little dependent on Steve.'

'A little!' Matt taunted. 'She won't even –'

Liz grabbed his wrist. 'Let Naomi finish, Matt, please.'

He shut his mouth slowly.

'It's common for patients to become dependent on their therapists. It can even be healthy, as long as it doesn't get out of hand. Well, I've been seeing a lot of Camilla, and I can reassure you it isn't. She likes Steve, and, of course, she trusts him. But it's nothing more than that. I know she's still hostile. And we might not have seen the worst yet. But try to concentrate on the positive things. She's talking.' She smiled, a sudden glow in the gloom. 'Even if it is only in monosyllables! And she's eating. She must have put on at least four pounds.' She waited for Liz's murmured confirmation. 'So, please *try* to accept that Camilla's in good hands. Look, I've got to go away for a few days. One of my old patients in New York is getting into trouble again. I should be back for next weekend. We can come down together then. Who knows, everything may look different. Meanwhile, try to live your normal lives. And not to worry too much.'

*   *   *

Matt stood staring from the window, watching an owl quarter the lawn in the moonlight. Each night since the visit to the clinic had been the same for him, jerking awake in the small hours, racked by the memory of Letzer's hand brushing Camilla's thigh, the conspiring glances. Above all, the indefinable sense that the man had taken *control* of Camilla. Naomi had called twice from New York, spending hours on the phone, trying to soothe his fears. Despite her efforts, he was unable to push from his mind lurid images of what might have happened *since* the visit. Irritable and fractious from the lack of sleep, his work schedule had once again fallen to pieces. Even the draft contract from Kowalski's people lay unattended on his desk, waiting until he was able to concentrate. He turned to the room. The moonlight cast deep shadows in the newly excavated hollows of Liz's face, emphasised the recent gauntness of her neck. With an intake of breath, he strode across to the bed and flicked on the light.

Liz's eyes focused slowly, first on the red glow of the clock, then up at his face. She squinted against the light. 'It's twenty past four. Whatever are you *doing*?'

He kneeled on the edge of the bed. 'I just *have* to go there, Liz. Are you coming?'

'No, don't. Please don't!' Camilla's voice was tiny, muffled by the pillow. Then, convulsively, she turned onto her side, flinging out an arm. 'No! No! It *hurts*!' As her head came off the pillow her voice was harsher, panicky. 'Stop it!' She repeated the words, this time as a full-blooded scream.

Her eyes jerked open as though in surprise at her own scream. She scrabbled back, kicking the tangled duvet to the floor as she cowered against the head of the bed. With her head clutched in her hands she screamed again, the pitch rising, her face upturned as though somebody stood above her. Her open eyes were staring yet unfocused. The scream trailed off in a choking gasp of pain.

Recoiling with another throaty sound full of agony and terror, she reached the edge of the bed. Oblivious, she dug her heels into the mattress and thrust again. She toppled, taking the bedside table with her. Its cargo of flower vase and water carafe crashed against the door in an explosion of smashing glass.

Camilla still lay, whimpering, among the wreckage, her eyes to the ceiling, when the door flew open. A woman appeared in the doorway. Camilla gave no sign of knowing she was there as the woman stepped quickly past her and held her thumb on a bellpush beside the bed.

Seconds later, Stephen Letzer appeared at a run. He wore a robe over shiny pyjamas. He paused for an instant in the doorway and then dropped to kneel at Camilla's side. Carefully, he pulled down the T-shirt which had ridden up over her thighs and tucked it behind her knees. Only then did he look questioningly at the nurse.

'Catherine, you found her like this?'

Catherine nodded. 'It seems to be another nightmare.' Letzer nodded slowly. 'Did you catch any of what she was saying?'

'Not much. *Don't. Don't hurt me.* There! She just said it again.'

Letzer leaned closer to Camilla, straining to make out the choked noises. At length, he took her by the wrists and lifted her hands clear of her face. 'Camilla,' he murmured, close to her ear. 'Camilla, wake up. You've had another bad dream. It's all right now. Nobody's going to hurt you. Not here.'

It was another minute before Camilla fully awoke, her eyes gradually coming into focus on Letzer's face.

She let her gaze roam slowly over the room, as if to reassure herself, and then, abruptly, reached and flung her arms around his neck. 'Oh, Stephen. Thank God, it's you.'

Expressionless, he gently prised himself loose. 'It's all right now, Camilla. There's nobody here but us.' He pushed himself to his feet, taking up the duvet as he did so. 'Here, let me help you back into bed.'

As she let him pull her to her feet, she once again let her eyes skitter over the room. Letzer caught the look. 'Can you tell us about it?' he asked softly.

'No,' she said, shaking her head hard. 'No. It's just . . . just the feeling. The memory of pain. And fear, Stephen.' She gripped his hand and pulled herself against him once more, letting her head fall against his chest. 'The sheer *terror*! I can't stand it.' She looked up, anxiety in her eyes, as he took a half-step back, making some space between them.

'Do you want a pill?'

She shook her head, her eyes fixed on his face. 'No,' she whispered. 'But I would like you to stay here. Will you?'

She felt his hand slide out of her grip. He hesitated for a moment before nodding. 'Okay.' He took another pace back and turned to the nurse, who was busy clearing up the broken glass. 'Catherine, would you mind? You can bring in the folding bed from the room next to my office and put it here.' He smiled wryly from her to Camilla, ignoring the glint of disappointment in Camilla's eyes. 'And I'll sleep in the armchair.' He sat Camilla down on the bed, still smiling. 'That way, whichever side you fall out there'll be one of us here to catch you.'

'Matt! Please!' Pale-faced, Liz pressed herself into the leather of the seat, one hand gripping the cloth of

Matt's sleeve as he swung the wheel, slicing within inches of the nose of the tractor, the tyres howling. The oncoming van roared past Liz's ear, its bumper gouging vegetation from the hedge. Letting out her breath with a hiss, Liz subsided into her seat.

'Matt, what's the matter with you? You could have killed us.'

Matt swallowed, glancing in the mirror. The slow-moving tractor was already lost to sight on the long bend. His own legs were trembling. He shook himself and reached for her hand. 'Sorry. That really was stupid.'

She laid a hand on his thigh. 'You mustn't let it beat you, Matt,' she whispered.

He knew too much alcohol and a succession of sleepless nights had left him depleted and off balance. The narrow escape with the van brought home with a jolt how badly his judgement was impaired. He drove on without another word until he brought the car to a halt in front of the house. The heavy overcast had kept dawn at bay. They sat for several seconds in the semi-darkness, staring numbly at the house. No lights showed in the windows.

Matt touched a hand to Liz's. 'Come on,' he murmured. 'We might as well know the worst.'

Red-eyed from the night drive, Matt's face had an added wildness as he strode across the deserted hall, with Liz in pursuit a half-pace behind, and took the stairs three at a time. His hand was on the doorknob when Liz managed to throw herself in his path. 'No. You can't, Matt. She's a grown woman.' Reaching back, she rapped on the door herself. 'Camilla? May we come in?'

Without waiting for a response, Matt heaved his way past her and threw open the door.

Letzer was on his feet, facing them from beyond

the bed. Surprise and anger mingled in his face.

Matt's own gaze went to Camilla. She was seated on the edge of the bed, her back to them, wearing a bathrobe. Her arms moved at her sides, as though she might have been pulling the robe closed. 'Camilla!'

She gave no sign of having heard him. His face working with a mixture of fury and anxiety, Matt launched himself around the bed towards them.

With an exclamation of alarm, Liz snatched at his arm. 'Matt! Please calm down!' He kept moving forward, Liz scrambling along beside him, trying to hold him, her voice beginning to crack as she pleaded. 'Don't, Matt, for God's sake. You're jumping to conclusions. Please –'

She broke off as Letzer stepped towards them, a palm raised. 'You can't do this.'

Matt stopped in his tracks, looking down at the upraised hand. He was three inches taller than Letzer, and perhaps twenty-five pounds heavier. 'Can't what? Talk to my *daughter*?' he said thickly.

Letzer did not flinch. 'It wouldn't do her any good. Not as long as you're in that state.'

Matt's chest heaved. Behind Letzer, Camilla had turned to face them. Matt let his gaze slide to her robe, her legs bare beneath it. He turned back to Letzer. 'This *state*?' His voice stalled, choked with fury. 'I come in here at seven thirty in the morning to find you in my daughter's bedroom . . . and you . . . You bastard!' He stepped forward, his hands coming up in front of him.

Letzer shuffled backwards, shooting a quick glance past Matt to Liz. 'You're making a mistake. It was a mistake to come here at all. Camilla's at a very delicate stage.' Real anger mixed with his nervousness. 'This could be unbelievably damaging. You have no right to take chances with her health like this. You could ruin –' He broke off as Matt took a handful of his sweater.

'Ruin what? Your chances of seducing my daughter?'

Camilla's angry sob of protest made them all look briefly round at her. She was cowering as though from the threat of Matt's violence, her hands to her mouth. The crouching posture loosened the robe, exposing her breasts. The sight brought fresh anger burning into Matt's throat. He dragged violently at Letzer's sweater, shaking the smaller man like a doll. 'Is that what you do here? We *trusted* you with our daughter, you bastard!'

Letzer regained his balance. 'I have never touched Camilla,' he said with outraged dignity. 'I respect her far too much for that. But I'm trying to tell you, she's at a critical stage.' He lowered his voice, as though to exclude Camilla. 'She's dependent on me, it's true. But that's only normal at this point in her treatment. She'll get through –'

Matt was no longer listening. 'She'll nothing! She's coming home with us. Now!' Shaking with rage, he thrust Letzer from him.

Reeling backwards, Letzer's heel snagged against a chair leg, sending him sprawling to the floor. His head hit the wall with a dry crack.

Matt was reaching for Camilla as she cowered, her eyes wide. At Letzer's sharp cry, she straightened. The look of loathing that flooded her face made Matt recoil as though at a blow. With her eyes, ablaze with hatred, drilling into Matt's face, she fell to her knees at Letzer's side, as he sat with his head cupped in his hands, groaning.

Matt stepped tentatively forward, his eyes searching the wall for any projection that might have caused the man real damage. There was none. 'Stop faking, you bastard.' His voice was quivering. He jabbed at Letzer with his toe. 'Get up before I *really* lose my temper!'

Letzer groaned again. Camilla rose slowly to her feet, her eyes, full of venom, still fixed on Matt's. Liz's voice came to him as though he were dreaming it.

'Camilla, please. Daddy couldn't help it. It was just temper. He cares so much. He just wanted to –'

'Get out!' Camilla's voice was a hiss. 'Stop screwing around with my life! I'm staying here. With people who *really* care about me.' She was screaming now, her face contorted. 'I never want to come back to that house. I never want to see you again, you . . . ignorant, bullying . . . brute!'

For a stunned moment Matt and Liz stood side by side, staring at their daughter. Then, blanched and silent, they turned and walked from the room, each supporting the other.

Annie Trevellyn watched from across the table as Matt drank a long mouthful of coffee and slumped back in his chair. He was unshaven, his wiry hair unkempt. The flesh under his eyes was puffy and grey. 'So, is there *anything* we can do?'

Annie shook her head. 'Legally, you're in a bind. Camilla's not a minor. You can't abduct her against her will.'

'Stop paying the bastard!' Roger's voice boomed from across the kitchen, where he was watching a rugby game on television, William and Mark at his side. 'If I know anything about the private medical industry, Camilla'll be out on her arse within twenty-four hours.'

Matt and Annie looked at each other from under their brows. 'Thanks, Roger,' Matt said sourly. 'It'd be a real comfort to know she was on the streets.' He sat straighter. 'Surely there must be *something* we can do?'

'As far as I know, there's only one way,' Annie said. 'Talk to Peter Monroe about getting her certified.' Her mouth twisted in apology in response to his sick look. 'Failing that, then I guess you've got no choice except to trust in Naomi, and hope she can bring Camilla round. The one thing I would warmly *not* recommend is that *you* try to visit her again. Women don't fall in and out of love with men on the basis of their boxing skills.'

Even though he detected no inflection in Annie's words, Matt's eyes went automatically to Liz's back, as she stood at the Aga. 'Don't worry. I won't. I sure would like to hear what Naomi makes of it all, though.'

As he spoke there came the sound of a car rasping to a halt outside. Matt had hardly risen to his feet when Naomi erupted into the room. Her smooth face was waxy with a film of perspiration. A few loose wisps of hair had escaped the tight chignon and straggled across her face. She ran straight to Liz and threw her arms around her. 'You poor things. You must be *distraught*. I'm sorry. I couldn't get a flight until late yesterday.'

Matt waved her to a seat. 'Christ, Naomi, we only spoke yesterday morning. We know we aren't the only people on the planet with problems.'

She ran a hand over his shoulder as she sat down, Annie shifting along the bench to make room for her. 'Thanks.' Liz poured her some black coffee, and she drank off half the cup before saying, 'Why don't you both sit down and tell me the whole thing from the beginning?'

She listened in total silence as they recounted the

visit. When they had finished she made no effort to disguise the deep concern in her face. 'This is my fault. I shouldn't have taken off like that.'

Liz shook her head. 'As Matt said, you have other patients. You couldn't have anticipated this.'

Naomi smiled gratefully. 'Unlucky timing, though. I *knew* Camilla was reaching a phase where it was on the cards. Frankly, I was expecting Camilla to sort of fall for me.'

'I wish to God she had,' Matt said morosely. 'At least *you* wouldn't have been trying to screw her.'

Naomi bit her lip. 'You know, I think you're probably wrong about that. A man in Stephen's position has lots of opportunities. I've *never* had even a suspicion that he was exploiting them.'

'You weren't there yesterday,' Matt retorted, looking to Liz.

'I still think you must be wrong.' A curious emphasis in Naomi's voice made Matt study her face more closely. For the first time he noticed that the smooth surfaces of her features seemed slackened. Faint traces of lines remained in her brow when she stopped frowning.

'We're not, Naomi. I promise you.'

'Mmm,' she said distractedly, as though in a reverie. Her dark, Mediterranean face had drained of colour.

Matt reached to touch her elbow. 'Are you okay?'

At his touch, her eyes jerked back into focus. Her smile was fleeting, abstracted. 'Sure. Jet lag's setting in with a vengeance, though. What do you feel we should do next?'

Liz answered. 'Matt insists we should take her out of there. Annie doesn't think we have a legal leg to stand on.'

Annie nodded. 'Unless Camilla were to be certified insane.'

Naomi recoiled, a hint of panic in her eyes. 'You can't be contemplating *that*! Camilla's not insane! You couldn't –'

Matt quelled her protest. 'Whoa! Of course we won't do that. But it means you're going to have to be our eyes and ears. Annie won't let me anywhere near the place.'

Annie laughed. 'Only to keep him out of court. I'm afraid Matt would beat Letzer up.'

'I'd better shoulder the burden, then. If Camilla *has* fallen for Stephen, making him a martyr would just be a disaster. A total fucking disaster,' Naomi repeated, under her breath.

As Liz handed round the soup she'd been making, Mark spoke for the first time, addressing Annie. 'There's another thing we were talking about last night. Supposing that weasel Letzer is just a gold-digger?' He glowered at Naomi, using the suggestion to goad her. 'What if he's getting his claws into Camilla for her money?'

Naomi's back stiffened. She looked from Matt to Liz, trying to read their faces, before meeting Mark's sulky scowl. 'Look, Mark, I know I'm the one who suggested Steve. I told you, he's had a lot of wealthy girls through his hands, a lot of them pretty dumb, but he's never done that.'

'Yeah?' Mark insisted. 'So he's an ace psychotherapist, just doing it for the public benefit. Is that why he charges two thousand pounds a week? Who knows, perhaps Camilla's the first girl he's come across that has her own –'

'Mark! That's enough. Naomi says he's not a crook, so let's take her word for it. He's not going to get anything more out of this family than the two grand a week.' Matt turned back to Naomi. 'When can you get down to see Camilla?'

She drew another deep breath. 'Tomorrow morning.'

Seven

The day was crystal clear, the sky swept by a biting easterly wind. Liz slid a hand into the pocket of Matt's coat, twining her fingers into his. With the other, she pulled the collar of her fur coat tight up under her chin. Alone among the weathered tables and benches of the pub forecourt they scanned the short high street. They had waited several minutes, their eyes streaming in the wind, before the black Volkswagen came around the curve of the lane beyond the village.

Naomi double-parked behind the Mercedes and leaped from the car. She pulled a cigarette from the deep leather bag that swung at her shoulder and, hands cupped, got it to light on the third match. With a quick, nervous smile, she strode towards Matt and Liz.

Watching her approach, Matt felt Liz's fingers tighten in his and the increasing pressure of her shoulder as she leaned tight against him. 'A complete fucking mess, isn't it?' he said softly.

'I can see that it must look that way,' Naomi answered, watching over her shoulder as the wind snatched away the cigarette smoke.

'*Look* that way? For Christ's sake, Naomi! You'd have to be blind not to have seen what's going on back there! She's head over heels in love with him. And she hates me.'

Naomi nodded. 'It certainly isn't going completely *right*,' she said, taking another nervy drag at the cigarette. She quickly raised a hand to quell Matt's derisive response. 'No, please. Don't make me feel more guilty than I do already. All this is *my* responsibility. I should have seen it coming,' she said, with sudden bitterness. She sucked once more at the cigarette, seeming almost to bite into it as she drew smoke deep into her lungs, and then threw it brusquely away from her. She shuddered. 'Can we talk about it inside?'

They made no attempt to push through the crush to buy drinks. Instead, they crowded into an empty corner behind a garishly winking one-arm bandit. Naomi's voice was barely audible above the roar of talk and laughter. 'If we go back to the very beginning of this episode, at least, Camilla was suicidal. She almost certainly wasn't just seeking attention, the classic "cry for help". It failed because she didn't happen to have a more effective instrument handy than those scissors. Even so, she made a very serious effort to kill herself. Because, for some reason she hated herself.'

'And now she hates me, too,' Matt said grimly.

She shook her head. 'Correction, Matt. She hates you. But she no longer hates herself. I know it's hard for *you* to see it that way, but in a case like this, that really is progress.'

'There's nothing like looking on the bright side!'

Naomi brushed aside the sarcasm. 'I know how terribly difficult it must be, but it's absolutely crucial that you view this from Camilla's standpoint, and not your own.'

Matt spoke through gritted teeth. 'Great. So I should be *ecstatic* that he's screwing our sick daughter if it makes her happy?'

Naomi took a long breath. 'Matt, I'm still trying not to believe that. It's hard, but I'm *trying*. But it would be plain stupid to deny that Camilla probably has fallen for Steve. I have to take the blame for that, though, not him. As I said before, it was always on the cards, and I should have been here to deal with it. Now it's up to me to retrieve the situation. As for you, try to concentrate on the positive things. She's talking again, she's eating, and, above all, she's loving. At this stage the fact that she's loving the wrong person isn't that important. Although I can see that must be very difficult for *you* to live with.'

A wariness entered Matt's eyes. 'Naomi, did that little quack say anything to you?'

'About what?'

He hesitated, looking at Liz. 'It's just that . . . I got the impression, on Saturday . . . just from his manner, that he was insinuating that I was so angry because I was *jealous*! Of him, for Christ's sake!'

A gust of laughter from a nearby group filled the pause as she looked momentarily at her feet. As the laughter died, she said, 'Look, this is a hell of a question, but I hope you can both understand that I *have* to ask it. Has there . . . has there ever been any . . . trouble . . . between you and Camilla?'

For an instant there was silence. Unconsciously, Liz again sought Matt's hand. 'Whatever is *that* supposed to mean?' she whispered.

In a deadened voice, Matt answered Liz's question. 'She's asking if I ever interfered with Camilla. Right?'

Naomi's hands came up to her face. 'Look, I'm sorry. I'm not suggesting anything. It's just . . . well . . . it's my *duty* to ask. The way she's been acting towards you is, well, *disturbing*. I've seen similar behaviour before. So has Steve Letzer.'

'From abuse victims?' Matt asked in the same toneless voice. Naomi averted her eyes. 'You don't have children, do you?' Naomi shook her head. 'Well, then, perhaps it's unfair to expect you to even conceive of my feelings for Camilla and Mark. It's something *I* couldn't have conceived of before we had them. All the clichés . . . not being able to hurt a hair on their heads, being ready to die for them, they're simply, literally, *true*. The thought of harm coming to one of them can still have me awake in the night, feeling physically sick. It would be impossible to want something for myself, even for an instant, that could harm them. Do you understand me?'

She nodded. 'Yes, I do. I'm sorry.'

Liz's eyes were squeezed shut. Tears glistened at their corners. Naomi took Liz's hand in both hers. 'I *had* to ask. You understand that, too, don't you? Please?'

Liz did not answer. The tears broke and slid down her face. Matt drew a deep breath. 'Sure you did. Now let's forget it.' He began mopping Liz's tears with a folded handkerchief. His back to Naomi, he asked, 'What really matters is, where the hell do we go from here?'

'Japan.'

Matt and Liz looked at her in disbelief.

Naomi nodded, a rueful half-smile on her lips. 'I'm serious. This has taken a lot out of you both. You need a break. Also, however much you love your children, you've still got a life, and your careers. And this promotional tour is all lined up now. It won't help Camilla in the long run to have you nursing resentments, blaming her for holding you back.'

'We'd never do –'

'Maybe *you* wouldn't. Others have, believe me. Anyway, why chance it? You can't do anything for Camilla for the next couple of weeks.'

Liz exchanged a glance with Matt. 'We couldn't possibly . . . Leave Camilla *here*? With . . . that man?'

'And me.' Naomi gave them the first really radiant smile of the day. 'I'll be practically *living* at the clinic while you're gone. Believe me, Stephen won't be able to so much as blow her a kiss, let alone seduce her.' She put a hand on each of their arms. 'Go for it. Take a break.'

Matt sighed. 'But we'll be half the world away. And there's the party.' In answer to Naomi's enquiring look, he went on, 'Our anniversary. The thirty-first of January. We always do a big party. Normally, it wouldn't have been a problem. Liz would have had it all in hand by now. But, with all that's been happening . . .'

'Worry about that when you come back. You don't have to have it. And they *do* have telephones in Japan. You're never going to be more than twenty-four hours away from Camilla. Doctor's orders. Go. Have fun.'

Matt stood at the window, holding the phone to his ear. With the other hand he mopped distractedly at his naked body with a bunched towel. Below him crawled the Tokyo traffic, already almost obscured by a thickening yellow smog. He dropped the phone back onto its rest. 'The damned machine again.'

Liz sat up in bed, wrapped in a satin dressing gown, pouring herself more coffee. 'Any message?'

'She missed us in Kobe. And everything's fine. There's no need to worry.' The jug rattled against his cup as he refilled it. 'So all we have to do is stay calm,' he said with bitter irony.

'Have you tried the clinic this morning?'

'Of course. And I got up and tried it earlier, at a quarter to two. Before five in the afternoon in England.' He balled up the towel and hurled it onto a chair. 'Still no answer.'

'Maybe there's something wrong with their phones.'

'Maybe pigs can fly.' The words came out with more vehemence than Matt had intended. 'Sorry,' he said, apologetically, sitting down on the edge of the bed and running a hand over his eyes. 'Being carted around nightclubs until two in the morning, night after night, doesn't agree with me.'

'Me neither. And I think at the next ladies' lunch when they ask me to stand up and speak about my life as the wife of a famous author, I'm just going to let out a single, ear-piercing scream.' She glanced at her watch and sighed. 'I'd better get dressed. The car will be here soon.' She swung a leg off the bed, parting the fabric of the dressing gown.

Smiling, Matt moved towards her, gripping the belt of the robe, restraining her. 'Not *that* soon.' He leaned to kiss her.

She let his lips touch hers for an instant, her own mouth unresponsive, and then pulled her head back. With a click of her tongue, she slid out of his grasp, tugging the dressing gown closed. 'There's not time. I need to take a shower.' Turning, she walked quickly into the bathroom.

He watched her go, his lips in a tight line. Usually, when travelling, they made love often, stimulated by the anonymity and privacy of hotel living. This time, they had not made love once since leaving home. Several times, overtired and unable to sleep for the thoughts of Camilla that gnawed constantly at him, he had prowled their rooms, watching Liz writhe and whimper, gripped by unendurable dreams. When he had tried to discuss them in their snatched moments of solitude, she had found excuses, taking refuge, as now, in some trivial piece of routine.

The snick of the latch seemed to Matt to echo around the room, turning his heart to cement. Never once, since long before they were married, had Liz locked the bathroom door on him. For the first time since his very first meeting with Liz, he had the sense of walking on quicksand that came of not *knowing* her thoughts, that there was something troubling her that she could not share with him.

'Fuck you, Letzer!' he said, choking.

Every window in the house was ablaze with light. Matt and Liz eased themselves from the hired limousine and stood, stretching and gulping the fresh Cotswold air, while the driver yanked their baggage from the boot. During the drive a sharp wind had chased away the cloud that had sat low over Heathrow. A waxing moon hung among the trees beyond the house. Matt looked around. Already there was a sprinkling of parked cars. He recognised them as belonging to people from London and other, more distant places, who had over-estimated their journey time. 'Feel up to it?' he asked, laying an arm tentatively over Liz's shoulders.

By way of answer, she gave a shudder.

He fished a ten-pound note from his pocket and handed it to the waiting driver. 'I guess staying the extra day *was* a mistake. Now we're home just in time for our own party.'

'You couldn't turn down twenty minutes' television. It wouldn't have been fair to the publisher. Or to you.'

She was looking straight ahead. He let his eyes linger on her for a moment more, and then, sighing, bent to pick up the first of the suitcases. He had hardly straightened when Mark came bounding off the porch and threw his arms around Liz. He turned and pounded Matt's back with the flat of his hand. 'Brilliant to have you back.'

'It's brilliant to *be* back, Mark!' Turning to look at his son he felt his chest constrict. If only Camilla would get better, life would be perfect again. He smiled. '*Really* brilliant.'

* * *

122

A long bath and two glasses of champagne later, the thirteen-hour plane trip had receded to no more than a bruising memory. Matt stood in front of the mahogany-framed mirror smiling at his fourth effort to coax his bow tie into shape. His preference for real knots instead of clip-ons must, over the years, have cost him two full days of his life. Satisfied at last, he pulled on his dinner jacket, smoothed the pleats of his shirtfront, and turned to where Liz sat at the dressing table with her back to him, putting in earrings. He picked up the champagne bottle that stood by the phone and waggled it at Liz's reflection. 'Ready yet?'

She shook her head. 'I'll wait. Shouldn't you ease up?'

'Of course, I *should*.' He poured a glass, his expression pensive. 'Happy anniversary.'

'I hope you're not going to get plastered.'

He stood up and crossed to rest a hand on her shoulder. 'No. But I do need to . . . find a level. Okay?'

She touched a hand briefly over his. 'Let's go down. Everybody's been here for half an hour.'

From the top of the main stairs, they found the hall thronged with people, spill-over from the drawing room and library. As Liz left his side to plunge into the crowd, Matt hesitated on the bottom stair, scrutinising the faces as he waved in response to the chorus of cheers.

Muttered snatches of book and film talk drifted to him from the corner where the London crowd had already begun to form a tight little caucus. From somewhere out of sight, Emma Trafford's laugh rattled the chandelier. Closer at hand, a group of Liz's charity circuit wives and their husbands were talking loudly. Overhearing them, Matt, who had never managed to develop an interest in horses, home furnishing or rugby union football, was aware of the familiar sense of detachment. Not seeing the face he sought, he stepped off the last stair and thrust his way into the drawing room.

He found Dick Field in a corner, deep in conversation with Annie. They did not break off their conversation until he was almost on them, making no effort to conceal that they had been discussing Camilla. Matt kissed Annie perfunctorily and turned to Dick. 'Hello, Dick. I was looking for Peter.'

'I ran into him at the hospital yesterday. He mentioned he wouldn't be here. Some long-standing dinner, I think he said.'

Matt frowned. 'Must have been bloody long-standing, then! He's known about tonight for as long as you have.' He was about to say more when a hand crashed onto his shoulder.

'Matt, can I have a word?'

Matt looked into the grinning, owlish face and broke into a broad smile. He turned to Annie and Dick. 'Andy Phillips. Andy's my London agent. Will you excuse me?' He let Andy draw him into a recess of the room.

Andy gripped his arm. 'Matt, Harry called just before I left the office. We're in business. Stan Kowalski's accepted our revisions, with no further argument. According to Harry, Kowalski's absolutely gung ho. The inside word from his people is that they've already scheduled the film for distribution in the summer of next year. Kowalski wants you to get over to Los Angeles as soon as possible, like next week, to sign the revised contract and talk over a few things. Can you?'

Matt locked Andy in a bear hug. 'Jesus, Andy, *can* I? I've waited *years* for this.' He released Andy and grabbed a full glass off a passing waiter's tray. He gulped down a mouthful, spilling drops down his shirtfront. 'Christ, did I need some good news. Sorry, I have to go and find Liz!'

Shouldering his way excitedly into the library in search of Liz, he failed to see William manoeuvring his wheelchair through the crush. He stumbled and fell across William's wasted thighs. William hooted with laughter as Matt threw his arms around his neck. 'Hey, William, it's finally on! The Kowalski studio! They're going to make a feature of my book. A cartoon, just like Disney.'

In his excitement William lifted his head and gave a shrill, rising laugh that made the conversation in the room falter. Matt was clambering to his feet as Roger shoved his way over, a flush of embarrassment in his face. His eyes flickered suspiciously between Matt and his son. 'William?' he said, looking vexed. 'What's that noise for?'

Matt took him by the arm, deflecting his irritation. 'It's a done deal, Roger,' he muttered. 'Kowalski wants me to go over to sign the contract.'

'Congratulations. I still think you should have held out for Disney, though,' he said, unable to keep the resentment from his voice. He watched peevishly as Matt wove his way into the crowd, and then turned back to heave William brusquely upright in his chair again.

By the time the party crowded onto the terrace for the fireworks Matt had secretly organised as an anniversary present for Liz, Matt's good fortune was the talk of the party. There could not be a single one of the ninety-odd guests who had not sought him out to offer congratulations. Standing hand in hand with Liz, waiting for the display to begin, Matt realised with a start that it was the first time in several weeks that he had got through an hour without once thinking about Camilla. The first shower of fireworks erupted, casting the terrace in a greenish glow. 'A *really* happy anniversary, darling. Especially with the Kowalski deal.'

Pulling her to him, he bent and kissed her on the lips.

For a moment, Liz's lips remained closed, unresponsive. Then, very gradually, they parted, turning it into a full-blooded kiss. Instantly aroused, Matt's arms went around her, holding her closer. He kissed her deeper, seeking the soft textures of her mouth. As the guests gazed upward at the exploding colours, Matt's eyes closed. He moved closer, his blood pounding as he felt her respond.

'Mr Stenner.' Blinking, he broke off the kiss and looked around. One of the agency waiters stood at his elbow. 'Sorry, Mr Stenner, but there's someone at the door asking for you.'

'Shit,' Matt breathed, reluctantly letting his arms fall to his sides. He kissed Liz's hair. 'Back in a second.'

Two men in sports jackets and slacks stood in the vestibule, talking to each other in low voices. At Matt's approach they fell silent, watching blank-faced as he strode across the hall. His heart lurched. Camilla! He almost ran the final few steps.

'Good evening, gentlemen. I'm –'

'Mr Stenner?' the younger of the two men asked briskly.

'That's right.' A strange sensation clawed at Matt's stomach. The man's manner was familiar, at once deferential and authoritative. 'It's about my daughter, Camilla, isn't it?' He stepped closer to the man, panic in his eyes. 'What's happened to her?'

'As far as we know, your daughter is in good health, Mr Stenner.' Some of the apprehension drained from Matt's face. The man coughed softly. 'Mr Stenner, I'm arresting you on a charge of committing incest with your daughter, Camilla, on various occasions between February and July 1985.'

Eight

Matt erupted from sleep with a startled cry, as though his nightmare were pursuing him into wakefulness. Shivering, he scrambled to his feet, clawing his soiled dinner jacket closer around him. The jacket was soaked with the chill sweat of his dream.

For a moment he stood transfixed, not knowing where he was. Then, abruptly, he let out another cry, staggering against the green-painted brick wall as the fragmented phrases reverberated in his brain, obliterating coherent thought. 'Section ten ... sexual intercourse ... a girl under the age of sixteen ... you knew to be your daughter ... Sexual Offences Act 1956 ... section twelve ... buggery!' The impact of the last word made him double over as though struck, a hand clutched to his head as if to pluck out the words. Images churned with the phrases. The steel mesh cage around the rear entrance to the police station, the sense of being confined like a dangerous beast. The bare holding room, stinking and stained with the vomit of the Friday night drunks. His initial relief at being led from there turning to mind-freezing shock as, with Annie at his side, he had listened to the custody officer reading the full details of the charges.

The memory brought from him another torn, wounded sound. Then, with a huge effort, he forced himself upright. A murky light filtered through the glass bricks in the ceiling. He looked at his wrist and grunted. His watch was gone, taken from him, along with his money, his bow tie, and his shoelaces. He pushed his feet into unlaced shoes and crossed to the washbasin. He doused his face in the icy water from the single tap, dried his hands on his trousers, and stretched out on the bare board platform that served as a bunk to wait. And to think.

The night before, in the turbulent hours before he had fallen into exhausted sleep, he had let himself believe that the whole episode was a mistake, that he would wake to find an apologetic policeman sheepishly returning the zippered nylon bag with his possessions. Now, staring at the featureless wall, he knew it would not be like that. In the hours since his arrest, the belief that Letzer was behind it all had crystallised to a diamond-hard certainty. And with it had come a further certainty, that the man had not acted hastily. He was cool and clever, and working to some kind of agenda. Matt covered his face with his hands. Along with his hard-edged anger lay the absolute knowledge that his nightmare had hardly begun.

The door of the cramped room set aside for lawyer interviews shut behind him with the heavy thud that had already become familiar. Beyond the glass partition sat Annie, still in the long dress of turquoise crêpe she had been wearing the previous evening. She eyed Matt's own soiled white dinner jacket and twitched her lips in a wry glimmer of a smile. 'How are you feeling?'

Matt spread his hands. 'I'm loving it,' he said flatly. He nodded at her dress, frowning. 'Didn't you manage to even get home? How about William? Roger must have been going bananas.'

'He wasn't delirious. Still,' she added, with a mirthless laugh, 'for once we can *prove* I didn't sleep with you. It might do him good to have to get William ready. I couldn't face getting home at two and then being back down here for the bail hearing. It was nearly twelve when I left you. Remember?'

He shook his head. 'It's a blur. What time is it now?'

'Nine thirty. The hearing's in about an hour. You're lucky. They have a special court here on Saturday mornings. In a lot of places you would have been stuck in a cell until Monday.'

He did not appear to hear. 'Did you speak to Liz?'

'As soon as I left here last night.'

'How . . . what was her reaction?'

'What would you expect? Devastated. Distraught. Angry. She was all for driving right down. I persuaded her not to. She would have been a danger to herself.'

Matt nodded. 'Thanks. Seeing me like this wouldn't have been a help. You said she was angry?'

Annie looked at him curiously from beneath lowered brows. 'With Letzer, Matt,' she said, very distinctly.

He shut his eyes for a moment. 'What happens now?'

'I told you. The bail hearing. I'll see you in there.' She smiled, gesturing down at her dress. 'At least I'll add a touch of glamour.'

Emerging from the police station after the hearing, they strode grim-faced through the Saturday shoppers, their clothes drawing amused glances as they hurried for the side street where Annie had parked. They were still settling in their seats when a motorcycle skidded to a halt behind them. The pillion passenger leaped from the moving bike and sprinted, camera in hand, for the police station steps. Annie gave Matt a sidelong look. 'They've smelled blood already,' she murmured.

Matt's voice was a whisper. 'Take me home, Annie, please.'

For perhaps half an hour they drove in virtual silence, Annie's sporadic efforts at conversation foundering on

Matt's trancelike indifference. When he finally spoke, his voice held a hollow, distant ring. 'Why did they take my passport?'

'You were lucky. They could have asked for sureties. Big ones. It's a good thing I asked Liz to have the taxi bring your passport down.'

'But it means I can't travel.'

'Well, of course. Would you rather have stayed in there?'

'No. I mean I won't be able to be in Los Angeles for the meeting with Kowalski.'

'Kowalski? The film deal? Can't he come here?'

He looked at her blankly. 'Stan Kowalski? Annie, half the population of Los Angeles would *kill* for five minutes of his time.' He shook his head slowly. 'And what will I tell him? I can't come because I'm on a child abuse rap? For Christ's sake, Annie, we're talking about the world's most successful producer of *children's* films!'

'Matt, you've got other things to worry about.'

'But this is the biggest thing I've ever done. It's an accolade, Annie. Harry's been working on this deal for *years*!'

She slowed the car, turning to look at him. 'Matt, do you understand just how *serious* these bloody charges are?'

'Sorry,' he said softly. 'It's lack of sleep. I don't know where I am. What do they carry?'

'Incest?' She turned her eyes back to the road. 'Life. For a victim as young as they're saying Camilla was, I think you could be looking at twenty-five years!'

Matt was still sitting in deep, despondent silence as Annie hauled the car against the verge to allow an open-topped four-wheel drive to gun past them, gouging soil from the bank as it went. With a soft exclamation, he reached the phone from the dashboard and dialled. Mark answered on the first ring. 'Dad! Where are you?'

'About three hundred yards up the lane. Is the gate open?'

'No. We had to shut it. There are –'

'Open it now.' He was still replacing the phone as they came out of the bend and confirmed his worst misgivings. A dozen carelessly parked cars were clustered around the gate. Men waited in groups, restless, parkas over their suits. At the appearance of the Audi, cameras and microphones seemed to spring into their hands.

Annie accelerated for the opening gates, scattering the reporters, who turned to lope beside the car, yelling questions, their faces thrust close against the windows. Flashes popped inches from their faces, making them blink. A moment later, Matt and Annie were into the safety of the courtyard, the gate swinging shut behind them. Annie grimaced as, in the mirror, she saw heads bob above the wall as photographers clambered onto the roofs of their cars and went on snapping.

Liz was already running full tilt across the gravel. He was barely out of the car before she threw herself on him, her outstretched arms around his neck.

They clung to each other for a long time, his lips pressing against her hair as he repeated her name, over and over. At length, he disengaged and stood back, studying her face.

He had been prepared for her to be worried, distraught, even. The reality was still a shock. Her red-rimmed eyes looked sore and inflamed. Her cheekbones, always sculpted, were thrown into gaunt relief where the flesh seemed to have been pared away beneath the pallid, waxy skin. Liz caught the look in his eyes and forced a smile. 'I spent the night in the kitchen, drinking coffee. It's not recommended for the complexion.'

Matt, folding her hand in his, led the way back to the house. Mark met him in the hall, throwing his arms around him for a long embrace. As they parted, Matt sniffed the air, frowning.

'Naomi,' Liz said. 'I asked her to come over. I just thought she might be helpful.'

In response, Matt twitched his eyebrows and pushed open the library door. Naomi spun to face him. She still wore her heavy woollen cape. A loose wisp of hair hung over one eye. A sheen of perspiration lay over her face. She took a last long draw on her cigarette, crushed it out with her fingertips and threw the remains into the hearth. 'Oh God, you poor thing.' She held him by the shoulders, taking in his wasted face, the smudged jacket. 'I came over the moment Liz phoned.' Her own eyes were reddened from crying. 'She told me the situation. It's awful. Just absolutely shitty.'

Matt moved away, taking her hands from his shoulders. 'The understatement of the fucking century. Didn't you see this coming?'

Her eyes were awash with new tears. 'No,' she said hoarsely. 'I didn't. Not exactly. I was –'

'Not *exactly*? What the bloody hell is that supposed to mean?'

She blinked hard and looked into his face. 'Please, Matt, don't jump to conclusions. Something like it was always possible. Some sort of accusation, I mean. Camilla even made a few remarks in my presence that got my guard up.'

Matt's nostrils flared. 'Got *your* guard up! When was this?'

She swallowed, forcing herself to keep her eyes on his. 'While you were away.'

'Why the fucking hell didn't you *phone* us? We'd have been home in twenty-four hours.'

She shook her head helplessly. 'I thought you both needed the break. I never thought it would come to *this* and I made Stephen *swear* he would tell me if anything came up.'

'And in the meantime he's dismantling our entire fucking lives.' His tone made Naomi flinch.

'Oh God, Matt, I'm sorry. I called Stephen as soon as I heard from Liz. He says it all came out so suddenly, and so . . . *completely*. He felt he had no choice.' She dropped heavily into a chair, her face bereft. 'It's not too late, is it? To stop it, I mean.'

Annie spoke from the doorway. 'It would have been a lot better if it hadn't got started,' she said drily. 'A *lot* better.'

Naomi sank deeper into the chair, her face in her hands. 'Oh shit! Can you all imagine what a . . . what an asshole I feel? I'm the one who *recommended* that man.' She looked up, her expression plaintive, the marks of her fingers still etched into the flesh of her broad face. 'I *trusted* him. He had always been so scrupulous. I can't believe he would go behind my back like that.'

Matt touched a hand to her shoulder. 'Forget it. He screwed you, just like he screwed us. That's water under the bridge. The question's only where in hell we go from here.'

Liz took his hand again. 'I was in a terrible state last night. Tell me again, what *exactly* are they charging you with?'

'You've got the jargon, Annie. Do you want to convey the happy news?'

Annie was about to speak when a commotion in the hall made her pause. A moment later, Roger thrust the door wide and propelled William's wheelchair into the centre of the room. 'Morning, everyone,' he grunted, off-handedly. He turned petulantly to Annie, looking ostentatiously at his watch. 'I thought you'd have been home hours ago. What about William's riding?'

Annie drew a deep breath. White spots appeared on her cheeks.

Matt stepped across and ran a hand through William's hair. 'Sorry, William. It's my fault. I'm in some trouble.' He made a point of including Roger in his smile. 'Annie's been helping me out. I didn't mean to interfere with your weekend. Sorry.' He turned to Annie. 'Thanks, Annie. You've been great.'

Annie, her eyes on Roger, indicated her dress. 'I'm not going to the damned stables like this. Can't you –'

'It doesn't matter.' William was beaming up into Matt's face. 'I can easily miss a week, if it helps Matt.'

Matt broke the instant of frigid silence. 'William, you're great. I really appreciate that.' He turned to Annie. 'Do you want to carry on?' Almost without a pause, catching the shadow behind her eyes, he laughed and went on, 'I have no secrets from Roger. You'll be able to read about it in tomorrow's papers, anyway.'

Matt drew Liz down beside him on the sofa and listened while Annie spelled out the charges, using the exact words the custody officer had used twelve hours earlier. As she spoke, the official language cold and yet intolerably charged, an icy stillness settled on the room. Matt studied Liz's face. Her oddly aloof behaviour on the Japanese trip had left him puzzled and disconcerted. In the midst of the mental turmoil since his arrest, what had begun as a fleeting apprehension had grown into a nagging doubt. Now, he watched every movement, every tic, looking for, but not finding, some sign that would confirm or allay his fear.

Mark lowered himself onto the sofa at his father's

side and slid an arm around his neck. At first Matt did no more than return the gesture, putting his own arm around Mark's rangy shoulders. Then, slowly, he turned and buried his face in his son's shoulder. He looked up again only as Annie was coming to the end of her speech. His cheeks glistened with tears.

'I suppose you should all know,' Annie said, her voice dropping to a whisper, 'the maximum penalty for incest in the alleged circumstances is twenty-five years.'

Liz's intake of breath rattled and died in the stillness.

Mark found his voice first. 'He's after her money!' He sprang to his feet, his eyes burning angrily into Naomi's face. 'It's obvious. The bastard's a gold-digger.' He stabbed a finger at Naomi. 'I'd like to throttle the little shithead.'

Matt rose and moved to his side. 'I'm inclined to agree with you. It's the only explanation. But beating him up won't change anything.'

Annie smiled. 'No. Basically, the charges stand or fall on Camilla's allegations. One way to throw additional doubt on them is obviously to discredit Letzer.'

'But, how can they even charge Matt without *evidence*, apart from Camilla's, a sick girl's, *word*?' Liz asked, her voice breaking.

Annie sighed. 'Do you remember, a few years ago, date rape was a big issue? There were a couple of cases that were all over the national press. There was no evidence in those cases, either, but they still went ahead.' She shrugged. 'The Crown Prosecution Service would scream to hear me say it, but they don't operate in a vacuum. If there's political pressure on them . . .' She let the thought die. 'Anyway, I don't see they have a hope of securing a conviction. Your defence would submit that, first, there's no evidence, so the case should be thrown out, and secondly, Camilla is "remembering" things that never happened, implanted in a vulnerable mind by an unscrupulous therapist.' She looked at Naomi. 'You must be familiar with some of the American cases.'

Naomi nodded. 'A lot of them. Some failed, some succeeded.'

'But is it *possible*?' Liz said. 'To make somebody really *believe* anything so . . . sordid . . . happened to them without their remembering it?'

Matt spread his hands. 'For that matter, could anybody *really* forget being . . . raped,' he forced the word out, 'by her *father*? It just isn't plausible.'

Naomi bowed her head. 'The American courts do admit recovered memory evidence. Personally, I believe both things are possible, genuine recovered memory, and false stuff. The problem is knowing which is which. Obviously, Camilla's memories are false. The question is, did they emerge spontaneously from whatever's going on in her own head, or did Stephen implant them? I can't believe he would be such a total asshole. He might have *behaved* like one, to us, but I'd still give him the benefit of the doubt. If he's a real *believer* in Recovered Memory Syndrome, then he has no choice. It's like religion. Start choosing the bits you want to believe in and your whole system falls apart. To him, Camilla's memories *must* be genuine.' She bit her lip. 'And he has worked with a lot of abused people.'

Mark grabbed roughly at her arm. 'Are you suggesting –'

'Of course not, Mark,' she said patiently, extricating her arm from his grip and massaging the place where his fingers had dug into her flesh. 'I'm only pointing out that to fight the charges effectively your dad needs to take account of Stephen's credentials. He has done good work with vulnerable young women.'

'Was sleeping with them always part of the treatment?' Matt asked bitterly.

Naomi's brow creased. 'Don't, Matt, please. You've no evidence of that. And don't ever forget that Camilla made a serious attempt to kill herself. There must be *some* reason for that. You can't really blame him for going with the one that fits the way he wants to see things.'

'Jesus, Naomi, I thought you were on *my* side!'

'Of course I am! But I have responsibilities to Camilla, too. I haven't had the chance to speak to her since this all broke, to try to find some explanation. She's clearly a very sick girl. Sicker than I realised. I need to talk to her. And to Stephen.'

'Why don't I come with you?' said Matt. 'If I could talk to Camilla, maybe I could . . .'

Annie's aghast expression made him falter. 'No! Forget that! Didn't you even *listen* in court this morning? It's a bail condition, for God's sake. Do you want to go straight back into a cell? The prosecution would just *love* it. Interfering with witnesses.'

'But surely, she's still my *daughter*. I'm not going to try to –'

'No!' Annie shouted the word. 'You can't approach Camilla. Or Letzer. Unless you want to get yourself into a lot more trouble than you're already in!'

Liz rose to her feet. 'How about me?'

'Well,' Annie said slowly, 'I don't see why not. If you *could* talk Camilla out of it, you would be saving yourselves a lot of grief. Not to mention an awful lot of expense.'

Liz turned to Naomi. 'Could you talk to Letzer? I'd be grateful if you could drive me down, too, if you're free. In my present state I'd be a danger on the roads. I heard that people who've just learned they have cancer feel like that.'

137

Roger gave a booming laugh, the first time he had made a sound during the conversation. 'Too true. I knew a guy who was told he had liver cancer. Three days later he pranged his Porsche on the Hammersmith flyover. Beat rotting to death, I suppose.' They all waited for Roger's renewed laughter to die.

Annie said, 'Liz's right. It's best if she and Naomi go together. You need some rest, Matt.' She touched a hand to her own dress. 'And I need to change into something more suitable for a Saturday afternoon.'

Fidgeting, Roger glanced at his watch. 'Right. I'm running late, too.'

Matt took the handles of William's wheelchair. 'Sorry, Roger,' he said with no trace of irony in his voice. 'I didn't mean to make you late for the game. Anyway, thanks to you, and you, William, for the loan of Annie. If she hadn't been there I'd still be climbing up the walls of that cell while they phoned around trying to find a legal aid solicitor who wasn't with the family in Safeway's.'

Matt and Annie installed William in the specially adapted Range Rover while Roger threw himself into Annie's Audi. She looked up briefly as he gunned it out of the courtyard in a spurt of gravel. Saying nothing, she turned her attention back to William, strapping him in and slamming the tailgate. Together, she and Matt walked to the driver's door. With one hand on the handle, she took Matt's hand in the other. 'Get some rest, Matt. Then you have to start thinking about getting a good lawyer. I'll try and think of some names, people who specialise in this kind of thing. Call me at the office and I'll let you know what I've come up with.' Her hand was tightening on the door handle when something in his face made her loosen her grip. 'What? Don't you want me to?' She stepped closer, her voice dropping to an urgent whisper. 'Don't kid yourself, Matt. If it does come to trial this could be a very dirty business. Your entire life will be turned inside out. In a lot of people's eyes you're already a pervert, as of yesterday night. You'll be . . .' Her voice trailed away. Her mouth had fallen open in silent protest.

Matt was shaking his head. 'You heard the dates, Annie. Nineteen eighty-*five*.' She shook her head slowly, her eyes widening in disbelief. 'Margaret Thatcher. Boom time for the banks. Roger was in Hong Kong all that year, rejigging the bank's dealing operations. The year Liz was doing the project for *Vanity Fair* in New York.' She moaned and took a half-step backwards, almost staggering, throwing a quick glance over her shoulder to where William sat smiling at them through the glass. Matt moved with her, closing the gap between them, reaching to touch her arm. His voice dropped to a whisper. 'Annie, I hardly slept alone that entire year.'

Annie's face had taken on a waxy pallor. 'Matt, I can't believe it. You can't make me *testify*!' She grabbed at the lapel of his jacket, her voice a panicky, urgent whisper. 'Think what it would *do* to Roger. I know you despise Roger. But I'm still *married* to him! He's still William's father. Think about William, for God's sake.' Matt had bowed his head, covering his eyes with his hand. When he looked up again, his tears glistened. Annie did not even notice, her own tears flying as she shook her head. 'He idolises you. Can you imagine what it would do to him to find out that all the time I was pregnant with him I was having an affair with *you*?'

'No, Annie. No. I lay in that cell thinking about it half the night. Somebody's trying to destroy my life. I'm not going to prevent *that* by destroying yours.'

'What then? What do you want from me, Matt?'

He opened his eyes again. Their faces were inches apart. 'No names, Annie. No other lawyers. I just want you to take my case.'

Nine

For some seconds Annie stared at him in mute dismay. In a barely audible whisper, she said, 'That's insane. It would just be . . . unprofessional! I'm much too close to you.' She spread her hands pleadingly, glancing back once more to give William a quick, stilted smile. 'For heaven's sake, Matt, we were *lovers*!'

He looked again into her pleading eyes. 'I've thought it through, believe me. Everything I am in the world, my family, my career, my friends, depends on beating this, Annie. And you're the best person in the world to do it.'

'But, don't you understand? I *can't*! It would be totally *unethical*.'

'I'm accused of *incest*, Annie. I couldn't give a fuck about the ethics.'

Her eyes were wild. 'But I was in love with you! I slept with you days before I gave birth to William. How could I possibly be objective?' Without warning tears began to flow again.

Matt looked towards the door of the house before taking her hand. 'You can't. That's why I want you to do it. You are the only person in the world who *knows*, absolutely, that I didn't do it. I know how hard that will make you try. Plus the fact that you're Liz's best friend. If she sees that *you* believe in me, it'll make it easier for her.'

The only sound was of their breathing as they both felt the weight of the irony of Matt's words. Matt broke the silence, smiling tentatively. 'Also, you happen to be the ideal *lawyer*. I made up my mind last night. I'm not prepared to have my family's future in the hands of a bunch of people who don't give a shit about us. I never understood the logic of a system where one bunch of people do the legwork and then when it comes to court they hand over to a barrister who hardly knows who I am.'

'The system works, Matt. You can afford the finest people in the country, people who specialise in this type of case.'

'Money isn't an issue. You *are* one of the finest, Annie. And you have right of audience. You can do it all, prepare the case *and* plead it in court.' He leaned closer so that their faces were almost touching. 'Please, Annie.'

She turned away, her hands over her face to hide her tears from William. 'From what I've seen so far, I'd be surprised if the Crown Prosecution Service even decide to proceed. If the only evidence they have is Camilla's allegations you won't need a genius to get you acquitted.'

He moved to her shoulder. 'An acquittal won't be good enough, though, will it?' She looked askance at him, her tears abated. 'Not proven beyond reasonable doubt?' He shook his head. 'That won't be enough, will it? If they were accusing me of armed robbery, okay. Middle-aged men making my sort of income just don't suddenly take to robbing banks. *Everyone* would assume it was a mistake, even the police.' He took a long breath. 'A taste for child abuse is different. It's more democratic. Rich people do it just like poor people! I may be acquitted for lack of evidence, but you know damned well that won't stop people keeping their kids at a distance. For Christ's sake, Annie, I write for *children*! Can you imagine the effect this is going to have?'

Annie nodded towards the drive where the press waited. 'That gang of vipers out there will see to that.'

'Right. So you can understand that it's not just a matter of winning the case. Letzer has to be *destroyed*. He's a charlatan, and the whole damned world has to know it.' He broke off, panting.

'Roger's going to be as jealous as hell,' Annie said softly, without looking at him.

He reached out, smiling, to take her hand. 'Thanks, Annie. Thanks a million.'

With a sudden sharp sob, she stepped forward and clasped her arms around his neck. Her cheek was wet against his. 'Oh, God help us, Matt. All of us.'

Stephen Letzer must have been watching for their arrival. Naomi's Volkswagen had hardly come to a stop when the door opened and he came striding down the steps towards them, then stood formally to attention, his heels together, back held straight. His face, like Liz's, had altered since they had last met. It was stricken and oddly changing, as though he were wrestling with some deep anger or grief that threatened to overwhelm him. His troubled smile had an edgy, tentative quality, as though he were somehow anxious for Liz's approval. Out of nowhere, an image leaped into her mind, making her stifle a wild laugh. His smile, his achingly formal posture were an echo of old boyfriends meeting her parents for the first time. 'Welcome, Mrs Stenner. I'm so glad you were able to make it.' She had come to talk Camilla out of sending her father to prison for a quarter of a century and the man was greeting her in the stilted rhythms of a prospective son-in-law.

Naomi had come round to Liz's side. 'Hello, Stephen.' She moved forward to kiss him. Letzer flinched, taking the kiss low on the jawline. Above his smile something unwelcoming stirred in his eyes.

'Nice of you to take the driving load off Mrs Stenner. The worry must be very distracting.' His smile gave way to a deep frown. 'Camilla's anxious to see you.' His voice fell to a murmur. 'The poor kid has been through a pretty wrenching time.'

'Camilla isn't the only one,' Liz replied, falling into step as he led the way towards the house.

He led them through the hall and stopped at a glazed door through which Liz could see the tiled floor of a conservatory, set with spiky plants in Chinese planters. Letzer put a hand on the doorknob. 'Please try not to let her get overexcited. She's stronger, but she's still a very disturbed woman.' He opened the door and stood aside. 'I'll be in my office. There's a bell if you need me.'

Liz gave him a long, appraising look and then stepped through the door. As Naomi made to go with her, Letzer laid a hand on her arm, his fingers sinking deep into the cloth of her sleeve. 'I think it's better Mrs Stenner does this alone.'

Camilla had been reading. At the sound of the door she dropped the book and rose, turning to meet Liz. For a heartbeat, Liz stopped short. Then, without a word, they ran to throw themselves into each other's arms. For a long time they remained crushed together, their cheeks pressing together, their tears mingling. At length, still choking, Liz pulled back to hold Camilla at arm's length, examining her.

Camilla had put on some weight, so that her clothes, a fresh T-shirt and jeans, had lost their borrowed look. Her hair, newly washed, had regained some of its lustre. Although still deeply drawn, her face had begun to shed its pallor, the dark bags beneath her eyes had faded. The biggest change, though, was in her demeanour. The neurotic vigour of her movements was more unsettling than the languorous slouch Liz had been expecting. Camilla spoke first, picking at the cloth of her T-shirt, making no move to wipe the tears from her cheeks. 'Thanks for coming.'

'It's okay,' Liz muttered inadequately. For some moments they faced each other, Camilla looking coolly back at Liz, waiting. When Liz at last managed to speak again her voice was a barely audible sob. 'Please tell me. How could you do this to your father?'

'Would *you* rather I had kept it quiet?'

The cleft in the centre of Liz's brow deepened. 'But, darling, you're speaking as if it *happened*. As if your father had really *done* those things. Don't you see? Isn't it clear to you? That man . . .' She hesitated, watching her daughter's unwavering gaze. 'Stephen . . . I'm not saying he did it to hurt you in any way, but can't you see that somehow he . . . well . . . he *put* these things in your mind? Implanted them. Maybe it's just that, trying to help you, he suggested things and you . . . I don't know . . . you somehow mistook them for reality.'

Camilla continued looking levelly into her eyes. 'But, Mummy, you don't know they never happened, do you? You weren't there,' she said flatly. 'You were *never* there.'

The words struck at Liz like stones. For a moment more she held Camilla's gaze and then, clapping her hands to her face, she dropped heavily into a chair. 'Oh God! I . . .' Some seconds passed in silence before she took a deep breath and straightened, squeezing the tears from her eyes with her fingertips. 'Camilla,' she said, very quietly. 'I know now I shouldn't have kept on working so long. I also know you've never understood it. I don't expect you to now. But for a long time it seemed important to me.'

'More than staying home to take care of Mark and me?'

'No, darling!' Liz shook her head, groaning. 'Don't say that. I was *working*. I had to. With your views you *must* see that. By the time Daddy and I married I was used to being a person in my own right. I just couldn't be an *accessory*, nothing more than the wife of a famous writer.'

'Is that what it would have been, staying home to protect us?'

Liz flinched at the uncompromising tone. 'No! I didn't . . . I mean Daddy wanted it, too. He *encouraged* me to keep working. And he was always there for you.'

'He sure was.'

Uttered as no more than the barest whisper, the words made Liz recoil against the back of her chair. She felt as though a steel band had tightened around her chest. Gradually she brought her breathing under control. 'Camilla, I can't pretend to understand what's happening to you, but I would give the world to make you feel less alone in it. Wouldn't it be a good start to tell me everything, all that you think happened, and when?'

For nearly half an hour Camilla talked, incessantly pacing the cramped conservatory. After some initial attempts to protest, Liz gradually lapsed into silence. She sat pale and immobile, her eyes locked onto her daughter's face as, without ever raising her voice above a whisper, Camilla recounted her story.

When she finished, a deep silence fell on the room. Liz felt the stillness crawl on her skin. 'Is that the story you told the police?' she asked at last.

'It's what happened.'

Liz sprang to her feet, spinning away from Camilla. 'No!' She spoke with her back to her. 'For God's *sake*!

Never! Not Daddy.' She turned back to face her daughter, her eyes stinging. 'You must see it ... you must tell them ... This man ... Stephen Letzer ... is behind this. How, Camilla? Some sort of brain-washing? Hypnosis, maybe?'

'Stephen isn't behind anything. Except that he helped me bring it all to the surface. What difference does it make *how* he did it? It's what *happened* that's important, isn't it?'

Liz stepped quickly towards her. 'Of course it makes a difference, darling. If he ... I'm not claiming he's done it deliberately. You obviously feel he's genuine. And I'll admit he seems to care about you. But maybe he ... unintentionally ... perhaps, he's confused you, so that you're confusing old fantasies with reality.'

'The dates, Mummy,' Camilla replied, wearily patient, as though explaining to a child. 'And you weren't there, so how can you tell me what happened and what didn't happen?'

Liz shivered. There was no reproach in the words. Only disappointment. 'But it just can't *be*, Camilla. Daddy could never have done such things. He simply *couldn't*.'

Camilla swallowed, seemed to hesitate. When she replied her voice was stretched to breaking point. 'Sorry, Mummy. But I know that he did. And I'm going to swear to it in court.'

It was dark enough for the car to bring the security lights clicking on as Naomi drew up in front of the house. Her hands remained on the steering wheel, gripping it hard. She did not switch off the engine.

Liz looked at her, her eyebrows raised. 'Aren't you coming in? Personally, I need a drink.'

Naomi gave her a tight-lipped smile. Throughout

the drive back, the anger that had been in her face when she emerged from Letzer's office to hurry after Liz as she stalked from the building had stayed in her. 'Thanks. I need to get home. I'd be bad company this evening.'

Liz sighed, reaching for the door handle. 'I know what you mean. Just thinking about that bastard has the same effect on me.'

As she swung her legs out of the car Naomi spoke again. 'Bastard is right! A total fucking bastard!'

The vehemence of her words brought Liz's head round and she was surprised to see Naomi's eyes glint wetly in the lamplight. 'Don't blame yourself,' she said hoarsely. '*You* can't help it if someone you trust lets you down, can you?'

For a moment they looked into each other's eyes. Then, Naomi smiled again, a quick little twitch of her lips. 'Bye, Liz. Love to Matt.'

Liz found Matt in the study, gazing morosely at the newspapers strewn on the desk. She stood at his shoulder, looking down. 'What a bunch of shits.'

'Who was the idiot who said there's no such thing as bad publicity?' He rose and kissed her. 'How did it go?'

She returned his kiss. 'I'll tell you every gory detail.'

He grimaced. 'Better get Mark in on it. He may as well hear the terrible truth about his dad.'

'Mark? I thought he was over at Jane's.'

'Binty West called. Jane's sick.'

He watched as Liz's eyes went slowly to the strewn newspapers. His photograph was on the cover of three of them. He put an arm around her. 'Exactly. Mark spoke to Jane at one. She was fine. Then, two hours later, her mother calls and the poor girl's gone down with a mystery illness. The dim old bird doesn't even have the wit to lie decently.' He gave a wry smile. 'The

Major must have come close to a heart attack when he picked up the paper this morning.'

Matt's arm tightened around her shoulders. 'The Wests just got in first, sweetheart,' he murmured. 'From now on, we had better get used to it.'

'How did Mark take it?'

'He was upset. About Jane, of course. But I think he was almost as pissed off at that pair of clowns on my behalf. I think if he ran into the Major he'd have trouble not whacking the old dolt.'

They found Mark at the kitchen table, eating cereal. Rachel was at the oven, checking a casserole. She turned at their entry, smiling at their surprise. 'I knew you'd all have too much on your minds to think about making any supper. I took this out of the freezer and ran over with it.'

Matt nodded. 'Thanks, that was thoughtful,' he muttered, turning to Mark. 'You okay? We thought you ought to hear her news.' He touched a hand lightly to Mark's shoulder. 'If you feel up to it. And Rachel. No reason why *Sun* readers should be better informed than you.' He took an opened bottle of wine from the fridge and sat down, pouring as he did so. 'So. How was it?'

The lack of response made him look up, frowning. Liz stood with her back to him, her fists clenched. With an anxious glance at Mark, he rose and moved to her, carrying a glass. He put the glass into her hand. He waited until she had drunk off a long sip, and then put his hands on her shoulders, needing more force than he had expected to turn her towards the table. 'Every word, darling, please.'

Liz sat down, her movements stiff and unco-ordinated. 'She says it started when she was just eight. She recalls waking up with a nightmare. One she had often, where she was drowning, in the dark. You came to her. I was in America.'

'She claims to remember all *that*? At eight years old?'

'Yes. So do I, Matt. All too clearly,' she added in a whisper. She looked into her glass. 'It was her eighth birthday. And I was in New York, doing a piece for *Vanity Fair*.' She drank off some more wine, spilling drops onto the table top. 'You were naked. You got into bed with her.'

'For Christ's sake, Liz, I'm naked half the damned time. So are you. It doesn't mean a thing.' He gave an exasperated toss of his head at Rachel's pinched expression. 'Come on. In the summer I often start *work* without bothering to put clothes on. When we're in France I sometimes don't wear clothes all day. So fucking what?'

'Don't swear at me, Matt. I know all that. I'm just repeating Camilla's story, as she told it to me.'

'Sorry.' He lowered his voice. 'So what came next?'

Liz looked around at the watching faces. All their eyes drilled into hers. For some time she hesitated, and then, with her eyes cast down, she murmured, 'You started masturbating.'

'Oh shit.' Matt's words were followed by a stunned, pulsating silence.

'That little bastard!' Mark's cry finally broke the quiet. 'I'd like to get that little shit face to face. I'd soon get the truth out of him. I'd –'

'What did I do next?' Matt asked conversationally, laying a restraining hand on Mark's arm.

Liz swallowed. 'That went on for a week or so, you doing it to yourself, then, after a while . . . making Camilla do it to you.'

Matt gripped Mark's arm, quelling a renewed protest. 'And? How long was it before I . . . went the whole hog?'

'Another month or so.'

He shook his head in disbelief. 'She remembers the detail of that, too?'

Liz nodded, her teeth grinding deep into her lip. 'Perfectly, apparently. I was still in America. The same trip.'

'Which hotel were you staying at?'

A note of weary sarcasm in his voice made her look at him sharply. 'Again, she claims to have a fix on the occasion. The evening of the village Easter egg hunt.' She wet her lips and blinked hard. Her face had drained to a dead white.

Matt stood up and took several aimless steps. His hands went to his face, his fingertips kneading the flesh above his eyes. 'Oh fuck,' he breathed. He repeated the words several times before slowly turning to face them. 'Could the two of us have a moment alone, please?' he whispered.

Matt stared sightlessly into the library fire. The light from the burning logs, the only light in the room, glinted on his glass as he drained it and then, with an exclamation, slammed it down, making it ring on the white marble mantel. From beyond the open door he could hear Rachel's voice, turned to a bray by embarrassment.

Until a few moments ago he thought he had considered all the possible consequences of what was happening. He had contemplated the wreckage of his career, the catastrophic effects on their social life, the loss of people they had thought of as friends, and come to some kind of accommodation with them. They could move, to the house in France, or maybe to America. It would take time, a lot more than a man nearing fifty wanted to spend at it, but they would make a new life, form new friendships.

He had even found a certain consolation in the idea

of not working any more; now that Mark was getting ready to go off to university, of having precious time to spend with Liz. There were a lot of cities to revisit together, a lot of coast and mountain still unwalked. And now, in that minute hesitation, the hardly measurable fraction of a second that preceded her denial, he had the sickening sensation that that, too, the entire rest of his life, had been torn from his grasp. Somewhere inside Liz, however deep she tried to bury it, the worm of doubt, the possibility that Camilla was telling the truth, remained alive!

Until that moment he had not understood that Liz could even imagine mistrusting him. She may not have understood it herself. And yet it had always been a stupid delusion to imagine she failed to notice the phone conversations brought to an abrupt end, or the subject clumsily changed when she had unexpectedly entered a room. Those times when, home unexpectedly, she had beaten him to the phone only to have the line go dead. It made no difference that it had all been a dozen years ago. The seeds of mistrust could lie dormant for decades. All it took was something to disturb the ground for them to sprout into new life.

Voices in the kitchen dragged him out of his reflection. Rubbing a hand over his face, as though to wipe away the thoughts, he hurried to join them.

'Hello, Matt!'

'Hi, William.' He sparred playfully with William, letting the boy land a fluttering blow to his stomach. 'Sorry to drag you over here and spoil your Sunday.'

Annie smiled from Matt to Liz. 'The evenings we allow. In dire emergency.'

'I know.' Matt smiled at William. 'Hey, William, why don't you go into the library with Mark? It's bad enough boring your mother with legal business on a Sunday. I don't see why you should suffer.' He watched

William's wheelchair roll out of sight. 'Where's Roger?'

'At home.' She left a weighted pause. 'There's rugby on satellite. New Zealand? South Africa? I don't know.' She grimaced. 'Apparently it's important. Much too important to be combined with taking care of William,' she added, half to herself. 'Now, what's the panic?'

Liz spoke. 'Look, Annie, Matt insisted I call you. He wants me to tell you what happened today at the clinic.'

Rachel drew up a chair for Annie and all four sat down at the table.

At each point that Camilla had specified dates, Matt felt he was being flayed alive by Annie's presence, yet he never once took his eyes off Liz. The fear that Liz might suspect the truth drummed in his head. Intently as he watched, though, he saw no flicker of suspicion in the bereft expression in her eyes.

Matt broke the silence which followed Liz's story. 'He's a cunning bastard, isn't he? I'll bet every one of those dates will check out. Liz will have been away. And I will have been here with the children. Alone.'

'You had an au pair at that time, didn't you? Wasn't she here?' Annie responded.

Alert to every nuance, Matt cursed inwardly at what he thought was a hurried note in her voice. 'That's right. Kristina Olsen. The Norwegian girl.'

'Are you still in touch? She might be a useful witness.'

Matt shrugged. 'We kept in touch for a couple of years. We could probably find her. She can't really prove I *didn't* do it, though. It's still basically Camilla's word against mine.' He turned to Liz. 'How the hell could he have got the dates? Surely he *must* have hypnotised her. Would hypnosis work like that?'

Liz shrugged. 'We'd need to ask Naomi.'

'I will,' Annie said briskly. 'But we're talking about a girl of eight, Matt. I'm not sure that, as far as the courts are concerned, they wouldn't consider a girl that age could simply recall something, if there was a trigger. Hasn't it ever happened to you, to have an image come suddenly to mind from your childhood?'

Matt stared at her. 'You're not suggesting –'

'No, of course I'm not. But maybe if Camilla did remember some specific things, let's say Liz's being away . . .' She paused, letting the shadow that fell on Liz's face pass. 'Then maybe Letzer could weave the rest into that by some process of suggestion.'

'But why, Annie? Why the fucking *hell* is he doing this to me?'

Liz leaned forward. 'Is he planning to blackmail us? Is *that* it? Are we going to get a phone call, tomorrow, some day soon, offering to drop the case?'

'That had occurred to me,' said Annie. 'The thing is, it's too late. It's in the hands of the police now. If he wanted to wring money out of you the time to do it was *before* calling in the police, not now. Unless Camilla's planning to sue you *after* you're convicted, for some sort of personal injury.' She spread her hands. 'This is Britain, though, not America. The sort of damages a court might award over here would hardly justify the risk.'

Matt gave them a lop-sided smile. 'I think we've underestimated your friend Steve.'

Annie cocked her head. 'How's that?'

'Come into the study.'

Watched by the three women, Matt leaned down and hauled open the heavy door of the old-fashioned safe.

Annie laughed aloud. 'Security conscious, isn't he! Three-inch steel, but no key!'

Matt smiled over his shoulder as he burrowed in the safe. 'Don't bother shopping us to our insurers. Liz's stuff's in the *real* safe, upstairs. This is just a fire precaution for family documents, wills, tax records, a few photos, passports, that kind of thing.' He sat up and dropped a buff folder, tied with red string, onto the desk. 'This, for instance.'

Annie leaned to read the label upside down. She glanced sidelong at Rachel. 'Patrick's trust?'

Matt began leafing through the folder. Rachel had sunk into a chair where she sat tight-lipped, looking at the floor.

'I don't think you've ever seen this, have you, Annie?'

'No, Patrick didn't ever talk to me about it. I presume if he needed legal advice he used the company's lawyers?' She looked questioningly at Rachel.

'I suppose so. He certainly didn't consult *me*!'

Annie made a show of ignoring the note of bitterness. 'I hope he consulted *someone*. Trusts can be minefields if they aren't properly drawn up.'

Matt folded back the document at the page he was looking for. He offered it to Annie, tapping a paragraph. 'You said it. What's your lawyerly opinion of *this*?'

She took the document and scanned it for thirty seconds in silence. At length, she looked around at the three of them, the corners of her mouth drawn down. 'I wish he *had* come to me.'

Matt shrugged. 'Me, too.'

'Does Camilla actually know about this?'

'I imagine so. I can't specifically recall discussing it with her, but I might have. After all, it's her money.'

Rachel was on the edge of her seat, craning. 'What is it? What's wrong? The children get the money when they're twenty-eight, don't they? I always thought it was quite straightforward.'

Matt nodded to Annie to pass the deed to Rachel. 'So did I. Until I reread what it says there. Liz and I are trustees, unless one of us becomes incompetent or unfit to secure their best interests. In which case you, Rachel, become trustee in our place.'

Rachel was still reading as she spoke. 'Except that each of them gets full control of their own share of the capital when they reach twenty-one!' Her head came up. 'But, Matt, Camilla's twenty-one next year.'

Matt leaned far back in his chair, steepling his fingers above his chest. 'So now you know why he didn't bother with blackmail,' he said. 'Because if they can get me sent down there isn't a court in the land that wouldn't agree that I was unfit to continue, according to the terms of the trust. Our dear friend Letzer stands to collect around two million pounds.'

Ten

Annie shook her head in disbelief. 'But whatever induced Patrick to put in a condition like that – especially anything so vague? I'm astonished that any lawyer would have *allowed* him such a phrase. It's bloody criminal.'

Matt looked for a moment at Rachel before saying softly, 'In his last months it wasn't easy to make Patrick see . . . reason.'

'But still, he couldn't possibly have anticipated anything as far out as this mess. What was going on in his head, for God's sake?'

'I tried to ask him.'

'And what did he say?'

Rachel sat rigid as a statue, her lips tightly clenched. Matt sighed. 'He was pretty far gone with the booze by then.' Rachel's jaw was set hard. 'Sorry, Rachel, but the fact is Patrick hardly sobered up once in the last six months of his life.'

'I knew he had a problem. I didn't know it was that bad,' said Annie.

'He had the accident at ten thirty in the morning. The post-mortem found he had already drunk a bottle and a half of brandy.'

Annie raised her eyebrows. 'But I still don't see why this weird clause.'

Matt shrugged. 'We neither. But then, there are quite a few things in it we thought were weird. For instance, there are whole pages about what happens if Liz and I divorce. And he specifically restricted any benefit to

Mark and Camilla. If we had had any more children they were excluded from the trust.'

Annie made a face. 'That looks plain vicious.'

'Too bloody right! Christ, can you imagine, trying to bring up a third child, and explaining that the other two were looking at a fortune while their little brother or sister was excluded? It's as if he were trying to tell us not to have any more.'

'Did you try to ask him about that, too?'

'Annie,' Matt murmured, 'you have to understand. For those last months, it was virtually impossible to get any sense out of Patrick at all, on any subject. My brother had been a drinker all his life, but,' he turned in brief, silent apology to Rachel, 'by the end he was an out-and-out lush. An alcoholic. A wreck.' Rachel began sniffing and clapped her hands to her face. Matt pushed a box of tissues absently towards her. 'The trust is a fairly complicated document. By the time I got a sight of it you couldn't have discussed a "Keep off the Grass" sign with Patrick. Also, I know the beneficiaries are our children, but it was *his* money. As to him restricting it to Camilla and Mark, that was never a problem. Liz had . . .' He caught himself and broke off, glancing quickly at Liz. She held his eye for just an instant before looking sharply away. Annie caught the look. Matt hesitated and then went on, 'We had already agreed not to have any more, anyway.'

The silence had lain for no more than a heartbeat when Annie said, 'You mentioned two million pounds. Was that just *Camilla*'s share?'

Rachel swallowed a sob. 'Probably more, now! They got half the money Patrick got when he sold the business. They got the same as me!' She sniffed back a sob. 'Just over two million pounds, in 1985!'

Annie nodded. 'If we *can* show Letzer's manipulating Camilla, it certainly gives him a juicy motive.' A

sudden smile lit her face. 'I think tomo...
dogs on your friend Stephen Letzer.'

Matt wove a path between the clusters of ...
ern women, like huge crows in the black cl...
swathed them from head to toe, who were ... ...g
from Harrods to climb into the column of waiting
limousines. He turned into the passage between a patis-
serie and an Italian restaurant. He was humming softly
to himself as he stepped into the lift and pressed the
button for Annie's fourth-floor offices.

His buoyant mood had lasted the three days since
the conversation in his study. In that time he had
gradually got to grips with the shattering facts of his
situation and had begun to feel he was once again
taking control of his life. Andy Phillips had been a
solid help. Since early on Monday he had taken the
weight off Matt, fielding the press. He had done such
a good job that the first wave of interest had already
begun to subside as the newspapers turned to other
stories. Each day, after Annie's court appearances, she
and Matt had cloistered themselves in her office, decid-
ing on their main lines of attack. They had quickly
concluded that there were two clear threads to Matt's
defence. First, they would simply deny the charges,
challenging the prosecution to make a case. With nothing more than Camilla's allegations to go on, Annie
was confident of an acquittal. The second strand to
their defence, designed to satisfy Matt's insistence that
he should not simply be acquitted but totally vindi-
cated, would be to cast doubt on Recovered Memory
Syndrome while at the same time totally discrediting
Letzer, branding him in the jury's minds as a con artist.

Matt and Annie had remained in the office until
late into the evenings, talking, telephoning and faxing,
setting in motion the trawl through computerised press

services which, supplied with a name, could
n up any mention that had appeared in the English-
speaking world over the previous thirty years, data-
bases that covered attendances at professional
seminars, college graduation records, anything at all
that might serve as a key to begin unlocking Letzer's
past. Guided by Naomi's suggestions, they had also put
out contacts to all the organisations with an interest in
cases like Camilla's. In both Britain and America,
private investigators, briefed by Annie, had already
started the legwork.

The offices where Annie and her partners worked
belied the fancy address. Instead of the clever lighting
and decorative receptionists of the smart commercial
lawyers Matt sometimes dealt with, there was faulty
strip lighting and a harassed woman in late middle
age, today gamely trying simultaneously to answer the
phone and work a photocopier. She smiled and nodded
towards Annie's open door. 'Go in, Mr Stenner. She
just got back from court.'

Annie's desk was a foot deep in papers and bulging
buff folders. A mug of coffee stood among a pattern
of wet rings. On the phone, she waved him into one
of the scuffed leather chairs facing her desk. Still speaking into the phone, she fished a sheet of paper from
beneath the wreckage and pushed it at him. 'Naomi's
stuff,' she mouthed.

By the time Annie slammed down the phone Matt
had read through the paper and finished the stewed,
tasteless coffee the receptionist had put in front of him.
'That's the stuff we dug up following Naomi's suggestions,' she said.

'I never imagined there'd be so many.'

'And that's only what we've turned up so far.
There'll be more. So far, though, we have the following.' She began ticking off on her fingers. 'Believers

160

– people who believe they're dealing with recovered memories of events so painful they had blotted them out. Unbelievers, mostly men, who are equally convinced the memories are false, implanted by overzealous therapists. Accused fathers, abused daughters, and, alas, sons, more of *them* than you might think, have all got their spokesmen. Therapists, for and against, each have theirs. There are groups of wives supporting accused husbands, and groups of wives supporting each other *against* accused husbands. We've even turned up a group of "retractors", young people who, having stirred up trouble by making the accusations in the first place, then decided they were wrong after all and withdrew them.'

Matt grimaced. 'That must make for a cheery home environment.'

Annie smiled. 'Mmm. The one thing they *all* seem to have in common is that they are just *dying* to talk about it.'

'At least we'll have a diversity of expert testimony to choose from.'

'Yeah. As a human being, it's depressing as hell. As a lawyer, I'm encouraged. We won't know until I can squeeze the evidence bundle from them, but the prosecution must be very thin on facts. Without facts, they rely on opinion. The more we can produce that undermines Camilla's, Letzer's, and all their other witnesses' credibility with the jury, the happier it makes me. What would make me happiest would be to turn up a case that we could hold up as an image of ours. One where we could prove the therapist had been in it for the money.'

Matt laughed out loud. 'Sure.'

'Well, I've told our people to talk to everyone they can contact. Who knows what might come up?'

Matt pushed the paper across the desk towards her.

'Annie, try *anything* that might have a hope in hell of helping. Please.'

'Most of them are in America. At Roy Erskine's rates, having his people talk to them all is going to cost a lot of money. I mean a *lot*. Most of their work is for big companies. They charge to match.'

Matt had met Roy Erskine and his partner, Larry Guenther, in Annie's office two days earlier, as they were passing through London on the trail of a shipment of counterfeit Estée Lauder. Roy Erskine was a balding, foul-mouthed ex-detective from the New York City Police Department. Larry was a quiet-spoken man, with a law degree from Harvard and the frame of an overgrown blond bear. Both of them had impressed Matt with their quick minds and no-bullshit attitude.

'I said *anything*, Annie. Please.'

Liz handed over the jar of home-made chutney and tossed the eighty pence into the Tupperware box she was using as a till. The woman dropped the jar into her shopping basket but instead of turning away to the bring-and-buy, or one of the craft stalls, she remained there, looking directly into Liz's face. Liz smiled invitingly, wondering if the woman wanted to buy something else. The woman went on staring. It was a face Liz knew slightly, somebody she had seen in the supermarket, perhaps, or maybe just a regular on the circuit of charity events like this one at Emma Trafford's house, one of the daintily spoken, but impoverished, bargain hunters. As the woman opened her mouth to speak, Liz knew with heart-sinking certainty that she was not going to ask for jam. She remembered a coolness in a greeting earlier, an acquaintance turning away in the post office yesterday, whom Liz just thought hadn't noticed her.

'Excuse me, but, er . . . aren't you . . . ?'

'Stenner. Mrs Matthew Stenner,' Liz intercepted, coolly meeting the woman's gaze. '*That* Mrs Stenner.'

Despite the crimson flush that seeped up from the woman's neck to infuse her face, she held her ground, continuing to stare at Liz. Then, with a snuffling sound, she wheeled and hurried busily away.

Liz watched her disappear into the room where the tombola stall was doing a roaring trade. A moment later she reappeared, peering round the door with another woman at her side. Brusquely, Liz reached behind her and yanked at the strings of the borrowed pinafore.

She found Emma in the huge, old-fashioned kitchen, bullying the caterers. She handed her the pinafore. Tears of anger stung her eyes. 'Emma, be a dear and find somebody else to do my stall. I have to go home. Before I hit someone.'

Liz parked next to Naomi's Golf and strode into the house. Guided by the sound of the deep, richly textured voice, she found Naomi in the library, the phone to her ear. At Liz's entry she smiled and gave her a finger wave. She raised her voice: 'No, I'm sorry, but Mrs Stenner isn't here, either. No, I have no idea when she'll be back. Goodbye.' She put down the phone, scribbling another name at the foot of a list that covered a foolscap sheet, and stood to lean across the desk and plant a kiss on Liz's cheek. 'Hello. Celia let me in. She'd been taking calls all morning so I said I'd help out. You look as though you've seen a ghost. Are you all right?'

'I'm fine.' Liz sighed deeply, her face a mixture of pain and fatigue. 'I really appreciate what you're doing. You must be neglecting your other patients terribly.'

'Don't worry. *Nobody* needs me more than you do right now. There's a girl in New York I might have to

163

take off to see if things turn bad. Otherwise, I've more or less cleared the decks to be able to help.'

Liz smiled wanly. 'Thanks.' She flapped a hand at the phone. 'I just couldn't face all this.'

Naomi gave an embarrassed laugh. 'I couldn't do less. When I think that but for me . . .' She let her words taper off. Then, smiling grimly, she waved the foolscap pad. 'You're right, though. God knows how so many people can be such cranks and still have the resourcefulness to get hold of the number.'

Liz frowned. 'Don't we have any *friends*?'

'One thing's certain, Liz. Now's the time you're going to find that out. There were a few calls from names I recognised. Harry? American? Isn't he Matt's agent? He sounded pretty agitated. He wants Matt to call him back as soon as he can. About the Kowalski deal? Apparently Matt can relax on the trip to Los Angeles. Kowalski won't be available for a while.'

'Damn!'

'Is that bad news?'

'Bad? Naomi, Matt's been *dreaming* about that deal for the last ten years. He'll be *devastated* if it falls through. It was the one thing he still felt he hadn't achieved.' As she spoke the left side of her face pinched into a grimace. She pressed the heel of her hand to her eye. 'Oh shit.' She smiled apologetically, her face colourless. 'That makes my day. I think I'm about to get a headache.'

Naomi stepped close. 'You go and lie down.' She nodded at the telephone just as it started ringing again. 'Let me take care of these crackpots. After all, I'm kind of a pro.'

It was after one when Matt reached the house. Naomi's Golf stood on the gravel, sparkling under a layer of frost. He slid the Mercedes into the garage and scrunched across the gravel to the back door, the cloud of his breath preceding him in the motionless air. He found Naomi curled up on the kitchen sofa, drinking coffee in front of the television.

'Hi, Matt. Another tough one? Should I get you a drink?'

'Tough enough. And yes, Scotch please.'

She crossed to the dresser-sized refrigerator and scooped ice into the glass. 'Is Annie making progress with the stuff I gave you?'

He took the glass and drank before answering. 'She sure is. At three thousand dollars a day plus that again in expenses, I expected them to be impressive. But they seem to be coming up with the goods. They've already turned up a whole bunch of stuff. Their people have already started interviewing.'

'And Stephen?'

'They're looking,' he said into his glass.

'Matt, what exactly are you and Annie expecting to find on Stephen?'

'Dirt. They're going through press cuttings, professional journals, anything at all that might shed some light on his past. And, if we're lucky, show up a nice dirty stain on it.'

'I'd really be surprised. I've seen him in situations where he's had opportunities to take advantage of women before. I'd swear he never has.'

'Taking advantage of Camilla isn't the issue. We could live with him sleeping with her. She'd probably get over it eventually, with your help, and ours. The problem is, he's screwing the entire family, and he's doing it for money. Maybe he never had *that* kind of opportunity before!'

She took a long breath, but didn't argue. It was a moment before she asked, 'How much is all this costing you?'

'Erskine's people? Depends how long it takes. I'm braced for a couple of hundred thousand dollars.'

'Shit!' After another pause, she continued, 'And the whole thing? Annie, everything?'

He refilled his glass. 'I haven't stopped to figure it out. Why? What choice do I have? To lie down and play dead?'

She pawed at the ground with a toe. 'Look, don't be offended – maybe you'll think this is too . . . well, too *American* a way of looking at it, too *commercial*, but if you're in for hundreds of thousands of dollars anyway, have you thought about *talking* to Stephen Letzer?'

He stared at her over the rim of the glass. '*Bribe* him? You think I should offer the bastard a pay-off?'

Naomi shifted, and picked at the edge of the tiled counter. 'Don't be angry, Matt. It's just that it hurts *me* so much to see the way this case is hurting you. And it's *crucifying* Liz. The more I've thought about it the more I think that if Stephen *is* out for Camilla's trust money, he might settle for a lot less. Especially without the risk that rides on a trial. I can't imagine Camilla seeing the case through without him behind her, can you?'

'Sure,' Matt said, slowly. 'And where does that leave me? In everybody's mind I'd still be Matthew Stenner, child molester.' He shook his head. 'No deals, Naomi. Not with that fucker.' He looked at his watch. 'Is Liz in bed?'

Naomi nodded. 'She went up hours ago. She was . . . very disturbed.'

'Disturbed?'

She reached for the woollen shawl that lay on the sofa and threw it around her shoulders. 'Look, it's late. I've got to go. Liz'll tell you about it herself.' She stepped abruptly forward and, craning against him, planted a lingering kiss on his cheek. He frowned, aware of the heaviness of her breast pressing into the crook of his arm. Awkwardly, he let his arm fall to his side. 'Good night, Matt.' Conscious of his movement, a faint flush had coloured her face. 'You should go to Liz.'

He opened the door silently, as eager not to wake her if she were sleeping as to discover the meaning of Naomi's mysterious reference. The bedroom was in darkness. He eased the door shut and crossed to the bed. 'Liz?' He whispered the name a second time. Getting no answer, he slipped out of his clothes, letting them fall to the floor where he stood, and got into the vast bed. She would solve the mystery for him in the morning. Deep beneath the duvet, he reached out for her, seeking the warmth of her in the darkness. He sat up abruptly. The icy beginnings of panic already clawed at his stomach as he reached to snap on the bedside light. The plumpness of her pillows was undisturbed. The bed was empty.

Fighting the panic, he leaped from the bed and ran for their bathroom. The bath was full. Unused towels lay on the mahogany washstand. He dipped fingers into the water. It was stone cold. Feeling he would choke, he turned and sprinted through the bedroom and out into the corridor.

A thin bar of light showed beneath Camilla's door. Matt burst into the room. Liz was seated on the floor, propped against the wall by the open door of the closet. Her shoulders were hunched, her arms folded across her chest, hugging a robe, his robe, close about her against the chill of the air. Books and soft toys lay strewn around her. She still held one book. With an involuntary cry of relief he threw himself into a crouch

167

in front of her. 'Liz. Darling? Are you all right?'

She looked up at him, her eyes coming only slowly into focus, red-rimmed and bloodshot. Her cheeks were still wet. The pale blue towelling of the robe showed dark where the tears had fallen. 'Yes.' Her voice came out high, a whoop. She nodded emphatically. 'Yes, Matt. I'm fine.' With the volume in her hand, she gestured wearily at the drift of books that lay around her. 'Stirring up some painful memories, that's all.'

He nodded, and leaned to plant a feather-soft kiss on her forehead. 'You shouldn't.' As he spoke, he looked around him at the closet and the scattered books. A wave of almost unbearably tender memories engulfed him.

The closet was crammed with boxes, the empty wine cartons that Camilla had always scavenged to store her books. From her earliest years Camilla had always been a precocious reader and writer. At seven she devoured at a sitting novels that an average ten-year-old would have struggled with. She was constantly in his office, looting paper for her elaborately constructed stories, illustrating them with drawings as precocious as her language.

He reached down to scoop up one of the slender notebooks, two dozen loose sheets held together with misaligned staples. The cover was decorated with an intricate design of flowers and insects, entwined around the title, 'The Happiest Ladybird by Camilla Stenner'. Tucked in the bottom right-hand corner was the date, December 1984. He riffled a thumb through the dog-eared sheets. Looking at the close-packed, childish writing that blackened every page some of the anxiety melted from his face, replaced by a distant smile. 'Look at it,' he murmured. 'Eleven chapters. They even have titles. She was such an incredible kid.'

As he turned back to her the expression on her face killed his smile dead.

'Matt, the police were here again today.'

He fell back onto his heels. 'What for?' he said at last.

'They were specially interested in knowing whether I had noticed anything odd about Camilla's behaviour as a child.'

He could feel the throb of his own pulse in the silence. 'And?'

'And nothing. I told them she had been a lovely child. A bit highly strung, but lovely. As far as I was here to see it, of course.' The sudden, bitter self-reproach that choked her voice caused his eyes to cloud with pain.

'What the hell's *that* supposed to mean?' he whispered, taking her hand in his.

'Just what it says. They were very insistent about dates. They went through my old expense records. They took some things away with them.' She sniffed, mopping the back of her wrist at her cheek.

He took her gently by the shoulders. 'Darling, you mustn't let them intimidate you. Those records won't show them anything new. We *know* you were away a lot when all this is supposed to have happened.' He gave a strained laugh. 'For Christ's sake, that's why Letzer *chose* those dates!'

He rose, pulling her after him, tugging the robe tighter around her. 'It's late. And you're frozen. Let's get to bed.'

For a moment her face was completely blank. 'Mmm. Of course. I'll just clear these away.'

Ignoring his protests, she scooped the books into their carton and picked it up. He watched as she pushed the box back into its place, needing to force it in. The movement made him smile despite the

169

apprehension that gnawed at him. The boxes took up more space than the clothes. Camilla's childish stories, school exercise books, letters from friends, programmes of pantomimes and plays, certificates for swimming, old birthday cards, even wrappings from presents that had particularly appealed, all were filed carefully away.

'Ready?'

Liz had her back to him. She stood for another second or two before looking suddenly down at the book she still held in her hand, as though surprised to see it there. She thrust it abruptly among the boxes and spun to face him. 'Yes.' She was crying silently, the tears pulsing from her eyes in waves.

They made their way back to their bedroom, walking slowly, like lovers or old people, each with an arm around the other, Liz still weeping soundlessly. Matt pushed open the door and flipped on the light. 'A good night's sleep will do us both good.' He started into the room and then looked down in sudden consternation. Liz had taken her arm from his waist.

'Matt, I'm sorry, I know it's . . . My head's *splitting*.' She hung back. Fear churned in his stomach as she forced herself to meet his gaze. 'I'm sorry,' she whispered, 'but . . . for tonight . . . I just need to sleep alone.'

Eleven

'Harry?'

'Matt? How are you? Not sleeping well, obviously.'

'Obviously.' Matt glanced at the study window, where the rising sun cast a pink wash over the clouds, and then down at the pad, where Naomi had listed the calls in a loose scrawl. Harry's name was almost obliterated among Matt's dense, angular doodles. 'In fact, I've been up since three. I've been trying to get you for two hours.'

'Sorry. I've been in a meeting. And right now I'm at Bernardo's, having dinner. I have some people with me.'

'Just tell me what's happening, Harry. There's no problem, is there?'

'Look, Matt, can I get back to you?'

'Harry, is it Kowalski? Has he heard about my problem?'

Harry's voice dropped to a murmur. 'You're a big name out here, Matt. The whole town's heard.'

'But, Harry, it'll all have blown over *long* before they even get the project moving.'

In the silence Matt could hear the sound of other diners, the clatter of cutlery. 'I tried to tell him that, Matt.' Harry paused again before saying softly, 'He won't take the risk.'

Matt had risen to his feet. 'For Christ's sake, Harry,' he pleaded, 'this was supposed to be a done deal. Kowalski was crazy about the idea.'

'He was. Sorry, Matt. The man's just plain scared.'

Matt let the receiver clatter back onto its rest and sank slowly back into the chair.

'No, don't do that, Shirley. There's no point in *you* taking flak. Let them have what they want.' There was a bone-deep weariness in Matt's voice. 'Just make sure you ask them for a receipt that I can pass on to Annie.' He put the phone down and stood for some seconds with his hand on the receiver. At length, he turned to where Rachel was looking curiously at him as she arranged tea things on a tray. 'Shirley Wood. My accountant. The police were waiting for her when she got to the office. They're taking all our old tax records.'

Rachel raised an eyebrow. 'Whatever for?'

'Belt and braces, I guess. Our expense records give a pretty fair picture of where we were, and when.'

'I didn't think you were arguing that you weren't *here*.'

He laughed drily. 'They're trying to make sure I *don't*.' He nodded at the tea caddy that she held open in her hand, his face brightening. 'Earl Grey? She feeling better?'

Rachel shrugged. 'It seems like it. At least she's speaking again.'

Matt smiled at his sister-in-law's brittle tone. For three days Rachel had been ferrying trays of food to Liz, where she lay nursing her migraine in the darkened bedroom, only to bring them down again, untouched, a while later.

'Rachel, I really appreciate the help. Without you, I . . . it would have been even rougher than it has.'

Rachel kept her eyes on the tray. 'Don't be silly. It's good to feel genuinely useful for once. Not having a family of my own . . .' She broke off, biting her lip.

Matt sighed softly. 'Is Liz . . . is she well enough to come with me?'

Rachel looked at him, appalled. 'I don't see how she possibly could. The poor woman hasn't eaten for three days. The last thing she needs is more stress. That's what brought this on in the first place.'

Matt let go the reproach, raising a hand in surrender. 'Sure. You're right. The last thing I want to do is make her worse. I just thought . . . it would make a difference having her there, in court, that's all.'

'Of course I'm coming.' Liz stood in the doorway. She had dressed formally, a dark blue suit over a cream silk shirt. Huge, opaque sunglasses made a stark contrast to the cadaverous pallor of her face. She stepped into the room. 'Unless you prefer to keep it between you and your lawyer.'

Even as Matt laughed, a shifting, uncertain note in her voice made him wish he could see her eyes better behind the dark glasses. He took her by the hand, drawing her to him. 'Thanks,' he murmured. 'It's great you feel up to it. I'm nervous as hell.' Removing the sunglasses, he leaned down to kiss her. A moment later they were clinging tightly to each other, oblivious to Rachel's shuffling embarrassment as their lips met in a long, hard kiss. The sound of a car door slamming in the courtyard drew them apart. They were still breathing hard, their arms loosely around each other, when Annie strode into the kitchen, sombre in the black suit and high-necked blouse of her court outfit. She smiled ambiguously from under arched eyebrows. 'I hate to break up the party, but Matt has to be in court at ten.'

They were already on the motorway when Annie reached into a black briefcase on the seat beside her and passed an envelope over her shoulder to Liz and Matt.

'I finally managed to get this out of the prosecution yesterday. Do you want to have a look at it?'

Matt took the envelope and withdrew several thin photocopied sheets, fastened at the corner with a string tag. He leafed slowly through the sheets, letting Liz read with him, then handed them back over Annie's shoulder and took Liz's hand.

'It's just copies of hotel registers from New York,' said Matt.

'Unfortunately they support Camilla's contention. You really were in New York, Liz, when she alleges Matt . . . when the alleged offences happened.'

Liz frowned. 'But they knew that already. I told them.'

Matt nodded. 'Plus, the police were at Shirley Wood's office, this morning, impounding our tax records. They would give them the same information, surely.'

Annie grimaced. 'That's bad news. They're really not taking chances on this case.'

'Well, you can't blame them for getting all the documentation they can,' Matt said, reasonably. 'Knowing they can't make a wife testify against her husband.'

Annie looked quickly over her shoulder. 'Matt, if this case comes to court, you're both going to learn a lot more about the law than you've ever picked up from television. In child abuse cases spouses are "compellable". If you want chapter and verse, look up section eighty of the Police and Criminal Evidence Act 1984. If they *want* Liz as a witness they *get* her.'

'But do I have to answer their questions?' Liz asked, craning forward.

'Yes, you damned well do! Have either of you ever been in a court of law?'

'No,' they answered in unison.

She stared grimly at the road. 'Well, if this *does* go any further, you'll see why I give all my clients two pieces of advice – don't lie, and don't be flippant. One,

174

honest people find it harder to lie under oath than you might think. Two, juries *hate* smart-asses, be they lawyers or witnesses.'

Matt was leaning forward. 'You said *if* it ever comes to court.'

She flicked him a grim smile. 'Look, I don't want to give you both false hopes, but the Crown Prosecution Service don't prosecute on a whim. They have rules to work to.'

'Such as?'

'Well, for example, a prosecution has to be judged to be in the public interest. Although child abuse *always* is,' she added, grimacing. 'However, they are also only supposed to prosecute if they have a "realistic chance" of conviction. To be absolutely honest, on what I've seen so far, I'm surprised the case has come even this far.'

'Don't they *have* a realistic chance?' Matt asked sharply.

She shrugged. 'I'll be making that point this morning, anyway. So far as I can see it's Camilla's word against yours.'

'And the hotel bills, proving I had the opportunity.'

'They prove you *had* it, not that you took it. Let's assume Letzer *has* planted the whole thing in Camilla's head. He would have had to use some sort of technique, hypnosis perhaps, to do it. It would be reasonable to suppose he would have been able to use the same method to revive genuine memories of when Liz was away, especially if they were related to events that mattered to a young girl. Her birthday, for example.'

Liz spoke, her voice thin with the strain of the last three days. 'You think they might just *drop* the whole thing? After putting Matt through this hell?'

Annie exhaled hard. 'I'm only saying they might. On a purely objective basis, they ought to, by their own rules, unless they've got better corroboration than we've seen so far. Unfortunately,' she added, icily, 'their own rules don't always seem to apply.'

Matt was hunched forward, his forearms on the back of the seat alongside Annie. 'Are you saying they have rules, but they ignore them?'

'It's not that simple. I told you before, strictly by the book they shouldn't have prosecuted either of the two big cases. But in the social and political atmosphere at that time, the CPS were under pressure. There were no witnesses or corroboration, just one person's word against another. Yet they got one conviction.'

'How could a jury *decide* a case like that?' Liz protested.

'Quality of testimony, I suppose. One story rang true to the jury, the other didn't.'

Matt's tone was sombre. 'You're telling us that's what my case comes down to, aren't you? Whether it *looks* as though I'm telling the truth, or whether Camilla is?'

Annie drew a deep breath. 'Not entirely, unfortunately. They have Liz's absences. And they won't have any trouble lining up expert witnesses.'

'Like Letzer?' Matt scoffed.

'Be grateful for Letzer. Until I saw the first witness statements I was afraid they might not ask him to appear.'

Matt raised an eyebrow. 'You *want* him to testify?'

'I'm *dying* for it. If we're right about him, then I need to have him up there as a prosecution witness where I can cross-examine him. That means I can ask leading questions.'

Matt laughed ironically. 'All my life I've heard the phrase "leading question". I finally need to know what it means.'

'It means questions that suggest the answers. It's the

difference between asking, "Who did you sleep with last night?" and, "Isn't it true that last night you slept with your sister-in-law?" The effect isn't the same, believe me.'

'I see what you mean.' Matt's momentary lightness faded. 'So, getting back to my case, how strong are the chances they won't proceed?'

As the moments ticked away before Annie replied, he felt the hope that had been forming shrivel inside him.

'I've been doing some homework,' she said at length, her voice very low. 'Not as strong as I'd hoped.'

Matt felt Liz's hand tighten in his. 'Why?'

'Policy. A couple of years ago there was a flurry of cases with the same basic elements to ours. Essentially, people claiming to recover memory of childhood abuse, usually while in some form of therapy. The accused naturally claimed the memories were not "recovered" at all but simply false, implanted by the therapist. Basically, they all failed, either on lack of evidence or unreliable prosecution witnesses.'

'And now something's changed?'

'Three years ago a man was accused of childhood abuse by his twenty-four-year-old son. The boy was in a bad way, homeless, on every kind of drug. A prosecution's nightmare as a witness. Dad, on the other hand, owned a chain of estate agents, and was a pillar of the Rotary club. They decided not to prosecute. Then last July he was overheard in the local swimming baths, offering schoolboys rides in his Jaguar.'

Behind her, they winced in disgust. 'So then they *had* to prosecute the bastard?' Matt asked.

'They had no witness. The son had killed himself in June.' They rode for some seconds in total silence before Annie spoke again. 'So, you see what I mean about the CPS working in a context?'

*   *   *

177

The magistrates' court was a surprisingly cramped, unimposing room. From where Matt stood in the dock he could have reached out and touched the CPS solicitor, an overweight woman in her early thirties, as she rose to address the two men and a woman who sat behind the raised bench. Dry-mouthed, Matt looked across at Liz, where she sat in the double row of tubular chairs. She held herself bolt upright, her knees tight together, her hands clasped in her lap. The pale knuckles, like her quick, taut smile of encouragement, were testimony to the tension that racked her. Five paces away, Annie sat looking down at her notes, waiting for the prosecution to speak, her own emotions impossible to gauge behind her impassive expression.

From the prosecution's first words Matt felt a knot the size of a fist in his stomach. They were not planning to drop the case. He gripped hard at the edge of the dock. In the windowless, oppressively hot space he felt he would faint. Liz's stifled cry brought the heads of the two other onlookers, a pair of badly shaven men in charity store clothes, snapping round. They sat gaping as she began crying silently. Matt tried to smile at her, and found he couldn't, sudden fierce rage welling inside him. With a hopeless gesture, he turned back, trying to focus through his blinding anger on the prosecution's words.

Having no jury to impress, the woman read her notes in a monotone, reeling off the dates of the specimen offences, picking out the salient points in the witness statements and reading the dates of Liz's stays in New York.

To Matt, the drab delivery only emphasised the renewed horror of the allegations.

'There has been some delay in compiling certain additional evidence, due to the main witness's rather precarious emotional state.' The woman looked across

178

at Matt. 'A state brought on, we are informed, by her recollection of these offences. However, with leave of the court, we would wish to put before it some preliminary reports which we feel already offer clear corroboration of the prosecution's case.'

The echo of her words roared in Matt's ears, drowning out everything except the anger and panic that fought in him. Corroboration? Of offences that had never happened? There could *be* no such evidence. And yet this woman's demeanour exuded certainty. The glitter of contempt in her eyes as she glanced across the few feet that separated them left Matt in no doubt. In her mind, at least, he had been tried and convicted already.

Although the woman was still talking, he could no longer distinguish words, only a rushing noise in his ears and a peculiar, light-headed sensation that the life he had known until this moment, and all that he had looked forward to, was somehow ending here, in this court. The room seemed to reel. In a new surge of panic, he gripped the edge of the box, fighting for balance. Slowly, as his vision cleared, he turned to look at Liz. She held a fist to her mouth, grinding her teeth into the bone, as though to stop herself from crying out. Her skin, already pallid from her migraine, had taken on a ghastly, mottled grey tinge. Fighting down the new, different fear that the sight sent pulsing through him, he forced his attention back to the court.

Annie was on her feet, demanding the magistrates' attention. The presiding magistrate, the woman, raised a hand, stopping the prosecution solicitor in mid-sentence.

'Thank you, Miss Varley. The defence wishes to address us. Mrs Trevellyn?'

'Your Worships, I must protest.' Annie's anger was not feigned. She wheeled to cast a furious look at the prosecution. 'The prosecution appears to be in possession of evidence which has not yet been transmitted to us, despite my repeated, virtually daily, requests. We *must* insist that this evidence be handed to us forthwith. We would also respectfully ask the court to put back this hearing to a later date, to give us time to consider this additional material.'

The magistrate nodded. 'Thank you, Mrs Trevellyn. Miss Varley?'

The prosecution solicitor was talking before Annie had time to sit down. 'The report I referred to is still in draft form, Your Worships. We received it only two days ago. It includes a number of photographs, of which we have requested prints.' As she spoke, she groped in a file and slid from it some photographs attached to a couple of typed sheets. 'I have the material here. If the court would like to examine it? And, of course, my friend for the defence.' She handed the documents to an usher, who passed them up to the bench.

Matt watched them huddle over the documents, saw with dismay their faces change as, one by one, they scrutinised the photographs. He wanted to shout aloud at the look of scalding disgust that the presiding magistrate cast at him as she handed the documents back to the usher, who crossed the room and offered them to Annie.

No muscle moved in her face as, without hurry, she read through the text. With no change of expression, she pushed the pages aside and picked up the first of the photos. She looked at it for a long time, longer than could have been necessary to take in the content of the picture. It was as though she were giving herself time, formulating her responses. At length, she put it down and looked at the others in turn, the scrutiny more perfunctory now. She proffered them back to the usher, not looking at Matt. 'Thank you, Your Worships,' she said quietly. 'This is obviously important material. I would want to have copies as soon as possible.'

The magistrate raised an eyebrow at the prosecution lawyer, who stood and gave a formal little bow. 'I'm informed that a set of prints will be ready for tomorrow, Your Worships.' She cleared her throat. 'Your Worships, I would suggest that the prosecution would need no more than a further two weeks to prepare this case for trial.'

The magistrate looked at Annie. She rose. 'Clearly, Your Worships, this is crucial evidence, the existence of which was unknown to us until this moment. With respect, I would submit that any decision on transfer for trial of this case should be deferred pending a further hearing before this court.'

The magistrate mused for a second or two and then, with a nod to Annie to sit down, began conferring with her colleagues in voices that did not carry beyond the bench. A few seconds later she signalled Annie to stand.

'Mrs Trevellyn, we have listened to what you say. However, it seems to us that, beyond obtaining your own expert opinion as to the significance of these pictures, there is very little in them that would affect the preparation of the defence's case. It seems to us unlikely in the extreme that the witness would permit you to effect any further examination! That being so, unless you have some more powerful arguments to offer us, we see no reason why this case should not be transferred forthwith for trial in the appropriate court.'

They walked to the car in silence, Liz sandwiched between Annie and Matt, clinging hard to their arms. It was not until Annie had nosed the car into the flow of the city centre traffic that Matt spoke. 'Are you going to tell us?'

Annie did not look round. Matt could see the flesh of her cheek stretch as she chewed at her lip. When she spoke they had to strain to hear her. 'It was a report by a man named Derek Worthington. I'm sorry to say it, Matt, but it's an indication of how seriously they're taking your case. He's the leading specialist on abuse-related injuries in the country. I saw him on the stand once. He was impressive. In fact, he's the very person I would have suggested *we* use.' She shrugged. 'Unfortunately, they got there first. It's one of the advantages of being the prosecution. Although they have to let us see all their evidence, regardless of whether they plan to use it or not, they still get to see it first.'

'But, Annie, the photographs? What *were* they, for God's sake?'

Annie's jaw muscles moved as, several times, she made to speak and then shied away, as though unable to find the words she needed. Finally, she swallowed and spoke, the words hurried. 'Camilla's anus.' She breathed deeply, shaking her head as if to deny what she had to say. 'There were scars. They are pretty old. Worthington examined Camilla. In his view there's no doubt at all. Those wounds were the result of penetration. In childhood.'

Twelve

Annie looked on, frowning, as Matt topped up Liz's glass, even though she had barely touched it. She cupped her hand quickly over her own drink. 'No more for me. I have to get back to William.' She watched, tight-lipped, as he shrugged and drained the bottle into his own glass. 'Does that really help?' she asked softly. He looked at her, pondering an answer, and then, without a word, drank off a big mouthful. Annie hurriedly put down her unfinished drink. 'I'd better go.'

She was still speaking as the telephone rang. Matt crossed the room in three strides and snatched it up.

'Hello? Peter? Thanks for calling back. By the way, are we still on for tennis on Saturday?' He paused, his frown deepening as he listened to Peter Monroe's words. It was a long answer to a short question. At length, speaking with forced cheerfulness, he said, 'Really? Okay. Well let me know if you *can* be free. I was looking forward to it.' He listened once more before giving a sour laugh. 'Well, not that great. That's why I was so desperate to talk to *you*.' He paused to drink some more wine and take a deep breath. 'To tell you the truth, it's a fucking disaster! Peter, they came up with something at court today, something so completely fucking ... preposterous!' Seeing the two women straining to hear, he flipped the phone onto loud-speaking and replaced the handset. 'An expert, Professor Worthington?' He made the name a question.

'Yes, of course. He's well known, used to be on the radio.'

'Well, they've had him examine Camilla, compile a report. There were photographs, of Camilla's ... backside. Peter, there were *scars*. This Worthington character's saying they are consistent with ... For Christ's sake, Peter, he's saying it's evidence I was *buggering* her.' His voice almost broke on the word. He gulped more of his drink. 'You wouldn't know, it was before your time, but Camilla had terrible constipation as a child.'

'I do know. I've had a look at her record,' Monroe answered, precisely.

'Have you? Great! We were talking about it all the way back here. It's the answer, isn't it? It explains the scars. It must have been when she was eight or so, about the time Camilla's claiming I ... did those things. She had terrible trouble with bleeding. We took her to Alex Lawton. In the end, we decided it was constipation. She was always a little bit that way as a child. Still is. The reason I called is we wondered if Annie – did you know Annie was representing me? – if Annie and I could have a look at the notes. Just from that period ... just to get dates right and ...' The sentence trailed off.

'Alex Lawton's notes record constipation, if that helps.'

'I know that. But Annie thinks it would be helpful –'

'Matt, Camilla's not a child.'

Matt wiped the back of his hand over his forehead. It came away filmed with perspiration. 'But she was at the time. We just want *sight* of the notes. Not copies ... I'm asking you as a friend, as *Camilla's* friend! That man is out to destroy her life, Peter.'

'I like to think I am Camilla's friend. But I'm also her doctor.' There was a long pause before Monroe went on. 'Look, Matt, it's only fair to tell you I had a visit today from the police. Sergeant Staples, from the Child Protection Team, at Crawley.' Matt felt as though an icy fist had clutched at his entrails. 'They tried to contact Alex Lawton. He died last year. So Staples asked me to look at the notes and do him an abstract. That's why I knew about the constipation theory.'

'Theory! Peter, it *was* constipation. Alex knew Camilla. He knew us all . . .'

'I'm sorry, but I'm not sure I ought to discuss this any more. I assume Annie will get a copy of the abstract. Goodbye, Matt. Sorry about Saturday.'

'Yeah. Me, too. Bye, Peter.' Matt reached to press the speaker button and turned to face the watching women. 'Fuck that!' he murmured, speaking half to himself. 'Seven months ago they came on *holiday* with us.' He raised his glass, found it empty, and opened the cupboard in search of another bottle. That, too, was empty. 'I'll be in the cellar,' he said, and strode from the room, leaving the two women staring after him.

Annie reacted first, taking Liz gently by the shoulders. She looked into the drained, unreadable face. 'You *must* believe in him, Liz. I *know* what you've heard today isn't . . . it isn't helpful, but you *have* to remember, it's just *opinion*. And from people who didn't know Camilla at the time. Alex Lawton was an experienced doctor, he knew Camilla, he knew Matt, he saw Camilla's injuries, not just twelve-year-old scars, and yet he had *no* doubts. Remember, too, Worthington's very reputation is a problem. I've seen it happen before. The police consult an expert in a particular field and he can't help assuming that the police wouldn't be asking him unless there were something wrong.' Annie drew back, gathering herself before turning back to Liz, who was gazing emptily into space. 'Ask *yourself*! Can you imagine *Matt* committing acts like that? God, Liz, you've *lived* with that man for more than twenty *years*. You must *know* with every fibre of your being that he couldn't do anything like that!' Annie's voice and body were trembling with passion.

A strange, distant expression came into Liz's face. 'I was away a lot, Annie.' The tic made the flesh leap under the almost translucent skin at the corner of Liz's eye.

Annie paled. 'But,' she said hoarsely, 'you can't believe Matt could have done *that*! He would never be capable of . . . the betrayal. Of everyone that was dear to him!'

In the silence Annie could hear the thud of her own heart beating as they looked into each other's faces, Liz's bony and boyish, with cropped blonde hair and light blue eyes, Annie's Mediterranean, the deep brown eyes framed by generous lashes, the whole framed by thick layers of dark brown hair.

At length, Liz smiled, a wan, unbearably poignant smile. 'I keep telling myself that,' she murmured. 'A hundred times a day.' She stood up and glanced at the wall clock. 'Thanks for what you're doing, Annie,' she said, suddenly brisk. Her smile widened, showing perfect, even teeth. 'But you ought to be going home. Don't forget, you've got a family of your own, too.'

Matt groaned and threw back the quilt. It was nine twenty. Rising, he walked stiffly into the bathroom. Studying himself in the mirror, he shuddered. Unable to sleep despite the drinking, he had lain awake until four. Then, finally, he had fallen into the deep sleep that had left him looking like this, pouchy-eyed and with the imprint of the pillow etched into his face.

Sighing, he began smearing lather over his stubble. He was still shaving when the phone rang, bringing him striding back to the bedroom.

'Hello, Matt. How are you?'

A strained note in Andy Phillips's voice made Matt frown.

'Okay, Andy, I guess. You? Tabloid reporters still crawling out from under your desk?'

Andy gave a brief, strident laugh. 'The worst seems to be over. For now.' He paused. 'Matt, Carrie just called.' Matt waited for him to go on. 'Anderson's are pulling the book.'

There was a second of absolute silence before Matt responded. 'I see. What about the advance?'

'They want it back.' Andy paused again. 'I tried, Matt. They're hiding behind the fact that you missed the deadline.'

Matt stared ahead of him, the phone dropping to his side. Kowalski had been first off the mark. After that, half the neighbours, the Wests, then Peter Monroe. And now Anderson's. They had made a fortune out of him and now that he had become a potential liability they were leaving him for dead. He raised the phone again. 'Thanks for letting me know, Andy.' He spoke flatly, fighting to control his voice. He stood for a moment longer and then slammed the receiver down, sending the phone clattering to the floor.

The young lawyers still at work at desks piled high with documents, looked curiously at Matt as he emerged from the lift and made his way to Annie's open door. She was on the phone as he appeared in the doorway. She looked him up and down, her face setting. 'Look, Roy. Matt's finally here. Let's talk again tomorrow.' Slamming the phone down, she took Matt by the arm and yanked him roughly into the room, shutting the door behind him. 'How many have you had?'

He sat heavily in a chair and held out a hand, rocking the splayed fingers. 'Not that many, really.' He laughed. 'It's just a bad time of day.'

She stood looking down at him, her eyes flashing. 'For God's sake, Matt, I'm taking a lot of flak from my partners over the time I'm spending on your case. I've been holding them off by telling them how good for the firm a high-profile case like yours will be. Provided we win it!' She waved a hand at his rumpled clothes and dishevelled hair. 'For that I need you fit and alert. Trustworthy! Not looking and smelling like a wino! What the bloody hell am I doing wasting *my* time if you can't even stay sober and get here promptly? I finally had to call Roy without you. I'd already kept him holed up in his hotel for an hour while I waited for you to arrive.'

He gave her a weary smile. 'Annie, please. It's been a bad day, even by recent standards.'

Some of the anger leaving her face, she regained her seat and poured a glass of mineral water. She pushed it towards him. 'What happened?'

He drank some water, and when he felt calmer, told her about the phone call from Andy.

Annie leaned closer. 'Matt, it would need more than losing a publisher to have you acting like a . . . wino. What else is up?'

He looked into the glass for some seconds before answering. 'Liz,' he said, at length.

Her eyes narrowed. 'The migraine again?'

He smiled to himself at her unconcealed scepticism. Annie had never believed in Liz's migraines. 'No! Well, yes, there's that.'

'What else?'

'I don't . . . Shit, Annie, I'm worried. After you left

last evening, she acted – I don't know – strangely.'

Annie's brows came together as she thought about Liz's parting words. 'Do you think she *knows* . . . ?' She let the words die away, glancing towards the door.

Matt shrugged. 'Maybe. I have a funny feeling it might be worse than that.' Their eyes locked for a moment. Then, Annie got up and stood at the window, looking down on the traffic. 'Oh shit.' She turned to him, blinking. 'You don't deserve that.'

Three or four seconds passed in silence. Then the phone rang. Annie took it up. 'Hello. Naomi? Yes, he is. I'll pass you over.'

Matt took the receiver. 'Naomi? Pretty lousy. How about you?' He listened for a moment, grinning lop-sidedly at Annie. 'Yeah well, I guess we should have known better.' He reached for Annie's pad and pencil. 'Okay, go ahead.'

Annie moved again to stand staring from the window as he noted the dozen or so names Naomi dictated. The list finished, he put down the phone and pushed the pad towards her. 'The names of the patients she's referred to Letzer in the past. She suggested yesterday it might be a good idea if you spoke to them, to see if he's tried the same kind of thing before.'

Annie gave the list a cursory glance. 'I'll see to it. Did you *see* Naomi yesterday?'

'She came over a while after you left.'

Annie's brows rose. 'What for?'

'She was upset. She went down to the clinic yesterday. Letzer's moved Camilla out.'

Annie nodded at a blue cardboard file. 'I was going to tell you that. She's moved into a rented cottage near Cambridge. The man we've had keeping tabs on Letzer called in yesterday. By the way, the bad news, from the point of view of the case, at least, is that he isn't spending his nights with her.'

'I get the impression that'll be a relief to Naomi.'

She made a face. 'You think there's something going on there? Isn't she a bit old for him?'

'Hell, I don't know. She's certainly an attractive woman. Of course, it might just be *professional* jealousy, because he moved Camilla out from under her, but she was climbing the wall last night. She was still pretty pissed off this morning. The place reeks of cigarette smoke.'

'This morning? Did she sleep over?'

He shook his head, laughing. 'Oh, Annie, don't. The way I felt last night, I was just glad to have some company.'

Annie leaned back in her seat. 'Do you really think she's attractive? I would have thought she was ... dumpy.'

Matt laughed aloud again. 'Heavy-set. *And* she slept in the east wing.' For a moment they looked silently into each other's faces. Matt spoke first, sitting up straighter in his chair and smoothing his fingers through his hair. 'How about filling me in on what Erskine had to say?'

Annie sat back, steepling her short fingers, tapping the ends of the squared-off, unvarnished fingernails together. 'First, on the Letzer front. It's pretty well all bad news, so far. There are seven Stephen Letzers currently in the New York phone book. They aren't him. Up to four years ago there was another one. The address is an apartment building for transients, people working in restaurants while they look for acting jobs, that kind of thing. A huge turnover. Nobody could remember a Letzer. They also didn't find any evidence, ads or anything, to indicate that anyone of that name practised any kind of therapy in the New York area prior to that time. Or since, for that matter. Which doesn't mean he might not have been doing it, of course, either under another name, or in some kind of workshop. There are a *lot* of those.'

'I can believe it. What else?'

'The worst part. They've checked out those qualifications you saw on his office wall. They're genuine, mostly from a couple of well-regarded distance learning schools.'

Matt snorted. 'Distance learning? Come on, Annie! Mail order!'

She shrugged. 'They're not exactly Harvard but they'll stand up.' She moved forward, lowering her hands onto the desk, and her fingers brushed Matt's. She left her hand there, their fingertips overlapping. 'You say you want to be *cleared*, not just acquitted. For that we need material that will *destroy* the man. His degrees aren't it, Matt. It's no use kidding ourselves.'

He stood up and went to the window. 'So, is there *anything* good?'

'There might be. They turned up an ad placed by a Letzer, S., in a new age magazine out in California. They didn't pick it up before because the thing only lasted about three issues.'

'Do they have any more details?'

'Not yet. Larry Guenther's flying out tonight, though.' She looked up at him. 'Matt, this is costing an awful lot of money.'

He stared down at the groups of laughing people hurrying for cabs and crowding into the restaurants. 'Whatever it takes, Annie. So long as they turn up something that will knock the jury sideways. From what you say, apart from Camilla, this case is going to be a parade of "experts", boring the jury stiff. What we need is for them to go out of that courtroom with one big fact in their mind, that the star prosecution witness is a really spectacular clunker. Tax evader, flasher – I don't give a shit. Just so long as they have it right in the front of their minds that they can't trust him an inch.' He turned slowly to look at Annie. 'What about the other stuff? Have they found us a carbon-copy case yet?'

'It's just possible,' she murmured. In two strides Matt was back in his seat, leaning eagerly across the desk. She hesitated and then smiled. 'I wasn't going to tell you until we had more. All we have so far is press cuttings. A few years ago, a woman started to sue her father for abuse. The usual story, a happy enough family, until she went into therapy and began "recovering" memory.'

'How did it turn out, for Christ's sake?'

Annie pursed her lips. 'It didn't. Four months later she placed an ad in the paper, apologising to her father.'

'What use is *that*?'

'Just that she was apologising to her father for the false accusation. You see, he shot himself a week before the ad appeared.'

A slow smile spread over Matt's face. 'Now, that sounds like something we could get our teeth into.'

Annie smiled. 'I've already talked to a few people. We'll make it front-page news. Provided Roy's people can find the woman.'

Matt was about to respond when the phone jangled. Annie grimaced with annoyance. It was now long after office hours. 'This is Annie Trevellyn.' From across the desk Matt could hear the buzz of anger in Roger's voice. Her eyes widened in horror as she looked at her watch. 'Oh shit! I *completely* forgot. I'm still . . . yes, of course with Matt.' As Roger's voice swelled, an angry flush seeped into Annie's face. Without waiting for a pause in his tirade, she broke in, 'That's plain silly. We're still working. I certainly can't be there in the next five minutes.' Roger's voice rose again, making her remove the telephone from her ear. 'Oh, fuck it, Roger! *Give* it away, then.' She slammed down the phone and sat breathing hard for a moment before looking up at Matt and shrugging. 'Sorry.'

'It's my fault. I shouldn't be allowing you to let my case take over your life.'

She gave a rueful little laugh. 'Did you have the impression we were getting along before that?'

Matt waited a moment before looking at his watch and saying, 'You'd better get home anyway. William will be waiting.'

'I was supposed to be at the opera. William's being looked after.' Abruptly, she rose and lifted her coat from where it lay on the chair behind her. Matt sprang to his feet and took it from her, holding it open for her to slip her arms into it. As she did so she twisted to look at him. The movement brought the light pressure of her body against his. 'If you still need company, how about taking me to dinner?'

As Annie drew the car to a halt, Matt was already reaching for the door handle. He fell back, a faint expression of surprise flickering in his eyes, as she cut the engine, leaving them sitting in silence in the thick darkness of the tree-lined street. It was a moment before he reached again for the handle. 'Thanks, Annie. That was fun. I haven't really laughed like that since this whole business blew up.'

Her eyes glistened in the shadow. Her hand touched his sleeve and rested there. 'I enjoyed it, too, Matt. I haven't had much to laugh at lately, either.'

'I know.' He sighed. 'Love to William.' His hand still on the door handle, he leaned down, letting his lips brush her cheek. 'Thanks again.'

The words were stifled as her mouth found his. Her

grip tightened on his sleeve as her other arm flew around him, pulling him to her, crushing her breasts against him.

Matt's head spun at the sudden, remembered sweetness of her. Her tongue forced its way between his lips, probing against his teeth. The heat of arousal swept through him. For a moment he hesitated, almost overcome by the delicious warmth and softness of her. Then, taking her by the wrists, he prised her gently away from him.

They sat without speaking, Annie with her eyes closed, her breathing a shallow pant. After some seconds, as it returned to normal, he bent to touch his lips to her hair.

'Thanks, Annie. For everything.' He hesitated another moment and then, swallowing, swung himself from the car.

Camilla woke in inky darkness, wakened by her own cry. Choking with panic and claustrophobia, she clawed the bedclothes aside and scrambled off the lumpy bed to stagger, whimpering, to where the dormer window showed a paler black. She threw open the window and leaned out, swallowing the night air in noisy gulps. For almost a minute she remained like that, oblivious to the chill on her naked body as she wrestled the panic under control. At length, raked by sudden shivers, she withdrew, slamming the window closed. Her teeth chattering now, she groped her way to the bedside chair and pulled on the man's sweater that lay there. Her breath still coming in shallow, rasping gulps, she pulled the sweater close around her, burying her nose in the wool, fancying that she could smell Stephen in it. A little calmed by the thought of him, she opened the door onto the narrow stairs.

The single room that served as living room and

kitchen was still warm from the wood-fuelled stove, a cosy contrast to the icy bedroom. Nevertheless, her hand still trembled as she reached for the spiral bound notebook that lay on the battered pine dresser. She laid the book on the table and made to sit down. Then, as though some force emanated from the book which made it impossible for her to come near it, she changed her mind. Her movements jerky and emphatic, she made a cup of instant coffee and forced herself to drink some. Reluctantly she sat down and opened the book. Clutching the stuff of her sweater to her face, she began reading her own close, meticulously clear handwriting.

As she read, the trembling grew stronger. Tears misted her eyes, hot, stinging tears of anger, fear and the renewed horror of the nightmare that had woken her. Eventually the tears broke and began pouring down her face. Her body leaped and twitched as though possessed. She crammed her white-knuckled fists against her teeth in the effort to still their tremor, and to gag the sobs that broke from her. Finally, she scrambled to her feet, upending her chair, and stumbled, gasping, to the phone. Hardly able to see through the streaming tears, she jabbed clumsily at the dial. She clutched the phone with both hands as it rang for a long time. When the voice came, irritable and thick with sleep, she gave a little cry of relief.

'Oh, Stephen! Please come! Straight away. It's just come to me, just now in bed. There's *proof*, Stephen. Proof!'

Thirteen

Camilla was still at the kitchen table, staring into a cup of cold coffee, skinned with the congealed milk fat, when the sound of the car brought her instantly to her feet. The door flew open as she reached it, and Stephen Letzer strode in, bringing with him a gust of the bitter March air. With a cry, she threw herself against him, her head cushioned on his chest. 'Oh, Stephen. Thank you for coming. I so needed to see you. It's been *horrible* waiting on my own. I've been –' She broke off obediently as he put his finger to his lips and disentangled her arms from around his neck.

'I'm here now. There's time.' As he spoke he leaned out to peer into the breaking daylight, his head cocked as though listening. After a moment, he shrugged and closed the door.

'What's the matter? You look worried?'

He ran a hand through his tousled hair. His clothes were a little dishevelled, his jacket collar turned up where he had dressed in a hurry. 'Just about you, my dear,' he said, still frowning. Then with an angry jerk of his thumb, he added, 'I think someone's followed me here.'

She glanced at the door. 'Who? The press?'

'Damned if I know. It could be. I even wondered if it might be –' He broke off with a sharp shake of his head.

'You don't think . . . my father?'

'Well, yes. It could be him. A monster like that . . . or perhaps he and his lawyer have cooked something up. Probably trying to catch me sleeping with you.' He nodded vehemently. 'That's probably what it is. I bet they'd love to pull that out of the bag in court: me seducing my patient.'

'I wish you would.'

He looked startled. 'No. That's impossible!' He put an arm around her shoulders and began shepherding her towards the kitchen. In a softer tone, he added, 'However much we would both like it to be different.'

They were in the kitchen before she asked, 'Did you think it might be Naomi that was following you?'

He turned away to make coffee. His back to her, he said, 'It's possible. She was pretty pissed off about me taking you away from her.'

'Well, after all, she's probably still taking Daddy's money.'

He spun to face her. 'Don't talk about that! I don't want to hear about that fucking bastard's dirty money! Ever!' He spun back to face the wall.

Shyly, Camilla moved closer. 'Are you sure it's only that?'

'What's that supposed to mean?'

She ran a finger down his back. 'I just wondered if you and Naomi were . . . if *she's* the one who's worried where you are.'

He turned around, thrusting a mug of coffee at her and laughing awkwardly. 'Maybe there was some . . . some attraction, somewhere. Once. There isn't now, Camilla, believe me. Not since . . .' He took her by the fingertips and led her to the table. 'Instead of that, let's just talk about what you remembered. Getting the poison out of your system is all that really counts. For now, anyway.'

Swallowing hard, she dropped her eyes and said, in a whisper, 'I'll try.'

*   *   *

The sound of a car engine brought Stephen Letzer out of the chair where he was dozing, and running to open the door. A blue Sierra was drawn up behind his own BMW. One man was already at the gate. The familiar bulky figure of the other was squeezing through the gap between the car and the garden wall. Letzer started down the path to meet them.

'Good morning, Sergeant, Constable. Thanks for coming over so quickly.'

Sergeant Staples nodded, ignoring Letzer's proffered hand. 'We came as soon as we could, sir. It sounds as though Miss Stenner might have come up with something a bit stronger for us.'

Since first reporting the assaults, Camilla had been making notes of what had happened. Using whatever fragments of memory each day's session with Letzer had dredged to the surface, she had been trying to build up a detailed picture. Letzer's technique centred on getting her to concentrate on specific events of the period – birthdays or outings – and then, by focusing very hard on these, to expand her memory to other things which happened at the time. She had already filled several notebooks with graphic descriptions of her father's activities. It would make impressive testimony, but the detectives knew that in a courtroom it would not be regarded as proof.

Letzer's face had darkened at the policeman's sceptical tone. 'A *lot* stronger! You'll see. This time it's *real* proof. That fucker Matthew Stenner is going to get what he deserves!'

Staples gave him a long, steady look. 'If you don't mind my saying so, Mr Letzer, you seem to be, well, *pleased* about the prospect of her father going to prison. In a doctor, I mean, a professional man, we're used to seeing a bit less . . . passion.'

Letzer flushed. 'Therapist, not doctor. But yes, I am

pleased. Why shouldn't I be? You've both seen enough abuse. You know what damage those bastards do. We're lucky. Camilla has recalled it. How many must there be out there who *never* remember, whose fathers are walking free!'

'So you're a real believer, are you, in all this recovered memory business?' asked the constable.

Letzer looked at the floor. 'I . . . I probably wasn't, well, sure, one way or the other.' He looked up again, defiantly meeting their eyes. 'Until I came across Camilla.'

When Letzer returned to the kitchen, Camilla clung to his hand. Her eyes were puffy and bloodshot. She smiled wanly at the police, half hidden behind Letzer's shoulder.

Staples smiled encouragingly. His voice was lower, warmer than before. 'Mr Letzer tells us you've had a flash of, well, enlightenment. You've remembered something that might be of help. Is that right?'

They had to strain to hear her response. 'I think so, Sergeant.'

Staples smiled again. 'That's wonderful. I wonder, would it be possible for you to tell us about it, er, alone?'

Seeing Staples' glance alight on Letzer, Camilla made a little sound in her throat. She edged closer against him, her grip on his hand tightening. 'No. I *need* Stephen with me. I . . . I couldn't bear to talk about it, not without him.'

The two policemen's eyes met for the shortest possible instant. Staples' chest rose and fell. 'It's your choice, Miss Stenner, of course.'

As she stepped from the silver BMW into the courtyard Camilla felt her throat constrict, choking her. She swallowed hard, still staying close to the car. Behind her, the Sierra rolled to a halt and the burly figure of Sergeant Staples eased himself out and strolled to her side. He looked from her to the house.

'Nervous, Miss Stenner? We'd still be happy to come in with you. We've got the search warrant.'

Tight-lipped, Camilla shook her head. 'No,' she said hoarsely, as Letzer came around to join them. 'We'll go alone.'

After a full minute, nobody had responded to their half-dozen rings. Letzer shook his head. 'Where's your key?' She fumbled in the bag slung at her shoulder and produced a small bunch of keys. Wordlessly, she held it out to him, her fingers slack. After three tries he found the right key, swung the door open and headed for the stairs.

'Camilla!'

The voice brought a shriek of panic from Camilla.

'Camilla!' Liz's voice was strained and thin. 'This is wonderful!'

They looked up. Liz had been making her way downstairs. Now she stood, transfixed, on the half-landing, a robe over her satin nightdress. For an instant the two women stared at each other and then both broke into a stumbling run to fall into each other's arms.

'Camilla, darling! You're back! I'm so happy.' Both were crying noisily, their tears mingling as their cheeks pressed together. Camilla drew back first, sniffing back her tears. 'Sorry. We let ourselves in . . . we didn't realise you were here.'

Liz smiled, smearing at her tears with a palm. 'Of course, darling. I've not been well . . . my head. But it's your *home* here. It always will be. I'm so glad you're back. I –'

'Mummy, is Daddy here?' As she spoke Camilla cast a nervous glance around her.

A faint flush came into the translucent skin of Liz's face. 'No. He didn't come home last night. He slept at the flat. He was with Annie until late, working on the case. Oh, darling, it's such a relief that *that's* all over, that you're back with us.'

Camilla swallowed. 'Mummy, I just came to . . . There's some stuff in my room that I want to pick up.'

Liz stared bleakly into her untouched tea. Across the kitchen table, Camilla, her face taut, her eyes red-rimmed, struggled briefly to buckle her bulging shoulder bag before abandoning the effort with a flounce of frustration and rising from her chair. In a jerky, convulsive movement, she leaned to kiss Liz on the cheek, mumbling, 'Bye, Mummy.' She swallowed and glanced wildly at where Letzer stood by the door. His expressionless face did not alter. She turned back to her mother. 'I'm sorry, too.' She hesitated for another second and then almost ran across the room, grabbing Letzer's hand and dragging him after her through the door, her eyes glistening.

Matt was singing softly along with the radio as he left the motorway traffic behind him. For the first time in weeks he was coming home to Liz with some good news. Just before midnight, as she drove him back to the flat, Annie had received a call from Larry Guenther. The man who had shot himself, the father of the woman who placed the ad, had been a fairly wealthy man, owner of two Toyota dealerships and a small office building in San Diego. His daughter had inherited everything, including an apartment in a smart suburb. Anyone with that much money was not going to be hard to trace. Already that morning, Annie had called to tell him she had a sympathetic journalist interested who was reasonably sure she could get the story into a series on the misuses of psychiatry which she was preparing for the late summer, chiming nicely with preparations for the trial. Roy Erskine expected to have an address for the woman within a week. Matt had already agreed to foot the expenses for the journalist to fly out to California to interview her.

A twinge of disappointment passed over his face as he approached the gates and saw Rachel's car standing on the gravel. He had been looking forward to more than simply telling Liz the good news. The strength of his arousal at Annie's kiss had left him shaken. It had been a stark reminder of how much the strain since his arrest had affected his and Liz's lovemaking. Lying awake into the early hours listening to the sounds of the London night, he had been making plans for a fresh start. Rachel had not figured in the plans.

He found Rachel alone in the kitchen. 'Where's Liz?'

She looked at him only momentarily before turning back to chopping vegetables. 'The library,' she said stiffly.

Liz was sitting with the curtains drawn, the room in virtual darkness. His heart sank as he kneeled at her side and kissed her on the lips. Her own mouth did not budge. 'Hello, darling. Sorry about last night. I was in no state to take a cab, let alone drive myself.' He frowned at her silence. 'What is it?' He stroked her forehead with his palm. 'Bloody migraine again?'

'No.' It was some time before she added, 'Matt, Camilla was here.'

Matt's face split in a grin. 'Liz! That's *fabulous*. What did she say? Is she coming home? Has she woken up to that quack?'

'Not really, Matt, no.'

Her tone killed his grin. 'What, then? What did she come for? Are we going to be a family again, or not?'

'Matt, I think I need some time to think.'

Puzzlement filled his face. 'Think? About what?'

She stood up abruptly and took two quick steps away from him. He was still crouching, looking helplessly up at her, when she added, in a voice that was breaking, 'I'm moving out, Matt.'

Fourteen

For several seconds the two of them remained frozen in the same postures, neither finding words. Slowly, Matt pushed himself to his feet, using the chair for support. He came to stand behind her and raised his hands, as though to take her by the shoulders. Then, changing his mind, he let them fall back loosely at his sides. 'Liz, I swear I didn't do it. Not any of it. Ever.'

Her head drooped forward as she brought up her hands to cover her face. Her shoulders rocked as she cried silently. After a while, she dropped her hands and walked a few aimless paces. The desolation in her face wrenched at him, propelling him instinctively towards her, reaching for her.

'Maybe not.' Her words brought him up short, leaving him standing uncertainly. His stomach heaved, as though he would be sick. 'That's what I tell myself over and over.' She began to cry again, only tears, with no sound. She shook her head, like a dog worrying at a rag. 'It's not just that, Matt. It's me, too. I was so selfish. I was never here for them. Not for you, either.'

He raised a hand, reaching at the air between them. 'No, darling. No!' With soft emphasis he added, 'You mustn't! Camilla is . . . she was always fragile. Nothing you could have done would have changed that. Letzer has just been clever enough to exploit your absences, that's all. You mustn't let him manoeuvre you into thinking you're to *blame*.' He stepped closer, daring to touch her shoulder now. 'You can't give the bastard the *victory*! What about Mark? What's *he* going to do?'

She shook her head, taking a dead-footed step backwards, eluding his grasp. 'I won't be far away. Rachel has agreed I can stay with her for a while.'

At the mention of Rachel, Matt's lips whitened. He threw a glance behind him at the door. 'I knew it! She's been poisoning the atmosphere, hasn't she? That juiceless old –'

'Don't, Matt,' she said, deeply weary. 'Rachel had nothing to do with it. But she's had enough troubles in her own life to understand what I'm going through. I asked her to come over because I didn't trust myself to drive in this state. Mark should stay here, of course.' She walked with a quick, nervous step to the door. 'I'll talk to him this evening.' She thrust open the door. 'I'm sorry, Matt. Really sorry.' The words were lost in a wrenching sob as the door slammed violently behind her.

Stephen Letzer watched the police car draw away before walking slowly back up the path to push open the cottage door. He found Camilla as they had left her, at the kitchen table, staring mutely at the books which lay open around her. He took her gently by the arm. 'Are you ready to go to work?'

She looked up, as though startled to find him there. Slowly, her lips curved into a tentative grin. 'Yes,' she whispered, pushing her chair around to face him.

Crossing to the window, he closed the curtains, shutting out the early spring sunlight to leave the room in semi-darkness. Returning to where she sat, he dropped to a crouch. 'Just relax, darling.' As Camilla gazed fixedly at the wall in front of her, he raised a finger and began moving it rhythmically from side to side in front of her face.

*   *   *

A shaft of sunlight knifed into the room, striking the pillow. Matt reacted as though he had been scalded, clapping a hand to his eyes with a moan. Gradually, he opened his eyes a crack to look at the clock. He groaned again; it was already ten thirty. In the ten days since Liz had moved out, restless nights, then oversleeping, had become par for the course. But with Mark gone off to school three hours earlier, who was opening his bedroom curtains? 'Liz?' he asked hopefully, pushing himself, still blinking, onto an elbow.

'Sorry. No. Just me.'

Matt squinted into the brightness, hauling himself to a sitting position. His face pinched in surprise. 'Naomi!'

She sauntered over to sit on the edge of the bed. 'Celia let me in. I hope you didn't mind me waking you. Not hearing from you, I thought I ought to see how you were. You *look* lousy. Have you been taking proper care of yourself?'

He lay back against the headboard. 'I'm okay. I drink. Wouldn't you?'

Naomi's eyes clouded. 'Matt, I'm truly sorry. I was just . . . devastated, about Liz.'

'How did you know?'

'When you didn't return my calls. I . . .'

'Don't take it personally. I haven't been returning anybody's calls.'

She gave him a fleeting smile. 'I don't.' She looked down at her hands again, twisting at a heavy silver ring. 'I just don't see how Liz . . . how she *could*. It's just so unfair. I told her so. I don't see how she could do it, at a time like this.'

He laughed through his nose. 'Fuck it, Naomi, it's precisely *because* it's a time like this. If she didn't think I was a child abuser she would still be here.'

A faint flush lent a deeper colour to Naomi's olive skin. 'Of course. I only meant . . . It's such an awful way to treat *you*, Matt.' As she spoke she raised her eyes to his.

It was a moment before Matt looked away. 'Thanks for the confidence. I need some. I think I'd better get up.'

He gripped the edge of the quilt and waited, his eyes on her, inviting her to leave. Her own gaze flickered down his bare chest to hover for a second at the point below his navel where the whiteness of the quilt contrasted with the dark swirls of his body hair. She rose slowly, smiling. 'I'll cook you some breakfast. You look as though a square meal would do you good.'

As Matt finished off the last of his breakfast, Naomi began fidgeting with her coffee cup. He had barely swallowed the last mouthful when she asked, 'Do you mind if I smoke?'

He shrugged. 'If you have to.'

She lit a cigarette and sucked deeply, letting out the smoke with a long sigh. 'Matt, how does it look? The case, I mean?'

'Okay, I guess. Erskine's people are working hard. They think they can come up with at least one good case for us. We've taken on some public relations people to help us exploit it. If we're lucky there won't be a juror available in the country by the time the case comes to trial who won't think Recovered Memory Syndrome is the bullshit of the century. Bailey Associates are bloody good. They've done great work on some real dogs. Remember Lord McIver?'

'Wasn't there something about him and women's toilets?'

'That's the man,' Matt laughed. 'He was *big* in that area. But you're about the only person in the country who remembers it. To most people he's now Lord McIver the selfless toiler for the homeless. Thanks to Tara Bailey.'

'Lovely lady.'

He shrugged. 'I need someone who knows how to fight dirty, not a Buckingham Palace spokesman.'

'Sure.' She drew again on the cigarette. 'Matt, how much is all this going to end up costing you?'

He grimaced. 'What's money got to do with it? I want my wife back. And my family. And my career. I don't give a shit *what* it takes, money or anything else. Letzer thinks he's got me dangling, that he's going to walk off with Camilla's money. Well, I'm not lying down for it. The bastard's going to have a fight on his hands. If we find he's had so much as a parking ticket, Tara Bailey will make sure it winds up on the front pages of half the papers in the country.'

'Matt, are you sure you aren't just whistling in the dark? Supposing they don't find anything? Isn't there a pretty fair chance you'll *lose* unless Camilla retracts?'

'From what she told Liz that seems to be about the last thing she plans to do.'

'Unless Stephen Letzer persuaded her to change her mind.'

He found no sign of mockery in her eyes. 'What the hell is *that* supposed to mean?'

Briefly she averted her face as though under the impact of his controlled anger. When she looked back at him, it was with a pained, pleading look. 'I know it's not my business, but again, how much is all this costing you – Erskine, Annie, public relations, the whole thing?'

He batted a hand at the air. 'God knows. Erskine's first bill came in the other day. That was already a hundred and forty thousand dollars.'

'Fuck! Who do they think they're dealing with? IBM?'

'They've had a lot of expenses, travel and so on.'

She laughed incredulously. 'Still! A hundred and . . . What's it going to end up at? Half a million? A million?'

He rose to put his plate in the dishwasher. 'As long as they get results.'

'But they *haven't*! For God's sake, Matt, they're bleeding you dry. And how about Annie? What does a firm like that charge?'

His shoulders rose and fell. 'She'll charge whatever she has to.'

Naomi rose to her feet and went to rest her fingers on his arm. 'Matt, be realistic. Annie has partners. She has to charge you the going rate. What's that these days, for a West End firm? A hundred and fifty pounds an hour? Two hundred? You must be looking at blowing a million dollars. With *nothing* guaranteed.'

Matt's eyes narrowed. 'The money's there. What do I have better to do with it, for God's sake?'

A flush suffused her face. 'Please, Matt, don't get mad at me. The idea came to me while I was talking to Liz. If Stephen Letzer *is* as unscrupulous as he looks, why don't I talk to him, see if he could be persuaded to . . . cooperate?'

'Why the hell would he do that while he thinks he's got a chance of getting his paws on Camilla's trust money?' She looked steadily into his face, not flinching at the flinty glitter in his eyes as realisation dawned, then turned instantly to renewed anger. 'Ah, no! Fuck that! No payoffs! No blackmail! I'm going to walk away from all this with my name *cleared*, not sneak out of it.'

'But, Matt, think about it. If I could persuade

Stephen to go public, to give us a written *admission* of what he's been doing . . .'

He thought for a moment. 'It is tempting,' he said slowly. 'After all, he'll get his money. I pay him off and he puts the whole process into reverse. Of course, Anderson's would love it. Instead of wanting their advance back they'd be clamouring for the manuscript. They'd probably print an extra hundred thousand copies just to ride the publicity, the sympathy for the innocent victim of a ruthless trickster. Everybody would be happy.' He grinned brightly and then let the grin slip abruptly away again. 'Except Liz.' He let the word hang for a long moment. 'To her, I'd stop being the man who definitely buggered her daughter, and be the man who just might have!' He sighed. 'Sorry, Naomi, I appreciate what you're saying, but it's all gone too far. There's only one way out now and that's to go to trial and to shoot Letzer down in flames. It's also our best chance of undoing some of the harm the bastard's done to Camilla.'

As he finished speaking, the phone trilled. Naomi, close by it, raised an eyebrow. At Matt's nod she picked up the handset. 'Annie!' Her face split in a smile. 'How are you? Sure, Matt's right here.'

Matt pressed the receiver to his ear. 'Hi. I was trying to get you all day yesterday.'

'I was in court all day, trying to get some bogus Barbie dolls restrained.'

'It's a comfort to know my place in the scheme of things. What's new?' At Annie's response he frowned and cast a half-amused glance at Naomi. 'Look, hold on a minute.' He laid the receiver on the counter. 'Naomi, I need to take this in the study. Can you hang this up for me?'

*   *   *

He settled himself in the old leather chair and waited for the snick as Naomi replaced the other receiver. 'She came over this morning,' he said. 'She thought I needed feeding. She's also put in a word for me with Liz. I don't get the impression it did much good.'

'Well, if that's really all?' He smiled to himself at the abrasive edge in Annie's tone. 'It wouldn't look good if the prosecution got wind of it!'

'Annie, cross my heart, all she did was cook breakfast.'

'If you say so. The last thing we need is her on the stand telling the world how five minutes after Liz moves out you're shacking up with Camilla's *therapist*, for God's sake.'

He chuckled. 'Annie, forget it. Apart from anything else, can you picture me with a woman that smokes?'

'She's given up before.'

He laughed aloud, letting the point lie. 'So what else is new? How are Erskine's people doing?'

'Pretty well, maybe. I was sort of saving it until there was something more concrete, but perhaps you need cheering up. It concerns the woman whose father did away with himself. She sold up his property, paid all the cheques into an account in her own name. Just three weeks later she withdrew the lot, in cash. A month after that, she placed the ad asking her defunct dad to forgive her. Then she disappeared off the face of the earth.'

'That's *good* news?'

'It is as of yesterday. They tracked down the Mexican maid. Apparently, the woman didn't sell all her furniture when she moved. She kept a few pieces and had them shipped out. Now they're looking for the haulage company. The bad news is, anybody with a van can go into that business. There seem to be, like, ten thousand of them in the yellow pages, and as many again that have gone out of business since. Still, Roy has found needles in haystacks for me before.'

'Great. He should get as many people on it as he can. Does he need any more money?'

'He'll yell if he does.'

'And Letzer? How are they doing on him?'

Some of the lightness went out of her voice. 'That really *is* a dead end, for the moment. And, Matt, there's more. First, the trust specialist here has looked over Patrick's trust deed.'

'And?' he asked, even though he already knew.

'If you're convicted there won't be a thing we can do. I wish to God Patrick had come to me.'

'So we wave goodbye to Camilla's inheritance. There'll still be enough to go round. Anything else? You sound suicidal?'

Annie's deep breathing was audible over the line. 'Well, first, here's some more good news. I got the report from Professor Blackstone.'

Tom Blackstone was their expert witness, the one they hoped would counter Worthington's evidence.

'It's pretty good. His view is that the scars *could* have been caused by constipation. If it was very severe!'

'Annie, that's terrific! Great! What the hell were you sounding so miserable about?'

'I got the documents this morning. The trial is for Chichester Crown Court.'

Matt frowned. 'So? Is there something wrong with Chichester?'

'No, of course not.' She hesitated. 'I also got the prosecution bundle – their evidence.'

'A problem?'

After another moment of silence Annie said, so quietly he had to strain to hear, 'Not a problem, Matt. A disaster. A total bloody disaster. Camilla's saying she kept diaries!'

Fifteen

Annie stood at the window, her bottom lip clamped between her teeth, looking on in silence as Matt, seated in her chair, hunched over the desk, scanning the photocopied sheets. His ashen face was stunned and expressionless. As he read, the blue eyes dulled, as though an inner light had been extinguished. A pang struck deep inside her as she watched. In the few days since she had last seen him the flesh below his jaw seemed slacker, his collar not fitting quite so closely. He had shaved hurriedly, leaving a patch of greying stubble the size of a coin on his jaw. He finished reading the last sheet and rose to his feet. With a slow step, he crossed the room to join her. Annie broke the silence. 'Are they genuine?'

He shook his head. 'I can't say for sure, but I guess so. Camilla did keep diaries. She was *always* writing – stories, poems, journals.' A sudden smile momentarily drove the despondency from his face. 'I used to have to put in a special order for notebooks for her, to stop her looting the office.' The smile faded.

'Had you ever seen them before?'

He sucked at his teeth. 'No, I'd remember, I'm sure of that. Although,' he added, his eyes widening in realisation, 'Liz was looking at something like this back when . . .' He broke off, covering his eyes with his hands. 'Oh God, of course. This is what Camilla came to the house to collect. She talked to Liz about it. That's why . . .' He drifted to the desk and picked up one of the photocopies. The text that covered it, in a small, uneven hand, was surrounded by a border. In the border, monstrous heads emerged from lairs, red mouths agape, showing jagged teeth. Between the monsters were little groups of symbols and rows of numbers. The numbers were easy to decode as dates. Without Camilla's accompanying statement the symbols would have been meaningless. With it, they told a tale of unspeakable horror. He threw the sheet back onto the desk with a shudder of dismay and loathing. 'That's why Liz left,' he whispered. 'Oh my God, Annie, how could she? How could Camilla let that ... bastard do this to me? What has he done to my daughter?'

She came quickly to his side. Glancing at the closed door, she took his hand in both hers. 'Don't, Matt. I warned you. It happens to everyone. The first time they see the prosecution bundle everybody's ready to commit suicide. Never forget this, Matt,' she said, speaking very softly, 'you *know* you're innocent. Anything they can produce that seems to say differently has an explanation.' A tight smile brushed her lips. 'Our job is just to find it.' She released his hand and moved to the desk. 'Now, with this material, the first thing we do is check its authenticity, even if it looks to *you* like something Camilla did at the time.'

'You think it might *not* be? That Letzer might have – I don't know – *hypnotised* her, or something, *influenced* her to write this ... crap? Would it even be possible?'

'As soon as I got this I spoke to a specialist. Her opinion, strictly off the cuff, is that it *might* be. She's never come across anything similar, though.' Catching the furtive disappointment in his eyes, she stepped closer. 'Matt, we *both* know it's crap.' As the silence between them lengthened she said briskly, 'I've already enlisted somebody – the man who did the work that

214

exposed the police officers caught falsifying interview notes, remember? He's agreed to come down to Crawley police station with me tomorrow. I told him you would be there.'

He gave her a sudden grin. 'My career's closed down for the duration, Liz has gone. I guess I don't have much to stay home for.'

'You're late!' Camilla threw herself against Letzer, making him stagger back against the garden gate. Recovering his balance, he quickly disentangled himself from her embrace, avoiding her kiss as he looked anxiously up and down the lane. Only after Camilla had closed the cottage door behind them did he allow her to cling to him, her head against his chest. 'I thought perhaps you'd had an accident or something! I've spent the last hour standing at the gate, just listening for the car!' Almost sobbing with relief, she went on in a rush, 'I know you'll think I'm stupid, but when you're not here I . . . I just can't function.'

He took her by the shoulders and eased her off him. 'How about a cup of coffee?'

She looked into his face, alarmed by something in his voice. 'I'll make some. What's wrong?'

He walked ahead of her into the kitchen. 'Naomi came to the clinic today.'

'What for?' Instantly she regretted the hectoring note in her voice. 'Hasn't she understood?' she asked, more mollifying. '*You're* treating me now. We don't need her hanging around any more.'

He let out a long sigh. 'I think she's finally beginning to understand that.' He half turned away from her, chewing at a thumbnail. 'She came to . . . she seemed to be offering me money.'

Puzzled, Camilla moved round to confront him. 'Money?'

215

'I wasn't going to tell you. She seems to think your family would be ready to pay me off.'

'What? Stephen, what was she suggesting?'

'I'm not sure you ought to hear this. The idea is that I persuade you to retract. That I persuade you all you've remembered is *false*.'

Her eyes widened. 'But that's ... What about the notebooks? Do they expect you to make me believe I *invented* all that?' Her voice had risen angrily.

He put an arm around her shoulders and bowed his head as though unbearably saddened. 'I don't know what they think. They've probably seen your statement, and the notebooks. They're desperate. Naomi mentioned a quarter of a million dollars. All he wants is for you to retract and me to sign a statement claiming to have implanted the whole story in your head.'

Camilla gaped, disgust and disbelief in her face. 'I can't believe he would ... How can he be so disgusting?' She began to cry. 'Oh God, Stephen, doesn't the man have any *dignity* left?' She turned to busy herself with the kettle, tears rolling down her face. 'Oh, how I *hate* that man!'

He remained silent, lost in thought, while she made the coffee. She brought the two mugs to the table, pushed him into one of the creaking Windsor chairs and settled herself on his knees. 'Stephen,' she whispered, wiping away the last of the tears, 'what are we going to do when this is over?'

'I don't know,' he said, his voice oddly distant. 'It partly depends if I end up with any money from selling the clinic.'

'Sell it? Why?'

'It's complicated. There's a loan. As a matter of fact, I put it with a real estate agent today.'

'What will you do, then? Afterwards?'

'A lot's happened in my life lately. I haven't really

worked it out. Travel some, maybe. After that, maybe study some more, do something useful. Work with disturbed children.' His grin belied a hardening in his eyes. 'No more taking advantage of poor little rich girls.'

There was a nervous edge to her laugh as she laid her head against him. 'That doesn't mean me, does it?'

He looked sharply down at her head and then away again, staring into space. 'Don't ever say things like that, sweetheart, please. Not even jokingly.'

Matt sat straight back against the leather of the seat, his eyes fixed on the road ahead. In the half-hour since they had driven away from the police station he had not uttered a word, as though the sight of Camilla's diaries had put him into shock.

Annie swallowed. 'He still has to run his tests, Matt, on the ink and the paper.'

'You know what they'll show as well as I do. Camilla wrote them, and she wrote them when she was a child.' He leaned towards her, gripping her arm. 'Eight years old, Annie! What could have been going on in her *head*, for Christ's sake?'

The break in his voice made her swivel to look anxiously at him. For the first time he was on the verge of losing his composure. She took a hand from the wheel and gripped his sleeve, her fingers biting into the thick forearm. 'Something, Matt, without a doubt. But nothing to do with *you*! For God's sake, we were *together*!'

He looked at her, agonised and perplexed. 'Why? Why in heaven's name would a child *invent* things like that?'

Annie's mind flashed back to the symbols and drawings, far more vivid than on the photocopies of the evidence bundle. Grotesque figures, some featureless, except for huge mouths, gaping in silent screams, others predatory and saw-toothed. Yet others, obviously male, their crudely drawn organs huge and menacing. Just thinking about them made her feel queasy and somehow unclean. Whatever their meaning, they were undoubtedly the product of a deeply disturbed mind. She glanced again at Matt. His face was haggard, deeply etched with uncomprehending distress. Pity clutched at her stomach as, for the first time, she saw something else, the bleak, bereft look of inexpressible loneliness. Instinctively, she took his hand. 'Matt, I used to keep diaries, too, in those days,' she whispered. She watched him slowly turn to let his shadowed eyes settle on her face. 'I dug them out last night.'

Her smile, wan and almost shy, brought a pang so sharp and unexpected that his hand went to his chest. For the instant of its duration the smile had fleetingly illuminated a time when they had both been twelve years younger, when there was nothing in the world he could not have. As the smile faded it left an after-image that left his whole being aching. 'I had a code, too,' she went on, her eyes on the road again now. It was some while before she was able to continue. 'I couldn't vouch for every single date Camilla mentions. But most of them. Enough to blow their case out of the water.'

Matt sat silent for some time before saying, without turning his gaze from the road, 'I really appreciate the offer, Annie. You understand why I can't let you do it, though, don't you?'

Annie, too, kept looking straight ahead. 'You don't think Liz ever . . . guessed?'

'I don't know,' he murmured. Then, a few seconds later, he said more briskly, 'Letzer still has to be the key,' he went on. 'Only our starting point has changed. There's no use trying to deny that Camilla wrote those things. We have to show the court that Letzer has hijacked them for his own purposes. Your detective character still hasn't got any evidence he's sleeping with Camilla?'

'On the contrary. Mind you, he also thinks Letzer knows he's being watched.'

'Yeah. He's a shrewd bastard, that's for sure.' Again Matt sat for some while in silent contemplation before saying, 'There's no real reason those sketches mean anything at all, except that Camilla was highly strung. She was always prone to nightmares, ever since she was a baby. She would hardly go upstairs alone until she was twelve. All he would have had to do was manipulate those symbols, to get Camilla to put that interpretation on something perfectly innocent.'

She sighed. 'You're right. Except that you saw his statement. Those sketches are the absolutely classic product of abuse.'

'But, Annie, we're going round in circles, for Christ's sake. The whole point is the man's a fucking *fraud*!'

Annie pursed her lips. 'It's not only *his* opinion, unfortunately. For heaven's sake, the study he's relying on most is the one the UN Children's Organisation commissioned three years ago. They match their findings exactly. You don't think we're going to convince the jury *they're* in this with him?'

He turned to her, his face blank with shock. 'Annie,' he whispered, '*you're* not wavering, are you?'

She glanced quickly at him, hardly turning her head. Her hand covered his. 'No!' He caught the glint of moisture in her eye before she had time to blink it away. 'I'm just trying to see it through the jury's eyes. On the evidence the prosecution are holding they must be thinking they've got a pretty reliable witness in Stephen Letzer.'

'Which is why we're spending hundreds of thousands of dollars to undermine him. Have you heard any more from America?'

She bit her lip. 'There's not much. Frankly, on the matter of tracking down Letzer, I'm disappointed in Roy. I thought by now he would have made more progress. They seem to have a lead on the woman, though. They tracked down the haulage company who moved her stuff. Roy's sent Larry Guenther up to Idaho to check it out. Let's hope she's still there.'

'Yeah, let's hope,' Matt said dully. 'How long do they have?'

Annie shrugged. 'It's hard to say. Plea and Directions is in three weeks. That's when they'll set a date. In theory, it could be any time after that. In reality, it'll probably be a few months. Abuse cases normally get priority but even so, they have to find court time. Given the fact that we're going to make every one of their expert witnesses absolute, I can't see the case taking less than two weeks, minimum.'

He raised his eyebrows. '*All* of them? You'll make them all take the stand?'

'Sure.' She laughed. 'We're going to *bore* the jury into submission.' She became serious again. 'I mean it. There are basically two lines we will take. One, discredit Letzer. For that we still rely on Roy, although even with nothing else I can sow some serious doubt. A man pushing forty, and no record of him having practised before. Working from a clinic that must have cost half a million pounds? Who is he? Where's he from? It's fishy to *you*, isn't it?' Matt nodded. 'Right. Well, I intend to make it smell funny to a jury as well. And if we can show the jury that Camilla came to the interpretation she did of her diary codes under his guidance, or, better still, under hypnosis . . . Then, two, we have to undermine the expert testimony. For that

I need the experts in the box where I can get at them. You'd be surprised how many prosecution experts turn out to be disasters. They are proud of their expertise, but they're proud of their independence, too. If you push them they'll recognise the limits of their abilities. I've seen a lot of them blow up in the prosecution's face before now.'

'You make it sound easy.'

She shrugged. 'Not easy. But not the disaster it looks to you right now, either.'

'Well, look, Roger, I'm sorry, but I'm just not going to be able to. I have to work and that's all there is to it.' Listening morosely to Roger's response, Annie fiddled with the old-fashioned glass inkwell she used as a paperweight, repeatedly lifting it and letting it fall back with a muted thud onto the leather-topped desk. She glanced at Matt before speaking again, her voice weary and impatient. 'Yes, Roger. That's right. He's here with me now. And will be for another couple of hours, at least. P and D is set for the twenty-eighth. Today's the twelfth. That gives us a deadline to apply for witnesses to be made absolute in three days' time. I'm in court for at least two of those days. So, surely, even *you* can see, Roger, that I have no choice? I have to do it *now*!'

Matt looked on in tight-lipped silence as she listened to Roger's reply with her eyes cast down. The simmering rage in her eyes was overlaid with a desolate look of bone-deep sadness. The lines that ran from her nose to frame her mouth were deeper than he had ever seen them. 'Well, *you* do it, darling. You might surprise yourself. Lots of men *adore* cooking.' As she listened she raised her eyes to look directly into Matt's. The undisguised anger in them glinted like a coin on a stream bed. 'Well, I don't care a *fuck* what you do!

221

Get them a bloody Indian takeaway!' She put the phone down with a crash, needing two attempts to find the rest. She was panting. After a moment she laughed and waved an apologetic hand. 'Sorry! I was expected home to cook curry for a bunch of rugby cronies.'

He smiled with one side of his mouth. 'I'm the one that should be apologising. I didn't know it was *that* bad,' he added in a whisper.

She drew back her lips in an ironic smile. 'We try to behave in public. Now, shall we get on with trying to save *your* life?'

Matt came instantly awake. Lying in the darkness, he reached for the water glass and groaned. Getting to bed so late he had forgotten to refill it.

On the way home, Naomi had called suggesting she come over and bring dinner. Depressed, with Camilla's diaries freshly in his mind, and Mark staying over with a friend after his rugby match, he had found the idea of company appealing. He had tried to keep the conversation on Letzer, desperate to find the key to discrediting the man. By the time he persuaded her to leave, close to one o'clock, he had made no progress. And the disappointment in her face as he walked her to her car had only added to his depression.

Slipping from bed he carried the glass into the bathroom. He drank off two glasses before refilling the glass a third time and padding back to bed. He slid beneath the quilt and spread himself luxuriantly, taking up the whole of the spacious bed as he tried to let sleep overtake him again. Ten minutes later, he knew it was not going to. It was not thirst that had woken him, but a nagging idea that circled in his brain, refusing to be still. He threw back the quilt and strode out into the corridor.

Cartons, spilling over with toys and books, lay on the floor of Camilla's bedroom. Kicking aside a pair of plush bears, he yanked open the door of the closet and began ripping the cartons of books from their places.

It took him only seconds to find what he was looking for. As he dragged out another carton, the notebook he had found Liz reading fell at his feet. Snatching it up, he strode down the back stairs to the kitchen.

Forty minutes and four cups of black coffee later he snapped shut the book and sprang to his feet. It was nearly five on the kitchen clock. In less than an hour Annie would be up, beginning the pre-office routine of bathing and feeding William. He hesitated only a moment before reaching for the phone and dialling Annie's number.

Sixteen

Annie's car slid to a halt in a spray of gravel. She jumped out and ran for the house. Bursting through the door into the utility room, she collided with Matt, already hurrying to meet her. They clung to each other for an instant before Matt pulled away, taking her by the hand. 'Mark's inside. I wanted him to hear this, too.'

Annie planted a kiss on Mark's cheek and lowered herself onto the bench beside him. She poured herself a cup of coffee and drank some, closing her eyes. 'Ah. You always made great coffee,' she said with a faint air of mischief. She reopened her eyes and looked directly at Matt. His eyes shone more brightly than they had for weeks. His face had lost some of the papery, exhausted look, regaining a little of its old vigour. 'So, are you going to show it to me?'

Grinning, Matt took a dog-eared notebook from the chair next to him and laid it on the table in front of her. 'Camilla missed this one. Liz had taken it out of its box.' He flipped it open at a page with the corner turned down and tapped it with a finger. 'It's there, Annie. The explanation of Camilla's problems.'

Annie looked at the open book. The left-hand page was covered with the dense, controlled handwriting she recognised as Camilla's. Halfway down the facing page the text ended abruptly. The bottom half of the page was filled with cramped, luridly coloured sketches. Frowning, her face set, Annie bent closer. 'What is it, Matt? What does it *mean*?'

He laid his finger on the pictures. 'Look at them. That's a *baby*, isn't it? And the red is blood. There, if you look, those are genitals, male and female, all covered in blood.'

She squinted at the sketches, her face pinched in distaste. 'It looks like it. But why? Why did she suddenly start drawing such . . . horrible things?'

Matt's finger moved to the top of the page. 'Look at the date. Rachel's miscarriage, Annie,' he breathed. 'Camilla *saw* it, remember?'

Annie's hand went involuntarily to her mouth. 'Oh my God! So she really *did*!'

Matt turned to Mark, his face sombre. 'It's something we've never talked about. Rachel's too sensitive about it. And it *was* horrible. Rachel was seven months pregnant. Everything was going fine. Then, one day, she was sitting here, at this table, and out of nowhere she started complaining of pains. She went up those stairs, to the bathroom. I was in the study, Mummy was here. Nobody was worried. After all, at seven months everyone assumes a woman's home and dry. The next thing, we heard Rachel calling. Mummy went up to see what was going on. She found Rachel on the floor of the landing, giving birth.' He swallowed. 'It was a hell of a mess.' His voice dropped to a whisper. 'The baby was dead. Strangled.'

Mark grimaced, a hand covering his eyes. 'Oh shit,' he murmured. He looked at Matt. 'And Camilla *saw* that? Eight years old, and she saw her aunt . . .' He broke off, shaking his head.

'She was playing in her room. She must have heard Rachel call.' He shook his head. 'She certainly took it very hard. She was so much looking forward to having a baby cousin. A girl, too.' His voice caught. 'At the time we weren't sure whether she had seen it or not, she wouldn't say. But now I see this . . .' He ground

225

his finger at the childish date code. 'February the twentieth, a fortnight after it happened. And she starts doing *this*.' As Mark stared at the notebook Matt's eyes flickered in a quick, sidelong look at Annie. 'And this must have been about the time she started having the nightmares, too.'

Catching his glance, Annie looked quickly away, reaching for the book. 'Can I take this with me? I'll start by getting Professor Blackstone's opinion.' She smiled, resting her free hand on Mark's arm. 'I wouldn't want to give you both false hopes, but I would say this puts a whole different light on Camilla's diaries!'

Larry Guenther pulled the rented car off the road and climbed out, arching his back, stretching clenched fists skyward, straightening the kinks from his muscles. Yawning, he reached into the car and lifted the folded map from the passenger seat. He spread the map on the roof and drew a small notebook from his inside jacket pocket. Laying the open notebook on the map he studied them both for a moment and then squinted into the valley below him. Far away, he could just make out a cluster of buildings through the haze, a smudge of smoke hanging motionless in the air above them. With a grim smile, he threw map and notebook back into the car. The recollection of the Latino haulage contractor who had moved the woman's furniture had been as vague as his book-keeping, with its illegible invoices in smudged pencil. In five days of quartering the twisting, empty back roads of northern Idaho this was the first time Larry had found a spot that seemed to marry the directions he'd been given with reality. He folded himself into the car and let it roll back onto the road, heading down into the valley.

*   *   *

The deeply rutted track emerged abruptly from among massive pines into an area that had been cleared to make small fields. A hundred yards ahead, across a stretch of bare earth hatched with the dried-out tracks of tractors, stood a cluster of shacks and weathered barns. The main shack was decently built from solid-looking pine planks with a shingle roof. Smoke rose from its stone chimney stack. A group of smaller buildings huddled around the main one. They ranged from neat, well-maintained cabins to ramshackle shacks cobbled together from discarded packaging materials. In the fields, neatly divided into small, unfenced lots, men and women – long-haired and dressed mostly in jeans and T-shirts, with a scattering of ethnic ponchos – were working the land. A few of the women carried children in cloth slings on their hips. Other children, slender, their faces grimy but glowing with health, played noisily in the alleys between the shacks.

'Welcome back to the sixties,' Larry muttered to himself as he stopped the car in front of the main building and unfurled himself from the driving seat.

As he slammed the car door, a pony-tailed man in soiled dungarees emerged from the shack and moved warily across the plank deck to meet him. Larry raised a hand in greeting, his face revealing none of the surprise he felt at seeing the six-inch wooden crucifix that swung from a lanyard around the man's neck. 'Good afternoon.'

The man inclined his head. His shrewd eyes scanned Larry and the car, looking for clues. 'Good afternoon, brother. What can I do for you?'

Larry pulled a card from his breast pocket and proffered it to the man. 'I'm trying to trace a Jill Stanakis. I'm told she came to live here about six years ago.'

The man's eyes narrowed. Over six feet and thickset, he appeared to be sizing Larry up. Larry followed his glance as his eyes went again to the men in the field. They seemed to have edged nearer.

'Look, there's no harm for Miss Stanakis. I just want to talk to her. About some trouble she had back in San Diego. She got ripped off. I'm representing somebody who's interested in her story, that's all.' He paused. 'He's ready to pay for it.'

Several seconds passed as the man unhurriedly looked him over. At length, he shrugged. 'Jill could use a break. I'll take you over there.'

When the telephone rang, Matt crossed the library in three strides and snatched it up, expecting it was Naomi but hoping it might be Liz. 'Naomi! I've been trying to get you all morning.'

She laughed. 'You're telling me. Nobody else got a look-in on my answering machine. What's up? Good news?'

'Not good, *great*! We've found out what triggered Camilla's diary entries.'

'Matt, that's just *wonderful*! What is it?'

Matt told her about Rachel's miscarriage and Camilla's subsequent nightmares.

Naomi was silent for some time before asking, 'Have you had an independent opinion whether that's a credible cause of the diary entries and all?'

'Annie's working on that today.' Anxiety entered his voice. 'Why? Don't *you* think it has to be the answer?'

'I have no idea. *Something* caused it. I guess that must have been pretty bad for her.' She paused again. 'Are you sure Camilla actually *saw* the baby born?'

'Until today I only wondered. To tell you the truth, it's all a bit of a blur. Christ, we had Rachel squatting on the carpet in a puddle of blood. All I remember is blind panic, running to phone doctors, ambulances, and whatever else.'

'Well, it certainly *sounds* like something that could have had serious effects on a sensitive girl. You've still got Camilla's own testimony to overcome, though, haven't you?'

Matt snorted. 'Christ, Naomi, thanks for the encouragement.'

'I'm sorry, Matt. I didn't mean it like that,' she said hurriedly. 'I just . . . well, want to be realistic.'

'Come on, Naomi. Annie was beside herself. She really thinks we're on to something. If we can undermine the diaries *and* blow Letzer out of the water, I'm in the clear.'

'God, Matt, if you knew how much I *hope* so,' she breathed.

He looked pensively at the phone for a moment, a faint smile on his lips. 'Thanks. Look, on the subject of Letzer, we're getting desperate. The man's got no background at all. He's out of nowhere. We have to give Erskine something more to work on. Can you try to think of *anything* concrete he might ever have let drop to you about his background, however trivial?'

She pondered in silence for some time. 'Shit, Matt, I already told you, I can't remember him *ever* talking about himself. All he ever talked to me about was, you know, professional stuff.'

'Well, how the hell did you get to hear about him?'

'I didn't. That is, we met. At a seminar, a while after I arrived in the UK. He hadn't been here long himself. I guess we just hit it off.'

'Surely he must have talked about his qualifications, what gave him his interest in all that stuff?'

'Well, no, now I look back on it. I mean, I always took him at face value. You don't . . . you just don't question a colleague's bona fides. Not unless you have some *reason* to think he's bogus.' The two of them were silent for a moment and then she gave a soft,

ironic laugh. 'Which I didn't. Then! And when I *did*
see his diplomas and so on, stuck up on his office wall
– which I always thought was a pretty poor way to
impress the British, by the way – they seemed perfectly
genuine. Not from great schools, but okay.'

'They are genuine. Erskine's people have established
that. But he didn't acquire them until he was in his
thirties. What we want is something, anything, to give
us a handle on him prior to that.'

'Okay, Matt. I understand. If anything comes to
mind I'll give you a call.'

'Thanks. Bye.'

He was about to put down the phone when she said
in a small, almost shy voice. 'Are you doing anything
tonight? I thought, if you were on your own, maybe
I'd come over and . . . I could cook you dinner.'

He drew breath slowly. In recent days, as the time
had passed since Liz's departure, he had caught himself
feeling desperately lonely. Naomi was good company,
and attractive. Although thick-set, there was no suggestion of flabbiness about her. Her legs were slender,
her hands were beautifully made, with long, tapering
fingers. She just was not Liz. He smiled wryly. 'Better
not. Mark's here this evening. You know he still . . .
Well, apart from anything else, he . . . he misses Liz
too much. Some other time maybe.'

Matt let himself into the house, feeling a twinge of
disappointment at finding it in total darkness. Even
though it was long after midnight he had been hoping
Mark would still be up. Now that friends no longer
rang, now that Liz had gone, the house seemed very
silent and lonely. And tonight, coming from the meeting in Annie's office, there was good news from Roy
Erskine to share.

He went through to the library, opened the French

windows and stepped out onto the terrace. Beyond the stone balustrade that marked the limit of the terrace, the gently sloping lawn was pale in the light of a three-quarter moon, leading down to the beeches, at last coming into leaf to hide the cottage annexe. He stood for a full minute, breathing deeply, relishing the early spring air, impervious to its chill. Then, taking a few steps onto the grass, he slowly turned to gaze at the house, its every detail thrown into sharp relief by the moon. His eye roved slowly over the moon-silvered façade until it reached the window of the corridor serving the children's bedrooms. A soft light, a habit dating from when Camilla had been afraid of the dark, and which they had somehow never discarded, shone from it. Without warning, a steel band seemed to tighten around Matt's chest, making him cry out. He took two staggering steps and sat down heavily on the balustrade, his eyes still on the house, his face pinched with the poignancy of his memories. They came as single, separate images, etched in his mind with absolute clarity as though he were only now living them. Moments when he had hurried past that very window, rushing to attend a child's frightened call. Times when, finding one of them bolt upright in bed, fighting back unfinished nightmares, he would hold them on his knees, pressing them close, murmuring comfort until the terror subsided and he could tuck them back beneath the sheets, never having been fully awake. The loving resignation with which he had changed bed linen after they had been sick, gently quarantining tainted teddy bears for laundering, knowing that he would not get off to sleep again for hours, with disastrous effects on the following day's writing output. And in all these memories, he was always naked.

As an adult he had only ever owned one pair of pyjamas, retrieving them from the undisturbed depths of a drawer when he went to stay with friends. Now, as the images flooded his mind, Mark and Camilla, snuggled, trusting and innocent on his knees, he was overtaken by a wild sense of horror. Was it possible that those moments, for him some of the sweetest memories of the children's infant years, were the seed that Letzer had corrupted into Camilla's allegations?

The image of Camilla that came to him was so strong he could feel her in his arms once again, the limbs as thin as twigs, the tiny corrugations of her ribs, the tickle of her fine hair as it moved with his breath. The power of the image brought a sudden surge of helpless rage coursing through him. He came to his feet, groaning. 'Camilla!' He spoke the word aloud, pleading, a hand outstretched as though she had been standing before him. 'You sweet, perfect thing. Don't you understand? Whatever he's made you believe, I could *never* have hurt you.' His hand was trembling. His voice tailed off to a murmur. 'Not ever.'

'Who were you talking to?'

He spun, startled, to face the voice. His heart bounded as the familiar silhouette stepped from the shadow of a shrub into the moonlight. He started forward. 'Liz!'

As he made to embrace her she shifted her stance, turning so that his kiss glanced clumsily off the side of her head. 'I thought I heard you speaking to someone.'

He held her awkwardly for a moment and then let his arm fall from her waist. 'Myself,' he said, disappointed at her wariness. He tried a smile. 'Who else do I have?'

Liz let the silence lie for a moment. 'Naomi,' she said, looking away from him.

He laughed. 'Come on!'

Still with her face turned from him, Liz said, 'I drove

over last night. There were a few things I wanted to pick up . . . Her car was in the courtyard.'

'Naomi *was* here. That doesn't have to mean I'm sleeping with her.' He took her by the arm. 'For Christ's sake, Liz, we were working on the case, that's all.'

'Yes. Of course.' She took a step away from him, moving into a pool of shadow.

Frowning, Matt made as though to move to her side. Something in the set of her shoulders changed his mind. He spoke softly, fighting to keep the unease that showed in his eyes from spilling into his voice. 'The news is all good, Liz. Erskine's sidekick, Larry Guenther, has run the woman to earth, the one whose father killed himself.' He moved an involuntary step closer. 'Liz, her case fits mine *exactly*! She got along perfectly with her father until some therapist got his claws into her and got her to "remember" that her dad had abused her. Being American, she sued her father. He couldn't stand the shame. The poor bastard shot himself. A couple of months later the therapist left town, ripping her off for every penny her father had left her – three or four million *dollars*!' His voice fell to a husky whisper. 'Liz, after her shrink disappeared, the woman, Jill Stanakis is her name, found virtual *proof* her father never touched her. She checked out his old credit card accounts. He *couldn't* have done it. He just wasn't *there*. Not unless he was calculating his life to the second like some character out of an old Hitchcock picture, anyway. Real people might do that once in a blue moon, to commit murder, but not abuse.'

'What happened to her?' Liz asked in a drab, deadened voice.

'Drinking, pills, all sorts of stuff, spending whatever money she had left. She's damaged her sight with the junk, though she can still see a little. Now she only drinks. She's been living on what from Erskine's report sounds like some kind of commune, a throwback to the sixties.'

'But how does it help, Matt? If it all happened in America, and the woman's a drunk?'

'They're drying her out. Annie's planning to call her as, well, I guess you could call her a *really* expert witness, if they can keep her sober enough to be up to it. Apart from that, though, Tara Bailey has one of her people out there now talking to her. Apparently, the woman's *great* material. Tara's already lined up the *Guardian* for a major women's page piece. She's got the *Sunday Times* on the hook, too, but they're only really going to get serious if we can find the therapist as well.'

'And? Are Annie's detectives on that case, too?'

The edge of bitterness in her voice made him wince. 'They aren't *Annie's*, Liz. They're just the best. And yes, they *are* working on it. They're working on it like hell. We need that article. We need the jury to walk into court with as much doubt about Letzer and the whole idea of RMS as we can put into their heads.'

'They're working on her description of him, I suppose?'

He shrugged. 'Of course.' He laughed. 'I agree it's not much. A fat man with a beard. Long hair, five feet eleven, thick glasses.'

'And three million dollars of somebody else's money! Get real, Matt! Two weeks on a health farm and fifteen minutes with a barber and he already wouldn't be recognisable, let alone if he spent a hundred thousand dollars of what he stole on having his face altered.'

For a moment Matt was silent, his eyes closed, fists clenching as he took several deep breaths through his nose. 'I know all that, Liz, better than anyone. But if there is *any* chance it can help I want him run down.'

'But if he swindled the Stanakis woman, why would he testify openly in court? It would be asking for trouble.'

Matt threw up his hands. 'Maybe. But it all happened years ago. He could have blown it all by now.'

'You're planning to *pay* him for his testimony?'

He whirled away from her, his hands thrown wide in appeal. 'For Christ's sake, Liz, I'm looking at twenty odd *years*! What do you want me to be? More Catholic than the fucking *pope*?'

'Don't talk like that, please,' she said sharply. 'You know I hate it.'

'Sorry. But what the hell –'

She stepped forward, cutting him off with a raised hand. 'How much is this all costing, without bribes to witnesses, I mean? Just Annie, and Erskine, and Tara Bailey?'

He looked at her blankly for a moment, before running a hand through his hair. 'I was going to call you about that.' He bit his lip. 'There's been a lot of outlay. I think we're going to have to sell something. I was thinking about the BP shares.'

'It's going to be ruinous, isn't it?'

His shoulders rose and fell. 'Cash flow's tight. Not getting the advance from Anderson's didn't help.'

She looked down, avoiding his eyes. 'Matt, I don't want this to go any further. There's been enough damage. It's one thing to see Letzer rip off Camilla's own money. I'm not prepared to see the rest of the children's inheritance go down the drain.'

He stared at her, shocked. 'Down the drain? Liz, we're talking about proving that I'm *innocent*, for God's sake.'

She blinked back tears. 'I didn't mean it like that, Matt. But I was at Annie's office. The evidence they

235

have, Matt, what Camilla wrote . . . it's so . . .' She began sobbing noisily. 'It's so *damning*, to a court.'

He took her by the shoulders. 'No, Liz! You mustn't see it like that. Please.' His own voice caught. 'What did Annie tell you? Surely you can see *she* knows it's all been cooked up?'

'Annie's a loyal friend, there's no doubt about that. She's told me over and over that I shouldn't believe in it. I'm *trying* so hard, Matt, but I just don't want to see the whole family dragged down by it all.' She shook off his grip, sniffing back the tears. 'I just wish to God Letzer had accepted my proposal, so we could all try to put this behind us.'

He seized her by the arms, hard enough to make her grimace. 'Your proposal? What proposal?'

She swallowed hard. 'I let Naomi offer him money. To go away and leave us alone.'

Stunned, he let his arms drop loosely to his sides. 'Oh my God. Can you *picture* how that's going to look in court?'

Seventeen

Walking down the steps of the Chichester Crown
Court building, Matt felt as though he were reliving
the childhood nightmare in which he wanted to run
but his limbs moved in slow motion, as though mired
in treacle. The drumming of the blood in his head
blotted out Annie's words as she walked beside him,
tight-lipped and angry. The Plea and Directions hearing had been a disaster from its very first moments.

The judge assigned to the case, Justice Davies, was
somebody Annie had clashed with before. A fleshy
individual in his early sixties with a cultivated voice,
he had the chapped, ruddy face of a sailor and the
vein-hatched cheeks of an all-day drinker. He had been
curt with Annie's pleas for more time, dismissing out
of hand her submission that they needed more time to
develop background on Letzer, testily suggesting that
they could find out all they needed to know from Letzer
himself when he took the stand. Without any solid
evidence from Erskine to show to the court that might
have cast doubt on Letzer's potential reliability, Annie
was forced to climb down. Instead of the six-to-twelve-
month delay Annie had been confidently expecting, the
case had been listed for the third of September. The
nightmare would become reality far sooner than Matt
had been braced for. In a little under a hundred days
he would be standing in the dock.

Reaching Annie's car, he almost fell into his seat,
still in shock, the words still rolling inside his head like
thunder, the clerk reading the arraignment, his own

reply, strangely disembodied to his own ears, denying the charges. Annie's voice, insistent, obviously repeating something, brought him slowly out of his trance. 'Huh?'

'I said, I warned you to take a barrister. Davies *hates* the idea of solicitors pleading in the higher courts. He thinks we're subverting the system.' She smiled wryly. 'And the system must be perfect, because it gave us him!'

He tried to smile in return. 'I wouldn't have believed it. The chauvinistic old fart.'

She inclined her head. 'But legally, he didn't put a foot wrong, unfortunately. Now, do you want to go home and sit in the car with a hosepipe to the exhaust, or come with me to the office and see what's new?'

He sighed. 'Let's go to the office. There's nothing to go home for. We *were*, or, at least, Liz was supposed to be hosting the British Heart Foundation lunch.'

'What happened? Did she call it off?'

'Not Liz. The committee. They decided that, after four years, an eleven-acre field wasn't enough parking space. They decided to hold it at Theo Seton's place.'

'Seton? Didn't they buy Jean Leighton's house, over at Cardley?'

'That's them. His father's Hugh Seton, of Seton and Starck, the estate agents.'

'It's a nice house, but there's no parking at *all*.'

'No.' He turned to look at her. 'You know what's most depressing about it? Dick Field is on that committee. He didn't even have the guts to call and tell me, or at least Liz.' He laughed and touched her arm. 'Don't quit now, Annie. You're the only friend we have left.'

Her fleeting attempt at a smile faded abruptly. 'How is Liz? Have you seen her? Is she showing any signs of coming round? I tried to make her understand, Matt.

As hard as I could, without . . .' She broke off, blinking.

'I know. I appreciate it.' He spoke without taking his eyes from the road. 'She comes over to see Mark. I . . . I make myself scarce.' His shoulders rose and fell. 'She's still got a lot of stuff of her own to work out. Being away so much, when the children were young. She's very . . . vulnerable about that.'

'I never understood how she could. To keep going off and leaving you alone like that, with the children. I could never have . . .'

'Perhaps it was different for you, Annie, with William . . .' He let the sentence trail away. 'And you didn't need to travel for your career.' He flicked a glance at her, taking in the clenched jaw, the solid grip of her hands on the wheel. 'And then, to be fair to Liz, for quite a while back there I didn't encourage her to give it up.'

Briefly, both were silent, letting the memories stir like mist around them. 'What are you going to do, Matt, when this is all over?' she said at last. 'Assuming you still have a choice,' she added, forcing a bright, momentary grin.

With his head pressed against the headrest, just out of her line of vision, he slowly turned to look obliquely at her. 'I want Liz back, Annie,' he said, his voice rasping in his throat. 'I want that more than anything else in the world.'

He saw her lips come tightly together, saw the bobbing in her throat as she swallowed, the tightening of her fingers on the steering wheel. Almost imperceptibly, she nodded. 'I'll move heaven and earth to help you have her,' she whispered. 'I promise you that.'

The days after the hearing seemed to pass in slow motion, taking on a surreal, meaningless quality, each indistinguishable from the one before, as though

Matt's mind refused to accept that with each day the trial grew closer. The day began at six, when he would rouse Mark and the two of them would swim, carving through the water in silent companionship for eighty or a hundred lengths before making themselves gargantuan breakfasts which they would eat on the terrace, enveloped in hooded bathrobes.

Matt treasured these moments. Mark must have been having almost as bad a time as himself. At school he must be an object of pity and curiosity. Quite a few friends had backed away. Jane was still loyal but their contact was reduced to snatched moments at weekends when she was able to slip her parents' leash. Despite Matt's pleas for Liz, Mark was hurt and confused by his mother's departure. Yet, through it all, he refused to admit the strain, anxious not to add to his father's load. He had become the last remaining fixed point in Matt's life.

Once Mark had departed to catch the school bus Matt would force himself into the study with the intention of working. Most days, though, he fell into a purposeless lethargy, dumping the hate mail, less of it lately, but still as obscene and deranged, into the bin, or rearranging the objects on his desk while the screen of the word processor stared blankly at him from across the room. The phone hardly rang at all now. When it did it was usually to cancel a long-standing invitation. The press interest had waned, too, no doubt a lull before the trial began. The film deal with Kowalski was stone dead. And, since Anderson's had backed away from the new book, no other publisher, in the UK or America, had shown a glimmer of interest. Even Andy had given up calling, his empty words of support all used up. Unless and until Matt could be proven innocent he was professionally a dead man. The few items that still came in from the cuttings service were occasional pieces psychoanalysing his work, purporting to analyse the perverted mentality that had created it.

Every couple of days he drove up to London to sit in with Annie, catching up on how things were going. Even there, though, he had the sense of being the odd man out, drinking endless cups of coffee in her office as she busily fielded calls from the people she had employed to travel the country interviewing and re-interviewing the string of expert witnesses she had lined up, repeatedly treading the same ground, trying to ensure that no potentially damaging detail was missed, no useful angle of attack left unexplored.

In America, Erskine had reached an impasse. Jill Stanakis had had a setback, somehow evading the team of nurses Erskine had on round-the-clock supervision and getting her hands on enough booze to reduce her once more to a stumbling, incoherent wreck. Hampton, the long-haired slob of a shrink, had dis-appeared off the face of the earth, along with Jill's three and a half million dollars. The woman who had fronted the real estate scam from an office rented by the hour, paid in cash, had most likely gone with him, leaving them with nothing more than a name, Bea Henderson, which appeared in no public record, and Jill's description of her as 'a red-headed bitch'.

Mid-morning, well into the second week since the hear-ing, Matt was jerked awake at his desk by the ringing of the phone. By the time he rubbed some feeling back into his face and reached for the loudspeaker button the answering machine had already kicked in, Liz's chipper tone coming to him with the unreal quality of film dialogue heard from behind a closed door. 'Hello,' he interrupted, still massaging his eyes. 'This is Matt Stenner.'

At the first sound of Roy Erskine's nasal twang he was instantly wide awake. 'Roy!' He was almost shouting into the phone. 'What's new?'

'Hello, Matt. How are you? Seems a while since we spoke.' Erskine's careful, low-key courtesy jabbed at some sensitive spot within Matt. It was as though even this man, who was sending him bills for hundreds of thousands of dollars, was having to watch his tongue for fear of letting show his deep-down sense that Matt was guilty.

'I'm fine,' Matt said, openly impatient. 'Do you *have* anything?'

'Well,' Roy said imperturbably, 'Jill seems to be doing better. She hasn't had a drink for four days. The girls taking care of her tell me she's managing to eat without sticking the fork in her eye. Anyway, your PR people seem to have done a good job getting her story out of her.'

'Hampton, Roy? Have you picked up any trace of that bastard?'

Roy laughed. 'I don't know. That Bailey woman's giving me a lot of flak over him, too. You've got a good outfit there, Matt. If I ever get in trouble I hope I'll be able to afford help like that myself.'

'I hope so, too, Roy,' Matt answered leadenly. 'Did you find Hampton?'

'Well, that's what I called you about. Larry found a friend with access to airline computers. The day after Hampton collected the money, *somebody*, using the name Green, bought two tickets to Fort Worth, Texas, paying cash. A couple of hours later, a Mr and Mrs *Harrison* bought tickets from Fort Worth to Monterrey, Mexico. They also paid cash. I don't have to tell you that paying cash for an airline ticket these days is a *most* unusual event.'

Matt was on his feet now, the phone pressed hard

against his ear. 'And you're telling me they're Hampton and the Henderson woman?'

'You said it, Matt, not me.'

Excitement flooded through Matt. 'You must have checked, for Christ's sake? Does anyone remember them?'

'We checked. It was years ago.' The hopeless note in Roy's voice told him the rest, dousing his excitement.

'So what now?'

'That's my question to you. You want us to fly down to Monterrey?'

'On the next available flight.'

Roy hesitated. 'This is, ah, getting expensive, Matt. We've got three nurses round the clock, on eight-hour shifts, just looking after Jill.'

'Roy, please, just get on the plane. That bastard could be the best chance I've got.'

'Sure, Matt. Larry and I were planning to fly down first thing in the morning.' Again he hesitated. 'Ah, look, Matt, you're in the papers again, you know?'

Matt frowned. A ball the size of his fist formed in his stomach. 'No! Which papers? Why?'

'Well, I guess it's a little early for your cuttings service to have reached you. It's a couple of the super-market tabloids we have here. They're saying the Christian Coalition have been studying your stuff.' Erskine chuckled, half apologetically. 'You probably hadn't realised it, but you're doing the devil's work.' The chuckle went out of his voice. 'They're calling for a boycott of stores that sell your books.'

Matt groaned. 'Oh shit!'

'You said it, Matt,' Roy answered emphatically. 'I've seen what this kind of thing can do. Does Bailey have an office over here? I'd say you might need some heavy-duty public relations help.'

'Thanks for the advice, Roy. I'll talk to my agent if he's still taking my calls!'

'Yeah, I would. In fact, I'd be surprised if you didn't hear from him as soon as they wake up on the West Coast. He could be in for quite a hit, too, I guess. These fundamentalists may look like a bunch of assholes from over there in Britain. But they can still get you delisted by every major chain store in the USA.' Roy hesitated again. 'Ah, look, Matt, no offence, but we're looking at a lot of outlay here. You know, the nurses for Jill, now Mexico, and all. Do you think you could . . .'

'How much do you want, Roy?' Matt asked with steely resignation.

Roy laughed, unembarrassed. 'Well, say a hundred thousand dollars? That would bring you up to date with, say, fifty thousand to spare as an advance.'

Matt ran a hand through his dishevelled hair. 'Give me till the middle of next week, I'll get it transferred.'

'Fine. Sorry to be –'

'Forget it. I appreciate your being upfront with me. Bye, Roy.' He was about to hang up when an afterthought stopped him. 'Hey, Roy, by the way, did you tell this to Annie? About Hampton? She'll be damned glad to hear it.'

'I tried. She wasn't answering on the mobile. She didn't show at the office this morning, either. I wondered if maybe she was sick. Wish us luck down South America way.'

Matt rang off and stood leaning on the phone, frowning. A moment later he took it up again and started dialling.

'Annie Trevellyn, please. This is Matthew Stenner.'

'Mr Stenner, I'm afraid Annie hasn't been into the office yet today,' the familiar brisk voice told him.

'Well, can you tell me where I can get hold of her? I've tried her home and her mobile. Neither of them is answering.'

'I know, Mr Stenner. I'm sorry. We had a call from Annie a few minutes ago. She's at the hospital.'

'Huh?' Matt pressed the phone closer to his ear. 'What's happened? Is she –'

'Not Annie, Mr Stenner. Her son.'

'William! What's the matter? He's not ... what's wrong with him?'

'I can't tell you much, Mr Stenner. A kidney problem, Annie said.'

There was a hollow where Matt's stomach should have been. William's face, radiant with his characteristic smile, the trusting, adoring eyes, filled his vision. He could feel the bony hand in his, see the rapture in the boy's face as they swam together, Matt gently supporting his shoulders as William paddled with frail arms, his afflicted legs trailing uselessly. Like every other parent of a spina bifida victim, Annie had lived in unspoken fear of the sudden, irretrievable kidney failure that could snatch her child from her. 'Did she say how serious it was?'

'Not really.' The receptionist's own voice cracked. 'But she sounded terribly upset. Not herself at all.'

Roy Erskine grunted as he emerged from the rented car and the Mexican sun struck like scalding liquid across his shoulders. He wished they could have held off until evening, but Matt Stenner needed information in a hurry. As long as he could keep on putting up the money they owed it to him to do their damnedest. After buying the information about the car smash from a desk clerk at the rental office at Monterrey airport they had driven straight down, which timed their arrival for the hottest part of the day. Fanning himself, he came around the car to where Larry Guenther and the policeman were already crouching by the trunk of a tree, examining a place in the bark where it had healed into fat lips over a weal.

'This where they hit?' Larry asked, fingering the wound.

The policeman shrugged and waved vaguely at the flat coastal plain. 'I was not here then. But there aren't so many trees. They were real unlucky, I guess.'

Roy looked around him. The road was a potholed strip running parallel to the coast, petering out at a cluster of fishermen's shacks in the hazy distance. Eastward, separated from them by a thin sand bar, was the gleaming blue of the Gulf. 'Anyone witness the accident?' he asked.

The policeman tapped the dog-eared folder under his arm. 'You saw. The lady reported the accident. It was evening.' He gestured again. 'Out here would be pretty dark. No people.'

'The report says the car caught fire, right?' The Mexican nodded. Roy squinted back down the road to the smudge that was La Santa. 'So she could walk the six or seven kilometres back to the hotel, but she couldn't get her boyfriend clear?'

The policeman shrugged. 'Have you been close to a burning car? It can be very frightening.'

'Maybe,' Roy answered distractedly, chewing at his lip. 'Apart from the woman's story,' he asked off-handedly, 'was there any proof of the victim's identity?'

'His passport, señor,' the policeman said with a flash of resentment.

Larry caught Roy's eye. 'But the car burned out?' he asked quietly.

The policeman jutted his lower lip. 'Probably it was in his coat. It was a convertible. Most likely he had taken his coat off and it was thrown out. You see strange things in car smashes, shoes found forty metres from the crash, that kind of thing.'

'Mmm. Can I take another look?' Roy took the folder and pulled out a black and white photograph of the wreck. He mused for a while in silence before wordlessly handing it to Larry while he ferreted again in the folder. 'No picture of the Henderson woman?' The policeman shrugged. 'Would there be anybody around who might remember her?'

'Not police. Nobody has been here that long. You could try the hotel.'

'Thanks, Chief. We will.'

The silver BMW turned into the hospital entrance, beneath the overhead 'Visitor' sign, and slotted into the car park. As Camilla reached for the door handle, Steve Letzer gripped the other arm. 'I still don't think this is a good idea. It could easily upset you.'

Camilla looked down at his fingers, which bit uncomfortably into her flesh, and then into his face. Her smile was strained. 'I know, but take my word for it, Stephen, I'm strong enough.' Twisting from the waist she leaned over and quickly planted a kiss on his pursed lips. 'Thanks to you!'

'You can't know how strong you are! And anyway, I want you to save yourself for the trial. You'll need every bit of your strength for that, believe me.'

She opened the door. 'Stephen, William's like our brother. Mark and I used to take him for rides on our ponies. Daddy would spend *hours* with him in the pool.'

He caught the look that came into her eyes and again reached to restrain her. 'You see! You can't tell what damage it might do. It's a terrible mistake.'

Firmly, she shook his hand off. 'Sorry, Stephen. I *have* to.'

He sat slumped in his seat as she swung herself from the car, his fingers drumming on the rim of the steering wheel.

'Please, darling, listen to me,' he said. 'Your mother should never have told you about him. *You're* still as sick as he is, even if you don't want to believe it any more. It's a trap. They *wanted* you to feel like this, to be reminded of a part of the past you can't help treasuring. Can't you see they're taking *advantage* of your sweet nature?' He hammered on the wheel with a clenched fist. 'I wish to God I'd never even told you about her call. I bet your father's behind this!'

She looked at him doubtfully. 'William being ill?'

'Of course not that. I'm sure the boy's sick. But your father could have put your mother up to calling the clinic. It's just another example of how manipulative he is, hoping to weaken your resolve so that you'll abandon the whole thing, let him off scot-free.'

She reached in and stroked his cheek. 'Trust me, darling, please. Seeing William won't change the way I feel. If I hadn't visited and if anything . . . You *do* understand, don't you?'

'Bullshit, Camilla. The boy's not dying! It's just another ploy.'

Her eyes clouded. 'Stephen! Mummy wouldn't do that. I'm not saying he *is* dying. But William has a long history of kidney trouble. His kidneys can only just cope. When he gets these attacks anything can happen.' Her eyes glistened. 'Sorry, darling, but I could never forgive myself.'

'Okay,' he said surlily. 'I'll come with you. Unless you don't want me there.'

She smiled through the incipient tears. 'Walk with

me to the reception, at least. Maybe you had better not come onto the ward.'

Roy Erskine stared into the shimmering haze, plucking at his sweat-darkened shirt in morose silence as Larry drove back to town, weaving gingerly over rutted asphalt that shone as though watered in the heat. The police chief's car was already lost to sight before Larry spoke.

'You thinking what I'm thinking?'

'I guess I am.'

'But, surely . . .' Larry gestured towards the smudge of dust that marked the passage of the police car. 'Wouldn't somebody have reported a disappearance? Wouldn't they have made the connection?'

Roy let his shirt fall back against his chest with a light slapping sound and jerked his hand at the nondescript dun hills that rose to their right. 'Come on, Larry. It's your first time down here. Over there they grow just about everything the complete drug user needs: coke, dope, magic mushrooms, peyote. Hundreds of kids, and not only kids, come down here to try stuff. And buy it.' He gestured to the opposite side of the car. 'That lagoon runs a hundred miles north, to the Boca Jesus Maria. From there it's around a hundred miles to the Texas coast. You want a vagrant, American size, American dentistry, that nobody in the world would miss. La Santa would be the place to look.'

Larry was silent for a long moment before he jerked a thumb over his shoulder, towards the United States. 'So you think Hampton's . . . ?'

Roy shrugged. 'As long as Stenner puts up the money, I think we owe it to him to keep on looking.'

The two nurses entered William's room, moving purposefully. Without ceremony, one of them interposed herself between Camilla and William and began busying herself with the bedclothes, talking to William as she worked with the noncommittal good humour of the profession. Camilla rose slowly, hardly able to bear to take her eyes from William's face.

Always pale, it was now an unnatural, milky white, the skin at the temples translucent. Wisps of thin, mousy hair stuck to his forehead. His eyes, normally glittering with mischief, were fixed lifelessly on the ceiling. She stooped to give a final readjustment to the flowers she had brought and scooped her small shoulder bag from the floor. 'Bye, William.' She reached down to take the hand that lay like a small, undernourished animal on the blanket. A tube, fastened to the shaved arm by a square of sticking plaster, ran to an anodyne grey box half hidden beneath the bed, the dialysis machine which had hauled William back from the brink. Blinking hard, Camilla bent and kissed him on the cheek. His eyes flickered an instant to her face before sliding back to resume staring at the ceiling. The pressure of his fingers was so faint that she was on the point of concluding she had imagined it when, about to turn away, she saw his jaw muscles clench with effort. Painfully slowly, his eyes slid back to meet hers. Then, without warning, he grinned. Although it lasted only a fraction of a second, it was the old grin, illuminating the room, the one that had captivated them for twelve years, which had won all their hearts, most of all her father's.

A sniff tangled in Camilla's throat, turning into an animal sound that became a sob. 'Get well,' she whispered. 'I'll come and see you again in a few days. I promise.' With another urgent squeeze of his hand, she wheeled and ran headlong from the room.

As she hurried, stumbling, along the corridor, clawing a tissue from her bag, pressing it to her smarting eyes, the image of the pale face, lit by that sudden generous grin, filled her consciousness, choking her. Since William's birth, herself still a child, she had understood that his life would be short. *How* short was a question she had never wanted to confront. She had never even really seen him as handicapped, accepting his incapacities in the context of his loving, outgoing nature. Learning from Liz, when she had returned her call, of his illness, and Annie's deep fear of a final, catastrophic kidney failure, she had understood for the first time. It might not be this time. It might not be the next. But each time the damage to his kidneys grew. William was doomed.

'Hello, Camilla.'

She froze, even her crying silenced.

'Sorry. Did I shock you?' The voice was a deep, gentle murmur. 'I didn't mean to. I was just going in to see William.'

Camilla's head came up slowly, her mind fighting for focus. Still too stunned to register more than dumb disbelief, she staggered a half-step backwards, as though she had been struck. 'Daddy!' In her surprise, a look of unforced, instinctive pleasure lit her face.

Matt had already started to move towards her, his hands raised to embrace her, when Camilla's smile was wiped away, replaced by shock, confusion, and then bitter indignation. 'What do you mean . . . ? How *dare* you!'

Matt fell back, his arms still outstretched. He stared at them with a curious, bereft expression and then let them fall to hang slackly at his sides.

'I *told* Mummy I was coming!' She almost spat the words at him. 'Didn't she *tell* you, for God's sake?'

'Yes,' he mumbled. 'She told me.' He spoke without taking his eyes from her, drinking in the sight of her body, lithe but no longer stick-thin beneath the loose

T-shirt, the trim, boyish legs below crumpled linen shorts. He opened his mouth to say more but no sound came, his throat swollen and constricted. Swallowing, he tried again. 'I knew ... it's not Mummy's fault. I ...' The inaudible words died again as he clamped his hands to his face. 'I couldn't help it. Sorry, darling. You ... you look well.' Without warning, he began to cry, as loud and uninhibited as a child. He pawed in his pocket for a handkerchief. 'I didn't mean anything ... I just had to *see* you.' The usually rich, deep voice was harsh, ragged with pain. 'Just *see* you.'

Camilla stood transfixed, watching dumbly as the big tears swelled and broke, skidding down his cheeks. Despite her fury she felt her own throat tighten. She clenched her fists, driving her nails deep into the flesh of her palms. She swallowed noisily, and tried to blink away the renewed stinging in her eyes. 'You knew! You did this to me *deliberately*!'

A spark of hope kindled in Matt's eyes. Deep beneath the anger and reproach in her voice he fancied he detected something else, too: a faint echo of mourning for a happier past. He dragged the back of a hand across his eyes. 'I just thought ... Oh God, darling. I don't know *what* I thought. Just if maybe I could *talk* to you, you would know that –'

'No!' She uttered the word under her breath and yet it held the hard-edged violence of a scream, making him recoil. 'I can't *believe* you could resort to this. Using poor William! I can't ... I can't ...' She broke again into crying, her whole body quaking with each sob. 'Can't believe you could be so ... obvious!' She broke into a run, lashing out blindly with an arm as she went, striking her father across the chest.

He took a few involuntary steps after her as she fled down the corridor and disappeared through the swing doors.

His eyes were still fixed on the wildly swinging doors, his face grieving, when they again flew open and Stephen Letzer burst into view. He ran three steps into the corridor and stopped dead. The fury in his face gradually gave way to a deep frown as he took in Matt's distraught, devastated face, glistening, in the harsh strip lighting, with unabated tears. The frown in turn faded, giving way to a sneer.

'God, Stenner, there's nothing you won't stoop to, is there?'

Letzer's eyes were filled with deep contempt. Matt, unblinking behind the tears, seemed to stare through Letzer, through the flapping doors, as though he were still seeing Camilla's narrow, athletic back receding ever further from him. Slowly, Matt blinked. For one negligent instant, his eyes focused on Letzer's face. Then, as though not even recognising the man, he turned and, the tears still falling, strode away towards William's room.

Matt sat with his head cupped in the splayed fingers of one hand. He held a plastic coffee cup in the other hand, staring into it as he mechanically swirled the cold dregs. Since the previous day's encounter with Camilla, his mind had been in a constant turmoil. He had spent the entire night pacing the library, drinking coffee and tumblers of brandy, numbly willing dawn to arrive. A swim with Mark had offered a brief respite. Then, after a morning's disastrous work, too dizzy and wretched to drive but too disturbed to want to spend the rest of the day in the house alone, he had taken the train to London and come to Annie's office.

At the sound of the door opening, he looked up, his eyes smarting and his head throbbing. Annie closed the door.

'Sorry to keep you hanging around. Three days out of the office leaves a lot of catching up to do.' She dropped a heap of ribbon-bound folders onto a chair and sat heavily on her seat. She looked at him with widening eyes. 'God, you look a mess.'

He sat straighter. 'I feel worse. You giving me a going-over for daring to see my daughter didn't help cheer me up.'

'It wasn't meant to. It was a *stupid* thing to do! Really crass. Don't you think I have enough on my plate in this case?' With tense, angry gestures, she opened a drawer and pulled out a document and tossed it onto the desk in front of him. 'Look!'

He squinted at it. 'What is it?'

'Read it. It came in this morning. It's additional evidence. They've tracked down the au pair, Kristina Olsen.' She jabbed a finger at the document. 'The second sheet. Her statement. *Read* it!'

Pulling himself together with an effort, Matt flipped over the top page and started reading. When he had finished he looked slowly up at Annie. 'Oh fuck,' he groaned.

Annie reached and took back the paper. 'My own thoughts entirely. Just what we needed. She remembers coming down to the kitchen at six in the morning and walking in on you.' She dropped her forehead into her hand and gave a despairing sigh that was almost a laugh. 'With no clothes on. And a fresh scratch on your back.' She raised her head wearily. 'As you said,' she murmured unemphatically, 'fuck.'

Matt let several seconds pass before speaking again. 'How's William?'

'There are no guarantees. The dialysis seems to be doing the trick.' She paused. 'This time.' Her hands flew to her face, her fingertips pinching hard at the bridge of her nose.

Matt let the silence hang for a while before asking, 'How's Roger taking it?'

'He's okay. Upset. But, you know Roger.' She gave a quick, ambiguous smile. 'His job keeps him busy.' She looked directly into his face. 'You know how Roger is, Matt. He loves William . . . in his way.' Her hands flew once more to her face.

'Would you . . . stay? If . . .'

Annie's abruptly raised hand made him falter. 'Matt, let me just deal with William. One thing at a time. Please.' She straightened, giving him a sudden, brittle smile as she took up the witness statement. She held it out, dangling over the drawer. 'My offer still stands, Matt. Nothing changes that.'

He gave a barely perceptible shake of his head. 'Thanks, anyway.'

Shrugging, she dropped the document and slammed the drawer shut. She stood up, glancing at her watch. 'Come on, if you want a lift. I promised William I'd be there by seven thirty.'

As Annie threaded her way through the tail end of the rush hour, Matt sat with his head pressed back against the leather, his stinging eyes closing, drifting in and out of sleep. Asleep or awake, his mind raced, a jostling garish nightmare of images of past and future. Annie had as good as told him that whatever happened to William in the short term, she and Roger were finished. She was prepared to testify and take her chances on William's reaction. Maybe she had already spoken to the boy, had some private reason to believe her relationship with him could survive the revelation. But it made no difference. Asking Annie to testify was impossible.

A familiar scene played in his mind: the dinner party where they had all met, just after Annie and Roger had moved in. By the end of the evening Liz had known that she and Annie would be friends. However, on the short drive home she had brought up the subject of Annie's attractiveness, harrying at the subject, at once anxious for and yet fearful of some more definite response than his noncommittal grunts. Already on that first evening, long before any inkling had dawned in his own mind that he was going to let himself fall for Annie, Liz had been on guard, instinctively wary of her dark beauty and quick mind.

Often, as her own friendship with Annie grew, she would return to the subject, picking at it, as though the current building between Matt and Annie somehow set some alarm ringing deep within her. And, of course, in answer to her question whether he found Annie attractive he would roar with laughter and say yes. Only slowly did he become aware that he was no longer pretending.

Liz laughed with him. But over the years, long after his affair with Annie had faded to a distant memory, she had continued to ask. And each repeated question, his every ironic denial, increased the scale of his treachery. From the first days of their relationship it had been clear, though unspoken, between them that they were totally faithful to each other. He would have found Liz's adultery intolerable. The few months with Annie were the only infidelity he had ever committed in their marriage. But, to Liz, he was afraid it would be unforgivable.

The sudden yawing of the car brought Matt awake. There was an instant of bemusement before he realised they had just turned into the courtyard of the house. Straightening, he glanced at his watch. 'Do you want a drink? There's time, if you don't have to be at the hospital for forty minutes.' He caught the grim set of

Annie's face and turned to look around him. He had missed Naomi's black Golf, parked in the shade of a clump of shrubs.

'You probably prefer to be on your own,' Annie said, smiling frostily.

He shook his head. 'Annie, I didn't even know she was going to be here. Come on. You have plenty of time.'

Annie checked her own watch and sighed. 'Ten minutes. Just time for some decent tea instead of the dishwater they serve at the hospital.'

In the kitchen Naomi, wearing Matt's apron, turned to greet them. Matt hastily covered his surprise with a polite gesture of enthusiasm. Seeing Matt's appreciative sniff, she gestured, smiling, to the stove. 'I couldn't get you on the phone so I spoke to Liz. She agreed it was time you and Mark had a square meal. Are you staying, Annie? There's plenty.'

Annie shook her head sharply. 'No, thanks. I'm on my way to see William.'

The smile fell from Naomi's face. 'God, yes. How is he?'

Annie's smile lasted only a fraction of a second. 'Thanks. Improving.' She looked around at Matt. 'Shall I make some tea?' Stepping past Naomi she began filling the kettle.

'Where's Mark?' Matt asked.

Naomi pursed her lips. 'Upstairs, I think. I'm sorry, he just doesn't seem to want to –'

Matt cut her off with a nod and strode to the stairs. 'Mark!' he bellowed. 'I'm home. And Annie's here.' He turned back to Naomi and shrugged. 'Believe me, I've tried.'

She was about to answer when the telephone rang. Matt was across the room and on it before the second ring.

'Hello? Matt?' At the sound of Erskine's nasal twang, he flipped on the loudspeaker and put down the handset. 'Roy? How are you? I just got in. Annie's with me.'

'Yeah. Look, we're still in Mexico.'

Matt exchanged a puzzled look with Annie. 'Why? Annie told me you found where Hampton died.'

'Might have died, Matt. Might have.'

'Or might *not* have?'

'Well, *somebody* did.'

'No games, Roy. Just spell it out.'

'Look, officially Hampton died in a car smash here. There was a body, there was identification. Except that he was driving a convertible Beetle, and he hit the tree at, at my guess, no more than fifteen miles an hour. He should have walked away, unless he was spaced out, or drunk. Also, it's hard to see why the car would have caught fire.' Static crackled in the pause. 'Unless somebody lit a match.'

'Roy, are you saying he was *killed*?' Annie's voice rose in disbelief as she strode to stand at Matt's shoulder.

'All I'm saying so far is that the old policeman in me doesn't like what he sees.'

While Roy had been speaking Mark had appeared in the doorway, his face sullen. Now, his face lit up as he ran to his father's side. 'Dad! This is incredible! If Hampton's still out there, all they have to do is find him!'

Matt laid an arm distractedly around his shoulders. 'Yeah. You hear that, Roy? That's all you have to do,' he called, smiling. 'Seriously, Roy, Tara Bailey will be baying for him. If you can give us Hampton she's pretty sure she's got some people at Channel Four who would run with it.'

'Yeah. Well, don't bet the deeds of the plantation

yet. There's something else, though. We talked to an old boy that used to work in the local hotel. He remembered them, Hampton and Henderson. They used to schlep a fancy document case around with them all the time. Cartier, or some big name like that, he thinks it was. Anyway, whatever it was it seemed too good for their clothes. Never seemed to put it down, even by the cesspit they call a swimming pool. Then, the night she checks out, she slams it on the desk and opens it, and he sees it's full of cash. One reason he remembers, it was the first time he'd ever seen what he thought was a female drug capo. Can you imagine? One of those pilot-type cases, stuffed with American currency. *Millions!*'

'Yeah. Jill's millions,' Matt murmured.

Annie leaned forward. 'Roy, did he give you a decent description of *her*?'

'Nope. A gringa, for sure. Big shoulders. Big hair. Maybe a redhead. Tallies with Jill's description, but no improvement.'

'And the man?'

'Fat. Hippy type, long hair, tall. No beard, but maybe he shaved it. A beard down here would be hot as hell. A funny thing, though, her boyfriend had been killed two hours earlier and she wasn't even red-eyed. He remembers being surprised. Christ, he was more upset than she was. She was kind of edgy, looking at her watch all the time, as if she was waiting for some kind of connection, but definitely no grief.'

Matt could not keep the excitement from his voice. 'How about luggage? Did he help her with it? Did he see who she left with?'

'No luggage. She left her stuff lying in the room. Just this big red buckskin briefcase with the money. Somebody came by for her in a little sports car. He couldn't give me the make. Sounds like it could be an

MGB, something like that. He swears the driver was a man, though.'

'Roy,' Annie asked, her voice neutral, 'what's *your* theory, so far?'

'It's only speculation, Annie, but try this: Hampton's just ripped off over three million dollars. For that sort of money Jill might even have been pissed off enough to put out a contract on him. So, he needs to disappear. What better way than to be officially dead. There are plenty of drifters down here, Americans, no known relatives, looking for a meal ticket. The couple buy one of them a few drinks, run the car into a tree, sit him at the wheel and torch the whole thing, leaving Hampton's ID handily undamaged nearby. The police here aren't looking for trouble. No proper autopsy is done. The perpetrators have fresh identities already set up. Hampton spends six weeks working out, loses forty pounds, gets a haircut, his own mother wouldn't know him. They're in the clear to go off and spend the money.'

Annie nodded, smiling sardonically. 'Sounds neat. Any idea where you go from here?'

Roy gave a bitter laugh. 'I was afraid you'd ask that. From Texas to Florida must be fifteen hundred miles. A zillion places they could come ashore from a boat and disappear into the blue.'

Matt pounded a fist into his palm. 'We *have* to find them. We can't get this far and just let it fizzle out. If we can find him, Tara Bailey can really get to work. Between his story and Jill's she could change the whole climate around this case! How about his old haunts in California? Surely a man can't just walk away from his past without leaving *some* clue where he's gone? Mail forwarding? *Some* damned thing!'

Roy's sigh was audible. 'I feel for you, Matt. In fact, Larry's already on his way up there. Don't hold your breath, though. It's all a pretty long shot. Our friend Hampton really worked this thing out.'

For some seconds after Roy rang off the four of them remained silent. Annie was the first to break the spell.

'Don't set your heart on it, Matt. Even if they find him, we can't really expect him to admit what he's done. Tara can certainly use it from a public relations angle, but it won't help the case directly.'

He gave her a crooked smile. 'Directly or indirectly, am I in a position to be fussy?' He let out a short, sour laugh. 'Who knows, maybe he's pissed away Jill's money by now. People like him are chancers. They don't invest in government stock and get by on the interest. I'll bet you that by now that briefcase is empty. He's probably desperately trawling for his next victim.'

'Maybe, Matt.' Annie looked at her watch and began to withdraw. 'I'm late. Bye, Naomi.' She was turning to leave when Matt's words, soft but quite distinct, made her spin back again.

'It was Gucci.'

'Huh?'

'The briefcase. It wasn't Cartier. It was Gucci.'

Naomi's eyes narrowed instantly to slits as she studied Matt's face, watching the muscles work beneath the skin as he struggled, against overwhelming fatigue, to string his thoughts together.

'Oh my God!' Naomi's hand flew to her mouth. 'Stephen!'

Eighteen

Matt was the first to react. He began laughing, a finger extended towards Naomi. 'That's it! You just beat me to it! An office decked out like a social security office and a briefcase like that. I remember thinking at the time it must have cost more than the bastard's clothes!' He struck the table with the side of his fist. 'Of course. He *is* doing it again, just as I said. He's using Camilla, exactly the way he used Jill!'

Annie looked at her watch and came to stand close enough to him that her leg brushed his thigh. 'Matt, I *have* to go. Will you call Roy back?'

Matt took her hand and stood up. He kissed her lightly on the cheek. 'I'm going to. Right now.'

Her face was sombre. 'It's still not *evidence*. You realise that, don't you? A shared taste in expensive briefcases won't prove anything to a court. I'll talk to Roy tomorrow, but meanwhile what we need him to do is to use what we just found out to get us some *admissible* material, stuff that I can use to discredit Letzer. If we can show the court that one of their prime witnesses is an impostor with a track record, we're home and dry.'

Naomi stepped towards them, her arm linked through Mark's. 'There's something else. Those figurines he keeps on his desk. I remember him *telling* me they were Mexican. He bragged about how valuable they were, what a great deal he had got. He must have bought them when he was down there, with the money he stole.'

'It might help me rattle him but it still isn't proof. For that, we are going to have to rely on Roy.' Annie looked at Matt. 'It's more expense . . .'

'I have to talk to Liz. There's some BP stock I was thinking of selling. Don't worry. There are assets,' he said with a self-mocking laugh. 'Just that with the boy-cott, not getting the advance from the Kowalski deal . . . or any *other* advances, while this business is hanging over me.' He grinned at each of them. 'You'll both get your money. Or do you want to play safe like Roy, and ask for it upfront?'

Naomi hurried to reassure him. 'God, Matt, it's not that. Money can wait. It's *you* I'm worried about. This must be costing you a fortune.'

He shrugged. 'What do you want me to do? Spend the next twenty years in a cell, gloating over how much I'm saving on groceries?'

She looked down, chewing her lip. 'No, but . . . Oh hell, let's just leave it to Annie's detectives, and hope they come up with something useful.'

Dinner finished, Mark rose and carried his plate across to the dishwasher. 'Thanks, Naomi. That was great.'

In the middle of making coffee, she turned to face him. 'Thank you, Mark. Do you want any of this?'

'Not for me. I'm going to go to bed.'

Naomi hesitated an instant and then stepped forward and kissed him on the cheek. He did not move away. 'Sleep well, Mark. And thanks.'

She watched the door close behind him before turning to Matt, smiling. 'I think I may have broken through.'

Matt refilled their glasses. 'I told you. He just needed time. You making the Letzer connection must have done the trick.'

She took up the tray with the coffee things. 'Can we

have this in the library? It's my favourite room in the house.'

Shrugging agreement, Matt rose and followed her from the kitchen.

Naomi set the tray on the low coffee table while Matt lowered himself onto the sofa. As she stooped to pour the coffee she raised her head to find his gaze had gone to where the loose, square neck of her dress sagged, letting him see deep between her heavy breasts. Without hurry, she stood and handed him his cup. 'You must think I'm pretty damned stupid.'

'Why?'

'Stephen. For letting him make a fool of me for so long.'

'You had no reason to doubt his credentials. He'd done good work for you.' As he spoke, he noticed for the first time how, in the last few weeks, the padding of flesh beneath her jaw had been pared away, leaving the beginning of chicken flesh.

She tried to smile. 'He just seemed such a *giving* person.' She swallowed. 'And he turned out to be no more than a tacky little shyster.' Her voice breaking with anger, she sat down heavily on the sofa. Matt was conscious of her thigh pressing against his. 'And *I'm* the one who introduced him to Camilla.' Her hand clutched at his. 'God, Matt, you must think the whole damned disaster's my fault.' She buried her head in his shoulder.

He freed his arm and put it around her. 'Of course not. Anyway, it all starts from this evening. Proving that Letzer used to be Hampton is all that counts now. Nobody's blaming you for being taken in by the bastard.'

She drew back her head to look at him. He could feel her breath on his face. 'Really?' she whispered.

'You're not angry with me?' She closed her eyes. 'Oh, Matt, I'm so relieved, I can't tell you.' A moment later, her mouth was on his.

The sudden weight of her toppled him, so that he was lying against the arm of the sofa. He felt her scramble around, her mouth not leaving his, until she was astride him, her fingers plucking at the buttons of his shirt, snatching it open. Hardly meaning to, he parted his teeth, letting her insistent tongue into his mouth. He was conscious of her fumbling with her own buttons and then felt the blood surge in his temples as the weight of her breasts, freed from the dress, spilled against his bare chest. Groaning, she took his hand and pushed it down, between her thighs.

For a moment, Matt remained like that, his senses reeling with the taste and feel of her flesh. Then, he pulled his hand free and, taking her by the shoulder, pushed her off him.

Naomi looked blankly down at him, her face flushed, her breasts hanging from the unbuttoned dress.

'Sorry,' he murmured.

She stared down at him, disbelief and anger flaring and then subsiding in her eyes. 'I thought you . . .'

He eased himself out from under her. 'I'm really sorry. It's not that I don't – you're a very attractive woman. It's just that, there's Liz.'

Anger welled in her eyes again, and was quickly controlled. 'I understand. Sorry. It's my fault. I made a mistake. I thought . . .' She broke off, standing up, and looked at Matt with a strange, glittering look in her eyes. 'Oh, what the fuck does it matter what I thought.' She buttoned up her dress. 'I suppose I'd better go.'

'You don't have to. You know, you've had a few drinks. There's a guest room made up.'

She smoothed the cloth of her skirt. 'Thanks. I'd better go home. I'll take my chances on a breath test.'

Neither of them spoke until she was in the car. She lowered the window. 'You didn't get around to telling me how you expect to *prove* Stephen Letzer and Hampton are the same man. The Stanakis woman's description of Hampton doesn't sound anything *like* Stephen.'

He looked down, one arm resting on the roof of the car. 'We won't have to rely on appearances, though, will we? Not if Jill can be in court to *identify* him.'

She frowned. 'I thought she was blind.'

'Nearly blind, not completely. But that won't matter, will it? They were *lovers*, for God's sake. She'll be able to identify his *voice*.'

She sat staring through the windscreen for a moment and then said, abruptly businesslike, 'Of course. Good luck, Matt. And thanks for a lovely evening.' Before he could respond the car bucked away across the gravel.

In the tiny built-on bathroom of the cottage Camilla let her robe fall to her feet and examined herself in the smeared mirror. She had no need to weigh herself to see that she had begun losing weight again.

In the three days since her meeting with her father the hollows had reappeared between her ribs. The recent bloom had gone from her face, the cheekbones pushing at the flesh, dark shadows once more under her eyes. The encounter with Matt had shattered the rhythm it had taken her so much hard work to establish. Once again, she was waking in the night, sweating and afraid, tortured by dreams that taunted her from just beyond the edge of memory. With a grimace, as though her body repelled her, she lowered herself into the bath, gritting her teeth against the scalding heat, as though only that could cleanse her of the night and the dreams.

She was still soaking when she heard the car draw up. With a look close to panic, she sprang from the bath and quickly dried herself, leaving wet patches that darkened her T-shirt as she pulled it on, and then fumbled her way into pants and jeans. Breathless, but satisfied that he would not see the thinness of her body, fearful of distressing him, she ran for the door and into his arms.

Letzer stood quite still, frowning, as she clung to him. Her heart drummed against his chest. She was shivering wildly, her teeth chattering, as though she had just been hauled from a shipwreck. He waited, his lips against her hair, until at last the shivering subsided and then, unhooking her arms from around his neck, he led her into the kitchen and sat her in one of the wooden chairs. His mouth twisted as he took in the cluttered table, the unstoppered coffee jar, the half-eaten food. He batted a hand at a fat fly that sipped from a pool of liquid on the oilcloth. Dirty crockery filled the sink. Wiping the grimace from his face, he bent to look at her. 'Another bad night?'

She nodded. 'Horrible dreams.' She took hold of his sleeve. 'I wish you'd stay.'

He straightened, drawing a long breath as he turned away from her. 'We've been over that. I can't. Your father has people watching me. It's just the ammunition they need to impugn my motives.'

'Well, couldn't I just come back to the clinic? I *hate* being here alone. I don't care about the photographers any more. Let's just give them their pictures and then they'll go away.'

He shook his head, his back to her. 'The clinic's practically sold.'

Her face lit up. 'That's good. Are you getting what you hoped?'

'Me? No. But we . . . I just want to get it over with. Forget it ever existed.'

A flash of panic passed over her face. 'You seem angry. Is it me? Is it something I've done?'

He smiled wearily. 'No,' he said, reaching to touch her outstretched hand and shaking his head emphatically. 'God knows it's nothing to do with you, sweetheart. Nothing at all.'

She rose and stood with her arms around him. 'Is it money, Stephen? Can I help?'

He stepped back out of her grasp, shaking his head. 'No! I don't want you even to suggest it! I'm just getting everything straightened out. All I want now is for this trial to be over, for him to be put away where he belongs.' He reached absently for her hand. 'I just want to get started on building a future. With you.'

She smiled, clasping his hand in both hers. 'Me, too. But you look so worried.'

He sat down on the arm of the decrepit armchair. 'I am,' he muttered. 'Worried sick.' He threw out an arm in a sudden sweeping movement that took in both the unkempt room and Camilla herself, her pallor, her trembling dependence. 'About you. This was what I was afraid of when I saw that son of a bitch at the hospital. I should *never* have let you go there.'

'I had to see William, darling. Daddy shouldn't have been there, that's all.'

Letzer's eyes blazed with renewed anger. 'Of course he damned well shouldn't. He knew that better than anybody!' Anger propelled him to his feet. 'He's set you back months! Hoping to save his own shitty skin.'

The force of his contempt for her father drove Camilla a faltering step backwards. 'I don't know. Darling, if you could have *seen* his face. I've dreamed of it ever since. The *pain* in it. I know what he did to me and yet . . . I can't help . . .'

'Feeling sorry for the bastard?'

She shook at the vehemence of his words. 'Well . . . yes. In a way.' She began to cry silently. 'Seeing Daddy like that has left me . . . confused. I don't see how I can possibly get through the trial . . . To sit opposite him in court and swear he did those things . . . Oh, Stephen, the poor man seemed so devastated. So *bereft*! I just can't believe he was only . . . acting!'

He stepped to her and placed his arm round her waist, pulling her to him. 'Perhaps he didn't need to.'

She looked up into his face, deeply puzzled. 'You mean he might not have done it?' she whispered.

'No. But it's a well-known phenomenon. Per-petrators can suppress things, too.'

Annie sank heavily into her office seat. She sat for a moment, her face in her hands. It was eleven fifteen, her working day was only just starting, and yet already she was totally drained.

'How was he?'

She looked at where Matt stood at the window, drinking coffee from a plastic goblet, his head half turned to her. 'Nothing new. The dialysis will put him back on his feet. Until . . . one of these times.'

'Are you coping okay?'

Annie flapped a hand at the heaps of folders on her desk. 'Work's going to hell, but my partners are being understanding.'

'And Roger? Is he pulling his weight?'

She filled her lungs slowly. 'He's having some diffi-culty coming to terms with the fact that his son has had another brush with death. In fact, he's just dis-covered the bank need him back in Hong Kong for a couple of weeks. He feels he shouldn't let them down,' she added flatly, keeping the irony out of her voice.

It was Matt who ended the few seconds of embarrassed silence. 'Oh Jesus, Annie.'

She sniffed. 'Just when you think nothing else can surprise you, eh? But you want to know how your fortunes are faring, not mine.' She worked a folder from a drawer and opened it, took out a sheet and, grimacing, passed it over to Matt. 'To tell you the truth, not that brilliantly.' She stabbed a finger at the paper. 'Roy's people aren't making much progress on tying up Hampton and Letzer. All they've come up with so far is the owner of the apartment Hampton used as a consulting room. Not much use, though. He'd never met Hampton himself. All he knows is what the building manager told him. The owner was only interested at all because Hampton left without claiming back his deposit. Apparently, in that sector of town that's about as likely as the second coming.'

'How about the manager? Didn't they talk to him?'

'He died. Two years ago. The current manager's sure about that. He dropped dead on the steps of the building.'

Matt let the report fall to the desk. 'The description of Hampton before he went to seed would fit Letzer.'

Annie pulled a face. 'Matt, it's vague enough to fit *me* if I were wearing trousers.'

He inclined his head. 'How about a photograph? Have they had any luck?'

'Not yet,' Annie answered, pulling the pile of that morning's mail towards her and flipping abstractedly through it, scribbling in the margins of some of the letters, putting aside those which required further attention. 'Jill Stanakis's father's suicide wasn't a big story. The only picture they turned up is this one.' She slid a grainy, faxed picture across the desk to him.

He looked despondently at the blurred image, a man

with a mane of dark hair holding a hand splayed in front of his face, hiding his features from the camera. 'Shit,' he murmured, before looking up at her again. 'What did Roy think of Naomi's idea? The graduation picture angle?'

Annie took her time before meeting his eye. 'He was impressed. He's got an agency working on it. There are an awful lot of high schools in America, though.'

'I think I can narrow it down. Naomi came up with something this morning. She has an idea Letzer once talked about having been to high school in Pittsburgh.'

'Naomi's finding a lot of ways to be helpful.'

The acid in her tone brought Matt's head up sharply. 'Ah shit, Annie. Lay off. She *called* me, at nine thirty this morning. She remembered it in bed this morning, *her* bed.' He shook his head, speaking low. 'You know how I feel, Annie. I want Liz back. Period.'

She looked at him for a little longer and then gave a curt little nod. 'I know.' She tossed aside the letter and took up another one, scanning it, her lips clamped tight.

'How long does Roy think that agency needs to turn up pictures?'

'Weeks, maybe months.' Her voice had fallen to a murmur.

'How about Jill? How long before she'll be fit to travel? Tara Bailey's really champing at the bit. She seems to have the entire press baying for the story.'

Very slowly she raised her eyes to look at him, allowing the letter she was reading to fall back onto the desk. 'Weeks there, too. She's a sick woman.'

He shrugged. 'We've got all summer to dry her out.'

'No, we haven't.'

A chilly tendril of apprehension unfurled somewhere inside him. 'What do you mean? There's plenty of time.'

Dumbly, she pushed the letter across the desk. He stared transfixed at the letterhead: Chichester Crown Court. He tried to read on and found the text swimming before his eyes.

'There's no time at all, Matt. The Shelford Pension Fund trial has collapsed.' Tears broke from her. 'Matt, they've listed you for the eighth of July. Ten bloody days from now!'

Nineteen

'Are you Matthew Richard Stenner?'

The words struck Matt's ears like fragments of hot metal. His throat constricted as if he would choke. His fingers tightened on the rail of the dock. He nodded, standing ramrod straight, forcing himself to look directly at the robed clerk. 'Yes.' The single word, once uttered, seemed to have nothing more to do with him, taking on an independent existence as it hung on the still air of the courtroom.

His eyes flickered to the back of Annie's head, quite motionless above the black gown. The briefest spark of stupid surprise at the new flecks of white in her hair, and then his eyes were again on the clerk of the court, his whole being concentrated on watching the man's broad, petty officer's face.

'Matthew Richard Stenner, you are charged in an indictment containing three counts. In the first count you are charged that, on a day or days between the first day of February and the thirty-first day of July 1985 you had sexual intercourse with Camilla Jane Stenner, whom you knew to be your daughter, who was then aged eight years, contrary to section ten, subsection one, of the Sexual Offences Act 1956. How do you plead? Guilty or not guilty?'

Matt's mouth seemed to be filled with ashes. 'Not guilty.' He heard the words echo around the room, and felt faintly curious at the sound, not aware of having spoken them.

'You are charged on the second count that, on a day

between the first day of February and the thirty-first day of July 1985, you committed buggery with Camilla Jane Stenner, a person under the age of sixteen years, contrary to section twelve, sub-section one, of the Sexual Offences Act 1956. How do you plead? Guilty or not guilty?'

The words of the charge seemed to break over Matt like great icy waves, threatening to drag him to his knees. He gripped the rail harder, his knuckles showing bleached against the brass. 'Not guilty.'

He looked around at the jury, trying to read their thoughts. The four men and eight women sat expressionless. Only one, a thick-set woman, dressed for the occasion in a dark blue suit and high-necked blouse, looked at him. Others stared into space, or were intent on the clerk, waiting for more.

'In the third count you are charged that on a day or days between the first day of February and the thirty-first day of July 1985 you had sexual intercourse with Camilla Jane Stenner, a girl under the age of thirteen years. How do you plead? Guilty or not guilty?'

'Not guilty.' Matt said the words quicker than before, a sense of relief that the worst was over. This charge would make no difference to the outcome, Annie had explained. It was routine in cases of incest, the prosecution's insurance policy in case the defence were to try to show that Camilla was not his natural daughter.

Matt looked sharply down, aware of something pulling at his sleeve. The prison officer who sat in the dock with him was urging him to sit. He sank slowly back into his seat.

Nausea had risen in him. He bit down hard, swallowing the bitter taste, fighting to bring order to his reeling senses. As though recovering from a blackout, he became dreamily conscious that the judge was speaking. He had the impression hours may have passed since the clerk had read the charges, though a glance at the clock above the press seats told him it was no more than a minute. Still fighting the nausea, he struggled to concentrate on the judge's words.

It was as though he were witnessing the scene from behind glass, a spectator, watching other people play out their private rituals. From his place at the elevated bench, the judge was launched into just such a ritual, leaning confidentially towards the jury, talking to them in a beautifully modulated voice that exuded relaxed competence. Each fluent sentence was perfectly constructed, each word meticulously weighted, as he laid out for them the implications of the case.

Matt hardly registered the meaning of his words. He was aware only of a growing sense of helpless horror as the judge, to put the jurors at their ease, made a small joke, drawing smiles from the jury and smirks from the two ushers. The urge welled in him to leap to his feet and shout a protest, to remind them that, while the lawyers played out their wry, masonic games, his life, everything he was and loved, was in jeopardy. As he fought down the impulse, the judge's words abruptly crystallised in his brain, as though he had suddenly spoken louder.

'So, members of the jury, although we all hope to finish it within the week,' he glanced, faintly condescending, at Annie, 'you shall be hearing a considerable amount of expert evidence and, in my experience, such cases do have a tendency to overrun. You should, I think, not expect to conclude your duty before the middle of next week.'

Matt looked down to where Annie sat, three paces from him, separated from the dock only by the table where her assistant, Hannah, was surrounded by a wall of ribbon-bound folders. Almost close enough for them to reach out and touch hands. Despite the physical proximity, he had the choking, nightmarish sensation that she was as separate from him as a face on a passing train. As though she sensed Matt's eyes drilling into her back, Annie turned, ostensibly to murmur something to Hannah, and she glanced up at him and smiled. The reassurance in the smile seemed to infuse his entire body, a confirmation that normality still existed.

The judge did not realise how prophetic he was being. To spin the trial out was exactly the strategy they had been discussing until the moment they had parted in front of the courtroom, Annie to robe, Matt to surrender to the court officers. Annie would use every device she knew to prolong the proceedings while they raced to finish drying out Jill Stanakis. Jill was flying in that day. Matt came near to smiling as he recalled Annie on the telephone, finally persuading Liz to agree to meet Jill and to supervise the team of nurses they had assembled to work in round-the-clock shifts. His half-smile faded as his attention was brought sharply back to the courtroom. The judge had finished his introduction and the prosecuting counsel was already rising to his feet.

Roland Barnes had long been a familiar name to Matt through newspaper reports of major trials. He was a tall man, made to look taller by the thickness of the pig-tailed wig and the sweep of his black robe. His fine-featured, mobile face was framed by wisps of wavy, greying hair which blended with the wig, so that far from looking absurd, it seemed part of the man. As he began speaking, Matt noted despondently that his voice was deep and warm, inspiring trust. Speaking as fluently as had the judge, never leaving a sentence unfinished, he introduced himself to the jury. Then, turning languidly, he introduced Annie to the jury, too.

Trying to listen with a juror's ears, Matt strained for the nuances beneath the formal courtesy. Despair and anger surged in him. A subtle, but unmistakable undertone of disgust made Barnes's message quite clear. Although obliged to go through the charade that Matt was innocent until proven guilty, they could already safely regard him as the loathsome and despicable beast the charges suggested.

The indictment was explained to the jury, the facts of the accusation reduced to dry details of names, times and places. Hearing it, Matt was once again overcome by the sensation of being caught in surf, the pounding in his ears, the sense that at any moment he would be dragged down by the irresistible undertow. He slumped forward, as though about to bury his face in his hands and then, abruptly, he straightened. His shoulders went back as, twisting his head, he glanced up at the packed public gallery. The sea of faces there swam in front of his eyes, no more distinct from each other than monkeys. Then, his eyes alighted on Mark, pressed into the middle of the second row. Matt's mouth twitched in a smile. A clamp seemed to tighten on his heart as Mark smiled back, tight-lipped, and then, disregarding the sidelong stares of the people around him, raised a clenched fist and brandished it in salute. Matt turned back to face the courtroom, the pain in his chest choking him, the faint imprint of his smile remaining on his lips.

Unhurriedly, hardly needing to look at his notes, Barnes outlined the main issues, meticulously outlining the case he intended to present, anticipating the lines of argument he thought the defence might adopt, already countering them. The man was impressive, languorous but thorough, never patronising the jury as he led them through the labyrinth of the case. By the time he finished, talking without a break for two and a half hours, Matt was sitting with his face in his hands, sunk into a deep, black depression.

Judge Davies's words roused him. 'Thank you, Mr Barnes.' He eyed the clock. 'It's twelve forty-five. An appropriate time to break for lunch.' He smiled indulgently at the jury. 'Please be back in your places at two. We'll have the first witness to the stand then.' He looked down at the usher. 'Miss Stenner, I believe.'

Matt's despondency flared into a sick panic. A maddened, unreasoning instinct took hold of him – to leap from the dock and flee the room, his life, the whole nightmare. Slowly, he became aware of fingers closed on his arm, pulling at him. Annie's face was less than a foot from his, smiling. 'Come on,' she said evenly. 'I'll buy you a sandwich.'

Liz shifted nervously, studying the flow of passengers from behind the dark glasses that hid her hollowed and reddened eyes. The hand-written card she held in front of her chest bore the word Stanakis in black marker. With her free hand she clung to Rachel's arm, her fingers biting deep. The flow of passengers had slowed to a trickle, those with swaying trolley-loads of baggage, a few, walking quicker, who had been delayed by customs. Liz pushed a few inches further forward, thrusting the card hopefully at the stragglers.

'She missed it!' Rachel said, pursing her lips. 'I bet you anything that's what happened. You would have thought that detective would have *phoned* us, wouldn't you?'

Liz was about to respond when a wheelchair emerged through the arrivals door pushed by a middle-aged woman in a dark blue skirt and white blouse with a name tag pinned to the breast. She paused, squinting at the card, and then, with a grim smile, propelled the chair towards Liz.

Liz gasped. Jill Stanakis was in her twenties. The woman in the chair looked fifteen years older. Stick-thin, she sat hunched, her head hanging, her bony hands twitching in her lap.

'Mrs Stenner?' At Liz's reply a relieved smile broke out on the nurse's face. 'This is Miss Stanakis.' She spun the chair towards Liz and pulled a docket from the bag that swung at her shoulder. 'Would you sign this, please?'

Liz looked up in horror at Rachel before taking the pen the nurse offered and dumbly signing where she indicated. Handing the docket back, she stooped to look into Jill's face. 'Is she all right?'

Embarrassment flitted in the nurse's face. 'She will be.' She dropped her eyes at Liz's frowning look. 'She's . . . she's *drunk*.'

Liz looked at her, uncomprehending. 'Drunk? I thought . . . Mr Erskine told me she was . . . she hadn't had a drink for weeks.'

The nurse's eyes watered. 'I'm sorry, Mrs Stenner. It wasn't my fault. She told me she was sick. She needed to go to the toilet. She'd been perfectly fine. Quite good company. I didn't see any harm, just letting her go alone. Just along the aisle.' She shook her head in despair. 'After a while I knocked on the door. In the end I had to call the stewardess. They had to break in.' She began sobbing. 'She was on the floor. She'd stolen a bunch of drinks from the trolley.' The woman fumbled for a tissue and buried her face in it. 'It wasn't my fault, was it? She was completely unconscious.'

They looked at Jill. Although no longer unconscious she appeared totally oblivious to what was going on around her, her head lolling on her shoulder. Rachel sniffed, drawing herself up to her full four inches taller than Liz. 'And *this* is what Matthew thinks is going to get him off!'

Liz swallowed. 'Annie seems to think she's the best hope he's got,' she said hoarsely.

'Camilla Stenner.' At the call Camilla started and clung to Letzer, resting her head on his chest. She shivered at the touch of his fingers as he unclasped her hands from his back and propelled her towards the waiting usher. He smiled encouragingly. 'Be strong, darling. It'll soon be over now.' Swallowing, she craned up to accept a kiss and then turned and walked quickly out of the witness room.

Matt's hand went to his face, ready to cover his stinging eyes, as he watched Camilla hesitate, looking to the usher for guidance, and then stride to the witness box, stumbling slightly as she mounted the step. He forced himself to remain stone-faced, fighting to keep a lid on his roiling emotions as he watched her refuse the proffered Bible and take the card bearing the words of the affirmation. Taut, high-pitched, her voice faltered, as though stretched to snapping point by the intolerable strain, ready to break on every word. Her complexion, too, was eloquent of the pressure she was under, the healthy glow she had exuded at their last encounter replaced once more by the sick pallor of neurosis.

'Would you please tell us your name?' Barnes spoke silkily, moving a half-step towards Camilla, smiling and relaxed.

'Camilla Jane Stenner.'

'And can you tell us where you live, Miss Stenner?'

Camilla glanced down at her hands. 'Lower Barton Cottage, near Kenningbridge, Norfolk.'

'Thank you. Miss Stenner, all of us here in this court-room understand that your testimony may ... ah ... that it may take some time. If perhaps you would prefer to sit down, I'm sure His Honour ...' He broke off looking up at the judge.

'No.' She straightened visibly. 'That's not necessary.'

Matt watched Barnes, beaming, turn apparently casually to the jury, letting them get a flavour of what a brave girl this was. 'As you wish. Miss Stenner, the man in the dock, Matthew Stenner, is your father?'

She turned to look directly at Matt, their eyes meeting for the first time since she had entered the room. 'Yes. He is.' Her words fell into the hush like pebbles in a lake.

'Miss Stenner, may I ask, how old are you now?'

'Twenty.'

'And your birthday is on the ninth of January, am I correct?'

'That's right.'

'So then, at the beginning of 1985, you would have been eight years old. In fact, on the ninth of January that year you had your eighth birthday party.' As he spoke of the party, he beamed again, as though the very thought of healthy, happy young children could not help but bring a smile to anybody's face. 'And that party was organised by your father.' He swung to face Matt, at the same time letting the smile fall from his face. 'Is that correct?'

'Yes.'

'By your father, because your mother was away on a business trip in America. Is that not so?'

'Yes, that's right. Mummy was often away at that period.'

'So, after the other children went home you were alone in the house with your father?'

'Except for my brother, Mark. And Kristina, the au pair.'

'Of course, there was the au pair. A young Norwegian lady, I believe. Kristina Olsen?'

'That was her name.'

'Did she sleep in a room close to yours?'

'No. Part of the house, the eastern annexe, was being restored at that time. Her room was in there. It's separate from the house, self-contained now, although at that time it didn't have its own kitchen.'

'So, a separate part of the house entirely. Would you say it was out of earshot of the main house?'

Camilla nodded. 'Yes.'

'And your brother, Mark, was six years old at this time. Did he have his own room, or did he share with you?'

'His own room.'

Barnes paused, giving the jury time to get the picture. Then he painted it for them anyway. 'So, there you were, a little girl, eight, just had your birthday party. Do you remember the occasion well?' He raised his eyebrows, smiling.

'Yes.' Camilla's fingers had tightened on the edge of the witness box.

'Yes. And when the party was over, at the end of the evening, you were put to bed. Your brother, too?'

'Yes.'

'By whom?'

'Kristina. The au pair.'

'What, to your knowledge, did Kristina do after you were put to bed?'

'Most evenings she went out. To classes, I think.'

'So you were effectively alone with your father.' He paused, feigning to refresh his memory by scanning a document on his table. When he looked up, his face was sombre. 'Miss Stenner, can I ask you to tell us, in your own words, exactly what happened that night?'

Matt could hardly bear to watch, and yet still less could he stand to look away as she began to speak. It took her two tries before any sound emerged. Even then, it was a husky whisper, barely audible. Judge Davies leaned forward, smiling gentle encouragement.

'Perhaps the witness would like to sit down now.' Camilla gave a jerky nod and sank onto the chair behind her. 'And, I know this is a great strain, but perhaps you could speak up just a little for the members of the jury.' Camilla nodded again, swallowed, and leaned towards the microphone on the edge of the witness box. When she found her voice it was stronger, less tremulous.

'I went to bed as usual, probably later than usual, because of my birthday. When Mummy was away Daddy often let me stay up later. He used to take me into the library and read to me. Especially if he was writing one of his own books. He would try bits out on me.' Her eyes flashed for just a fraction of an instant to Matt. He recoiled, a hand going to his eyes, as though he had looked at the sun. Her voice fell to a whisper. 'It was a way he had of making me feel special, his special girl.'

Matt stirred in his seat, making the dock officer turn sharply, a hand raised ready to restrain him. He wanted to cry out, to shout his version to the court and to the world, that it was true, but it was no more nor less than that. Those winter evenings, reading aloud, with Camilla snuggled against him on the huge sofa, watching the flickering log fire, had been some of the most precious memories of his life. Until Camilla had uttered those words he had always thought it must be true for her, too. Gradually, as she went on speaking, he sank back to rest his elbows on the edge of the dock, his head sinking into his hands.

'So on this evening, your birthday, you went to bed, a little late, after a session snuggling on the sofa with your father. And what happened then?' Barnes's voice was velvety, just loud enough for the transfixed jury to hear.

'I went to sleep.' Her voice cracked.

283

The judge leaned down towards the usher. 'A glass of water for the witness?'

Camilla took the water from the usher and drank thirstily, swilling it in her parched mouth. 'Then I remember waking up. It was dark. There was someone on the bed. At first I remember thinking it was Mark, my brother.'

'Excuse me, Miss Stenner, you said *on* the bed?'

'I meant in it. Right next to me. Touching my skin. My nightdress was rucked up.' She broke off again, taking another deep gulp of the water.

Matt shook his head slowly, his hands still covering his face, as though they could protect him from the scalding effect of her words. Outrage, incomprehension and despair boiled in him, making him dizzy and feverish. And beneath it, glittering through the rest, was an implacable hatred for Letzer and what he had done to them all. Barnes was putting another question to Camilla, smoothly apologetic. 'I'm sorry, but I must press you. *Touching* you? Can you tell the jury just *how*?'

'With his hand, first. I remember that's when I knew it wasn't Mark, when I tried to move it. It was so big. And then . . . then . . . he . . . he moved up closer against me. Sort of snuggling against me.'

'Did you struggle at this point, or call out?'

'No, not really?'

'Why not?'

'Well, I wasn't really worried. After all, it was my *father*. It didn't occur to me . . . I was eight . . . that he would *do* anything, anything *wrong*.' Looking out between splayed fingers, Matt saw how, at the mention of the word father, the eyes of several of the jurors swivelled to look at him, resting on him for a second before turning again to Camilla.

'Miss Stenner, before I ask you to describe further

what happened that night, can you tell the court, was there anything in your father's previous behaviour that might, in retrospect, have been leading up to what happened?'

Annie was on her feet. The judge motioned to Barnes to pause. 'One moment, Mr Barnes. You object, Mrs Trevellyn?'

Annie twitched her gown closer around her. 'My learned friend is asking the witness to speculate on the defendant's motives, Your Honour.'

Judge Davies looked to Barnes, an eyebrow arched.

'Your Honour, I don't believe my friend's objection is justifiable. I was merely trying to establish whether, in the witness's *experience*, the events she is describing came as a total surprise or whether she had, in her own mind, already grounds for expecting some such occurrence.'

Davies looked from one to the other before smiling wryly.

'Perhaps, Mr Barnes, you could rephrase your question to take account of the defence's objection.'

Barnes inclined his head as Annie resumed her seat. He turned again to Camilla. 'Miss Stenner,' he asked with exaggerated urbanity, 'had anything occurred prior to that night, that gave you grounds for misgiving?'

Camilla mused for a moment. 'No.'

'Miss Stenner, didn't he frequently come to your room?'

'Oh, yes. Whenever I had a bad dream, or something.'

'And how would he customarily be dressed on those occasions?'

'He wouldn't be. That is, he wouldn't normally wear anything.'

'You mean he came to your room naked?'

'Yes. But I never worried about it. That was just Daddy.'

Barnes looked down, only momentarily put off his stride. 'I see. Were those the only times he let you see him naked?'

Matt's fingertips clawed at the flesh of his scalp. He and Annie had gone over this ground a hundred times. He had told himself aloud, even muttering the words as he entered the dock that morning, that this man was paid to do a job, that there was no personal animosity in it at all. Now, watching Barnes work, the insidious, subtle skill with which he staked out his ground, Matt could feel his own searing contempt for Letzer spreading like a stain to include this man, this total stranger who was taking money to destroy everything he, Matt, held dear – his freedom, his family, his reputation.

'No. He would walk around the house without clothes on all the time, on his way to the pool. And at bathtime he would often get in with me, or invite me to get in with him.'

On the edge of his seat, Matt writhed like a trussed animal. He wanted to jump to his feet and *scream* at the judge, the jury, the reporters scribbling notes, and Camilla. To make them understand somehow that, although every word Camilla said was strictly true, the meaning they were all putting on it, which he could read in the pinched faces of the jurors and the ironic, predatory smiles of the reporters, was standing things on their head. What they were visualising as they listened to Camilla's account had *nothing* to do with what had really been happening. Of *course* he loved to see his children's lithe little bodies, loved to hold them, to kneel at the bathside and watch them frolic in the suds. And, yes, after a run, he would sometimes share a bath with them. If he had ever thought about

286

it at all he had supposed it was what every father who enjoyed his children would do. But between that and the insinuating touches and dank, furtive lusts that Barnes alluded to was an unbridgeable chasm, so deep and wide that in his most fevered imaginings he could not conceive of crossing it. He had tried! Many times in the depths of the sleepless nights since his arrest he had stared from his window trying even to *imagine* how a man might find such desires within himself. The effort alone made him sick to his stomach, in the grip of a loathing that left him shaking. Barnes's voice came to him again, echoing strangely as though reaching him through a tunnel.

'And you did get in with him, didn't you? At eight years old, younger, perhaps, there was nothing wrong in taking a bath with your father, was there? It killed two birds with one stone, didn't it? Even though there was an au pair on call who would have been pleased to take the task off his shoulders, if only he had asked her?'

Annie was on her feet again. Davies rested one veined cheek in the palm of a hand, concealing the beginnings of a smile. 'You know better than that, Mr Barnes,' he said, without waiting for Annie to speak. 'Rephrase it please.'

Barnes dipped his head. 'Was it part of Miss Olsen's duties to bath you?'

'I don't really know. I suppose –'

Barnes cut her off with an upraised hand. 'I know you want to answer as truthfully as you can, Miss Stenner, but please don't feel obliged to speculate. Just the bare truth will do very nicely. You don't remember.'

Matt swivelled to study the jury, looking for clues to how they were responding to Barnes's effort to establish himself as the embodiment of fair play. Not one of the twelve faces, at once empty and intent, gave any clue to the thoughts behind it.

'On the occasions when you did not take baths with your father, who bathed you?'

'Mummy did it, if she was home. When she was away it was mostly Dad . . . my father.' The correction drove a hot spike into Matt's heart.

'Not Miss Olsen?'

'No. As I said, she went out most evenings.'

'And your father didn't ask her to stay home and do a chore which most of this world's au pairs can never escape?'

'I suppose not.'

'Quite. Miss Stenner, during the period over which the offences are said to have occurred, your mother was away a great deal, is that not so?'

'Yes. She spent a lot of time in New York. Working for magazines there.' Speaking of Liz, Camilla's eyes flickered automatically to the public gallery, as though seeking her. Matt followed her gaze, saw Mark smile as his eyes met his sister's, and then watched the smile fail and turn to a pleading look as Camilla turned away again.

'Let us return to the matter of the person "snuggling up" to you. Can you resume your story from that point, please?'

'Well, he put his arms round me. I could feel his breath . . .' She broke off to drink some more, gripping the glass tight with both hands as she drained it. The usher hurried to refill it. 'Oh God, I can remember it so *clearly*.' Her voice fell to a hoarse whisper. 'It smelled of tobacco, and . . . I didn't know what it was then. I do now. It was alcohol!'

At her words Matt's head dropped as though he had been struck. He looked up again to find Annie's eyes on him. She had just time to give him a smile and a discreet thumbs-up sign before Camilla resumed speaking. In a halting voice that sometimes faded to nothing, compelling the judge to coax her to repeat herself, she began detailing what had happened to her, beginning with the unconsummated, drunken fumblings of that first night to, a few nights later, the absolute trauma of the first penetration.

For a moment Matt felt nothing but a curious internal hollowness, as though he had been eviscerated. Then, all at once, revulsion, anger, rebellion surged in him, making it a physical effort not to leap to his feet, to shout and plead with Camilla, to beg her to admit she was wrong. He wanted her to see him cry, to implore her to remember the truth. To hear her admit that, yes, she did have many nightmares. Terrible, haunting dreams that would have her sitting up in bed, her face contorted with screaming. And he would come to her, running, and lie down alongside her, soothing her until she could find peaceful sleep again. And that the rest, every word of what she had just told the court under oath, was no more than an evil fabrication, implanted in her mind by an unscrupulous impostor.

Then, gradually, as Camilla continued her testimony, as the horror of her story gripped the court, reflected in the pale, rapt faces of the jury, his anger subsided, pressed down by the sheer weight of the realisation of what was happening to him, leaving his body numb, his mind in a kind of trance, the only defence left against the nightmare around him.

Camilla spoke for a long time. Occasionally, she would falter and break off. The court would wait in enthralled silence as she grappled with her emotions. Then, after sitting silently for a moment, her eyes clenched shut, her lips moving as though repeating some mantra to herself, she seemed visibly to find the inner resources to continue, moving on to the next outrage.

Inexorably, never raising her voice above a husky whisper, needing almost no prompting from a sombre Barnes, she wove the fabric of fact to clothe the allegations.

In the box, his head sunk in his hands, Matt flinched as she catalogued dates and childish references that set his own memories churning, a litany of birthdays, major toys, camping weekends and holidays. He watched, agonised, as the jurors scribbled notes, frowning in concentration. They could not help being impressed by the tide of specifics. Each date, each corroborating event, contributed authority to the charges against him.

'And during this period, Miss Stenner, you recall being taken to the doctor on a number of occasions?' Barnes's hushed voice was apologetic, deeply respectful.

'Yes.'

'Can you tell the ladies and gentlemen of the jury the *reason* for those visits?'

'I was suffering from bleeding.' Her voice quavered. She cleared her throat, two rasping coughs. 'Anal bleeding.'

A collective embarrassment seemed to go through the courtroom like a soft breeze. In the public seating people shifted position, coughed.

'Did the doctor, as you recall it, prescribe any medication for your symptoms?'

'Yes. I remember him telling me it was something against constipation. I remember it because I had never heard the word before. I asked him what it meant.'

'And do you now believe his diagnosis to have been correct?'

'Oh, I believe I really *was* suffering from constipation. I remember Mummy and Daddy discussing it, making me eat lots of dried fruits, purées of figs, things like that. I *hated* them! But that wasn't the reason for the bleeding. That was caused when he . . . penetrated me. It hurt me. It hurt a lot.' Camilla had bowed her head so that her chin was against her chest. For the first time in her testimony tears came to her eyes.

'I'm sorry, Miss Stenner, I know how extremely painful this must be for you, but could you please speak a little louder, for the jury.'

She raised her head, her chin jutting. She flapped away the tears with the back of a hand. 'I could feel . . . *tearing*. I used to *beg* him to stop.'

'And what was his response?'

'He just used to grunt, and put his hand over my mouth.'

Barnes stood motionless, letting the words hang in the hush. At length he turned back to the bench, glancing at the clock. It was four twenty. 'Your Honour, I wonder if this might be a suitable moment to adjourn. Then, tomorrow morning I would like to pass on to the first exhibit.' His pause was barely perceptible, just enough to gather the attention of the one or two jurors whose eyes had been on Matt. 'That will be Miss Stenner's own childhood record of these events.'

Twenty

Drained and punch-drunk, Matt descended the steps of the court building in Mark's wake as his son shouldered his way angrily through the knots of smirking onlookers. Matt stared straight ahead, fighting the urge to look back, knowing that Camilla and Letzer were still in the lobby, waiting for him to leave. Amid the blur of faces he was fleetingly surprised to see Naomi loitering on the edge of the crowd. He had not noticed her in the public seats. Seeing him look at her, she raised a hand, her smile strained. Her eyes were puffy and reddened, as though from crying. 'Things to do,' she murmured and turned away.

Annie, in street clothes now, hurried to Matt's side and caught him by the elbow, propelling him on. 'Bad day?' she murmured, her smile tentative.

'Could it have been worse?' he asked, unable to keep the bitterness from his voice.

'Frankly, yes. To begin with, they didn't throw any surprises at us. Believe me, that's always a relief in itself.'

'Great.'

'Matt, the first day of a trial is always like that. It's like the first time you see the evidence bundle. It's the prosecution's day. By the time they finish, you can't visualise yourself ever being acquitted. You'll feel better tomorrow, when I've finished cross-examining her.'

He looked at her in silence for a moment. 'She'll still be my daughter, Annie. Seeing my best friend put her through the wringer isn't going to cheer me up much.'

They strode across the car park in silence for a moment. 'There was good news, too, though. Remember?' She laughed at the doubt as he studied her face. 'The smell of tobacco. I bet Letzer's kicking himself over that. It happens all the time when people aren't telling the truth. They start overembroidering, trying to make themselves sound more convincing.' She laughed again. 'You? Smoking? Come on. Be glad. They made their first mistake. There'll be more.'

Reaching Annie's Audi, he paused with his hand on the door. 'Cigars, Annie. In those days I used to smoke Monte Cristos. Only when Liz was away, of course,' he added. He waited for Mark to slip into the car. 'Another of my little infidelities,' he murmured, with bitter irony. 'I used to smoke one before I went to bed. If I ever *did* go to settle Camilla in the night, I must have reeked of the damned things.'

Annie was still for a moment, her eyes on his face. 'Shit!' she murmured, before swinging herself into the car.

On the short walk from the court building Camilla had clung to Stephen Letzer's arm, not uttering a word. Twenty yards from their hotel she broke into a run, zig-zagging through the shoppers to hurl herself through the revolving doors into the lobby. She stood quite still in the dimness, one hand on the back of a chintz-covered chair for support, trembling and panting like a hunted deer. Letzer burst through the door two paces behind her and sprinted to her side. He looked quickly into her face and then hurried to the reception desk to retrieve their two keys.

Camilla followed submissively as he took her by the hand and led her through the deserted lounge, and along the corridor to her room. Rushing inside the moment he turned the key, she tore off the dark glasses and floppy cotton hat and hurled herself onto the bed. Burying her face in the bedclothes she allowed the dam to break. The tears came in awesome, heaving gasps.

Kneeling at the bedside, a hand resting lightly on her shoulder, Letzer let the minutes pass, waiting until she had cried herself out. As the crying subsided, he lifted her head and wiped away the tears with a corner of the quilt. 'Do you want to tell me about it, sweetheart?'

She spoke in a whisper, her voice almost inaudible, lost in the folds of the quilt. 'I'm not sure if I should. The judge said I mustn't discuss it with anybody. I . . .'

His lips pressed gently on hers, cutting her short. 'I'm not *anybody*, darling.' Smiling, his face inches from hers, he gestured at the room. 'There's only us.' His lips brushed hers again. 'I want to *know*, darling. I can't bear the thought of you in there . . . of not being with you.'

Camilla gave him a fleeting, strained smile. Blinking and shaking her head, she pushed herself to a sitting position, bunching the pillows behind her and drawing up her knees. 'Stephen,' she whispered, 'I can't go back there tomorrow.'

He put a hand behind her head. 'You can. You can be stronger than you think.'

She shook her head in violent contradiction. 'No. You weren't there. You didn't see his face today. It was . . . it was horrible. The way he looked at me. As if I were tearing his heart out.'

'I'll bet. Don't you think he knew exactly what he was doing? You *mustn't* let it work for him. Making *you* feel like the guilty one, him the poor, misunderstood victim.' He looked away, hardly able to contain his revulsion. 'They are just such *contemptible* people.'

Camilla hunched forward, agony etched into her

face. She still shivered, despite the stuffiness of the room. 'But . . . Stephen . . . I *know* Daddy so well. He was so close to me. I can't *believe* it was just an act.'

'It was, though, darling.' There was an implacable certainty beneath Letzer's whisper. 'And you *know* it. Did they get to the diaries?' She shook her head. 'Well, when they do, the jury will know it, too. The diaries are *real*, Camilla. *They* don't lie. Every vicious, brutal moment of it is in there.'

She looked at him, a pleading, panic-stricken expression in her eyes. 'But, perhaps . . . you told me some doctors believe they *forget*!' Her words came in a tumbling rush. One hand snatched at the lapel of his immaculate, pale summer-weight jacket, the knuckles white. 'Perhaps that's what happened. Perhaps he did do it, but it was . . . well, not really him. Perhaps he's just – I don't know – sick. The idea that he might go to prison for so long . . . Couldn't some sort of *treatment* help him?'

Letzer shook his head. 'Believe me, sweetheart, I've read every piece of literature there is on those bastards. Nothing works. Nothing.' He spoke close to her ear, his voice a rasping whisper. 'Not with people like that. What he's trying to do to you is typical. They deny, and deny, and deny, until you start to think that *you're* going crazy. They are cunning, ruthless bastards, and they'll resort to anything to stay on the outside, where they can offend again.' He drew back, cupping her face in his hands, looking deep into her eyes. 'I wish to God there were some other way, that you didn't have to go through this. But there isn't. Be strong for just one more day. After tomorrow it will be easier. But you *must* see it through.'

'Stephen, why is it so important to you? Why can't we just let it . . . Wouldn't it be better if I just never saw him again?'

He took her by the arms. 'It's not *me*, darling. It's for all the other children a man like that might damage. Never forget them.'

Before Annie had even brought the car to a halt Mark and Matt had the doors open, ready to leap. They ran through the house, and hurried across the lawn towards the copse of ancient beeches that hid the cottage, a Scandinavian log house erected by the previous owner to house an ailing relative. Liz and Rachel had spent two full days making it habitable. Until the pool extension, with its additional bedrooms above, had been completed several years earlier, the cottage had been useful in housing a variety of long-stay guests, academic friends on sabbaticals, foreign families exploring the region, family members between houses. For the last half-dozen years, ever since Mark finally stopped using it as a playhouse, it had stood neglected. Every few months Matt would vow to have it dismantled. Right now, it was a godsend, the perfect place to lodge Jill, close at hand but safely cut off from the house and its abundant liquor supplies. They knocked, waited for the sound of a brisk young female voice, and entered.

The agency nurse was sitting in one of the unmatched armchairs Liz had resurrected from forgotten corners of the house, scanning the job ads in a nursing magazine. Rachel sat at the pine table with the *Telegraph* in front of her, the crossword partly done. Liz had been sitting across from Rachel. At Matt's entrance she had risen and was standing, still holding the book she had been reading. Matt rushed across and kissed her. She accepted the kiss passively, tilting her head to take it on the cheek and not the mouth. 'Thanks for collecting Jill. You, too, Rachel.' Rachel's head dipped in acknowledgement. 'Where is she?'

Liz jabbed a finger at the ceiling. 'She was tired. There have been journalists in and out all day.'

Matt grinned. Tara Bailey's people were earning their money. 'Is she asleep?'

'No!' The voice, like sandpaper on glass, made them spin to face the stairs. Jill stood on the top step, dressed in a sweatshirt, jeans and trainers. The clothes were new, provided by Erskine. 'And you can stop talking about me like I was a head case.'

The nurse had let her magazine fall to the floor. She was up the stairs in three strides, taking Jill firmly by the hand. She came down backwards with Jill stepping tentatively in her wake, gripping the banister hard. Matt stepped to meet her, grasping the scrawny hand that hung loose at her side. 'Hello, Jill. Pleased to meet you at last. I'm Matt Stenner. How are you feeling?'

She looked in the direction of the voice, her eyes screwed up in a hopeless effort to remove the thick mist from her vision. 'Like shit. Did you bring anything to drink?'

Matt gave a discouraged laugh. 'Sorry. Jill, would you like to sit down? I want to talk to you seriously.'

'Yeah? Well, give me a drink first. Just a little one, to help me concentrate.' An involuntary shudder buffeted her, rattling her teeth.

'Tea or coffee?'

She stared into space for a moment and then gave a laugh that crackled like crumpling parchment. 'Ah, shit, coffee, then. Black.'

With a nod to the nurse to prepare the coffee, Matt took Jill's hand, led her to one of the wooden kitchen chairs and lowered her into it. She perched like a sick bird, her head pulled into her hunched, narrow shoulders. He pulled up another chair and sat in front of her, leaning forward so that she could feel his breath. 'Jill, can you see me?'

'I can see you're there. A shape. Can't see shit of what you look like, though, if that's what you mean.'

Matt looked over his shoulder at the watching group and grimaced. As he looked back Jill shuddered again, pulling her clenched fists hard against her navel, as if her guts hurt her. 'Look, Jill, you've just *got* to pull yourself together. And fast, too. For a few days. That's all we need. Can you do that?'

She gave another cackle. 'No.' She held a hand out flat, palm down, letting him watch it jerk and leap. 'See. Give me a drink. In this state I can't even *think*.'

'No. For Christ's sake, Jill, get it into your head. The deal is, for the next few days, no booze.'

'And you get this into *your* head. If I can't drink, I can't think.'

'No, Jill, sorry. Surely you can get it together for a few days. You were doing fine back home.'

'Back home's different. Travelling makes me nervous.'

Matt looked up at Annie, wondering. Finally, he leaned closer to her, cupping her bony hand in both his. 'Look, Jill, how much money did that bastard Hampton steal from you? Three million dollars? Four?'

She shrugged. 'Who's arguing for half a million? They stripped me bare.'

'Would you like to get back at him?' She gave another dry, dismissive croak of laughter, not bothering to reply. Matt looked again at Annie. 'Would it help you straighten up for a while if we offered you the chance to do just that?'

Her eyes narrowed shrewdly. 'What's that supposed to mean?'

'Larry Guenther already told you what's happening to me?'

'They say you've been screwing your daughter, right?'

298

'That's what I'm charged with, Jill. The same as your dad was charged. And the whole thing's been put together by my daughter's shrink. He's got my daughter head over heels in love with him. Familiar story, so far?' She dipped her head, like a bird taking a crumb. 'Good. Jill, the man who's trying to rip off my daughter's trust fund calls himself Stephen Letzer.' She shrugged. 'Jill, we know Letzer *is* Lewis Hampton.' He glanced at Annie before adding, 'We have proof. All we need is for you to come to court and support that proof by identifying his voice.'

Stupefaction seeped into her face. 'Holy shit.' A moment later the surprise was replaced by panic. She began shivering violently, her hand leaping and twitching in Matt's. She shook her head, so hard that the flesh of her cheeks swayed. 'No,' she gasped. She looked around her nervously, her tongue running over her lips, a hand half raised, as though seeking a drink. 'No. I couldn't.' Her whisper was like a wire brush on rust. 'Not if it's Lewis. I always thought I could but . . . I know I'd go to pieces.' She drew back, pulling her hand free from Matt's grasp. 'I didn't come here for that. I was just going to stand up and say my piece about my experience, and what happened to Dad. You'd better forget it. Forget about me. Let me just get back to the settlement. I can get along there. They take care of me.'

Matt looked up at Annie, a wildness in his eyes. He grabbed Jill's hand again, sliding off the chair onto one knee, his head almost touching hers. 'Please. Please, Jill. I know you loved him. It must hurt like hell. But try to think of the lives he's damaged. First you, and your father. Now Camilla. Me. And he'll do it to others, more helpless young women, every time he sees an opportunity. Again and again, over and over.'

She was shaking her head rhythmically from side to

side. 'I'm not sure I could, Matt. Those wounds have been a long time healing.'

He held both her hands now, his big hands dwarfing hers. 'It's not the money, is it, Jill? He could have had that, couldn't he? But the bastard broke your heart. And your father's, too. And now he's doing it again. To my daughter, and to me. Picture it, Jill,' his voice fell to an insistent whisper. 'Imagine, him in bed with Camilla, making love to her, and then lying there afterwards, whispering all those beautiful promises. The same empty, cheating words he must have whispered to you, just the same way, taking advantage of your vulnerability, just the way he's doing to Camilla. Do it for *her*, Jill, and for the others, the ones he hasn't even met yet.'

She was crying soundlessly, the tears rolling down the prematurely lined cheeks. 'Part of me wants to. There's a part of me always knew he'd do it again, that he's a man who *likes* to hurt people.'

'You can, Jill, you can. You can expose the bastard for the crook he is. All it takes is for you to stay on the wagon, just for three or four days. Can you do that?'

She sat straighter, stifling the tears. 'Ah, okay, fuck Lewis Hampton. I'll try.'

Matt leaned on the door of Annie's car as she lowered herself into her seat. The jubilation he had felt as he left the cottage still showed in his face. 'We're going to nail the bastard, aren't we?'

'I hope so.'

Something in Annie's voice pulled him up. 'What's that supposed to mean?'

Annie jutted her bottom lip. 'She isn't exactly the perfect witness. And she's been making money out of the interviews, hasn't she?'

'How else did you want us to persuade her to cooperate? You would have eaten me alive if I'd given her money directly.'

'You're damned right, I would. But it's still not good, Matt. Now I see her, it's obvious that Barnes will need about two minutes to take her apart. If he gets wind of it, we're dead in the water. He'll make it look as if she's doing the whole thing with a view to selling her life story.'

'We'll have to take our chances. Unless you can show me another way to get me out of this nightmare.'

Annie was silent for a moment. 'I can help you out of part of it.'

He looked down at his feet. 'No.'

Annie glanced towards the house. 'Liz doesn't believe in it, does she?'

'In Jill?'

'The whole thing. She doesn't believe in our theory, Letzer and Hampton, the whole thing. I can see it in her eyes. She's trying, but she can't go with it. You know why, don't you? She's afraid the diaries are genuine. As long as she thinks that, Matt, nothing's going to change her mind.'

He stood silent, unable to think of an answer.

'Let me tell her, Matt,' she murmured. 'Take the chance.'

He remained silent for a while longer. Finally, sighing, he said, 'She's coming to court tomorrow. Let's see how it goes. If it still looks as bad tomorrow evening, it's out of my hands.'

Smiling joylessly, she started the car. 'It's a deal,' she whispered, blowing him a kiss.

Matt watched the jury file into court, already into a routine, entering in the order in which they sat, smiling and murmuring asides to each other as they took their places. Only two among them ventured glances at Matt. They had already mastered the trick of emptying their faces the moment they turned to the court. The two who looked openly at him, a young blond man with sharp, eager features, and wearing a cheap grey suit, and a thick-set, bald man in his fifties with the worn, uncertain look of long-standing unemployment, gave no hint of the revulsion he knew must already be in them.

Roland Barnes was preoccupied, leafing through a sheaf of papers. Before the judge's entry, he had returned Annie's greeting with a perfunctory smile, hardly troubling to conceal the condescension in it.

The judge glanced around the court, satisfying himself all was in place. 'May we have the witness in now, please?'

Matt's stomach knotted as Camilla made her way, looking straight ahead of her, to the witness box. She had clearly not slept. The dark hollows around her eyes were shocking against the blanched skin, giving her a wrenching death's-head beauty. She nodded mutely as the judge reminded her she was under oath, shook her head when he leaned to ask if she preferred to sit, straightening and gripping the edge of the stand. As Barnes turned to her, preparing to resume his examination, Matt could sense every heart in the room going out to this tragic, dignified figure. He dropped his head in his hands as, with a theatrical swirl of his gown, Barnes turned to the Crown Prosecution Service official behind him and asked for the first of the diaries.

Camilla stared dumbly down at the diaries with Barnes's invitation to examine them pounding in her ears. Slowly, she prised her fingers loose from the edge of the stand. Her arm seemed heavy as she began desultorily turning the pages. Her eye ran over the entries. Stories, some running into a dozen or more pages, with their arbitrary chapter divisions, punctuated the painstaking record of the microscopic crises and minute pleasures of an infant's life. Her chest contracted as the jumble of memories flooded back once more, moments of aching happiness mingling with the hurt, bright, incandescent spots in the dark landscape of betrayal. She scarcely heard Barnes's questions, answering automatically in a drab, emotionless voice as he established for the jury the authenticity of the diaries. Only when Barnes turned to the sketches and symbols, reading out page numbers for her and the jury, did she become aware of the jury scrabbling to find the pages among the photostat sheets in their folders while Barnes waited, a hand on his hip, and Annie sat tight-lipped, her pen poised over the foolscap pad on her table. The image of Matt swam at the edge of her vision. The urge to look at him was almost irresistible, forcing her to cock her head awkwardly away from him.

'Miss Stenner, when did you recall the existence of these diaries?'

'During the time I was being treated by Stephen – Stephen Letzer.'

'The therapist whom your parents engaged to treat you after you had attempted to kill yourself?'

Annie sprang to her feet. The judge nodded, turning wearily to Barnes, who inclined his head, smirking pleasantly at Annie. 'Miss Stenner, who engaged Mr Letzer's services?'

'My parents.'

'And at what point was that?'

'After ... after ... I tried to kill myself. I wasn't responding to the treatment I was getting.'

'Was Mr Letzer known to you prior to your parents' retaining him?'

'No.'

'I see. And did your parents, in suggesting that you should see Mr Letzer, indicate to you whether he had sought them out?'

'It was made quite clear. He was recommended to them, by Naomi. Naomi Butler, the therapist I was seeing at the time.'

'So, it was put to you that they had sought *him* out, rather than the other way around?'

'That's right.' Camilla drank water, draining the glass, and held it out for more.

'And what were the circumstances of your suddenly remembering these diaries?'

'I just remembered. During therapy.'

'Quite. But perhaps you could explain to the jury what the therapy consisted of. For example, were you under any kind of, well, influence? Medication of any kind? Or perhaps, as the defence might perhaps suggest, some form of hypnosis, or suggestion?'

'We just used to talk. I never took any kind of drugs with Stephen. He never hypnotised me, either.' Six paces away, Annie's thick eyebrows twitched and she hurriedly scribbled a note.

'Thank you.' He grinned wolfishly at Annie. 'And now, Miss Stenner, I'm afraid I'm going to have to ask you to bear with me while you explain for us the detailed meanings of the contents of these diaries.'

For the rest of the morning Barnes led Camilla, page by harrowing page, through the diaries, apologising repeatedly as he had her explain the repulsive meanings of sketch after sketch to the spellbound jury. It was a risk. Several times Camilla was forced to sit and rest while she fought tears. Twice she appeared close to complete breakdown, forcing Matt to fight down a surge of hope that she might abandon her testimony altogether. Each time, she had plunged him back into his profound despair by recovering her composure,

304

even refusing the judge's suggestion that she continue sitting, doggedly hauling herself back to her feet.

As the lunchtime recess approached it was plain from the jury's rapt faces, with two of the women staunching tears, that Barnes's dangerous strategy had paid off handsomely. At that moment nobody in the courtroom could doubt that Camilla was a deeply damaged woman, fighting bravely to overcome savage injuries. Injuries that went beyond the physical hurt to leave deep scars on her soul. Injuries that he, her father, had callously inflicted.

The waiter hovered at Matt's elbow, eyeing their untouched plates uncertainly. At a curt nod from Matt, he began scooping them onto his tray. As the four of them waited in silence for him to finish, Matt could feel the prurient looks of the scattering of other customers crawling over him like slugs. Opposite him, Liz stared sightlessly down at the table. The skin of her face looked thin and papery, drawn tight over her cheek-bones. Fatigue and hurt were etched into the flesh around her eyes. As the waiter retreated, leaving them alone in the secluded alcove, Matt covered her hand with his. It was as cold and lifeless as marble. 'Thanks for coming. It helps.'

It was some time before she looked up. 'That's okay.' She turned to Mark, at her side. 'God knows, I couldn't let Mark sit through this on his own.'

Below the table Annie's knee touched briefly against Matt's in a gesture of encouragement. She leaned towards Liz. 'Liz, I know it was hell for you this morn-ing – for all of you – but you *mustn't* jump to con-clusions.' A sudden passion lit her face, surprising after the silent morosity of the meal. 'Never let it out of your mind, Liz, not for a second, this whole *case* is fabricated! Everything you heard this morning has

305

been constructed, piece by piece, by Letzer.' Liz looked at her dumbly, with the same hurt eyes. Annie craned nearer, sending the vase, with its single rose, flying, not even seeing it. 'You'll see it, Liz. Be strong for a few days more.' She addressed them all. 'Roy's turned up a graduation picture of Hampton, from a high school in Oregon. It'll be here today. Also, they've drawn a blank on Letzer. *Nobody* of that name was ever registered at a high school. A few other Letzers, but they've all checked out. *Our* Stephen Letzer never existed at all until 1989. He was almost thirty years old, by then! We've obtained some telephoto shots of Letzer. As soon as Hampton's picture arrives we'll be having them compared. Our clever Mr Letzer is in for a very big shock.'

She turned back to Liz. The intensity of Annie's gaze seemed to impale her. 'Matt didn't do it, Liz. You have to believe that.' Liz made no response, continuing to stare at her, hollow-eyed, expressionless. Without warning, Annie half rose from her chair, and leaned forward until her face was only inches from Liz's. 'He *couldn't* have!' Beneath the table Matt's leg forced itself against hers. He raised a hand as though to restrain her and then let it fall back, willing her back into her seat. Abruptly, Annie sat limply back. 'He *couldn't* have,' she repeated, in a vehement whisper.

Sobbing, she stood up and rushed from the room.

'Mrs Trevellyn?' Davies's smile was faintly bored.

Annie got to her feet, automatically tucking a loose strand of hair back into place. The touch of her hair somehow added to her unaccustomed nervousness. To Barnes, and to the judge, the lack of a wig marked her out. As a solicitor with a Higher Court Certificate she had as much right as Barnes to appear in such a case. Yet she knew from a dozen tiny signs and minute condescensions that in their eyes she was an interloper, breaking the rules of the club. Past experience of Judge Davies had also convinced her that he resented it all the more for her being a woman. Normally she would have revelled in such knowledge. Now, looking around the packed courtroom, composing herself, she felt a deep sense of inadequacy. Turning to find Camilla's eyes fixed on hers, her misgiving gave way to a sudden, stomach-churning panic.

She saw with absolute clarity how wrong she had been to succumb to Matt's emotional blackmail, not to have insisted they take a barrister, leaving her own commitment to Matt to be channelled into the preparation of the case. A stranger would not now be feeling what she felt, the past dragging at her shoulders like a physical weight as she faced this young woman whom she had watched grow up. A stranger would not have wanted to run to Camilla, to shout to the world that her father was innocent, that she could love him again as he had always deserved to be loved. As she still loved him herself.

'Miss Stenner,' she began, her voice echoing in her ears, 'you told the court that your therapist, Stephen Letzer, never used hypnosis on you, is that correct?'

'Yes, it is.'

'Quite. Later we shall be hearing testimony from experts that it is in fact a simple matter for a trained hypnotist to implant what I believe is called a hypnotic block in a patient. This means the patient retains no memory whatever of having been hypnotised. If this were so, you could not be certain it had not happened to you, could you?'

The judge's chapped cheeks creased in a smile as Barnes sprang to his feet.

'Your Honour, the witness cannot be expected to speculate in this manner.'

'Yes, Mr Barnes. Mrs Trevellyn?' He arched an eyebrow at Annie as she got to her feet again. She bowed.

'You are aware that Mr Letzer displays a diploma in hypnosis on his office wall?'

'Yes. But he would never have used it on me. Not without my agreement.'

'I see.' Annie smiled warmly. 'Even though expert opinion might insist you have no way of knowing, you are nevertheless ready to say on oath that Mr Letzer did not hypnotise you. Because you *trust* him?' She looked at the jury as she emphasised 'trust', leaning just heavily enough on the word to leave it lying in the jury's minds.

'That's right,' Camilla answered firmly.

'If we could show you that Mr Letzer is, in fact, an inveterate liar and cheat, would you reconsider that trust?'

Camilla cast a searching look to the gallery. 'No. He isn't a liar,' she said, her voice breaking with emphasis.

Annie's smile was thinner. 'But if he were, a very big one, and if we could demonstrate that fact to you, would you then reconsider, or would you continue to have confidence in him?'

Barnes was on his feet again. Without waiting for the judge, Annie bowed. 'Don't answer that, Miss Stenner.' She paused, letting the jury absorb the exchange. 'You and Stephen Letzer are very . . . close, aren't you?'

Camilla's glance flew again to the gallery. She nodded. 'He's helped me face all of . . . this.' She flapped a hand at the courtroom.

'Of course. But it's more than that, isn't it? You said yourself you are at the point where you would believe him, even if we showed you he was an inveterate liar. Miss Stenner, are you in love with Stephen Letzer?'

Watching through splayed fingers, Matt saw the panic veil Camilla's eyes. Again, her glance went to the gallery. He wanted to reach out, to take her hand, to tell her the whole truth, anything to spare her this agony.

Annie's voice was calm but implacable. 'That's the truth, isn't it, Miss Stenner? Stephen Letzer was being paid by your family to treat you for psychological problems. He betrayed them, and you, by taking advantage of your vulnerable condition and making you fall in love with him?'

Camilla looked down at the floor, her face working. 'No! It's not the way you make it seem. It's . . . I'm very fond of Stephen . . . I . . .' She pressed her hands to her watering eyes.

'Perhaps, Mrs Trevellyn, the witness would like to sit down?' the judge asked, his voice kindly, but his eye flinty as he looked at Annie.

Trembling with the effort, Camilla stemmed the tears. She shook her head, pulling back her shoulders. 'No!'

Annie turned to the judge. 'I think I've exhausted that line of questioning in any case, Your Honour.' She turned slowly back to Camilla. 'Miss Stenner, you're a wealthy woman, aren't you?'

Camilla shrugged. 'I don't have capital of my own.'

'But you do receive a substantial income, from a trust fund, don't you?'

'I suppose so. But it's all controlled by my father.'

'Until when will that situation persist?'

Camilla frowned, genuinely puzzled. 'Until I'm twenty-eight, I think. We never discussed it much.'

'But there are circumstances in which you wouldn't have to wait so long, aren't there?'

Camilla's frown deepened. 'Are there?'

A momentary frown touched Annie's brow. 'You are familiar with the terms of your uncle's trust fund?'

'As I said, I know that at twenty-eight I can take

control of my share. What else is there to know? Daddy always handled it.'

Annie flicked a glance at Matt. He gave her a doomed shrug. 'Miss Stenner, do you at least know the value of your share?'

Camilla shook her head. 'Not really. Quite a lot. The fact is, until ... until ... all this ... I never really thought about money, not in the sense of the future. I always had everything I needed. I knew Daddy was earning a huge amount from his writing, that there were investments. I just sort of supposed ... well, that money wouldn't be a problem.'

Matt could see the calculation behind Annie's eyes, could see her thinking it out, wondering about changing tack. 'Miss Stenner, the current capital value of your share of your Uncle Patrick's trust is about ... two million pounds.' She paused, letting the figure settle among the jury. 'You knew *that*, at least?'

Camilla splayed her hands. 'It seems a lot. I had no real idea.'

Annie looked down at her notes, giving herself time. Camilla's answers resonated with the matter-of-fact spontaneity of truth, and yet she had no choice but to pursue the questions to their conclusion, unsure now that this would bring her out where she had expected to be. 'Really?' The sarcasm was ugly in her own ears, bringing with it another flash of anger at Matt for forcing her into the situation. 'And are you also unaware that there is a condition in the trust deeds which gives you *immediate* control of your share ... if your father,' Annie turned and gestured towards the dock, where Matt hunched intently forward, his face in a permanent grimace of pain, 'Matthew Stenner, were to be convicted and go to prison?'

Sheer, dumb surprise filled Camilla's face. 'What? Of course I didn't know that!' Instinct overcame her as she turned to look directly at Matt. 'Why would . . . ?' She broke off, her face pinched in puzzlement.

Annie looked down at the floor and then slowly, theatrically, raised her eyes again. 'Miss Stenner,' her voice was just enough above a whisper to be audible while forcing the court to an attentive hush, 'please help us all to understand. A deed, detailing the conditions of a trust worth over two *million* pounds to you . . .' She turned, her gaze traversing slowly over the jurors' faces, briefly holding each one's eyes, '. . . a fortune, this document lay in the open safe in your father's study throughout most of your lifetime. And yet, neither as a child, nor even as a teenager, with all the curiosity about the future that that age brings, you never once *read* it?'

Camilla shook her head. 'I was never really interested. I told you, I knew Daddy was rich. Somehow Patrick's trust – it never seemed . . . really *mine*, I suppose.'

Annie paused again. The path of her attack was crumbling under her feet yet she had no choice but to continue. 'Did you tell Mr Letzer of the existence of the trust?'

Camilla reflected. 'I don't think so. He knew I had an income.'

'And as you *never* spoke to Mr Letzer of the trust, despite being so close, it naturally follows that you could not have told him of the condition whereby, if he could only devise a way to get your father convicted of a crime, you would within months come into two million pounds. Is that correct?'

A desperate look of pleading entered Camilla's face, as though she were about to speak to Annie as an old friend. An instant later it had gone, beaten back as Camilla's eyes clenched shut, her fists bunched in frustration. 'Yes, it is!' she said at last. 'Stephen *never* let me talk about my money.'

'Unless perhaps under hypnosis,' Annie murmured, making the words reek with scepticism. She quickly raised a hand, before Barnes was even halfway to his feet. 'You needn't answer that, Miss Stenner, of course.' She glanced down at her papers. 'Now, just before we move on to examine your notebooks, I would like to take you over another point. Please forgive me if it's distressing to you, Miss Stenner, but do you remember your aunt's miscarriage?'

Camilla frowned. 'Yes.'

'She miscarried in your house, on the landing close by your bedroom, didn't she? You were present when it happened?'

Camilla nodded, perplexed. 'Yes.'

'It was a very traumatic experience for your aunt, wasn't it?'

'It must have been. I don't think she's ever fully recovered from it.'

'Quite. There must have been a lot of blood, on the carpet, the walls?'

Camilla shrugged, still frowning. 'There must have been. I just remember a lot of shouting, Mummy and Daddy running about with towels and things.'

'Your aunt was several months pregnant when it happened, wasn't she?'

'Seven, I think.'

'Yes. What happened to the foetus, immediately, I mean?'

'It was lying there. Mummy wrapped it in a towel.'

'Was it alive?'

'Of course not.'

'So you were there, barely eight, watching a baby, your long-awaited cousin, lying dead, strangled in its own umbilical, your aunt screaming in distress, blood

312

and fluids all over the place. Miss Stenner, wouldn't it be reasonable to assume that an experience like that, in a girl so young, and so ... sensitive as we know you to have been, would have had deep-seated psychological effects?'

'I was very sad afterwards. All I can remember at the time was being very curious, and quite angry when Mummy made me take Mark away.'

'I see. It's quite possible it could have had subconscious effects, though, isn't it? That the shock might have been so severe that you suppressed the memory of it, just as you claim to have suppressed the memory of the alleged offences?'

Camilla spoke very quietly but unwaveringly. 'In that case, I suppose I would have written about *that* in my diary, wouldn't I?'

Annie looked at Camilla in silence, taking two long breaths before saying, 'Precisely. And perhaps you did. In fact, I would like now to move on to your diaries.'

With steely, patient tenacity, she led Camilla again through the notebooks. At each drawing, each cramped pictogram, she plied Camilla with questions, probing and pressing, ready to pounce at the first hint of inconsistency. She found none.

As the afternoon wore on, Matt sunk deeper and deeper into impotent despair. Camilla's subdued dignity in the face of Annie's relentless, sometimes bullying, attack, had the jury eating out of her hand. The strain showed in her increased pallor, and the way her fingers curled around the rail, only loosening their grip to turn a page or take frequent drinks. Nevertheless, despite sometimes trembling so badly that she spilled the water, she never quite lost her composure, speaking in a soft clear voice as she insisted on the particular significance of each diagram. Entranced by her restraint and courage, the stout woman juror and her neighbour, a lank-haired, slack-faced woman in her twenties, with fingertips yellowed with nicotine, were unconsciously smiling, faint dreamy smiles of sympathy.

Matt made an involuntary sound that was almost a groan, audible enough to make the judge look to him sharply, as a sudden flush of panic rose in him. He *knew* that every word Camilla uttered was false, every word of it scripted by Letzer. And yet, watching her, he knew, too, that it was almost impossible not to be convinced. His eyes went to Annie, fastening on her as she stood, her profile to him as she stooped to make a note. The sight of her calmed his panic. More than ever he was glad he had made her represent him. Now, in the face of Camilla's studied responses, no stranger could have remained convinced of his innocence. Annie *knew* he was innocent, just as he knew. He repeated the words over and over, clinging to their meaning like a drowning man to a spar. Alone in the world, Annie would still be certain of him. Without that, he was no longer sure he would be certain of himself.

As he made himself look into Camilla's face, the thought struck him with the force of a revelation: the person on the stand was not his daughter. Not the real Camilla. She had become a manifestation of Letzer. In Camilla, Letzer had found exactly what he wanted. They had brought to him a loving, gentle creature and, finding her wounded and malleable, he had taken over her whole being, insinuating himself into her mind and spirit. Matt's hands shook in anger and revulsion. Letzer had made Camilla his thing. He would use her, plundering everything he wanted from her until he cast her off, as he had Jill, broken and beyond repair. Except that, with Jill's help, they were going to break the spell.

314

Seeing the judge's eyes slide up to the wall clock he turned his wrist to stare at his watch. It was four thirty-five. Already they had overrun by five minutes. The judge was letting his impatience show.

Annie, too, glanced at the clock. It had been a harrowing afternoon for her as well. 'Miss Stenner, I'm sure most of us, as children, experienced recurrent nightmares. Flying, for example, or shouting and not being heard. Did that happen to you?'

'Yes. Everybody has that, don't they?'

'Probably. And isn't it a fact that these nightmares can be so graphic that, on waking, we are still under their spell? Sad, perhaps, or frightened. Has *that* ever happened to you?'

Camilla made a movement of her shoulders. 'I think so, yes.'

'So sometimes, you agree, you have woken still under the influence, as it were, of a dream, convinced it was real. With your *emotions* affected by your dream?'

'Sometimes, yes.'

'I would like to put it to you that that is exactly what happened with the alleged offences. That they were fantasies, dreams, but so powerful, so horrible, that you woke up believing they had happened. Is that not so?'

Camilla shook her head, her hair flying. 'No! Not at all! I already told you! Sometimes I would be . . . bleeding. His . . .' Her body shook in a spasm of uncontrollable loathing. 'His *semen* was on me!' She was trembling, grinding one fist against her mouth. 'It was horrible. Silvery! Shiny! As though slugs had been climbing on me!'

Annie stood with her head bowed, her teeth sunk into her lower lip. She brushed a hand across her face before looking up. Her voice caught in her throat as she tried to speak. She began again. 'Silvery? Shiny?

Miss Stenner, you told the jury, in answer to my learned friend's question, that you never actually *saw* your father while he was committing these acts. He always turned off your night-light. The alleged offences you said took place in *total* darkness.' As she spoke Annie took up her notepad and flipped back through the closely written pages. She tapped a passage with her finger. 'You said, too, that you didn't dare to turn the light back on again in case he was still there, lurking, waiting to come at you again. Miss Stenner, were you telling the truth?'

'Of course! I never did dare to turn the light on! I saw it in the light from the window. Sometimes there would be a chink in the curtains.'

For just an instant, Annie let her gaze brush over Matt's. A strange, milky light of disquiet glittered in her eyes. 'Miss Stenner, these things happened at night, did they not?'

'Well, yes. But late in the night. Later on, in the spring, it was almost dawn. It would be starting to get light.'

Annie leaned down, making a show of studying her notes. Her hands were flat on the table, supporting her. Her head reeled. Rising nausea hit the back of her throat, flooding her mouth with the bitter taste of it. She turned laboriously back to face Camilla. Her skin was grey. She could feel the blood rushing in the veins of her neck, as though it were draining out of her. 'Miss Stenner, are you claiming that these . . . alleged things happened at *dawn*? Did you have a clock in your bedroom? A *luminous* clock, we would be forced to suppose, since you told us everything that happened did so in total darkness?'

Camilla nodded, frowning at the faintly quavering note in Annie's voice. 'It was *always* just before dawn. I didn't need a clock. It was always around the time the milk lorry came past.' She glanced up at the judge. 'There's a dairy farm next to the house. The lorry always used to come past at five thirty. The driver used to eat breakfast in his cab in a lay-by at the edge of our wood. He still does, as far as I know.'

'Thank you, Miss Stenner.' Annie hardly knew what she was doing. Her words seemed to float to her ears from a great distance away. 'That is all, Your Honour.'

She sat down heavily, almost missing the chair, sending it skidding backwards, its rubber-tipped feet screeching on the woodblock floor. Her head spun. With just time to snatch a handful of tissues to her mouth, she was sick.

Twenty-One

The sounds of the courtroom came to Annie like a half-remembered dream. She must have stood for the judge's withdrawal and sat down again without even knowing it. She was only vaguely aware of Hannah, scrambling to clear up around her. At Camilla's words her mind had gone reeling back to those first nights with Matt. It had been very soon after their affair had begun. The image flooded back so strongly she could see him in front of her, taste him, smell his body. She could feel again his strength as he turned her over, hear her own first whimper as he dragged her hips back and down, positioning her for what he intended. His breath was a quickening pant, warm on her neck as he bent low over her, his shoulders twice as wide as hers, whispering, cajoling. She heard again her own refusal, at first whispered and then louder, adamant in the face of his pleas, and yet half afraid to refuse, scared of losing him. The courtroom chair moved under her involuntary movement as she relived the moment when she had pulled away from him, denying him what he wanted. She flushed as she recalled how grateful, how absurdly, childishly relieved she had been that he had accepted her refusal. Once or twice in those first nights he had tried again, persuading, cajoling, but never forcing, always gentle and amused in the face of her timidity. Then, after a while, he had let it drop.

Abruptly, she rose and, with Hannah hurrying at

her side, too sensitive to her moods to speak, she strode from the courtroom.

Matt had not seen Annie vomit. The moment Camilla had spoken, he had squeezed his eyes shut, as though trying to shut out the implications of her words. He sat, with his head bowed, his fingers clamped over the edge of the dock, the knuckles white. For a long time he could not move. He felt like a miner trapped in a rock-fall, a sense of suffocating blackness, of debris, pressing in all around him. The rough hand of the custody officer yanking at his arm brought his head up, his eyes slowly opening. He looked stupidly around him in time to see Annie striding from the room. Above him, Liz and Mark were now alone in the gallery, Liz clinging to Mark's arm as she looked down, her face an unreadable mix of emotions. With a stilted salute to them, he walked woodenly out of the dock.

Alone in the robing room, staring into the mirror, Annie heard Camilla's answer screaming shrilly in her head.

Five thirty!

Every single day during his year in Hong Kong, Roger had phoned her. And like everything Roger ever did, it had to be at the time that best suited *him*. He would call at lunchtime, from his office, his voice muffled by the sandwiches he ate at his desk. And so, each night, she would set Matt's alarm for four forty-five. Sliding from his bed, she would dress silently, kiss him as he sleepily watched her, and slip from the house to drive the few minutes home.

At five thirty, showered, dressed, and still thinking dreamily of Matt, her skin still feeling the heat of him, she would be in her kitchen, a cup of coffee at her elbow, to take Roger's call. And now, for the first time, the question sprang at her. Could it be that he had not gone back to sleep after all? Could he have taken her refusal to give him what he sought so easily because . . . because he knew that he could obtain it at any time, only a few steps down the corridor?

Quickly, she wet a handful of tissues and pressed the coolness of them to her temples and eyes. Gradually, her turbulent thoughts subsided. She looked hard at herself in the mirror, asking the questions again, but coolly now, images of the Matt she had known for so long flashing through her mind, displacing the ugliness. She pictured him as she had seen him with his children, with Liz. And with herself, for a while as a lover and then as the staunchest of friends through the difficult years with Roger. Most of all, she saw him as he had been with William. The uncountable hours he had spent with William in the pool, coaxing the boy to make use of his withered, uncoordinated limbs. Or wrestling with him on the lawn, as lithe as a kitten despite his size, reducing William to helpless laughter, happy in a way Roger had never wanted, or known how to, make him.

She opened her mouth wide, stretching the muscles of her jaw, and worked her shoulders, shaking out the tensions that lay knotted under the skin. It simply could not be. She repeated the words aloud, watching her own lips in the mirror. It was just not allowable to admit even a twinge of doubt about Matt. She had loved him as she had never loved anyone, before or since. Her breath came in a long, slow sigh as the question she had never dared put openly to herself finally forced its way to the surface. Had he ever loved her? Or had he only ever been using her, a convenient stand-in for Liz? As he was using her now, perhaps, in making her defend him, using her guilt for his own purpose?

*　　*　　*

The sense of relief as Annie swung the car around the last bend in the lane, bringing the house into view, was palpable. The long drive up from Chichester had taken place in virtual silence, each of them drained and disturbed by the events of the day. Annie had driven like an automaton, silent and whey-faced, deep in her own thoughts. Next to her, Mark, as silent as Annie, exuded a dangerous tension, as though at any moment he might explode into a blind rage or hysterical grief. In the rear, Matt lolled, exhausted, his head against the leather. Liz sat next to him. Overwrought from the day, she had gratefully accepted Annie's suggestion that she leave her car and ride home with them. She sat as she had throughout the journey, straight-backed and watchful, the strain apparent in the fluttering of the tic which narrowed her left eye to a squint, and the tight set of her jaw. Her hand lay unmoving on the seat, her fingers curled in Matt's, lifeless and unresponsive, held but not holding.

Annie had hardly brought the car to a halt before Rachel appeared at the front door and began moving with her stately, swaying walk down the steps to meet them. Seeing her, Matt came suddenly alive. He sprang from the car and sprinted across the mossy cobbles towards her. 'Rachel, what's up? Is it Jill? Has something happened?'

'No. She's asleep again. Still getting over her trip, I imagine. The nurse is with her!' She proffered a brown envelope she had held half hidden in the folds of her skirt. 'I signed for this.'

Matt spun back to where Annie was already pulling away, brandishing the envelope at her. 'Hey! It's the picture! Hampton!' With the others jostling excitedly at his shoulder, he extracted and held up a single photocopied sheet.

Disappointment stunned him. The page, cut from a

high school year-book, was densely covered with a dozen or more bleary passport-sized photographs, each with a caption beneath. Matt stared despondently at the one Erskine had ringed. Dark hair hung to the shoulders. A wispy, adolescent beard blurred the chin. The thick-lensed granny glasses made it impossible to discern the eyes. He scanned the caption. 'Lewis Hampton. Lewis knows he doesn't have John Lennon's talent. But he'd settle for the royalties!'

Annie was the first one to find words. 'Sounds as though he was making enemies already.'

Matt didn't laugh. 'I'm fucked, aren't I?' He let his arm drop to his side. 'Letzer doesn't even wear glasses, for Christ's sake.' He took Liz by the hand. 'Can we go inside? I need a drink.'

They were halfway across the hall when Liz said, in a whisper, 'He wears lenses.' Matt's head jerked around to look at her. Her eyes shone with a strange excitement. 'Men never notice things like that. I saw them, when we were in his office, when he stood against the window. You know I've always disliked them, especially on men. They've always struck me as a sign of vanity.'

'Liz, are you absolutely sure?' Matt asked.

'Of course. There was even a bottle of lens fluid on his desk.'

'You see.' Annie took the sheet from Matt's hand and tilted it to the light. 'Take my advice and don't start losing even more sleep. My office will have a copy, too, to send away for enhancement.' She made a *moue* of distaste. 'The agency mostly works for the tabloids, working up long-range shots of celebs taken by snoopers. We use them occasionally, usually in especially nasty divorce cases.' She handed the picture back to him. 'You'll be amazed. By the time they've programmed out all that hair, so that he's got cheekbones and a chin, and taken the glasses away, there will be the youthful Letzer.' She tapped the caption. 'Dreaming of a fortune, if not the fame he's about to acquire.' She handed the sheet back, looking at her watch. 'Look, I can't stay. I'll be late for William,' she said, suddenly brusque.

Matt glanced automatically at his watch. They had made good time on the journey back. She would be at the hospital twenty minutes ahead of her usual time. Reading his look, she quickly averted her eyes. 'What about tomorrow, Liz . . . ?' She broke off, made uncomfortable by something in Liz's eyes.

Liz looked quickly at Matt. After a moment of hesitation she said, 'Could you pick me up?' She hesitated again before adding, 'I'll still be at Rachel's.'

As she spoke, Liz's eyes locked onto Annie's. For a long moment the two friends remained staring into each other's faces. Annie felt dizzy, as though she would fall. In that instant she was certain Liz had at last understood everything. Triggered by the mounting doubt about Letzer's integrity she had finally let herself make the connection, the connection Annie had wanted, and feared, when she had defended Matt in the restaurant. 'Of course. Bye.' She strode quickly away.

Inside the house the phone rang. Mark dashed to answer. Seconds later, he reappeared, running. Annie's car was about to sweep out of the courtyard when he banged a hand on the roof. 'Annie! It's Roy Erskine. For you.'

She took the call in the kitchen, the others pressing eagerly round her. 'Roy? We got the picture. Is that really the best you can do?'

'Afraid so. Pretty poor, isn't it? Experts tell me it's probably not a professional job like the others, but a do-it-yourself, from a booth. Don't complain, though. The reason is, Hampton was in hospital the day they had the photographer in to do the graduation pictures.'

'You sound as though that's supposed to be good news.'

Roy chuckled. 'It might be. He was being treated for a football injury. The hospital record shows he broke his tibia in two places.'

Annie frowned. 'Roy, Letzer isn't going to submit to an X-ray to enable us to prove he's somebody else.'

'I know. But if the dead man down in Mexico *doesn't* have the broken leg, then Hampton isn't dead. Seems to me you've got more chance of convincing the jury that Letzer and Hampton are the same man if you can also show Hampton's death was faked.'

'My God, Roy, that's for sure. But, Roy, we've only got a few days at most. You're never going to get an exhumation and an affidavit out of the local police in that time.'

'Maybe you're right, Annie. But I've sent Larry down there today with a bagful of Matt's money.' He laughed softly. 'Let's hope there are still some things money *can* buy. If you offer enough of it!'

Annie slotted the car into the garage and turned off the motor. Instead of getting out, she sat quite still, staring sightlessly at the wall. It was a little after one o'clock. The drive from the hospital should have taken her twenty minutes. In fact, she had driven around for nearly two hours, winding at random through the narrow lanes, fighting to make some sense of the day's events. Time and again, saying it aloud over the muted hum of the engine, she had told herself Matt *must* be innocent. Anything else was unthinkable. And each time, in the silence that followed, the same disturbing thoughts forced their way insidiously back into her consciousness.

Until today Matt had not needed her faith. She *knew* he was innocent. Now, faith was all she had left. She knew now that he *had* had the opportunity. And she could even provide a motive. She groaned aloud. Until a few hours ago she had felt that ultimately she was in control, knowing exactly what she was doing. Her offer to give alibi evidence would have thrown the trial into total confusion. Davies would probably have tried to refuse to admit it, invoking the convention that alibi evidence should have been produced before the trial ever began. Nevertheless, she could almost certainly have convinced him, or at least an appeal hearing, that her evidence was admissible. Since four thirty that afternoon that was dead in the water. Even perjuring herself for Matt, an idea that had come to her more than once during her drive, was out of the question. Roger would never have let them get away with it.

Another image flooded her mind. Liz's intense, clouded stare as Annie had been about to leave the house before the call from Roy.

She laughed aloud, short and high-pitched, at the irony of the situation. Liz, who had doubted Matt and had tried to buy Letzer off and avoid the trial, had seen her doubts swept away by the knowledge of Annie and Matt's affair. She, Annie, whose testimony until that afternoon could have cleared Matt, had nothing left but blind faith. Shivering with a sudden chill, she climbed quickly from the car and ran to the house.

Locks of hair, damp from the shower, clung to Annie's forehead as she paused at the bedside, listening to the rasping of Roger's breath. Soundlessly, she lowered herself into bed beside him. Instead of immediately giving way to fatigue, she sat for some time, letting her eyes become accustomed to the pale summer darkness, watching. In sleep, Roger's big, domed head seemed heavy as stone, pressing deep into the pillows. His jaw hung slackly, a silvery glint of saliva at the corner of his mouth trembling in the stream of his breath. A shift in the light from the open window as the moon emerged from a film of cloud seemed to penetrate his sleep. His breath caught in his throat with a phlegmy sound. He opened his eyes, without raising his head from the pillow, and caught the gleam reflecting on her cheek. He moved his big hand under the sheet and squeezed her thigh. 'No sense crying. The boy couldn't be in better hands. Done all *we* could.' His head fell to the side, his eyes closing again, instantly asleep.

Annie looked at him for a long time and then, brushing the tears away with her hand, she settled beneath the duvet, turning her back to him, and buried her face deep in the pillow.

'Professor Worthington, perhaps you could begin by telling us your qualifications.'

Matt watched poker-faced as Barnes smiled expansively at the jury, inviting their attention. It was not hard to understand his satisfaction. Just taking the oath, Worthington had already impressed them. Tall, burly, with a broad, battered face, mildly unruly brown hair, and a readiness to smile, he exuded dependability. Now, his response to Barnes's invitation, as he listed a string of degrees, his voice, deep and unhurried, with its flattened northern vowels, completed the picture of understated competence. Matt studied the faces of the jurors as the man spoke. The average age must be around forty. There could be no more than three of them too young to have heard first-hand the weekly radio series the professor had chaired for years, advising listeners with problem children. The prosecution probably calculated that, in addition to being one of the country's leading experts on child sexual abuse, his fame would counter any tendency for the jury to be impressed by Matt's own celebrity.

'Professor Worthington, earlier this year, you were asked to examine Camilla Stenner, is that correct?'

Worthington nodded. 'Yes.' He was already fishing a pair of half-moon spectacles from his breast pocket.

Barnes proffered a document. 'And this, I believe, is your report of that examination?' He waited for Worthington to scan the pages and nod. 'Good.' He turned to the judge and jury. 'Pages seventy to seventy-four in the bundles, Your Honour.' The jury scrambled to find the pages. Only when the rustle of paper had died away, leaving the courtroom hushed, did he turn back to Worthington. 'Professor Worthington, would you be kind enough to summarise for the court the findings of your examination?'

Matt felt breathless, trapped, as though Worthington's slow, careful testimony was being piled on top of him, crushing him under its weight. He hardly followed individual words, conscious only of the sense of horror filling the room like a foul stench as the familiar, fruity voice rolled on, describing in dispassionate detail the extent of Camilla's scarring, and the injuries that she must have sustained. His testimony was made all the more impressive, and all the more shocking, by the man's bluff, plain language.

Barnes let him speak uninterrupted for twenty minutes, silent and apparently pensive as he let Worthington's natural authority do his work for him. He only intervened when Worthington began speculating as to the extent of any bleeding, holding aloft a thin sheaf of eight by ten photographs.

'Your Honour, I wonder if this might be an appropriate time to exhibit the originals of the photographs.

I think it's important that the members of the jury should see them now. I also think it important to remind the court that these photographs are recent, and that it is not in dispute that whatever the *cause* of it may have been, the scarring which is visible in the photographs results from injuries suffered over a dozen years ago.'

At the judge's nodded approval an usher took the pictures from Barnes and, after carefully labelling them with their exhibit number, handed them to the jury.

Matt squeezed his eyes closed. Blood drummed in his ears. He clenched his fists, seeing the photographs in his mind, fighting down the urge to be sick. Barnes had timed his thrust to perfection. He had let Worthington set the scene for him, so that by the time he produced the pictures he appeared almost as a disinterested observer. Instead of the snake-smooth manipulator, orchestrating a carefully contrived attack, he was transformed into a mere messenger, inviting the jury to worship, with him, before this undisputed authority.

The jury members could not contain their shock. Disgust ran through them in a slow wave, in the wake of the circulating pictures. Several of them, passing the pictures on, looked up at Matt from under lowered eyelids, no longer even remembering to keep the loathing out of their eyes.

'May I ask you, Professor Worthington, whether at any time in your career, from the time you began in medicine, through the years when you were, as it were, paediatrician to the nation, courtesy of the BBC,' he paused, shamelessly milking Worthington's media status, 'during all those, what, thirty years of practice, did you ever encounter tearing such as the jury have been asked to look at in those photographs, to which you felt able to attribute any cause other than anal –'

He broke off as Annie sprang to her feet. The judge

nodded, smoothing a stray wisp of grey hair wearily back behind his ear as he turned to Barnes. 'You know better than that, Mr Barnes. Try again, please.'

The indignation Barnes had been cranking up was still in his face as he bowed. 'I'm sorry, Your Honour.' He was playing to the jury now, knowing they were with him. 'I, ah, got carried away. Professor Worthington, with the benefit of your long and distinguished experience in the field, what, in your opinion, would cause such injuries as Miss Stenner suffered?'

Matt's eyes were glued to Worthington. He saw the man's thick chest dilate, tugging at the buttoned tweed jacket, and then they were looking directly into each other's eyes as Worthington peered over his spectacles as if trying to read him. Hope leaped in Matt. The broad face held none of the bleak hostility he had seen in the jurors. He merely looked curious, faintly dismayed, as though wondering how Matt could conceivably have come there. Matt returned his gaze, his eyes aching with the effort to make them tell it, to let the man know he was innocent. He found his mind running in random, futile paths. Their ages were only a few years apart. Given half an hour of conversation they would unearth a dozen people they both knew, a score of restaurants they both had eaten at.

Worthington's chest fell as he spoke, his words a sigh. 'Anal intercourse. The common word for it is . . . buggery.'

Annie rose slowly to her feet to cross-examine. Watching Worthington testify, she had become aware of a choking, oppressive feeling. At first, she had put it down to the heat in the courtroom, which overwhelmed the labouring air-conditioning, and had already prompted the judge to suggest that he and Barnes remove their wigs. Now, turning to face

Worthington, the nagging oppression resolved itself suddenly into an enveloping sense of defeat. Worthington's physical and intellectual presence dominated the courtroom. He simply radiated flinty integrity. She knew with absolute certainty that she was not going to shake him in the essentials of his statements. Even to try too hard would make her, and their entire case, look cheap and foolish.

'Professor Worthington, is it your experience that constipation, especially severe constipation, can be a cause of . . . splitting and bleeding from the rectal area?'

Worthington shook his head. 'I've never seen anything on that sc –' He broke off in response to Annie's sharply raised hand.

'Please, Professor Worthington, if you could confine yourself to answering the question.'

Worthington sucked at his teeth, chafing at the restriction. 'Yes. Constipation, or its relief, can sometimes give rise to such symptoms.'

'It can result in scarring?'

'It can certainly cause wounds, which might lead to scarring, but not on anything like the scale in those photographs.'

Annie looked ruefully down at the floor. He had got it out anyway, before she could stop him. 'But it can leave visible scars?'

'It's not impossible.'

'And the extent of that scarring would depend, surely, on the exact extent and nature of the sufferer's problem? In other words, you could not predict exactly how bad it might turn out to be in a particular case.'

'That's of course true, but there are sensible limits to these things. I would *never* expect anything even resembling what Miss Stenner displays.'

'But it varies enormously from sufferer to sufferer?'

'It varies, yes, but in my experience it's never more than slight, superficial splitting.'

Annie shuffled some notes, playing for time as she sought another approach that might give her a fingerhold in the smooth rock-face of his evidence. 'Professor Worthington, you are aware that Miss Stenner was treated for constipation at the time of the alleged assaults?'

'Yes. I saw her old medical records in the course of preparing my report.'

'And, having seen those records, you regard them as valid?'

'I accept that constipation was among her problems. It would follow from –'

Once again, Annie's out-turned palm cut him short. 'Thank you. That answers my question. Professor, please confirm for the court that your special area of expertise is in child abuse?'

'Yes.'

'Not the stomach and bowel, the digestive tract?'

'Not as a speciality, no, although –'

Once again, Annie's upraised hand cut him off. 'Professor Worthington, you know that Miss Stenner's general practitioner at that time was approaching retirement, a man with thirty-odd years' experience, who had known Miss Stenner from birth? Had attended her birth, even?'

'Yes. I know that.'

'And are you saying that now, at a dozen years' remove, *you* can make a more reliable diagnosis of her condition than *he*, a very experienced doctor, was able to do at the time, and with the advantage of being able to examine Camilla's injuries, rather than just the scars?'

'Time teaches us things. Views of child abuse have

changed. Our knowledge is better. At that time it was widely believed that it only happened in . . . shall I say . . . less privileged families. Now we know differently. We know it cuts across barriers of income or class. I believe a doctor today, faced with the same symptoms in a child, would respond very differently.'

'May I ask you, Professor, do you have children?'

'Yes. A son and a daughter. Grown up now.'

'But, had you found one of them as children, showing signs of emotional disorder, would you have sought first the opinion of an admired and respected general practitioner, a doctor of what I might term the old school, or would you have entrusted them to a young, inexperienced therapist with mail-order qualifications from dubious American colleges?'

Worthington laughed aloud. 'I couldn't begin to answer that.'

'Try, Professor, please.'

Worthington hitched his glasses up his nose and smiled genially. 'I would probably have gone for the doctor.'

'Thank you. Then let me cover one last point, Professor. You told us just now that abuse is now recognised to be common in all classes. Would you agree that in the past there has been a tendency for it to be, as it were . . . pursued more diligently where it occurred among the less privileged?'

Worthington shifted, uneasy for the first time. 'I wouldn't want to denigrate the work of the police, or anybody else, but I would be inclined to agree that it has perhaps been easier for somebody . . . ah, better placed in society . . . to have the powers that be take his or her word for things.'

'But that situation is changing, isn't it? Would you say that today there is a welcome trend for more equality in the eyes of the law, and of the social services? A greater determination to pursue offenders, regardless of their social prominence?'

'I think that's true. I hope so.'

'I'm sure we all hope so.' Annie paused, pretending to study her notes, letting the silence fill the room. When she resumed, her voice was lower, serene. 'Can I put it to you, Professor, that the defendant, Matthew Stenner, is a victim of this new-found zeal? That it is precisely because of the defendant's prominence that he finds himself in the dock? Isn't it in fact the case that the Crown Prosecution Service, with the best intentions, saw Miss Stenner's allegations, which, I remind the court, were totally uncorroborated at the time they were made, as a heaven-sent opportunity to display their even-handedness? Isn't the defendant, Matthew Stenner, a victim here, too? A victim of his own standing? Of political correctness gone mad?'

Barnes was on his feet, a hand extended. The judge nodded curtly. Irritation glinted in his eyes as he leaned towards Annie. 'Mrs Trevellyn, you are well aware that the witness cannot possibly be required to answer any such questions!'

Worthington glanced up at the judge and drew himself up taller. 'I can only tell you that, as far as *my* report and my opinions are concerned, they are based on the facts as I have been able to observe them.'

Annie smiled courteously and gave him a little bow. 'Thank you, Professor. I have no more questions.'

The usher followed Worthington from the court. Peter Monroe was called next.

'Dr Monroe, you are Miss Stenner's GP?'

'That's right.'

'And before coming here you familiarised yourself with her past notes, especially those written around the time she was seven and eight years old?'

'Yes.'

'It's a hypothetical question, Dr Monroe, but what would your reaction be if today somebody brought a child into your office suffering symptoms similar to those Miss Stenner was suffering from when your predecessor saw her?'

Monroe's voice caught in his throat. He took a hurried sip of water. 'I would be obliged to alert the social services. Immediately.'

'Would you have any regard for the social standing of the family concerned in making that decision?'

Monroe gnawed at his lip. 'No. I'm afraid experience has shown that doesn't have any bearing where abuse is concerned.'

'I see. Dr Monroe, turning to Miss Stenner's medical notes, as recorded by your predecessor. The defence suggests that Miss Stenner really was experiencing . . . ah . . . bowel trouble at the time. Do you accept that that is probably so?'

'There's no reason to doubt it. The question would be *why*.'

'Indeed. And, in your experience, what might have been the reason, in this particular case . . . ?'

Annie was on her feet. 'With respect, Your Honour, my learned friend is plainly asking the witness to speculate.'

Without waiting for the judge, Barnes, back on his feet, bowed to Annie. 'My apologies. My friend is perfectly correct, Your Honour.' He turned back, smiling graciously, to Monroe.

'Dr Monroe, in the course of your . . . twenty, is it? . . . years of general medical practice you must have encountered many cases of chronic constipation. Could

334

you list for us the causes you have identified over the years, please?'

Monroe hesitated, ordering his thoughts. 'Diet, first. Certain kinds of medication – some cancer treatments, for instance. Emotional disturbance.' He hesitated, as though reluctant to pronounce the word. 'Abuse,' he said, at length. For the first time he looked at Matt, a quick sidelong glance.

'Of all those, Doctor, would any be likely to be accompanied by severe lacerations?'

'Only the last, in my view.'

A ghost of a half-smile played on Barnes's face. 'You are well acquainted with the Stenner family, I believe?'

'Yes, I am.'

'From what you know of them, is it likely that Miss Stenner as a child suffered any dietary deficiency?'

Monroe permitted himself a smile at the absurdity of the suggestion. 'They probably have the healthiest diet of all the patients on my books. Healthier than my own.'

'Does the record show she was on medication, other than what might have been prescribed for the constipation itself?'

'No.'

'Is there anything in Miss Stenner's records to indicate she was being treated for cancer?'

'No, of course not.'

'Is there any mention of emotional or psychological problems prior to the onset of the alleged incidents of abuse?'

'None. Though I have to say that from my personal knowledge of the family, I do believe Camilla was always inclined to be . . . I suppose highly strung would best describe it.'

'Mmm. So, in your opinion, Doctor, what does that leave as the most likely cause of her problem?'

'In the absence of any of the other things, abuse. The constipation perhaps caused directly, as a physical effect, or, I think more likely, a psychological symptom arising out of the emotional upset that would be expected to accompany the abuse.'

'Dr Monroe, shortly before Christmas last year you were called to attend to Camilla Stenner at her home, were you not?'

'Yes.'

'What was the reason for her needing your attention?'

'She appeared to have tried to commit suicide.'

Barnes paused before speaking again, his own voice hushed. 'Did you think it was a serious attempt, or the more common "cry for help"?'

'I took it seriously. She had stabbed herself in the wrists with a pair of scissors. There were puncture wounds, quite deep. She was lucky not to have hit an artery.'

'Did you see much of her following that incident?'

'Not much. Shortly afterwards her parents handed Camilla in to the care of therapists, I believe.'

'Doctor, had there been any previous history, anything that might have seemed to lead up to this, be a foretaste of it?'

'She had something resembling a nervous breakdown as a teenager, I believe.'

'You believe? Were you not asked to treat her?'

'No. Matt and Liz talked to me about it. I visited them at home a couple of times, but basically her mother nursed her through it. Liz is a very competent woman.'

'So, on two occasions she was manifestly not a well person but you, as her doctor, were not really called upon, except in some vague consultative role?'

Matt watched Monroe hesitate. His body swayed as

though he were kicking at the inside of the witness stand. At length he gave a curt nod. 'I suppose that wouldn't be inaccurate.'

'Why do you think that was?' Monroe shrugged. Barnes took a step closer. 'Could it have been that they were anxious you should not see too much of her when she was vulnerable, in case –'

'Your Honour!' Annie called furiously. Barnes deferred, a contained smile on his face.

The judge blew out his cheeks. 'Mrs Trevellyn is right, of course, Mr Barnes.'

Barnes was on his feet again in a theatrical swirl of black cloth. 'My apologies, Your Honour. I withdraw the question, and in fact I have no more questions for Dr Monroe.'

Annie rose slowly to her feet. She poured water into her glass and the carafe clinked hard against it, the noise shockingly loud in the silent room. She drank half the glass at one swallow, paused, and then drank some more. She looked over her glass at Matt, who sat drawn but dispassionate with one hand covering the lower part of his face, masking his expression. A bolt of sheer hatred shot through her, the force of it almost making her gasp out loud.

Peter Monroe and his wife, Sarah, were close and valued friends, part of the group of intelligent, unbigoted people it had taken years to get to know and appreciate. In summer they played tennis together, in winter they played bridge. They ate at each other's houses, swam in each other's pools. For the first time, as she prepared to cross-examine Peter, with Worthington's evidence still echoing in her brain, reinforcing everything Camilla had said, she knew with leaden certainty that the faith was broken, she could no longer believe in Matt's innocence.

With sudden clarity she saw how the pieces slotted together. Matt had manipulated her from the start, insisting she keep her evidence in reserve, hoping she could win him an acquittal without his having to risk losing his family. He had played ruthlessly on the past, reviving feelings he knew were still there, renewing pain she had spent years trying to dull. Had he already been using her, way back then? Had their affair, the love she had believed in so deeply, been no more than a sham? Paedophiles were notorious manipulators, showing incredible patience and cunning, sometimes spending years preparing the ground for what they planned. Could their whole affair have been no more to Matt than an elaborate alibi, its whole purpose to ward off precisely the kind of charges Camilla was making? For a split second, the world went black, as though she were about to faint. By sheer strength of will, she looked into Matt's face. The eyes were still impassive, the rest of his face still hidden by his hand. For a moment she stared fascinated, as though momentarily ensnared in the memory of how she had loved his hands, the strength in the fingers, twice as thick as her own, the spiky tufts of hair that she liked so much to brush with her lips. She turned away, inhaling deeply, picking up her notebook.

'Dr Monroe, in addition to being Camilla Stenner's GP you're also that of the rest of her family, are you not?'

'Yes. Matt and ... er, Mr and Mrs Stenner, and Mark are all patients of mine.' The clipped formality of Peter's reply added to the sense of unreality for Annie.

'Since when?'

He looked to the ceiling, calculating. 'About four years.'

'And before that time would it be fair to describe your two families as friends?'

Monroe swayed as though once again swinging his leg, out of sight below the panels of the stand. 'Yes.'

'Good enough friends to have spent holidays together?'

Annie felt an insane urge to laugh at the absurdity of it. The families regularly took holidays together. And her own family had been with them.

'That's correct, yes.'

'You have a daughter, Annabel, two years older than Camilla Stenner?' Monroe murmured agreement. 'And is it not the case that throughout their teenage years, and long before that, your daughter and Camilla were very close?' Again Monroe murmured agreement, dropping his eyes, seeing quite clearly where Annie was leading him. 'In fact, throughout those years you very frequently allowed your daughter to spend nights at the Stenner house?'

'Yes.'

'Did your daughter stay at the house on many occasions when you knew Mrs Stenner would be absent, when you knew that Mr Stenner would be alone with them overnight?'

'That is certainly true.'

'Dr Monroe, would you have allowed your daughter to go to that house at *all* if you had *ever* had the slightest misgiving about Mr Stenner's behaviour?'

Monroe swallowed hard. 'No, of course not.'

'So, as a close friend of the Stenner family, a trained doctor, vigilant in such matters, you have never seen any reason to curtail your daughter's friendship, or her visits to the house?'

'No.'

'Nothing in Camilla's behaviour aroused your ... apprehension?'

'Well, she was always inclined to be ... brittle ... highly strung. But I can't honestly say it ever worried me, not from a medical point of view.'

'Did you read anything into that "brittleness", as you term it?'

'Not at the time, anyway.'

'And now?'

'Well, it's possible it could be a result of ... earlier experience.'

'But it's quite common for a person to simply *be* highly strung without any need for the "earlier experience" you invoke?'

'Of course it is, yes.'

'And that's what you thought it was with Camilla?'

Monroe spread his hands. 'I had no reason to suspect anything else.'

Annie half turned to the jury. 'Precisely. You missed the signs, didn't you, Doctor? Because you're only human, after all. And isn't it possible, now that you are aware of these allegations being made, and I would remind this court that they are no more than that, that being only human, you find yourself *retrospectively* putting a new interpretation on hitherto innocent acts?'

Monroe bit his lip. 'I don't believe I am doing that.'

'Ah, but you are, aren't you?' Annie spoke sharply. 'Your earlier answers, regarding Camilla's medical records, were an example of just that kind of thing, weren't they?'

Monroe hesitated, blinking. 'I don't agree. I tried to give a clinical opinion.'

Annie brushed aside the self-loathing that had invaded her. 'Quite,' she answered, deliberately applying just a hint of amused disdain. 'A clinical opinion which revises another experienced doctor's opinion, purely in the light of unproven allegations.' She shook her head slowly, inviting no further response from

Monroe, before continuing. 'And at the time your daughter was regularly an overnight guest with Matthew Stenner, did she ever say anything, or behave in any way, or do *anything* that might have given you grounds for even the slightest unease?'

'No. Never.'

'Your daughter is aware of this case, is she not?'

'Certainly.'

'And since Mr Stenner's very well-publicised arrest she has no doubt taken time to reflect on those occasions. Has anything come to mind, has she said anything to you, that would now give you cause for retrospective concern?'

'No.' He drew a deep breath and looked across at the dock, his eyes boring into Matt's. 'Annabel firmly believes Matt is absolutely innocent.'

Twenty-Two

Larry Guenther rubbed his stinging eyes. On the entire two-hundred-mile drive, in pitch darkness, from Monterrey to La Santa his rented Toyota had been the only car with a full set of lights. Blinking away the grittiness, he looked around as the policeman re-entered the office and sauntered across to slump in the chair opposite Larry. 'Sorry, Mr Guenther. The Alcalde is not there. I tried his home.' He glanced at his watch. 'Even though it's very early. He is in Mexico City.'

Larry rested a hand on the slim black document case that lay on the table. 'Couldn't you arrange it yourself?' Larry let his eyes linger on the case. 'Without any other authority, I mean?' He tapped his hand on the case. 'My client's life depends on it. He would . . .' Larry broke off to crane around, ensuring the door was closed. '. . . be very grateful. Very.'

The policeman's eyes followed Larry's to the bag. His tongue flicked over his lips. He seemed about to speak and then swallowed. He shook his head hard. 'No, señor.' He shoved himself to his feet and turned sharply away. 'I can't,' he murmured, more to himself than Larry. 'No exhumation. I never dealt with anything like that. It would need men. No,' he repeated emphatically. 'Not without authorisation from the Alcalde.'

Larry rose to his feet. As he did so he slipped a hand into the bag and withdrew a thin sheaf of fifty-dollar bills, not quite hidden in his big paw. 'I understand, Chief.' He riffled the corner of the wad with his thumb.

'Can you at least give me an address where I can get hold of him, in Mexico City?'

'Miss Olsen, can you tell us what your connection is to the Stenner family, please?'

Annie hardly heard Barnes's question. Since the cross-examination of Peter Monroe she had been doing no more than go through the motions, unable to put aside her simmering, impotent fury at Matt and what he was putting her through. Fortunately, the two witnesses who had taken up the first half of the afternoon had been no threat to their case. The first woman was the author of a book on Recovered Memory Syndrome, the other, who claimed to have recovered memory of abuse herself, ran a self-help group for victims. Both of them had been so patently eager to promote their view, so prone to overstatement, that Annie had been able to stay virtually on autopilot and still leave them both floundering, contradicting themselves wildly. If anything their testimony weakened the prosecution case. The Olsen woman would be another matter. With a palpable effort, Annie forced herself to concentrate.

Old affection and present dismay mingled in Matt. Twelve years ago Kristina had been a pretty girl, heavy-boned but athletic. Now, still a young woman, she was matronly, thick around the hips and breasts, the coarse but sculpted looks lost under the weight of flesh around her jowls. The waist-length, red-blonde hair that Camilla had so much envied was now a dull auburn bob. Only the smile remained unchanged as she answered, in almost unaccented English.

'I worked for them as an au pair.'
'When was that?'
'July of 1983 until June 1985.'
'Where did you sleep?'
'My room was in the east wing of the house.'

'Did that connect with the main house?'

'Yes. Through the kitchen.'

'Was it part of your responsibilities to bathe Camilla, and Mark?'

She pondered, smiling. 'No. Not really. They did it themselves. I was usually out in the evenings.'

Barnes paused, the trick he used to let the jury know he was setting something up. 'What time did you normally come home?'

'Sometimes early, perhaps at ten o'clock.' She smiled at him, suddenly girlish again. 'Sometimes very late – the next morning.'

'How did you get into the house? I mean, by which door?'

'There was a door to the wing where I slept. It was good because I didn't have to disturb anybody.'

Barnes grinned his wolfish grin. 'You mean anybody in the house would not necessarily hear you come in?'

'Yes.'

'When you came in, did you go straight to bed?'

'Usually, yes.'

'Do you recall any *particular* occasion when you did not go to bed straight away?'

She glanced at Matt, flicking her tongue over her lips, and nodded. 'Yes.'

'Can you tell us about that?'

Seeing the faint smile on Barnes's lips, Matt frowned, edging forward on his seat.

'It was one night when Liz, Mrs Stenner, was away. I came in at about a quarter to six.'

'How do you know it was that time?'

She fluttered her eyelids. 'I had been with my boyfriend. He worked at the hotel in the village. He had to get up at a quarter past five to start preparing breakfasts at six. It just took me a few minutes to get home.'

344

'So you returned to your room at five forty-five. And then?'

'I was hungry. I went down to the kitchen.'

'The main kitchen?'

'Yes. And when I walked in, Matt . . .' she glanced across at Matt and immediately lowered her eyes, '. . . Mr Stenner was there, making coffee.'

'Did he see you?'

'No. He had his back to me.'

'Did you notice anything special about him?'

'He wasn't wearing any clothes.'

'I see,' Barnes drawled, smiling down at his notes. 'Did you notice anything else? Anything *unusual*?'

'Yes.' She paused, looking again at Matt, her eyes watering suddenly. 'He had two scratches, side by side.' She twisted, reaching to touch a point far down her shoulder blade. 'Here. They were bleeding.'

'Miss Olsen, you did say that Mrs Stenner was abroad that night?'

'Yes. Definitely. I remember how surprised I was.'

Barnes turned to Annie, smirking broadly. 'I have finished, Your Honour.'

Annie rose wearily to her feet, her head bowed. Eventually, she looked up at Davies, who sat with his chin cupped in his hand. It was easy to imagine he was smirking, too. 'I have no questions, Your Honour.'

All the way back from Chichester to the house hardly a word had been spoken in the car. Once home, Matt eased himself out and, catching Liz's eye, he hesitated and then turned back. 'Annie,' he said tentatively, 'don't you want to come and see how Jill's doing? Tomorrow's her big day. She was getting pretty agitated this morning.'

Annie spoke over her shoulder. 'You and Liz talk to her. I have to get to the hospital.' She turned to look him full in the face. 'Frankly, Matt, it's been a shitty day.'

He opened his mouth to speak again and then, thinking better of it, withdrew and closed the door. Annie was slipping the car into gear when Liz came around and indicated to her to lower her window. She stood for a moment, waiting for Matt and Mark to move towards the house, out of earshot.

'Thanks for what you're doing, Annie,' she whispered. 'For everything.' Her voice grew husky. 'Having to talk to Peter like that must have been hell.'

'Yes.' Abruptly she covered Liz's hand with hers, squeezing it with all her strength. 'By the time this is over I won't have a friend left.' Her eyes moistening, she threw the Audi into gear and sent it bucking from under Liz's hand.

At the sound of the door opening the nurse dropped her book and came to meet them, smiling. Behind her, Jill lay flat out on a sofa, one arm trailing on the floor, jiggling her fingers to the beat from her Walkman. She raised a hand in greeting, waggling her fingers lazily before letting it fall back.

'Hi, Jill! How are you doing?' Matt looked enquiringly at the nurse.

'She's doing *very* well. She's getting stronger by the hour, aren't you, Jill?'

Jill swung her legs off the sofa and sat up. 'Don't talk about me as though I were a pet. I'm okay.' Standing, she tugged off the Walkman and cast it aside. 'Look at me.' She stood in parody of a model girl pose, one skinny leg thrust forward. It was true, in the new clothes they had bought her, and with the lank, prematurely greying hair layered by the girl who came to cut the family's hair, she looked a different person from the one who had stumbled off the plane. The daily

346

walks the nurses cajoled her into taking had put some life back into her sallow, indoor complexion. The three or four pounds she had put on still left her pitifully thin. Laughing at the pose, Liz took her hand. Her laugh faded. The skeletal hand trembled like an injured bird, jerking and scrabbling in Liz's palm. She looked hard into Jill's face and shot Matt an alarmed look. Underneath the bravado she was a bundle of twitching nerve ends. 'Are you scared?' she asked quietly.

Jill's vacant, virtually sightless eyes were watery. 'Mmm.' She pulled her hand out of Liz's grasp. 'Scared as hell,' she said, in a rasping whisper. 'I wish I could just get shit-faced and stay that way until this is all over. Can you imagine what it's doing to me? Being in the same room with Lewis, after all this time? I go to pieces just thinking about it.'

Matt crouched in front of her, taking her by the arms. 'Liz will bring you one of her sleeping pills, so that you can get some decent rest. Just hold out like this for another twenty-four hours, Jill. That's all. It will be the end of the nightmare, for both of us.'

She looked into his face, a strange sadness in the empty eyes. She reached up and touched his face with fingers like broken sticks. 'For you, Matt,' she breathed. 'Not for me. Lewis won't ever be over for me.'

They returned to the house to find Mark slumped in the kitchen with the day's mail spread out on the table. Matt poured drinks for himself, Liz and Rachel. Then he wandered across to poke through the post. He smiled mirthlessly. 'You shouldn't even look at that stuff.'

Mark shrugged. 'It's educational,' he said, his voice strained. 'To see what crippled bastards there are out there.' He gestured to the letters, some single scrawled pages of insults, some multiple pages of closely written invective, all of it totally deranged. Matt scooped it up and carried it across to throw it in the bin beneath the sink. Stooping, he brushed against Rachel. She recoiled in an involuntary display of loathing. He turned away from her without a word, leaving her trembling and tight-lipped with embarrassment.

They were halfway through a stilted, joyless meal, when the doorbell rang. With undisguised relief, Matt put down his fork and walked out to answer it. A moment later he returned with Naomi at his side. Her face was drawn, her olive skin a muddy, sallow shade. At the sight of Liz and Rachel she flushed. 'Hi. Sorry to come by in the middle of a meal. I didn't think you . . .' The sentence trailed away as she looked from Liz to Matt.

Matt pulled out a chair, laughing sourly. 'It's the condemned man's last meal. Rachel cooked it for us,' he added, smiling brightly at his sister-in-law. 'Sit down. Do you want a drink?' He was already reaching for a glass as she shook her head. 'What's wrong?'

Naomi's glance slid over their faces. 'Could I . . . It's kind of delicate. Can we talk privately?'

Matt shook his head. 'There are no secrets.' Under the half-bantering tone he glanced across the table at Liz. 'Not any more.'

'Okay. Look, I shouldn't be here, but I thought I had to come. I just can't sit back and see you go through this. Surely you can see as clearly as I can that it's crucifying you all.'

Matt frowned. 'You're telling us! But what the hell do you think we can do about it now, except win? We've got Jill. And we've got Roy Erskine. He's doing a great job. He's going to have some surprises for Letzer, and for Barnes.'

Naomi shook her head, as though in despair. 'But

supposing you *don't* win. Where does it leave you all?'

'In deepest, deepest shit.'

Naomi swallowed. 'Look, I know what you think, Matt, but I came here to *beg* you to think again. Why not let me talk to Stephen and ask him to name his price?'

Matt laughed. 'Oh shit, haven't we been over that enough already?'

'But I don't believe you're considering carefully enough the effect on *Camilla*! Even if *you* can face the idea of going to prison, *she'll* probably never get over it, living with the *certainty*, in her mind, that you did those things. If we could persuade Stephen to just *disappear*, I'm certain Camilla wouldn't let the thing go on. Without him behind her, pushing her, she would see reason. You could all get on with your lives. And, sooner or later, Camilla might come to believe she has been wrong, about him, and about you.'

'The hell with that.' Matt rose and walked over to the waste bin. He delved inside and brought out a handful of the crank mail. He threw it onto the table in front of Naomi. 'And put up with this for the rest of my life?' His glance slid for an instant to Rachel. 'This is just the ones that bother to write, the truly nutty ones. But don't you think the whole world out there thinks pretty much the same thing? Shit, Naomi, I've hardly a friend left who wants to know me, my publishers won't talk to me, my agents don't return my calls, from being a hot Hollywood property I've become a dirty word, and you want me to sneak out from under it and slink away?' His hand found Liz's. For a moment Liz did not react. Then, slowly, her fingers tightened round his. 'No. Be in court tomorrow. We're going to do this properly.'

Naomi rose slowly from the table. Her face was deeply flushed. 'I'll be there.' She swallowed. 'That's the other thing I came to tell you. The police came to see me. They're going to call me as a witness.'

Matt broke the shocked silence. 'A witness? To what, for God's sake?'

She looked squarely at Matt. 'I did a lot of work in America with male abusers.'

'What kind of work?' Liz asked, puzzled.

'Men who have difficulty facing up to their desires,' she answered, her eyes not moving from Matt's face. Her faintly ironic smile turned to a brief, sardonic laugh. 'But I mustn't keep you from your meal. Bye.'

Dropping Liz's hand, Matt took three quick strides after her. Then, his face congested with anger, he spun and came slowly back to the table.

After Naomi had gone none of them had any appetite left. Rachel was the first one on her feet. Liz followed her and the two of them busied themselves with the dishes while Matt continued sitting with Mark at his side, finishing off the bottle of wine. When they had finished clearing up, Rachel turned to Liz. 'We'd better be going. It's an early start tomorrow.'

At her words Matt looked up, startled. He jumped to his feet and crossed to where Liz stood. For a moment neither of them spoke. Then he took her hand. 'You're not going? I thought ... You've been so supportive. Since ... since ...'

She shook her head, looking at the floor. 'Sorry. I ... it's too soon.'

He took her other hand. 'I'll sleep in the guest room.' He jerked his head. 'For Mark, too,' he murmured.

She raised her wounded eyes slowly to his. 'Don't crowd me, Matt. I still have a lot to ... to get accustomed to.' She withdrew her hands and kissed him chastely on the lips. 'I'll see you early tomorrow.' She crossed to where Mark had also risen and took him in a long embrace, burying her face in his hair. 'Good night, Mark.' She withdrew, her eyes shining, and, hurrying across the room to join Rachel, she let her fingers brush Matt's. 'Be careful not to scratch yourself tonight.' She ran from the room before the tears began to roll.

Despite the hour, the rising sun was already hot on their backs as Matt and Liz crossed the sloping lawn towards the guest cottage. Matt sought Liz's hand, entwining his fingers in hers. 'I hope to God she's going to be okay.'

'What happens if she isn't?'

He closed his fingers tighter in hers and did not answer.

The nurse came out to meet them. Matt eyed the doorway anxiously. 'How is she?'

'Nervous. She's been in and out of the bathroom since she got up. She's in her bedroom at the moment, afraid to come down.'

Liz stepped past her. 'I'd better go up and talk to her.'

Matt had been pacing the sitting room for ten minutes before they came down, Liz coming backwards, leading Jill by both hands, coaxing her down each step.

The nurse had done a good job of getting Jill into crushed linen shorts and an apricot-coloured polo shirt. She had even managed to put some lipstick on her, though it looked a little garish against Jill's papery pallor. Matt realised with a pang of shame that she looked about the way he had hoped, decent enough to be credible, damaged enough to be pathetic. He moved to meet her off the stairs.

'Hi, Jill, how are you feeling? If people have feelings at this hour?'

Jill looked at him with her unfocused eyes. She swallowed. 'Scared,' she croaked.

Matt took her hand. 'Don't be. It'll be over in thirty seconds. Just long enough to hear him sworn in. Annie insists we get you out of there before he starts to give evidence, or we can be in big trouble. He won't even know you're there.'

'Yeah? Well, I still wish to God I could just get shit-faced.'

Matt laughed softly. 'A few more days and you can stay drunk for a year. Champagne. Thirty-year-old cognac. Whatever you want.'

She gave a bitter laugh. 'You'd be pissing your money away. These days my taste runs more to cleaning products.'

He laughed aloud. 'I'll buy you the top brands. No own-label stuff. Right now, we'll settle for coffee. Let's go up to the house.'

They were nearly at the bottom of the second pot of strong, black coffee, Jill gulping down two of the big breakfast cups to every one of theirs, before they heard Annie's car draw up outside. A few moments later she stepped into the room, her face set and unsmiling. Her voice when she spoke to Jill, though, was warm.

'Hello, Jill. How are you feeling? Nervous, I bet? Well, don't be, please.' She gave Matt a sour glance. 'Even if *I* am. Just stay close to Liz, and for God's sake keep your head down. And swear to us you'll stay quiet, whatever you may be feeling. The last thing we need is for you to attract the judge's attention.' Her glance flicked to Liz. 'And for heaven's sake make sure you're out of the gallery before he starts giving his actual evidence. That's crucial. Do you understand that?' Her face fell back into stony immobility as she watched Jill swallow and nod.

'Coffee?' Matt was already pouring, pushing the jug of hot milk towards her. 'To steady your nerves for the big day.'

'The biggest,' she said desolately. She remained in the doorway, making no move towards the table. 'Thanks. I've already had as much as I need.'

Matt nodded, frowning. He stood up, draining his own cup. 'I guess we should be moving. Jill?'

Jill stood up and grabbed at the pot, pouring the last of the coffee into her cup and draining it noisily. She rattled the cup back into the saucer and wiped her lips. The bright lipstick smudged, giving her face a faintly comic look. 'Sure. Yeah. I guess so.' She clasped her hands together in an effort to stop them trembling. The recently acquired bloom drained abruptly from her face. With a groan, she clutched her hands to her stomach. 'Oh, fuck! I need to be sick.'

Liz stepped hastily forward. Snatching at her hand, she dragged her, stumbling, towards the lavatory only to be brought up short by the sound of running water and of Mark singing to himself.

Turning, she set off up the stairs at a run, the whimpering Jill staggering in her wake. She hurled open the door of her bathroom and bundled Jill inside, quickly guiding her to the basin. Jill collapsed to her knees in front of it.

'Will you be okay? Shall I stay?'

Jill shook her head, mumbling, her face wreathed in pain, one hand resting on the edge of the basin, the other still pressed to her stomach.

Liz moved to the door, looking anxiously back at the hunched, frail figure, its thin, pale limbs protruding absurdly from the crisp new knee-length shorts and shirt. 'Shout when you're ready.' She closed the door on the first sound of retching.

In the kitchen Annie was still waiting by the door

as Matt, Mark now helping, stacked the dishwasher. They looked up as Liz re-entered.

'She's being sick. I'm not surprised. The thought of seeing somebody you used to be in thrall to . . . it must be pretty intimidating, mustn't it?'

Matt looked sidelong at Liz as he fumbled with the dishwasher, searching for some sign of irony. Her face was unreadable, half turned away as she listened for sounds from the back stairs. 'Jill!' she shouted, one hand on the doorknob. 'Jill? Are you all right? Do you need anything?' She leaned into the stairway, her head cocked. 'Jill?' She moved up two or three stairs, still calling. Halfway up the flight she broke into a run.

She rattled the bathroom door. 'Jill? Are you all right?' The others jostled in a knot behind her. She shook the door, grasping the knob with both hands. 'Jill!' They were all shouting now. With a grunted warning, Matt shoved them aside and lashed out with his foot. The latch gave on the third try.

Rushing headlong into the room, he found his first response was to apologise. She was seated on the toilet. He had even begun backing out in embarrassment before he realised she was fully dressed. Her head lolled against the hand-basin. Her hands trailed loose at her sides. His foot struck against something, making it ring. With a cry of anguished protest Matt fell to his knees at her side. He picked up one of the empty bottles that lay around him and stared at it. Four ounces of Habit Rouge Eau de Cologne, drained dry. He pawed at the other bottles. Liz's toilet waters. All of them drained. Only his aftershave, lying directly under her slack hand, where it had fallen when she passed out, had a half-inch of fluid still in it.

Liz kneeled beside him. Tears stung her eyes as she put an arm over his shoulders. 'I'm so sorry, Matt. Really sorry. I didn't think.'

354

He stared, transfixed, at the litter of bottles. 'None of us did, darling.' He was almost sobbing himself. 'None of us did.' Without looking up, he called hoarsely, 'Mark, get a doctor, quick.' His eyes went again to the bottle in his hand. 'And an ambulance.'

'Mr Barnes, I believe you have a matter you wish to cover in the absence of the jury?'

Barnes inclined his head. 'Yes, Your Honour.' He accepted a sheaf of typed sheets from the Crown Prosecution Service official behind him. 'We would like to introduce a new witness, whom the police interviewed only two days ago.' He passed a copy of the typed sheets to Annie. 'Miss Naomi Butler. She was the person who treated Miss Stenner before Mr Letzer was called in. As you can see, it's a fairly brief statement.'

Annie was immediately deeply engrossed, her head resting on her hand as she scanned the three pages of type. When she had finished she looked up at the judge, waiting to catch his eye. The moment he raised his eyes from his own copy, already looking expectantly at her, she was on her feet. 'Your Honour, there's material in here I would wish to discuss with my client. Subject to discussion with my client, I may have to ask for two or three days to prepare our position.' Annie studied the judge's face, struggling to keep her own neutral. Added on to the weekend, they would give Larry the time he needed to arrange the exhumation of the crash victim. She had spoken to Roy early that morning. The Mexican police chief had agreed to fly over and testify. Official endorsement would mean ten times more to the jury than a hired investigator and a photocopied document in Spanish.

As the judge deliberated, she looked out of the corner of her eye at the dock. Matt's face had an expression she had never seen before. It suddenly seemed as ravaged, as eroded by inner pain, as a cancer victim's. His eyes seemed to have grown more prominent, the skin of their lids purplish and translucent. The bone of the eye sockets thrust at the skin, as though the skull had begun to assert itself beneath the flesh. His knuckles looked knobby and arthritic where he gripped the rail. It struck her with sudden, sickening force that the suffering in the face was real. The best actor in the world could not fake that look. It was more than a renewed fear of gaol, of life as a 'nonce', shut away in a special wing for his own protection, his only company men whose pleasure had been the murder or rape of children, the despised dregs of any prison, enduring constant abuse, harassment and sudden violence from the other inmates. Matt was not a physical coward. What was etched in his face could only be the deep grief and mental torture of the innocent.

She turned back to the judge, her face hot with a scalding wave of guilt.

'Mrs Trevellyn, I've considered this statement very carefully.' He paused, letting his eyes roam around the court, a faint smile on his lips, as though he were enjoying the tension. 'And frankly, I see no grounds for granting any such request. The witness's statement seems to me a straightforward account of what she saw, together with some expert opinion, which, I agree, appears to cover some interesting new ground. If you aren't able to deal with this by the time Miss Butler is called, then I shall have to consider granting you further time.' He pushed the typed sheets decisively into a folder, dropping his eyes from Annie's. 'For the moment, however, I'm going to ask you to try. I'm disinclined to put the jury to the inconvenience of a long adjournment unnecessarily, in what is already threatening to be a longer case than expected, unless you can offer me some very cogent reasons.'

Matt looked on grimly as Annie stood with her head bowed. They had spent the drive down discussing this moment. Annie had a choice. She could explain about Jill, and her relationship with Letzer, but then all element of surprise would be lost. Letzer would learn Jill was here and he'd be free to disappear back to America without giving evidence at all. It would weaken the prosecution, but not destroy it. Alternatively, she could let Letzer come to the witness box now and take a chance on Davies allowing her to recall him when Jill was ready. He did not have to, but he would know that if he refused, an appeal would almost certainly succeed. That route enabled them to discredit a witness who was already established as integral to the prosecution's case. The big risk was if Letzer were to testify, do damage, and then disappear before they could blow him apart. Annie raised her head. 'I've nothing to add at this time, Your Honour.'

'Mr Letzer, could you tell the court your title and qualifications, please?'

Liz watched in a kind of fascination, taking in the man's every gesture. He stood straight-backed, his hands resting on the edge of the stand, shifting constantly. Every few seconds one hand went to the knot of his discreet silk tie, or picked a fleck of imaginary lint from the dark blue cloth of his suit. He looked thinner than she remembered him from the clinic, his shirt collar bunched under the tie, as though his neck had shrunk. Beneath his eyes puffy crescents reached down to his cheekbones. The muscles of his throat worked incessantly as he swallowed. Despite the banker's uniform, he exuded lack of ease. 'I'm a psychotherapist. I also do counselling. I'm a trained stress counsellor.' He reeled off a series of degrees, all the time unable to keep his eyes from darting to the public

357

gallery, scrutinising the faces with a hunted, panicky hunger.

When he had finished, Barnes smiled. 'In simple terms, Mr Letzer, what would you describe as your special field?'

'Disturbed young people. Especially disturbance with its origins in abuse during childhood.'

Again Letzer searched the public seats with his eyes. For an eerie moment Liz felt he was looking straight at her, and then his gaze moved on, not recognising her, still searching. Then, behind Liz's shoulder the door creaked softly. Liz watched a suppressed smile soften his expression, effacing the look of hunger.

As she stared down at the witness box, a soft, fleeting pressure of a hand on her shoulder made her start and jerk around. Camilla was squeezing along the row behind her. Her face working with barely controlled emotions, Liz snatched at Camilla's sleeve, pulling her down until Camilla's hair brushed her lips. 'How can you, darling?' Her voice was pleading, distraught, but so soft as to be inaudible two seats away. 'How can you bear to *sit* here, listening to this?'

Camilla gulped noisily. 'I have to, Mummy. Stephen wants it. He says I have to hear it all, to know the truth.' She tried to pull away, gave up as Liz clung to her. 'It's the only way, Mummy. The only way I can be whole again.'

Liz released her grip and watched desolately as her daughter shuffled past the nudging onlookers to take a seat at the far end of the row, eyes already fixed on Letzer.

Annie sat smiling to herself with quiet satisfaction as Barnes went through the generalities, working to establish Letzer's credentials as a qualified professional, caring and yet dispassionate, a man on whose professional judgement the jury could rely. It was the middle of the morning before, without changing from his affable, man-to-man tone, which had made their exchange into a discussion between two intelligent, worldly men, he moved to the main thrust of his questioning.

'Can you please describe how you first came into contact with Camilla Stenner?'

'She was referred to me by her parents.'

'What appeared to be wrong with Miss Stenner at that time?'

'She had attempted suicide. She was depressed, and didn't seem to be recovering.'

'Did they offer any clue as to what had triggered the depression?'

'The parents speculated that it was the result of a love affair going awry.'

'Was that a likely cause, in your opinion?'

'I had no opinion at that stage. It was certainly plausible. People have been known to attempt suicide for such reasons. They mentioned a previous episode, several years earlier, which did apparently *coincide* with a romance breaking up.'

'But, as far as you were concerned, when you agreed to treat Miss Stenner, you had formed no judgement as to the source of her . . . emotional disorder?'

'That's correct.'

'So the possibility of abuse had not at that stage entered your mind?'

He paused, weighing his words. 'My mind was entirely open.'

'Mr Letzer, when Miss Stenner was handed into your care, how would you describe her state, physical and mental?'

'Physically, she was undernourished, though she was

by then eating enough to keep her weight stable. She was lethargic. Mentally, she was withdrawn, uncommunicative. Depressed.'

'And what was the nature of the treatment you applied to Miss Stenner?'

Letzer glanced again at Camilla as his fingers clawed at his neck, lifting the knot of the club tie away from his throat and letting it fall back. 'Essentially, I talked to her. We would have several sessions a day of therapy.'

'And where did this take place? Was it in private?'

'My method is to treat patients wherever they seem responsive. I have a consulting room at the clinic. Some sessions took place in there, some in her room. It was in private in the sense that only the two of us were present, but the door would be open. That was my policy.'

'So you spoke to Miss Stenner, several times a day, trying to win her confidence, and coax her back to health?'

Letzer glanced up at Camilla before answering. 'That's exactly right.'

'And did you succeed, would you say?'

He licked his lips. 'I suppose so, though I might not put it as simply as that.'

Barnes smiled urbanely. 'Well, did her general demeanour improve? Did she shake off her depression?'

'Up to a point, yes. I thought she was beginning to make real progress. I was reasonably optimistic, except that she began to show increasing hostility to her father.'

Barnes stepped in quickly. 'This was *before* she made the allegations at the heart of this case?'

'Yes. And then, after a while, she told me . . . she told me of . . . what she had been through.' Letzer swallowed and looked down at the floor. His fingers tightened on the rail, as though he might fall, overcome at the recollection.

Matt's eyes were on the jury. Over the last days one or two of them had become emboldened enough by their sense of his guilt to look squarely at him. The stout woman was doing it now, allowing the flesh around her eyes to pucker faintly, in a microscopic, but unmistakable declaration of distaste. Concealed behind the panelling of the dock, he drummed a fist against his knee. The man had them eating out of his hand.

'What was your immediate response?'

Letzer grabbed the glass and took a long drink. He squeezed his eyes shut and then opened them again. 'I was shocked. Appalled. I . . . I suggested to her that she must be mistaken.'

Barnes took time off to put his notes down and make a show of reordering them, giving time for the words to settle. He took them up again with a slow, respectful gesture, reminding Matt for an instant of an undertaker. 'How would you describe Miss Stenner's manner at that point?' he asked, his voice soft in the hush.

'Distressed. Very, very distressed.' Letzer's voice was muffled. 'I could not get her to even hear what I was saying. She just began crying. A terrible, heart-breaking sound. I would say keening would be a better word than crying.' His fingers curled tighter round the edge of the stand. 'And she was shaking. Uncontrollably.'

'What did you do then?'

'I shouted for Catherine, our nurse.'

'And then what happened?'

'I tried to calm Camilla down, to get her to talk coherently.'

'And was she able to do so?'

Letzer sighed deeply and looked up into Camilla's face. He nodded slowly, his eyes clenched shut. 'Yes,' he rasped, reopening his eyes. 'She was. After a while.' He was manifestly struggling with the memory. 'She told us her father had repeatedly had sexual inter –'

Annie sprang to her feet. 'Objection, Your Honour. Hearsay.'

The judge nodded, raising his eyes to the jury. 'Yes, Mrs Trevellyn. Members of the jury, you will ignore the witness's answer.' He looked wearily at Barnes. 'Go on, Mr Barnes, please.'

Letzer had closed his eyes. His teeth dug deep into his lip. Barnes looked at him with a faintly curious expression, as though waiting to see if he would cry. At length, he leaned closer to Letzer, lowering his voice confidentially. 'Mr Letzer, my friend, Mrs Trevellyn, may later point out that you knew you were dealing with a young woman who had a history of emotional problems, and had recently made an effort to kill herself. So, tell us, did you take Miss Stenner's behaviour at that point to be that of a rational person, in command of her faculties?'

Matt watched in impotent fury as Letzer took two slow, deep breaths before looking up at the jury with a perfectly judged air of sincerity, raking them with a clear, unblinking gaze. 'Yes. Absolutely. Cam . . . Miss Stenner's behaviour was entirely consistent. I simply do not believe the reactions I saw could have been faked.'

'Even by somebody with Miss Stenner's record of emotional troubles?'

'In my experience it would be normal to expect someone who has suffered that kind of abuse to be disturbed in some degree.' He wiped a hand over his face. 'To me, it's a tribute to her personal strength that she managed to stay so . . . normal, for so long.'

Annie had hardly begun rising before the judge nodded and turned to fix Letzer with a penetrating gaze. 'The witness will confine himself to answering the question.'

Barnes was looking down musingly, fiddling with his folder, giving the jury time to savour Letzer's show of emotion. 'Mr Letzer, did it strike you as strange, or improbable, Miss Stenner abruptly recalling past events in this way? Especially events as . . . momentous . . . as these, having apparently suppressed them for all those years?'

'To tell you the truth, it did. The whole concept of RMS – Recovered Memory Syndrome – has caused a heated debate in the psychiatric world. I used to be a sceptic myself. Until I saw it happen in front of my eyes.'

'And that's what happened in this case? She *recovered* the memory of past events?'

Letzer turned to look up at the gallery. Camilla's gaze was locked onto his, the adoration in it palpable. Letzer turned back to Barnes, his smile fading only slowly. 'Yes,' he said calmly.

Barnes smiled too as he half turned to the jury. 'So, although there are differing views in the rather – how shall I put it? – esoteric world of psychiatry, you, without wanting to claim that all cases are genuine, firmly believe it exists?' Barnes had leaned heavily on the word esoteric, putting down a marker as to how he intended to approach the defence's expert testimony.

'Of course. I'm absolutely *convinced* it's genuine. I've seen it *happen*. Whether it's common enough to merit the term syndrome, I wouldn't know. I do know that Camilla genuinely remembered those things, with no help from anyone.'

The judge again responded to Annie's movement. 'Once again, I have to ask that the witness restrict himself to answering the questions.'

Letzer nodded. 'I'm sorry, Your Honour.'

'Mr Letzer, how would you describe your relationship with Miss Stenner?'

'Er, Miss Stenner and I are close, I think.'

'How close, in your view?'

He put a hand to his mouth, coughed, and swallowed hard. 'Ah, very close. I hope.'

'How much time did you spend with Miss Stenner in the month, say, prior to this trial?'

'A lot. I saw her every day.'

'Professionally? By that I mean, were you treating her?'

Letzer shook his head. 'No.'

'You were seeing her as a . . . friend?'

'Yes.'

'Mr Letzer, I'd like you to look at some notebooks.' Barnes paused while the usher took up the diaries and placed them in front of Letzer. 'Mr Letzer, do you recognise these?'

Without touching the notebooks, he said, 'Yes. They're Camilla's diaries.'

'How are you familiar with them?'

'Camilla was working on them, before the trial.'

'Were you present when she did that?'

'Sometimes, yes.'

'And while present, did you offer your opinion as to the meaning of any of the items contained in them?'

Letzer looked up from the diaries and fixed Barnes with a frank, open stare. 'Of course not! Camilla didn't need my help.' His gaze swivelled to Matt, his fingers tightening on the edge of the witness box. 'The meaning was all too clear!'

'At the time you were treating Miss Stenner, prior to her making the allegations against her father, and for many weeks afterwards, you were unaware of the existence of Miss Stenner's diaries?'

'Absolutely unaware.'

'And when you became aware of the content of the diaries, what was your reaction, your *professional* reaction?'

'That if I had ever had any doubts about Recovered Memory Syndrome, they blew them away! To my knowledge it's the first time in an RMS case that there's been contemporaneous evidence this strong!'

Twenty-Three

Throughout Letzer's examination Annie had watched the jury carefully. There was no doubt about it, he had impressed them, coming across as a sincere and authoritative witness, deeply moved by his patient's plight. He had even seen some of them glance up with him to the gallery, noting for themselves the commitment in Camilla's look. She smiled inwardly. It would make the impact of taking him apart all the greater. Over her years as a trial lawyer she had often been struck by how much juries resented finding out that they had been strung along.

'Mr Letzer, you are a qualified hypnotist, aren't you?'

His tongue ran over his upper lip. 'I've taken some courses.'

'You have at least one diploma on the walls of your office, haven't you?'

He inclined his head. 'Yes.'

'Was it earned by serious study or is it just to impress susceptible people?'

He bridled. 'It's genuine. I worked hard for it.'

'Quite. But a moment ago you had only "taken some courses". You are in fact a well-*qualified* hypnotist, aren't you?'

His laugh had a distant tremor of uncertainty in it, as though he knew where Annie was leading but was not sure how to head her off. 'Well, it's a fairly alternative field. The qualifications are, well, not necessarily very demanding.'

'But that doesn't stop you proudly displaying your diploma among your many others, does it? Is it an inferior qualification?'

He writhed inside his suit. 'No. But, well, in a sense there's not much to *learn* about hypnosis. It's as much art as science. The important thing is knowing how to use it.'

'Because in the wrong hands it can be dangerous?'

'Ye . . . Yes, it can,' he finished lamely.

Annie gave him a bright smile. 'You listed those other qualifications for us. Can you tell us the names of the institutions where you studied for them? One by one, please.'

The flesh of his left cheek hollowed as though he were gnawing at the inside of his mouth. 'The American Institute of Applied Therapies and Psychiatric Sciences.'

Annie let the silence dangle in the room as she looked slowly from Letzer to the jury and back again. 'Perhaps you could repeat that, Mr Letzer. I feel it might not have a familiar ring for some of us.' She stood waiting, a trace of a smile on her lips for the jury to see as he repeated it. 'I see. That isn't what you could call Ivy League, is it?'

He raised his hand from where it rested on the rail and let it fall back. 'It's a well-respected college.'

'Oh, I'm sure it is, Mr Letzer. How long did you attend there?'

Her half-smile returned as he raised his chin. He decided to get it over quickly rather than let her drag it out of him. 'It's not a residential college. It's a college of distance learning.' Before Annie could twist the knife, he added, 'You study by correspondence.'

Annie nodded gravely. 'I see. So the impressive list of credentials you gave are in fact,' she lingered for a moment, 'mail-order degrees?'

A faint tinge of colour rose in his face. 'Yes, but good ones. The Institute is highly respected. It's for people who can't attend a regular college, older students, who have regular jobs, women with small children who can't get out of the house.'

'And which was your case, Mr Letzer? Did you have a job?'

'I worked.'

'At what?'

He spread his hands and laughed. 'Anything that would pay enough to live on and still leave time for studying. I was cramming in a lot of courses. It was pretty close to a full-time job.'

'Mr Letzer, did the range of things you did at that time, while you were studying, include working as any kind of therapist or counsellor?'

He frowned, looking uncertainly up at the judge. 'No. How could it? I wasn't qualified.'

'So, to be quite clear, you did not begin doing counselling or therapy of any kind until what date?'

He screwed up his face, thinking. 'I finished my forensic psychiatry courses in summer 1989.'

'And then you set up professionally?'

'Yes.'

'Where?'

'San Diego. That's in California,' he added, smiling at the jury.

Annie looked down at her notes, gathering herself. She had seen the curiosity gathering almost imperceptibly in the faces of some of the jurors at the undercurrent of unease in Letzer's answers. 'How did you advertise your services?'

He sipped water. 'I didn't. I preferred to work by word of mouth.' The last words came a little too quickly.

Her lips pursed, Annie selected a sheet of paper from

her table. A two-inch-by-one-inch block of type was pasted in the middle. 'Mr Letzer, this is an advertisement from a magazine which existed for a few years in California from the late eighties. It offers counselling, therapy, and . . . hypnotism. The name is Steve Letzer. Would that be you?'

He looked momentarily nonplussed. 'Well, yeah. I guess . . . it must have been.'

'So you did advertise. Although you stopped in late 1990. Why was that?'

He grinned. 'I don't remember. I was probably getting enough work by word of mouth.'

Annie smiled easily. 'I see.' She took a piece of paper from Hannah's outstretched hand and glanced at it. 'This is a letter from the American Association of Psychiatry, one of the best-known professional bodies in the field, are they not?' She waited, forcing Letzer to nod a response. 'According to their letter there are over eleven hundred college-educated, fully qualified psychiatrists offering counselling services in the San Diego area. Most of those advertise. But you, with your mail-order qualifications, saw no need to do so. You relied on word of mouth?'

He nodded. 'Yes. I did.' He took another hurried sip of water. 'I wasn't certain I'd be staying on in California.'

Annie smiled, an eyebrow raised as she turned to the jury. 'No? So you were already planning to leave California, prior to 1991?' She turned back to him, still smiling, her manner relaxed and affable, as though she had decided not to press the point. 'Could that be because you thought you had, in the old California tradition, struck gold?'

'I don't know what you mean.'

'No? What names did you use while you were living in California?'

'My own.' He picked at the cuff of his jacket.

'What is that?'

He picked up the glass and put it down again without drinking. 'Letzer. You know that. Stephen Letzer.'

'You never used the name Lewis Hampton?'

'No,' he snapped. 'Never.' His voice caught on the second syllable, obliging him to say again, 'Never!'

'And does the name Jill Stanakis mean anything to you?'

He shook his head. 'Not a thing.'

'I see,' Annie purred. 'Did you, through your word-of-mouth work, or in any way at all, have any involvement with anybody who displayed Recovered Memory Syndrome? Let's agree to call it RMS.'

'Not directly, no.'

'Indirectly?'

'I studied the literature. I attended seminars, sat in on support groups. The subject interested me, a lot.'

Annie drew a slow breath. 'Mr Letzer,' she said patiently, 'did you offer therapy, counselling or any kind of treatment to any such person displaying RMS before setting up practice in Britain?'

'No.'

'Absolutely never?'

'Never.'

Annie turned with a sweeping motion to face the jury, the theatrical movement underlining Letzer's answer, fixing it in the jury's mind. 'I see.' She turned slowly to face him as she said, 'Earlier on, you mentioned a person called Catherine, saying that she was a nurse at the clinic. Does she no longer work for you?'

'No.'

'Why? Don't you need staff any longer?'

Letzer's eyes dropped. 'Not really. The clinic hasn't really done very well.'

'Isn't it true that you have put it on the market?'

She watched his head go back as she caught him off balance. Hannah's team had done good work. Annie had received the news as a scribbled note from Hannah on their way into court that morning, a dividend for the tenacious groundwork, including almost daily phone checks with estate agents.

'Er, not me. The owners.'

'Of course. You don't own the building, do you?' Annie waved another piece of paper. 'According to this copy of the entry in the Land Registry, the building is owned by the Bellhope Foundation.' She looked up at the judge, smiling sweetly. 'It's a foundation registered in Liechtenstein, Your Honour. The sort of thing people use to minimise tax liabilities, or, of course, to hide their identities.' She looked at Letzer. 'Can you tell the jury who's behind the Bellhope Foundation?'

He shook his head, defiantly meeting her eye. 'No.'

'No, you can't say, or no, you *won't* say?'

'I can't. I rented the premises. I dealt with an office in Vaduz. A lawyer.'

'Mmm.' Annie nodded slowly, not hiding her pleasure at the turn things had taken. 'Would it not be unusual for a young man, with very little professional experience, to come to England to start a business and find himself talking with Liechtenstein lawyers?' She held up a hand as he was about to speak. 'That wasn't a question, Mr Letzer. You're a free agent, of course.' She put down the piece of paper, letting her eyes roam over the faces of the jury. Three of them were making hurried notes. 'Mr Letzer, coming back to your skills as a hypnotist . . .' She glanced back, picking up the faint smiles among the jurors at her jibe. 'Did you use hypnosis on Miss Stenner at any time?'

'No.' His jaw jutted as he made the assertion in a ringing voice, all the previous hesitation banished. 'Certainly not.'

Annie raised an eyebrow, an ironic smile touching her lips. 'In the course of your studies, by correspondence and otherwise, did you come across the notion of the "hypnotic block"?'

'Yes. Of course.'

'Would you be kind enough to explain to the jury exactly what you understand such a term to mean?'

His eyes flashed angrily at Annie as he sipped more water. 'It's pretty simple. While a subject is under hypnosis, the hypnotist makes suggestions, gets the person to do certain things. Then, before bringing the subject round, he implants the block. It just means talking to the subject in a certain way so that when he or she comes round they can't recall what they did while they were under.'

'Isn't it also true that the subject has no memory of the fact of even having *been* hypnotised?'

'If that's what the hypnotist wants. But I think it's important to add that it's regarded as unreliable. The block can fail at any time.'

'Yes, indeed it can. But isn't that likely to happen only years later?'

'It might. Then again it can happen quite soon, if some event triggers it.'

'But usually a very long time after the event?'

He nodded reluctantly. 'Yes.'

'By which time the hypnotist could be in another country, using a new identity.'

'I *object*, Your Honour!' Barnes was on his feet, his robe billowing. 'That is a gross and unjustified slur.'

Exasperatedly, the judge peered down at Annie. 'Mrs Trevellyn, you will withdraw your last comment.' He looked sternly at the jury. 'And you, members of the jury, will put it out of your minds.'

Annie bowed. 'I withdraw the remark, Your

Honour, with apologies,' she purred, as Barnes regained his seat. 'In summary, then someone who had been hypnotised and had a block put in place would have no memory of having been hypnotised when they came round. Broadly correct?'

'If the block works, yes.'

'Which it probably would, if done by a qualified person?'

He nodded. 'As you say, probably.'

'And that person might easily swear, even under oath, that he or she had never been –'

'Your Honour, I really must object.' Barnes was rising, leaning across his table towards the judge, a hand outstretched in protest.

'Your objection is justified, Mr Barnes. Mrs Trevellyn, I really will not have you asking witnesses to speculate in that manner.'

Annie gave a tiny, contrite bow. A glance at the jury, busy scribbling notes, assured her there was no need to labour the point further. 'My apologies, Your Honour, I was trying to make what I thought was the valid point –'

'I'm sure the jury took your point, Mrs Trevellyn. Go on, please.'

Annie settled her robe over her shoulders. 'Mr Letzer, when did you first learn of the existence of Miss Stenner's diaries?'

'Some weeks ago.'

'How?'

'Camilla simply remembered them. During a therapy session.'

'Quite. I accept that you did not use your skill in hypnosis, despite having laboured so hard to acquire it, but did you use any *other* technique, beyond just plain *talking*?'

'Camilla was always totally conscious.'

Annie let her eyes stray to where Matt sat. She saw him hunch forward, knew that he, too, had sensed the hesitancy behind the careful choice of words. 'That doesn't quite answer the question. Did you use *any* technique? Perhaps I can phrase it better. What areas of your training or knowledge were you calling on in the period leading up to her allegations?'

'Just counselling, enabling her to look deep inside herself.'

'You're sure of that?' Annie looked up to the bench, where the judge sat skewed towards Letzer, as anxious as everyone else in the room to see where Annie's questions were leading. 'Mr Letzer, you said you had a nurse working for you at your clinic?'

'Yes.'

'Please will you remind us of her name?'

'Catherine. Catherine Morgan.'

'And she no longer works at the clinic?'

'No. She left to join her sister. In Canada, I think.'

Annie smiled and nodded as she turned the pages of her binder. Finding the page she wanted, she took her time reading it before looking again at Letzer. 'Did Miss Morgan sometimes sit in on your sessions with patients?'

'Sometimes.'

'And was Miss Morgan ever present when you used hypnosis on patients?'

'She might have been. Not on Camilla, though. I never –'

Annie's upraised hand cut him off. 'Thank you. Was Miss Morgan ever present during your sessions with Miss Stenner?'

His frown deepened as he slowly nodded. 'I suppose she might have been, occasionally.'

Annie looked briefly down at her notes again. 'And did you ever talk to Miss Morgan about a technique known as EMDR? Eye Movement Desensitisation and Reprocessing?'

Annie kept her gaze on Letzer, watching the shadows pass behind his eyes. Erskine's Canadian associates had tracked the Morgan woman down. She had given them the information Annie was now using, but had refused to come over to give evidence. From his face Letzer did not know that.

'I might have. We talked about a lot of things.'

'Did you talk about EMDR?'

He shrugged. 'I might have.'

'Could you tell the court what the technique is used for?'

He grimaced. 'As far as I've read, it seems to have some success in treating Post-Traumatic Stress Disorder.'

'Would that involve helping people recall events they had otherwise suppressed?'

'Yes.'

'I see. And can you describe how, practically speaking, the technique is applied?'

He made a vague gesture. 'The practitioner moves a hand in front of the subject's eyes. I believe the idea is that the movement might mimic the eye movements made in dreaming. I'm not sure how it's supposed to work.'

'You're not sure. You have read about the technique.' Annie smiled warmly. 'Is the name James Sparkman familiar to you?'

He screwed up his face, as though making a careful search of his memory.

'Let me help you. The Professor Sparkman who used to work at Watford General Hospital.'

'I seem to recall the name.'

'Good. Because did you not phone Professor Sparkman as late as January this year requesting information

375

following the appearance of an article in *The Times* by Professor Sparkman? And did you not order a ticket for a seminar on EMDR scheduled for March this year, giving the number of a Visa card in your name?'

As Annie finished speaking, Matt looked quickly at the jury, looking for the tiny changes of expression that would tell him they, too, had noticed the minute hesitation as Letzer composed his face.

'I, er, it's possible. I don't remember.'

'Mr Letzer, why have you been concealing the extent of your interest in this technique from the court?'

'I haven't!' A deeper flush rose from his collar to suffuse his face. 'I suppose I must have ordered tickets. I try to keep up with *any* developments in my field. It doesn't follow I went to the seminar.'

Annie simply smiled. It was a full three seconds before she continued. 'EMDR is still very much at the evaluation stage, isn't it? According to the literature I have seen, nobody yet understands how it works. Is it not a fact that it can leave some patients severely disturbed?'

'So I understand.'

'But you nevertheless used it on Camilla Stenner?'

'You have no proof of that.'

Barnes, who had been rising to object, dropped back into his seat as Annie bowed in acknowledgement. At length, she took a step closer to him. 'Isn't it true, Mr Letzer, that you are a man who is ready to be carried away on the tide of any new fashion in your field, RMS, EMDR, hypnosis, anything that can't be properly evaluated, that enables you to bluff your way through it?'

He was quivering with anger. 'No! That's not true! I've *studied* –'

Annie went on as though he had not spoken. 'Isn't it true that EMDR, like certain aspects of hypnotism, and, above all, like RMS is, to use a rather old-fashioned term, "hocus-pocus"? Isn't it the fact that you're a liar and a fraud, who has found a niche preying on wealthy young women?'

His panicky eyes flew from Annie to Camilla, and to the judge. 'You have no right to say that! I spent years studying. You're trying to distort everything. Nothing you can say will hide the fact that these things *happened* to Camilla! It's all there, in the diaries!'

Annie's sharply raised hand came too late to prevent him finishing his outburst. 'Try to confine yourself to answering the questions, please,' she said imperturbably. She gave him another of her bright smiles. 'Now, let us indeed turn to the matter of the diaries. You were present when Miss Stenner collected the diaries from her parents' house, were you not?'

'Yes. Camilla would only agree to go if I went with her.'

'Despite the fact that you were also accompanied by police officers?'

'That was Camilla's decision, not mine.'

'Of course. Is it a measure of the success of your treatment of Camilla that she needed you to hold her hand when the police were available to do it?'

'I told you, Camilla wanted me along.'

'Mr Letzer, who let you into the house?'

'Camilla had a key, but Mrs Stenner was in.'

'Wouldn't it be normal for a mother to have known of the existence of diaries kept by an eight-year-old child?'

'Your Honour!' Barnes was calling even before he was fully on his feet. 'Mrs Stenner is not a witness in this case. My friend really cannot speculate in this manner.'

Davies lifted his chin from his cupped hand. 'I

consider that to be a permissible question, Mr Barnes, the mother of so young a child . . .'

Annie dipped her head in acknowledgement.

'I suppose it would.'

'Thank you. Were you aware of what happened to the diaries after they were collected from the Stenner house?'

'Camilla took them to the cottage she is renting.'

'They were not handed directly to the police? They are, after all, the crux of the prosecution case?'

'That was none of my business.'

'No, of course not. Were you aware at that time of what those diaries contained?'

'No.'

'However, during the time you were seeing Miss Stenner, while she was, as it were, working on the diaries, you came to understand that they had a very important bearing on this case, did you not?'

'Of course.'

'Mr Letzer, you are an intelligent man. You have degrees to prove it. They aren't only important to the case, they're important to *you*, aren't they?'

'How do you mean?'

'To your knowledge, is this the first case where allegations arising from RMS have apparently been supported by contemporaneous *written* evidence?'

'To my knowledge, yes.'

'As the therapist prominent in the case, this could have a considerable effect on your career, could it not?'

'I object, Your Honour! The question is totally irrelevant.'

Davies sighed. 'Yes, Mr Barnes. The witness will not answer that question. Go on, Mrs Trevellyn.'

'Thank you, Your Honour. Mr Letzer, did the diaries, when they turned up, and if taken at face value, dovetail neatly with your own conviction that Miss Stenner was experiencing RMS – *Recovered* Memory, and not *False* Memory, which is the name many distinguished specialists give to this so-called phenomenon?'

'You're suggesting I influenced Camilla, to make a name for myself?' His fists clenched. 'I don't care about that. All I'm interested in is that *he* should pay for all he did to . . .' He began to shake from head to foot. Annie could hardly contain her dismay as he clapped a hand to his face, hiding his eyes. '. . . For the *pain* he caused to that poor . . . child.' The last word emerged as a racking sob. As he lowered his hand, settling his shoulders back, moisture glistened on his cheekbones.

If it was a performance it was an almost unbelievably good one. Her face closed, unsmiling, Annie said, 'Please confine yourself to answering the questions, Mr Letzer.'

She moved on to cross-examine him about the diaries, going over the same ground as Barnes, laying traps, trying to show that he could have influenced not only the fact of Camilla's recall, but the very content of what she thought she recalled. Repeatedly she returned to the meaning of the symbols, to show that they were open to a thousand different, and innocent, interpretations.

Each time he met her head-on, recovering confidence, totally unshakable in his assertion that *all* the interpretation had come from Camilla's constantly improving memory of events, during the days spent in isolation in the cottage.

The judge was eyeing the clock, preparing to rise for the lunchtime break. Annie caught his eye, indicating with a nod that she was nearly at the end of the questioning. 'So, in summary, Mr Letzer, the jury is asked to believe that *all* of the interpretation of the symbols

379

was the result of Miss Letzer's memory, alone and without any intervention from you?'

'Definitely.'

Annie gave him a brief grin. 'Quite. But you will agree that, since the two of you were alone, in that isolated cottage you took care to rent, where there would be no Catherine Morgan to witness events ... some people might think there would have been a temptation for you to ensure that Miss Stenner's recall coincided with your, ah, expectations –'

'It wasn't like that! That wasn't why we took that cottage. It was somewhere Camilla could be away from ... from interference.'

Annie bowed graciously. 'No doubt. But you *were* frequently alone with her there. You have already agreed it would have been possible for you to have used hypnosis without Miss Stenner remembering that fact. You are asking the jury to take your word that you *didn't*, aren't you?'

'I guess I am,' he said, tight-lipped. 'But I'm telling you again, I didn't do that. I would never do that to Camilla. It would be like stealing a part of her life. And enough's been stolen from her already!'

'Your sentiments are commendable. But, you will appreciate that, if the jury has to take your word in these crucial matters, it is important to establish that you are a thoroughly *creditworthy* individual, won't you?'

He looked nervously around the court before answering, as though suspecting an ambush. His eyes lingered for several seconds on Camilla as though he drew strength from her. He straightened his shoulders. 'Obviously. And I resent the suggestion that I would lie, especially about anything affecting Camilla.'

Annie was not looking at him. 'Mr Letzer, do you believe Camilla Stenner is in love with you?'

380

His fingers tightened for a moment on the edge of the box. Releasing his grip, he fiddled with the documents that lay in front of him, suddenly concerned to align their edges. Annie was preparing to repeat the question before he looked quickly into the gallery and back at Annie, squarely meeting her eye. 'Yes. I believe she is.'

'Don't say it so quietly. I would think you would want all the world to hear.' She let her eyes play for a moment on the gallery before turning back to Letzer, a congratulatory smile on her face. 'Miss Stenner is a wonderful young woman. You must be very proud.' Letzer nodded, unable to keep his face from lighting up. Annie's smile disappeared, leaving him grinning at the jury. 'Even though, according to the most basic rules of your profession, you had an absolute *duty* not to let it happen.'

Letzer's smile turned to a sick smirk as he saw the trap close around him. 'It shouldn't happen, it's true. I just . . . Camilla is so *special*, we –'

'Specially vulnerable? Specially damaged? Are those the easiest to seduce?'

'No! You've no right to say that!' He was leaning over the front of the witness box, his face contorted in protest. 'I . . . *never*. . . we've . . . we've never slept together. I could never take advantage of Camilla like that. Never! We . . .'

Jurors reared back instinctively at the vehemence of his protest. Once again, his anger was either genuine or he was a supremely good actor.

Annie cut her losses. 'Do you love Miss Stenner?'

He looked up into Camilla's face, his features working with emotion. 'Yes,' he said, the word catching in his throat as a barely audible croak. 'Yes. I'm deeply in love with her.'

Annie swept the jury with her eyes. 'With her,' she

said distinctly, 'or with her two-million-pound trust fund?'

The lank-haired juror swivelled to look at her neighbour. Her audible gasp brought a sharp look from the judge.

'That's despicable. I love Camilla for herself. I don't want to hear about trust funds, money or any of that stuff.'

Annie sighed. 'Unfortunately, in these courtrooms we hear a great many despicable things, and we encounter despicable people,' she added icily. 'Do you expect to continue your relationship with Miss Stenner, after this case is over?'

He looked tentatively up to the gallery. 'I hope so,' he murmured, his eyes still on Camilla.

'Are you aware of the *terms* of Miss Stenner's trust fund?'

'I know the trust exists, and that's all. We . . . I . . . there's been no reason to talk about it.'

'Well, let me clarify matters for you. Should Miss Stenner's father be convicted in this court, Miss Stenner takes control of her share of the trust at twenty-one. If he is convicted it will be in part on your evidence today. It will also be on the evidence of Miss Stenner's so-called diaries. Or, rather, on what she *says* those diaries mean. Let me remind you that the only person with whom she had contact while she was studying those notebooks was you. Should the jury return a guilty verdict, the girl you say you love, the vulnerable, disturbed woman whose affections you have won, will dispose of something over two million pounds sterling. Three million dollars. But in all the times, as lovers, that you talked of the future, you never became aware of that?'

Something odd seemed to be going on inside Letzer. His knuckles whitened where he gripped the edge of the box. In place of the angry flush, his face was drained and pasty. His upper body swayed slightly, as though he might faint. He remained in the same posture for perhaps two or three seconds before slowly shaking his head. His eyes half closed, he muttered his answer through clenched teeth. 'No.' It was no more than a whisper. He turned his eyes once again on Camilla, the plea in them clear for the whole courtroom to read. 'Camilla never told me.' He repeated the words in a whisper, as though talking to himself.

Annie's eyes roamed over the jury, trying to read reactions in their blank, inscrutable faces. Her heart sank as she watched the fat woman, back in her blue suit today, sneak a look up to the gallery, where Camilla sat. The faintest hint of a smile tugged at the corners of her mouth. She looked like the kind of woman who hung around churches to watch other people's weddings, the perfect audience for Letzer's bogus love story. His cleverly judged shows of emotion had been an uncomfortable surprise, sending Annie's strategy awry. She had been expecting a much cooler, more cynical response. She took a deep breath. At moments, even *she* had found herself half convinced that he genuinely loved Camilla.

'Mr Letzer, are you a truthful man?' Annie asked.

He hesitated, openly weighing his words, before lifting his head and saying in a level voice, directly to the jury, 'I have my shortcomings. But I'm on oath here. And I would *never* lie where Camilla's welfare was concerned.'

Annie's raised hand had been too late to stop him completing his answer. Once again, he had played it cleverly, leaving an impression of a man who was flawed but frank. 'As you say, you are on oath.' She began turning to the bench, as though she had finished, when she turned back abruptly, as if on an afterthought.

'Oh, just one last question. Have you ever been to Mexico?'

He hesitated for a long time, sometimes looking up at the gallery, sometimes down at his hands where they fidgeted with the water glass. Finally he nodded. 'Yes.'

Annie was swept by a deep, overwhelming lassitude. She had not realised how certain she had been that her question would take him off guard, and how much she had been depending on his denial. He was still talking, laughing now, as though at a fond memory.

'Oh, it must be, I don't know, three years ago. I drove down for a couple of weeks, for some sightseeing. I picked up some statuettes, Mayan stuff. I was sure they'd be fakes. They turned out to be *genuine*! Worth a thousand times what I –'

Annie's listlessness had dissipated. 'Just answer the questions, Mr Letzer,' she said, sharply now. 'You reminded us all just now that you are on oath.' She waited for him to acknowledge her words, his brow furrowed.

'Three years ago. Was that the only time you were in Mexico?'

'Yes.'

Annie looked quickly at the jury to ensure that they picked up the quaver in his voice. Calmly, she pulled out the fax that had come in from Erskine's New York office the previous night. 'Would you please look at this document. In 1991 you were registered in New York as the owner of an MGB sports car. Did you own such a car at that time?'

He put the glass to his lips and, finding it empty, put it back down again with a crash. 'Yes.'

'What colour was it?'

'White.'

'What happened to it?'

'I . . . It was old. I guess I scrapped it.'

384

'In America?'

'Well, yeah. I was living in California in '91, so I guess . . . yeah.'

'Mr Letzer, you already said, on oath, that you had been to Mexico once in your life, three years ago. That would be in, what, 1994?' He dipped his head, keeping his eyes down. 'You were not in the town of La Santa in May 1991, then?'

He swallowed. 'No.'

'But your car was, wasn't it?'

He bit his lip and shrugged. 'Was it?'

Annie looked around her as she flipped over the page. 'Would you now look at this document?' She drew from her folder the faxed copy of the statement from the Mexican police. 'Could it have been your car, Mr Letzer, that was found burned out in a remote spot not far from the Mexican town of La Santa?' She looked directly at the jury. 'A coastal town, very handy for getting back to America by boat.'

'Well, I told you, I scrapped it.'

'But not in Mexico?'

'No. Who knows? Anybody might have got hold of it. It was a junker.'

Annie nodded. 'Had you ever heard the name Lewis Hampton?'

Letzer's head moved back as though at a blow. He recovered quickly. 'I don't think so. No.'

'Was he not practising as a therapist in San Diego while you were living there, and involved in a major swindle, stealing the money of a young woman he was treating, who had fallen for him?'

Letzer shifted his shoulders. 'You told me yourself, there are hundreds of therapists in California.'

'But did this one not leave town the moment he had stolen this poor woman's money? You, Mr Letzer, seem to have disappeared at the same time.'

'I never heard of the man.'

'Was that same man killed in a car accident, also in La Santa, in Mexico, a few days after you both left San Diego?'

Annie watched in astonishment as the colour ebbed from his face. His shoulders drooping, he stood for several seconds with his head bowed, grasping the rail. When he looked up he signalled for a glass of water and drank deeply. His hand was shaking. He began to look up at the public seats and then pulled back, forcing his eyes on Annie. 'Why are you telling me this? It's nothing to do with me.' A film of perspiration had broken out on his face.

Annie nodded slowly, and turned, smiling grimly to Judge Davies. 'No more questions at this time, Your Honour.'

Twenty-Four

'How did it look from up there?' asked Annie.

Liz stopped toying with her salad and shrugged. 'I don't see how you could have done any better. He's a damned good actor. I watched Camilla when he was making those declarations of undying love. The poor girl's completely besotted. I must say, if I didn't know better, I'd have been convinced *he* was, too.'

Annie nodded slowly, letting her fork drop onto her untouched plate. 'There's no doubt about it, he wrong-footed me. I didn't expect him to be that good. The jury were eating out of his hand. But what did you make of it at the end? On the one hand he seemed *ready* for the Mexican tack, which took *me* by surprise. I thought that was the point where I would rattle him. But he was cruising until I mentioned the Hampton persona. That's the weakness, and he knows it.' She smiled into Liz's wan, eroded face. Tentatively, she reached out and put her hand over Liz's. When Liz did not pull it away her smile widened. 'It's going to be all right, Liz. Believe me. Once we get him face to face with Jill he'll fall apart. I guarantee it.'

As she spoke, her smile faded. Matt, who had left the restaurant in order to make his call away from the eager ears of the other lunchers, came striding across the room, the phone dangling slackly at his side. His face was sombre. Annie raised her eyebrows. 'How is she?'

He lowered himself into a chair and poured himself the last of the half-bottle of wine. 'Hard to say. She won't be out before the beginning of next week, anyway.'

Annie spoke so low her words hardly carried across the table: 'There's no *doubt*, is there . . . ?'

'That she'll recover? They don't think so. Although, the way Rachel tells it, I think she hopes so.' He drank some wine and ran a hand over his eyes before laughing, genuine amusement mixing with the bitterness. 'After all, she's never been comfortable with me, has she? She's always acted as though I'd done something that she couldn't quite put her finger on. Now, seeing me accused like this, I think she's happy at last. It's the first really cheering thing to happen to her since Patrick died. It's a good thing Mark's there. The sinister old bag would probably sneak Jill a bottle of gin just to see me go down.' His laughter dying abruptly, he looked bleakly into Annie's eyes. 'Because if Jill *can't* get into that witness box, that's surely where I'm headed for the next twenty years, isn't it?'

At his words Liz gave a soft moan. 'Oh God, I shouldn't have left her alone. I ought *never* to . . .'

Matt's arm coiled around her, pulling her to him. 'Don't! Please! Any of us would have done the same. She said she was being *sick*. No grown woman wants a stranger watching her vomit.'

Annie was looking hard for some good news. 'There's still the photo. And Larry. And if Roy's people can keep coming up with stuff like the MGB . . .'

'Yeah, well, it'll all help.' He sighed. 'But there's no sense kidding ourselves. Without Jill I'm dead.'

Annie sat silent for a moment, then shoved her chair brusquely from the table. 'We had better be getting back. Davies hates to be kept waiting, especially by a woman. Even more especially by one with only a Higher Court Certificate!'

*   *   *

'Ms Butler, you have already listed for the court your professional qualifications. Would you like to tell us what post you held from 1981 until 1990?'

'I worked at Stockton General Hospital in St Louis, Missouri.'

'Is that a hospital with a good reputation?'

'In psychiatry? It's regarded as one of America's leading hospitals.'

'I see. What precisely was your title?'

'From '87 until I left to do research I was Assistant Director of Psychiatric Resources.'

'Thank you. We'll return to your work there a little later.'

As Barnes turned to select another sheet of notes Matt leaned forward in the dock, studying Naomi. In place of her usual ethnic-tinged wardrobe she wore a crisp suit of pale green linen and a silk, high-necked blouse. Her hair was gathered into a chignon. Instead of the usual heavy silver jewellery she wore a lone ring on her right hand, set with tiny rubies, and a single strand of pearls. Waiting for Barnes's next question she let her eyes stray to Matt's face and gave him a brief flicker of a smile. He smiled back behind his hands. She looked and sounded a picture of competence. Anything positive in her testimony would be worth its weight in gold.

Barnes turned back to Naomi, smoothing a grey curl back under his wig with a fingertip. 'Ms Butler, you were the person the defendant originally called in to treat Miss Stenner after her attempt at suicide, is that right?'

'Yes.'

'In the course of treating her, how much time did you spend at the Stenner house?'

'I was there virtually every day for several weeks. Quite often I overnighted there.'

Barnes feigned surprise. 'Ah! Did you? So would you say that you got to know the family well?'

'Very well. We became friends, I think.'

'Ms Butler, in your professional experience, are there indicators, accepted clues, which would *alert* experts to potential problems within families, sexual abuse problems specifically?'

'Yes. For example, if a child seemed especially fearful, or withdrawn. Certain kinds of behavioural problems. Eating disorders, of course. Anorexia, for example, would be a classic indicator. Not on its own, of course, but in a particular context it might make a specialist, a social worker or child psychologist look closer.'

'Were you aware that Miss Stenner had suffered a bout of anorexia while still in her teens?'

Naomi nodded. 'Liz told me about it.'

'And when she told you, did you speculate on a possible cause?'

'Of course. That would be part of what I had been invited in to do.'

'What possible causes came to mind?'

'There were a number of possibilities. Some people are probably just born neurotic, some are made neurotic by damaging experiences; betrayal, peer group pressures, parents fighting, divorce. Abuse,' she added, her voice suddenly husky.

'You knew, of course, there had been no divorce, and you had no reason to suspect brutality on the part of the defendant towards his wife. In fact, he was a pillar of his community, was he not, a highly regarded man, a world-famous writer, whose whole body of work might be seen as evidence of a life-long interest in children . . . ?'

'Your Honour! I must ask my learned friend to withdraw!'

Without waiting for the judge to speak, Barnes bowed and offered Annie a slow, reptilian smile. 'Your Honour, I will gladly do as my friend suggests. I assure the court no aspersion was intended. None at all.' He turned back to Naomi, the smile slowly dissipating. 'Let me just ask you, Ms Butler, did the context lead you to suspect any *particular* cause?'

Naomi hesitated. 'It wasn't my main role. I had really been asked to try to help Camilla out of what seemed to be deep depression. However . . .' As she spoke she was twisting the ring on her finger, wrenching at it, tugging it up to the knuckle and driving it back down again. '. . . it did strike me that Matt was very . . . jealous of Camilla. Unusually possessive. That again doesn't mean anything in itself, but it is a frequent predictor of an abuse situation.'

Matt stared in total disbelief. His sudden movement to the edge of his chair had made the dock officer, seated alongside him, jerk out a hand, ready to restrain him. It was unnecessary. Slowly, as disbelief turned to outrage, Matt sank back into his seat, twisting to look up into the gallery.

Liz was staring at Naomi, the same look of stunned incredulity in her eyes. Gradually, as though feeling his eyes on her, she swung her head to look at him. She flicked convulsively at her face, brushing away a tear that tumbled suddenly over her cheekbone. Without taking her eyes from his, she silently mouthed the single word, 'No.' More tears came.

'Ms Butler, I would like to return to your work at Stockton General Hospital. You mentioned that the hospital was highly regarded for the work being done there in the field of psychiatry. That's a wide area. Can you tell the court if this was in a particular field?'

'Yes. The principal area of research was into sex offences.'

'Did you, personally, have a speciality?'

She drew a deep breath, unable to resist a fleeting glance at Matt, who sat pale and immobile, hunched forward in his chair. 'I ran the section dealing with adult abusers.'

'Was that only trying to cure them, or was there more to it?'

'Partly it was treating their problems directly, trying to help them, and partly my work was research. We were particularly looking at underlying causes, looking for predictors, examining how abusers managed their own responses.'

'And with reference to that area of abusers managing their responses, did anything particularly striking emerge from your researches?'

Again, she flicked a glance at Matt before answering. 'Well, yes. We were the first, though other researchers have since supported our findings, to identify the phenomenon we dubbed PFD, Post Facto Dissociation.'

Matt felt a further stirring of apprehension and anger. Barnes was smirking happily. 'Could you explain that, please?'

Naomi set herself, looking at each juror in turn, as though weighing up an audience at the start of a lecture, gauging their attention. 'First of all, for our inquiry, we selected a group of perpetrators against whom there existed virtually irrefutable physical or other corroborative evidence, evidence so strong there was virtually *no* room for doubt. Among that group, after conviction, over eighty per cent continued, when interviewed, to deny the offences. This, of course, is not surprising. Life in prison for child abusers can be very harsh, even dangerous.' She stared straight ahead as she spoke the words, not allowing her eyes to stray to Matt. She drew breath, taking her time, working her audience with the skill of a seasoned lecturer. 'Of course, our initial assumption was that this denial was simply a form of cowardice, a conscious lying, in the effort to avoid the odium they knew attached to the offences. However, we were puzzled when this denial continued through prolonged deep therapy with almost half this group, thirty-four per cent of the total. We were even more perplexed when most of these also sailed through polygraph tests.'

'Those are lie detectors, aren't they?' Barnes intervened, helpfully.

'That's correct. However they measure only physiological responses, perspiration levels, and so on. It's well established that trained people can fool them, and abusers are notoriously manipulative people. So, with the subjects' consent, we moved on to inhibition-lowering techniques. The first one we tried was alcohol. In controlled conditions, subjects were encouraged to get drunk. Although their inhibitions did indeed drop, and although they became garrulous and indiscreet on many subjects, none of our final thirty-odd per cent admitted to their offences.' She took a leisurely drink from her water glass. In the silence Matt heard her swallow. She had the entire courtroom hanging on her every word. His own blood was pounding now, rising in volume with every word she spoke, like a hammer beating against the inside of his skull.

'We then moved on to other substances – truth drugs, if you will. Some of them, about a third of our sample, then admitted their actions. Under very deep, and extremely carefully controlled hypnosis another twenty per cent admitted their guilt. I should say that the tests under hypnosis were not done by us. They were carried out by members of the American Medical Hypnosis Society, highly reputable, qualified physicians who had no prior knowledge of the offences, so that there could be no question of the hypnotist influencing the outcome. This left us with about sixteen per cent of all offenders, who continued to deny. Our conclusion was that these sixteen per cent, plus probably many of the others of the original sample were in fact not really lying in the common sense of the word. That is, there was no *intent* to deceive. What we concluded, what I believe others have also now concluded, is that these men – they were all men, by the way – had no conscious *knowledge* of their offences, and so could not be said to be lying. They had quite simply, in a sense, *forgotten*. They had repressed the memory so deeply that their denial was, to them, simply the truth as far as they knew it.'

Matt's stomach churned. In a surge of anger he half rose from his chair, slumping heavily back as the dock officer snatched roughly at his sleeve. Barnes's next words came to him as though from very far away.

'And did this ... er, process of forgetting happen quickly, or gradually, over a long period?'

'In many cases, very quickly indeed. It was a difficult experiment to do since few offenders are caught within such a short time lapse. However, what results we were able to obtain showed that over half of the subjects repressed all knowledge within forty-eight hours.'

A tremor of shocked surprise rippled through the room.

'In your study, did you find any correlation between social class and the ... repression?'

She nodded. 'To our surprise, we did. The higher the socio-economic standing of the perpetrator, the more likely it was to occur.'

'I *see*.' Barnes let the words roll off his tongue as he looked slowly around at the jury, his head wagging in agreement. When he turned back to Naomi he had assumed a look of innocent puzzlement. 'And how would such a person, in your opinion, respond under oath, to the question, "Did you commit such or such an offence?"'

The blood thundered in Matt's ears, almost drowning out the words. He clung to the edge of the dock, like a drowning man. Without it he would have fallen to the floor. He buried his face in his sleeve, as though to shut out the meaning of what she was saying.

'He would have no choice *but* to deny it. He would be genuinely angry, absolutely as though he were innocent. Because, in his own mind he would *be* innocent.'

Almost sobbing with the effort, Matt raised his head. The jurors were no longer looking at Naomi but directly at him. Nausea clawed at his stomach. The whole room began to sway. Naomi's words seemed no longer to be coming from any particular direction but from everywhere at once, deafening, filling the room.

'He would go to his grave believing in his own innocence.'

From her seat on the rickety bench Camilla heard the front door open and close. She sprang to her feet, sending the book that lay unopened across her knees sliding to the ground, and ran headlong across the lawn. She almost collided with Letzer as he emerged from the open back door, a scowl darkening his face. Her own brows knitted as she took his hand in both hers.

'You've been gone for an *age*. What's wrong?' She moved closer, so that the length of their bodies touched. 'Not bad news?'

He laughed, leading her back to the bench. 'That's what I get for leaving the mobile at the hotel. It didn't occur to me when we rented it to ask if this place had a phone. I must have driven fifteen miles. The first booth I found, some idiot had ripped the phone out.'

'But, why were you looking so worried? Is there bad news? Is it about the sale?'

He dropped onto the seat, leaving her standing, his hand still in hers. 'No, it's not that. In fact there was a message from the agency. They're showing a couple of people over the place next week.'

She sat down, close against him. 'What is it, then? You looked suicidal.'

He shook his head and leaned against her shoulder. 'Nothing. Not now that I'm back with you.' Anxiety remained etched into her face. 'Sorry. It's Naomi. She's being a pain in the ass. She must have called a dozen times.'

'What does she want?'

A shrill note of alarm had crept into Camilla's voice. For a moment he stared, uncomprehending, into her face. Then, with an abruptness that made her blink, he said, 'I have no idea!' He pushed himself to his feet and walked across the lawn to examine a rosebush. 'Talk shop, I guess. Or for me to tell her how well she did on Friday. As a matter of fact, she *was* pretty impressive, wasn't she?' Getting no answer, he turned to look at Camilla. She was gnawing at a thumbnail, her face clouded, the muscles working beneath the taut skin. He took a step closer. 'Well, she was, wasn't she? I thought she did a tremendous job. She really saw off that Trevellyn woman.'

'Don't talk about Annie like that! Please, Stephen,' she added anxiously. 'She's a friend.'

He snorted. 'Oh, sure. Some friend! Defending *him*!'

For a while she did not answer, staring straight ahead of her. At length, she whispered, 'God, Stephen, it's a mess, isn't it? Not just Daddy. Mummy, Mark, Annie – this is tearing them all apart, isn't it? *We're* tearing them apart.'

He strode to her, dropping to one knee. 'Not us.

Not you. *Him.* He set it all in motion, all those years ago, the very first time he touched you.'

She rose abruptly to her feet, moving two paces from him, leaving him looking up at her, deep disquiet in his eyes. 'But who does it help to put him through this? The past isn't important any more. I have *you* now. I just want to think about the future.' Her fists clenched helplessly. 'And you've seen how he looks. Supposing Naomi's right and he really *doesn't* remember it? What's the point of it all? He'll just go to prison still believing he's innocent. What will it achieve, except to hurt Mummy and Mark even more?'

He rose and came slowly to her, gently pulling her round to face him. 'No, darling. You mustn't see it like that. That's what he wants you to think.' His face was inches from hers, his eyes aglow with conviction. His fresh, minty breath wafted a stray strand of her hair. 'You owe it to all the others. Remember there are tens of thousands of them out there, millions perhaps, just like him, biding their time, waiting for their opportunity. With some it will be their own children, with others it will be the child of a neighbour or relative, somebody whose trust they might have spent years cultivating, watching their target ripen. With others it might be total strangers, an infant picked up in the park, or snatched into a car on their way to buy sweets.'

She shuddered, trying to pull away. 'Don't! You mustn't! Don't compare Daddy to . . . to those . . .'

He held her by the shoulders, flexing his knees to bring his face on a level with hers. 'Those what, darling? Do you think he's any different? *Please* see it through, darling. For all those who haven't been victims yet. Or perhaps just don't know they have been.' He dropped his voice to a whisper. 'We have to win this case for them, Camilla. So that all the filthy bastards with their "let's keep it our little secret" will know that the day their victims remember and speak out, nobody will be able to laugh at them any more. Nobody will dare try to tell them that some nutty therapist just pasted it into their minds for fun. Because people will remember Matt Stenner and know it's for real!'

Matt stepped through the open French windows into the shade of the room they had christened, years earlier, the sun room, although it was no sunnier than any other room in the house. It was a room he hardly ever came into, his routines keeping him to other parts of the house. The main item of furniture in the room was the baby grand piano they had bought second-hand when Camilla had expressed an interest in learning to play. It had taken the local piano teacher six months to transform Camilla's unlimited enthusiasm, though admittedly small talent, into tearful antipathy. Since then, the piano had functioned as nothing more than a plinth for a forest of formal, silver-framed family photographs. Crossing to the piano he sat down and laid his cheek on the cool, black-lacquered lid. Almost immediately, he felt himself sliding into sleep. In the moment before sleep came, he jerked fully awake again, roused by the horror that had haunted him in the twenty-four hours since Naomi's testimony. For two nights he had read, swum, drunk coffee, anything but sleep and face again the nightmare that lay in wait, that would bring him awake again minutes later, the bedclothes drenched in sweat. The nightmare that screamed to him that the evidence was there, in the photos, and the diaries, and that he had had the opportunity. Awake, he could cling to reason, know that he was a victim of Letzer's scheming. Asleep, the horrors gained the upper hand.

Slumped onto the piano stool, he stared at the pictures. Tears stung his eyes. Camilla, five years old, smiling shyly out at him, one of Liz's T-shirts trailing to her feet, or as a gap-toothed eight-year-old astride her bike. Mark, too, looked out at him, a laughing-faced child, or a boy of twelve or thirteen, already strapping and handsome.

Matt reflected again that prison life, with its daily humiliation and ostracism, the constant threat of sudden retribution from the other prisoners, held no particular fear. What scared him was that, after the privileged years when his profession had allowed him to observe every day, every nuance of his children's development to adulthood, he was going to lose them. They would pass from youth to middle age without his being there. There would be grandchildren he would be unable to know. It was the thing he feared about death. Not the pain of it, if there were to be pain, but losing the knowledge of his family.

He reached for another photograph. Patrick had been eighteen months older than he. They had been inseparable right through their teens, sharing games and clothes, having crushes on the same girls. Later, as young men, their interests had diverged, Matt into engineering, and then writing, Patrick into electronics, building a business that by the time of his death at thirty-seven was worth millions. A mournful smile touched Matt's lips as he stared at the picture, taken on a terrace of the villa Patrick and Rachel had owned in Italy, against a background of cypresses and tan hills. Patrick was as tall as Matt, though without the breadth across the shoulders. A frisson ran through Matt as, for the first time, he saw the resemblance to Mark in the well-defined cheekbones and bony jaw. The smile, too, with the rakish, off-centre charm of a forties film star, and the mannerism of standing with one foot thrust forward, were uncannily like his son's. He felt a fresh pang of regret at Patrick's loss. Going to prison would have been easier knowing Patrick was there to support Liz and the children.

'There you are! Didn't you hear me call?' Matt spun to face the windows, his burdened eyes brightening. Liz stood silhouetted against the light, the strong sun outlining the slender shape of her legs through the cloth of her skirt. 'We've been looking all over for you.' She stepped into the room, frowning as her eyes grew accustomed to the dimness.

'I was dreaming.' He rose and kissed her. For the first time in what seemed many months, she did not pull away. 'I didn't know you were here.'

She took a short step back, keeping hold of his hands. 'Rachel stayed at the hospital with Jill. I invited myself to tea.' She looked him up and down, her smile clouding. 'What have you been doing with yourself? You look awful.'

He shrugged, looking down at himself. He was dressed only in shorts and unlaced running shoes. 'I was up all night.'

She stepped closer, looking into his eyes. She bit her lip. 'Matt, don't. Naomi's research may or may not mean anything, but as far as we're concerned it's bullshit.' Her little laugh had a brittle, distant quality. 'You never touched the children. Keep that fact in your head, as I should have kept it in mine, for God's sake.' She released her grip on his hands and moved deeper into the shadow of the room, her back to him. 'You couldn't have. You know that. And so do I.' Her voice had thickened as she fought back tears.

He stood helpless, his hands hanging at his sides, surveying the ambiguities of her last words, the ironies making his head spin. She believed in him again, when he no longer believed in himself. Because she had understood that he had been with Annie? And Annie, having risked her friendship with Liz to convince her of his innocence, had seen her own belief in him destroyed. Indecision and lack of sleep were making his head spin. Whether to let Liz continue to believe in his innocence for reasons that he knew were no longer valid, or tell her the whole story, and let Naomi's testimony wreak the same havoc on her as it had been wreaking on him since yesterday? He opened his mouth and closed it again without speaking, too confused to ask for or offer explanations. He stepped forward and took her by the shoulders. 'Shall we go and have that tea?'

'Yes.'

They had taken two steps when he took her by the hand and turned her to face him. 'If you're not doing anything special, I could cook us dinner, too.'

She nodded. 'I'd really like that.'

Twenty-Five

Reciting the words of the affirmation from the card, Matt studied the faces of the jury, wondering wryly whether refusing to swear on the Bible was adding to the stack of evidence against him. He had talked it over with Liz on the drive down. Her opinion was that he *should* take the oath, that it would help make him look a more dependable citizen. He knew what she meant, but despite her urging, he had been unable to do it, rebelling at the hypocrisy of it.

'Mr Stenner,' Annie began, her voice measured, low-pitched, 'you are charged with committing sexual inter-course and buggery with your eight-year-old daughter. Let me begin by asking you one fundamental question. Did you ever commit any of the offences with which you are charged?'

The words struck him like a flail. In all their rehearsals Annie had never prepared him for this question. His whole body swayed in agonised denial as his face contorted into an instinctive expression of revulsion. 'No!' he said, finding his voice with obvious difficulty. 'Of course not! Never!'

Nodding pensively, Annie turned to the bench. 'As you know, Mr Stenner, the prosecution have submitted in evidence against you notebooks purporting to be diaries written by your daughter at the period the alleged offences took place. They are, of course, relying on statements from your daughter, heavily influenced by Mr Letzer, as to the meaning of certain annotations and drawings in those books. Very heavily indeed.' As she spoke she gestured to the usher, who took the notebooks from where they lay, numbered, on the exhibits table, and handed them to Annie. She passed them to Matt. 'Have you seen these notebooks before?'

'Yes, at the police station.'

'And before that?'

'Probably. I certainly saw a great many like them. Camilla was always writing. She got through more notebooks than I did.'

'Would you agree that they are in Camilla's handwriting?'

Matt scanned mechanically through the top book. He nodded, gazing down at the close, uneven text. 'Of the time. I think so, yes.'

'Would you look through the books and examine some of the sketches and what appear to be gibberish annotations?' She gave him some page references and waited in silence as he flipped through the books. 'Are those things familiar to you?'

'Specifically those ones, I can't say. But I saw many like it. There was a period when Camilla did them all the time. My wife and I used to call it her "black period".'

'But you were aware of these items at the time your daughter was executing them?'

'Of course.'

'She did not hide them from you?'

'Not that I recall. We always looked at what she was doing. Doesn't everybody, at that age, at least?'

'Did you attach any importance to them at the time?'

'We certainly used to worry a bit about the drawings. They seemed so . . . depressing. But then Camilla was always prone to troubled thoughts. She was afraid of the dark. She used to lie awake at night worrying that the house might catch fire, or that "things" would be coming after her.'

Matt was cruising now, following the advice Annie had given him during their run-throughs of the questions, answering firmly, but taking care not to appear overconfident. Her strategy was to work on the worst-case basis that Jill would never be fit to appear, even though during the weekend she had made enough progress to have been walking around her room. Annie planned to take him through events at that time, trying to offer the jury a plausible alternative explanation for the prosecution's most crucial evidence, the books. If Jill did appear, she would blow the prosecution's case away. Once Letzer was exposed, Davies would have no alternative but to terminate the case. If Jill relapsed, or backed out, then their last remaining chance of keeping Matt out of prison was to establish reasonable doubt, even if it did leave the rest of his life in shreds.

'Did these drawings and so on coincide with the time at which these dreadful offences are alleged to have taken place?'

He stared at her, musing, for a second or two. 'Yes. Now I look back on it, they did.'

'Mr Stenner, is it true that during the years these notebooks lay undisturbed in your house, you could at any time have put your hand on them and destroyed them?'

'Of course. They were stacked in the closet in Camilla's room.'

'Nevertheless, although you and your wife saw these drawings, and were disturbed by them, it never occurred to you *to* destroy them?'

'Why should it have?'

'Well, you tell us, Mr Stenner, please. Why *didn't* you destroy them?'

'Because there was no reason to! I never touched Camilla! How could it ever have occurred to me that the day would come when Camilla would be led into putting such a twisted interpretation on them?' His chest was heaving. 'For God's sake, I'm not an imbecile. If I *had* been doing what I'm accused of doing, and Camilla suddenly started drawing these,' he tapped the books, unable to keep the revulsion from his face, 'I can't conceive that I would have left them lying around for five minutes, let alone for twelve years.'

'Quite.'

For the next hour, Annie led him through Camilla's childhood, her history of nightmares, the repeated bowel problems, the unpredictable, withdrawn behaviour, her troubles at school. As each of Annie's softly articulated questions relentlessly built up a searingly intimate picture of Camilla's problems, Matt's firm, well-rehearsed responses gave little clue to the turbulence and self-loathing churning within him. Despite everything that was being done to him, his instincts were screaming their revulsion. Every question seemed an unbearable intrusion, an invasion of his family's most private spaces. As he gave her the answers she expected, almost verbatim as they had discussed them, he was aware of the intolerable weight of Camilla's eyes on him from her place in the gallery, as though her gaze were eating away at his flesh.

And all the time, reciting his answers in the same firm, clear tone, he had the queasy, disorienting sensation that had haunted him through the weekend, the sense that he was looking down on himself, Naomi's testimony like a jagged, toxic fragment lodged deep in his brain.

By the time Annie sat down, a little after eleven thirty, he was exhausted and dispirited. It had been the worst ninety minutes he had ever spent in his life, worse than the first night in the police station, months earlier, when outrage had somehow fuelled him, carrying him through. Now he simply felt dirtied and drained, in a state of total emotional exhaustion.

He watched blankly, hardly comprehending, as Barnes rose to his feet and gave him a slow, amiable grin.

'Camilla, in her evidence, told us that when, as a child, she cried in the night, you would often go to her naked. Is that true?'

Matt looked at him blankly, as though in shock. A second or two passed before he answered. 'Yes. Yes. I would have.' He glanced up at Liz, frowning.

'Do you own pyjamas?'

'Yes,' Matt answered, speaking very low.

Barnes grinned cheerfully. 'A little louder, Mr Stenner, please, so the jury can hear you. You own pyjamas, but do you wear them?'

'No. Not since I was twelve or so. I keep a set as a kind of courtesy, for when I visit friends.' Matt grinned, trying to lighten what he could see was on the brink of degenerating into a disastrous exchange.

'I see. So you are alert to the sensibilities of grown-up friends, but you have never seen the same need in the case of a vulnerable young girl, perhaps just awakening to sexual matters?'

'I don't wear pyjamas now. I didn't then. I wasn't about to ferret them out of the drawer at three in the morning. Camilla was my *daughter*, for God's sake.' He bit his lip, angry at himself for allowing Barnes's deliberate sneering to succeed.

'Indeed she was.' Barnes dropped his voice in a parody of confidentiality. 'Mr Stenner, do you own a bathrobe, too, or a dressing gown?'

'Of course. A bathrobe.'

'Of course? Mmm. And where do you keep it?'

Matt's head throbbed. He felt breathless, trapped. 'In the bedroom.'

'More precisely, please.'

'Behind the door.'

'I see. So, putting it on would have taken you, let's see . . .' Barnes mimed the act of donning the robe, holding his left hand in front of him, ostentatiously looking at his watch. 'Shall we say two and a half seconds? Can we agree on that?' He waited for Matt's tight-lipped nod. 'Good.' Barnes was patronising him, playing with him. 'So your robe hung there, to hand. You could have picked it up in passing, even put it on as you walked, so that you would not have lost those two and a half seconds that must have been so precious to you, but you did not bother to do that, even to save your daughter from possible embarrassment?'

'Camilla wasn't embarrassed. She was used to seeing me without clothes on, around the house, or in the pool.'

'You say she wasn't embarrassed. Did you know that, or did you just *assume* it?'

'Look, she was a child. It was normal for her to see us like that.'

'So you assumed, because *you* did a thing, it must be acceptable. *You* were the judge, in other words, of her emotions?'

'Of course I was!' he answered, immediately angry with himself for the note of truculence in his voice, for letting himself rise again to Barnes's bait.

'So you were in the habit of assuming you knew how she felt. You were her father and you knew best. You could have eliminated even the *possibility* of doing her any damage by simply putting on the handy bath-robe, but you chose not to?'

'You're twisting everything,' Matt said, fighting to retain his composure. 'What we did was perfectly innocent, and normal, and there *is* no sinister explanation for it.'

Barnes made an ironic bow and showed his teeth.

'My apologies if you feel I'm doing that. I assure you I'm really only trying to establish the facts. Now, to clarify something for the jury: the pool you mentioned, it's at your home, isn't it? A rather nicely equipped indoor pool?'

'Yes.'

'And when you swim, you swim naked?'

'It depends. If I'm alone, usually, yes.'

'And when your children were small, you all swam together?'

'Of course. As a family.'

'With swimming costumes or without?'

Matt shook his head, angry and depressed at the turn the questioning was taking. 'It depended,' he said wearily. 'When the children were very small, probably we didn't bother. Later, we usually did.'

'Usually?' Barnes arched an eyebrow. 'Let's return to your night visits to your daughter. Normally, would it be you that went to Camilla, if she was disturbed in the night?'

'No. If Liz, my wife, were there she would normally go, especially when I was working on a book project. I can't work well if I don't sleep well.'

'So you really only did it when your wife was away, is that it?'

'In general, yes.'

'When you were alone with your children?'

'I was practically *never* alone with them. The au pair, Kristina, was almost always there.'

'Although we've heard from Miss Olsen that she was often out very late.'

Matt looked exasperated. 'I mean she was ... around. I didn't know whether she was in or not.'

'Where did she sleep, Mr Stenner?'

'The house has a rear wing with a self-contained flat. That was hers. She told you all that herself.'

'But now I would appreciate hearing it from you, Mr Stenner. As we just heard, there may be subtle but important differences.' He grinned wolfishly. 'From her quarters, would you say one could hear normal conversation from your daughter's bedroom?'

'Conversation? No.'

'What then? A shout? A cry of pain? A scream?'

Matt's face muscles worked with the effort to control his anger as, eight feet from him, Barnes watched his struggle, an amused smirk on his face. Below the level of the witness stand Matt's fists clenched and unclenched. 'There never *were* any cries of pain. No screams, either.'

Barnes nodded encouragingly. 'I'm sure you're right. But, had there been, would the au pair have heard them, or not?'

'She would have heard a scream. A shout, perhaps not. How would I know, exactly?'

'I don't know, I don't know.' Barnes paused to look down at his notes, the smirk slowly fading. 'Mr Stenner, would you say you've always been a healthy man, a man who likes to keep himself fit?'

Matt nodded warily. 'I've always exercised.'

'And as a fit, healthy man, in the prime of life, at, what were you then – thirty-five? – did you often find yourself waking in the night with an . . . ah . . . forgive my bluntness, with an erection? Perhaps especially when your wife had been absent for a few days?'

As Barnes spoke, Matt had been looking at Annie, trying to read in her eyes some clue as to how he should respond. At Barnes's words, she jerked her head sharply away from him, busying herself with the papers on her table. Visibly off balance, Matt looked momentarily up at Liz before saying, in a strained voice, 'I suppose I would have. Don't most normal men?'

'We are only here to examine *you*, Mr Stenner.' He

409

smiled distantly as his emphasis brought an angry flush to Matt's face. 'Was it then also *normal*, or wise, for you to go to the bedside of this precious little person, terrified as you've assured us she already was by nightmares, naked and with an erection?'

Matt hesitated. Annie was still making a show of being engrossed in her documents. The picture of her filled his mind. He saw again her arm, pale in the moonlight, thrown at a careless angle across the quilt, her dark hair masking her face, as he slid, silent and anxious from the bed. 'Look, by the time I reached her room I wouldn't have ...' The pitch of his voice was misjudged, forcing him to clear his throat noisily. 'It just wouldn't have been ... Or perhaps on those occasions I wore the robe.' He knew it was not true. In his anxiety to avert discovery, his need to reach Camilla's room before she lost patience and came pattering along to push at his door and find Annie in his bed, he would never have taken the time to snatch the robe from its hook. Even Barnes's two and a half seconds would have been courting catastrophe.

'But you can't remember doing so?'

'You're asking me about things that I might have done twelve years ago. I was doing nothing wrong. There's no reason why I *would* remember details like that after so long. I undertook to tell the truth on this stand. To tell you I remember every night of my life would be plain stupid.'

Barnes bowed in mocking deference. 'Commendable. Do the details you *do* remember include taking your daughter back to your room with you, to *your* bed?'

Matt's intake of breath was audible. 'Oh my God! I'd forgotten it until you brought it up now. I did take her into my bed, very occasionally. It was always close to dawn. They were the worst times for Camilla's dreams. I would hear her crying. She would be completely inconsolable. I couldn't stop her, couldn't get through to her at all. She would pull away, hiding under her duvet, as though she were still in a nightmare, and I was some kind of monster that had just stepped out of it.' He flinched at the memory, as though it were a physical pain. His voice sank to a murmur. 'It was horrible, like a form of hysteria. In the end, I used to carry her back to my bed. It seemed to work. She would curl up in Liz's place, clinging to her pillow. That seemed to be the only thing that would calm her down.'

The last words were barely audible. The queasy, haunted feeling had returned to grip him. His tongue felt as swollen and dry as a plague victim's. The room seemed to sway in front of his eyes, forcing him to snatch at the rail for support. It was true. He had taken Camilla to his bed, often at dawn, after Annie had gone. The memory of it, of the comfort he had found from the close warmth of her small body, in the empty hour after Annie had gone, stabbed at him like a blade thrust into his eye. He became aware, as though watching from the bottom of a lake, of Barnes nodding in feigned sympathy with his plight.

'I see. May I ask, Mr Stenner, did your erections persist while your daughter was in your bed, lying in your wife's place? You see, your daughter's recollection is of being assaulted at that hour, yours is of consoling her. Is this coincidence, do you think?'

Matt raised a hand in a helpless gesture. He was still looking for words when Barnes continued, 'Or is it, Mr Stenner, just two people's very different interpretation of the very same events?'

A choked, whooping sob from the public gallery, brought every head in the place snapping around. Matt made an involuntary wounded sound in his throat.

Instinctively, he began to reach out an arm, halting, the gesture half complete, in an attitude of impotent pleading. Above him, Liz was on her feet and fighting her way along the row. She trampled on feet, almost staggering onto the laps of the gaping spectators as she scrambled blindly for the door, a hand clasped hard to her mouth, her face contorted.

'Members of the jury, we'll rise now. I would be grateful if you could all be back in your places by two fifteen, please.' Judge Davies turned to look down at Matt. 'I remind the witness that until such time as he has completed his evidence he should speak to nobody outside this courtroom.' Davies rose, and with a curt bow to the room, turned and disappeared through the door behind him.

Matt closed his eyes, swaying slightly on his feet. It was as though for the last three hours he had been inside some monstrously noisy machine and someone had just switched off the motor. He continued standing, his eyes tight shut, letting the stillness seep through him, waiting as the court emptied around him.

He paused at the top of the court steps, his eyes screwed up against the sun's glare as he sought Liz. She was seated on a grassy mound thirty yards from the court steps. Annie sat beside her, her arm around her shoulders. Matt hesitated for a moment longer, and then strode across towards them.

At his approach Liz raised her eyes. They were red-rimmed, her face deathly pale. For an instant she stared blankly into his face, as though not knowing him, and then, with a whimper, she scrambled to her feet and flung herself forward, her arms around his neck, almost knocking him to the ground. The sour smell of bile was on her breath.

'I'm sorry, Matt. I had to leave. I needed to be sick. I couldn't *stand* what he was doing to you. It was just so . . . horrible. So *vicious*!'

Before Matt had time to respond, Annie was alongside them, prising Liz off him, alarm in her face. 'Liz! Stop it! You *can't*!'

In response to Annie's silent plea, Matt eased Liz from him and, without speaking, pressed her gently back into Annie's arms. At Annie's nodded signal he walked three paces away and sat down. Annie did the same, pulling the weeping Liz with her. In the distance a knot of onlookers sniggered.

Choking back her sobs, Liz spoke, loudly enough for Matt to overhear. 'Sorry, Annie. I couldn't stand what that man was doing to Matt.'

Annie tightened her arm around Liz. 'The worst's over, Liz. Barnes has nearly finished.'

Liz lifted her head and gazed across to where Matt sat, staring down at the grass. 'We don't have a chance do we, if Jill *does* let us down?'

Before Annie had time to find an answer the attention of all three of them was caught by a figure hurrying towards them. Matt recognised one of the young lawyers who kept late hours in Annie's office. He was still twenty paces away when Annie scrambled to her feet and broke into a run. She snatched the big buff envelope he proffered and half ran back to join Liz, thumbing open the envelope as she came. Matt had risen. He moved an involuntary pace closer, watching intently as Annie inserted a hand and drew out a set of black-and-white eight-by-ten photographs.

As she went through them, the eager light in her eyes gradually faded and died. Still holding up the photographs, she looked from Liz to Matt. 'A pity,' she murmured, at length.

Liz and Matt stared at the pictures she held fanned

in her fingers. Five different versions of the same face. They could have been almost anybody. Only one, at a stretch, might have passed for a younger version of Letzer.

Annie waited in silence as they clung to each other. Liz pointed to the one that was least unlike Letzer. Her voice quavered as she spoke. 'If he's had surgery? Straightened the nose, taken some of the flesh off it. Probably had his entire face reshaped, jaw, cheekbones. Everything!'

Annie shook her head slowly. 'Yeah.' Her eyes were on Matt as she said flatly, 'I'm sorry, Liz. It was a terrible picture for them to start with. It was asking too much of the system. Twenty years is too long. It's all that hair on the original, it just gives the computer too much scope for guesswork. It doesn't have the shape of his eyes, none of the bone structure. All you can see in Roy's photo is his nose, and as you say, that's about the easiest thing to change.' She looked abruptly at her watch. 'Better be getting back.'

The two women walked side by side with Matt trailing in their wake, still within earshot. They had gone several paces before, tentatively, without looking at her, Annie slipped an arm through Liz's. 'Don't worry, Hannah got a call from Mark just before the adjournment. Jill's improving by the hour. And don't forget Larry. He thinks he'll have the certificate by tomorrow. Plus, Roy phoned through another little nugget this morning.' She threw Matt a wry smile over her shoulder. 'They've finally started to earn their money. I told you they would. They've tracked down somebody who remembers seeing Hampton outside his building with a girlfriend. They were sitting in a car, arguing. You know what car it was?' She looked from one to the other, grinning broadly. 'A white MGB! The witness remembers because he used to have an MGB himself.

Roy will bring the man's statement over with him. He's sent a copy to Larry, too, to see if it will help get some more cooperation from the Mexican police. Meanwhile, Hampton and his girlfriend happen to have been seen driving around in the same car as Letzer. A nice little coincidence for the jury to get their teeth into.'

Camilla's toe snagged in a fold in the threadbare carpet where a retaining clip had gone missing. Without even extending a hand to save herself, she sank to her knees, her weight dragging on Stephen Letzer's arm. Instead of trying to get up again, she let herself sag against the wall and began crying, the noise a soft, wrenching mew.

With a harassed look back towards the lounge where a scattering of tourists lingered over a late afternoon tea, Stephen Letzer shoved the two room keys into a pocket and reached to pull her to her feet. Camilla was a dead weight. Bending, he slid his arms under her, lifting her bodily, and carried her up the single flight of stairs and along the dim, dusty-smelling corridor to her door. Without putting her down, he manoeuvred the key into the lock and entered the room. Kicking the door closed, he laid her carefully on the bed where she stayed, inert and weeping.

He ran to the bathroom, returning with a soaked towel. Wringing it, letting the water cascade to the floor, he dropped to his knees and began mopping her forehead. Worry seemed to be eating away at his face, etching the youthful contours, ageing them. His brow was gathered into a deep vertical furrow above nervous, flickering eyes. 'Darling, it's all right now. It's over for him. Today was the hardest of all. From now on it won't be anything like as difficult. A few more days, that's all. And you'll have finally closed the book on this whole filthy business.' He stroked her shoulder as her body twisted in mute protest. His voice dropped to a hypnotic purr. 'Trust me. You'll see. You *need* to hear, for it all to be out in the open. You need to see him led away to really *know* it's over. You'll be able to start living again. *Really* living, darling. You'll be your real self again, for the first time since you were seven years old. We can start all over. Just the two of us.'

Slowly, as though in great pain, she raised her head to look at him through splayed fingers. 'Oh God, Stephen,' she said in a husky whisper. 'I *can't*. I just don't think I can bear any more. You saw him. Even this afternoon, with Annie trying to be *kind* to him, he was almost breaking down. This is just . . . *torturing* him. It's breaking him *apart*. Whatever he did to me, it's so long ago. It seems, so, so, cruel. He always seemed such a . . . *fine* man, so proud and strong. I never *imagined*, never wanted, to see Daddy put through anything like what that Barnes man did to him this morning. It was like . . . like watching an animal being torn apart by dogs.' She drew a sobbing breath. 'I saw that happen once. To a cat. It left me with some of the same empty feeling here.' She put a hand to her abdomen. 'It seemed so *pointless*.'

He dropped the towel and bent so that his face was close to hers. His eyes held an eager glitter. 'It will never be *that*, darling,' he crooned. 'I would never ask you to go through this if it were pointless. Please try to remember, you have to persevere, for all the others.' As he spoke he jumped to his feet and snatched a copy of the *Guardian* from the dressing table. He thumbed through it and thrust it open in front of her. 'Look! Look what they've managed to do! Could you believe they would sink so low?'

Camilla pushed herself onto an elbow and peered through her tears at the article. It was on the women's page, headed with a photograph of a thin, myopic woman. The headline was 'Recovered Memory. Lost inheritance'. Camilla looked from the paper to Letzer. 'Who's Jill Stanakis?'

'God knows. That's not the point. The point is, the article is there to undermine the whole idea of RMS. Don't you see, this is what we're fighting against? We're like anybody who comes along with a new idea. We have to fight the prejudice, and the ignorance.' He hurled the paper from him in disgust. 'Don't these people, the journalists who write this garbage, understand? Every molester in the country must be cheering them on.' He was panting now, breathless in his conviction. 'You are going to change the way people think, darling! Because you've been so brave they're going to see, to have *proof*! Don't you see how important it is?'

She shook her head, her face exhausted and desolate. 'I don't *care* about that, Stephen. It's Mummy and Mark, too. I just want the hurting to stop.'

He bent lower, his cheek against hers. 'It *will* stop, darling. When people like your father begin to understand that they are going to get caught . . .'

Twenty-Six

For the next few days Matt lived in a state of suspended animation. The parade of medical experts Annie had assembled, despite her best efforts in examining them, seemed as irrelevant as mechanical dolls. Under the shrewd, velvety cunning of Barnes's questioning some of them ended up proving worse than useless, falling headlong into every trap he laid, letting him lure them into offering opinions that were of more help to the prosecution than to Matt's defence. The man they had procured to rebut the evidence of anal penetration, a man with a reputation which on paper was almost as solid as Worthington's, turned out to be a disaster. Watching him fumble and prevaricate Matt realised with a yawning sense of loss how much hope he had had riding on the man. Before the case he had given them explicit assurances that he could testify to cases where damage as extensive as Camilla had suffered had occurred in the absence of penetration. Within minutes Barnes had had him back-tracking, prevaricating and uncertain, forced to admit that he did not have sufficient first-hand knowledge of the cases to be able to assure them that there had indeed been no assault. By the end of his cross-examination Barnes practically had the man agreeing that Matt was guilty.

Only in the evenings, when Annie dropped them at home and sped off to join William, home again now, did life seem real, taking on a vivid, almost unbearable intensity. While Mark and Rachel continued to take shifts at Jill's bedside, Matt and Liz would have dinner together in the kitchen. Matt would open the best wines he could find in the cellar and the two of them would eat together. Often, they would cling to each other in silence, each happy just to drink in the other's presence. At other times they would talk incessantly, about the past, and about the future, never, as though repelled by some tacit dread, about the case.

Slowly, over the days since the start of the trial, the elation that had come with the first realisation that Letzer and Hampton were the same person had gradually been eroded. Now, as witness succeeded witness, as the evidence piled up, as Jill progressed with agonising slowness, and Erskine still had no hard evidence, the gamble became more and more desperate. Although neither would voice it openly, each now knew they could lose.

They talked of Liz's future plans, intense and committed as a pair of adulterers, trying to project themselves beyond the unimaginable chasm to a time when they could once more be together.

On the Wednesday evening Mark returned from the clinic early. He burst into the kitchen, flushed and jubilant. For the first time a doctor had been ready to commit himself. Although her health was still precarious, Jill had improved enough to risk a short appearance.

Matt sprang up to clasp him in a hug. 'Short will be plenty! Did he say when? Did Jill say anything? Is she ready to do it?'

'Well, she's obviously, like *mega*-scared, but she says she wants to try. I think she feels ashamed of herself. She wants to show you she can do it.'

'How soon? Annie doesn't think Davies will stand for a request to wait for her to sober up any more. She's convinced he's got his knife into her as it is.

Apparently, he's notorious. He doesn't like solicitors pleading in the Crown Court, taking bread out of barristers' mouths!'

'But surely he can't let his stupid prejudices affect the *case*! It wouldn't be fair!'

Matt laughed softly and covered his son's hand with his. 'Fair, Mark?' He looked into Mark's face, offering the sight of himself, the ravaged eyes, the pallor, the slack skin at his throat. 'Do you think there's anything fair left? He's convinced we've lost anyway. *We* may know Letzer's a sleazy little con man, but he was a hell of a convincing witness. To the judge, we're basing ourselves on nothing more than the fact that he owns a particular briefcase and once drove an MGB.' He sighed. 'At best, he'll probably tell us to bring her on whether she's ready or not. He's only human. Annie's done a good job. If it weren't for the diaries, we'd be home and dry. Remember the jury's faces when Camilla was in the witness box? *With* the diaries we have to come up with something that blows their whole case to pieces. If we don't, you'll spend the next quarter of a century talking to me from behind glass.'

Mark reared away, clutching his fists to his temples. 'No, Dad! What about Larry Guenther? When you show them that the body that was buried wasn't Jill's therapist?'

Liz put down her glass and stood up. She wrapped her arms around Mark, pulling his head down onto her shoulder. She sniffed back tears. 'Mark, the body has still to be exhumed. We just don't have that evidence yet. And as long as the jury are convinced those diaries mean what Camilla swore they meant, the rest is just worrying at the edges.'

Mark shook his head, his words muffled by Liz's shoulder. 'Annie should have done more. Surely she could have made them see what a fucking ... *evil* dude he is. You only have to look at the smarmy . . . shithead.'

Liz smiled ruefully at Matt. 'Mark, we *know* the truth. We know Daddy. They only know what they see and hear in court. Annie did what she could. Jill just has to identify his voice, period. Anything less than that is just so much hot air, however many experts or character witnesses we produce. And, anyway, it doesn't look as though Guenther *is* going to come up with the dead man. Roy Erskine called this afternoon. Guenther's sitting it out in Mexico City, waiting for the bloody mayor to emerge from his conference. The man won't give him the time of day. They've taken Dad's money, and they've come up with *nothing* for it,' she added bitterly.

Matt shook his head. 'That's not true, darling. The stuff on Letzer was damned good. And don't forget who found Jill in the first place. And they're still trying. Don't give up on them.' He smiled wanly. 'Not for another forty-eight hours.'

Mark straightened, lifting his head from Liz's shoulder. 'But, I don't understand. If the judge knows what Jill's going to say? Surely, if he knows the full story, he *must* help!'

Matt sat back in his chair and rubbed a hand wearily over his eyes. 'But that's just the point, he doesn't know.' He raised a hand, quelling Mark's protest. 'Annie, Mum and I talked it over until our heads spun. If Annie tells the judge, then she would have to make the application for Letzer's recall at the same time. Letzer would be told he was going to be needed. In his position what would you do then?' He nodded at the realisation in Mark's face. 'Precisely. You'd be on the first plane back to the States, out of reach of a perjury charge. We decided it was best to take a chance and wait. Obviously, if push comes to shove we'll *have* to come clean with the judge. If we can, though, we want to hold on so that Annie can make the application while Letzer's sitting up in the gallery, holding Camilla's hand. Then he can't run. Or, at least, if he does, our point's made.'

'Supposing he just doesn't happen to turn up anyway?'

'I'm fucked,' Matt said flatly.

'He'll be there, Mark.' Liz spoke very quietly. 'You've seen the look on his face. He's rubbing Dad's nose in it. He couldn't bear to miss a day.'

Matt laughed bitterly. 'It's part of his plan. Naomi had a theory about that.'

'Naomi!' Mark exclaimed. 'Her stupid theories! I wish *she* had gone home, before she started spouting them in court.'

Liz nodded assent. 'Perhaps she has gone. Good riddance. Giving that evidence, it was as though she really *hated* us.'

'Maybe she does,' Matt said, almost to himself. 'Anyway, she predicted he'd want Camilla to sit through it all.' With his elbows on the table, he dropped his head into his hands. 'Learning to hate me is going to make her whole again,' he said, choking.

Thursday morning. In Britain it would already be past noon. Larry walked up the steps of the party building, built to resemble the steps of a Mayan temple, moving slowly, trying not to break into a sweat. Although it was not yet nine o'clock the smog was holding the sun's heat as though it would never let go.

Pausing in the cool of the cavernous reception area to get his breath, Larry scanned the shirt-sleeved officials manning the circular reception desk. Seeing one who fitted the description Chief Alvarez had given him, he strode to the desk. The name tag was right.

'Señor Guttman?' The man looked at him through glazed, expressionless eyes, his belly thrusting against the counter, and then nodded noncommittally, as though preparing to claim that his tag was a mistake. 'Larry Guenther. Chief Alvarez warned you to expect me.'

Larry slid a hand into his jacket pocket and felt for the slimmer of the two unsealed envelopes. He slid it out, doubled over in his palm, and passed it to the official. Expertly, the man thumbed it open and squinted at the contents. His smile turned to a warm grin. 'Just a moment, Señor Guenther. I'll see if the Alcalde can find time for something so important to Chief Alvarez.'

Friday morning had brought a squally south-westerly wind and with it, thick banks of low cloud. A hail flurry slapped against Mark's window, bringing him instantly wide awake. It was four thirty. He had anticipated his alarm by fifteen minutes. By the time he descended to the kitchen, a little before five, his parents had already emptied the coffee pot. Side by side at the table, their fingers intertwined, they both looked sick, their eyes deeper shadowed than ever, as though they had not slept at all. Impulsively, in a gesture he had not made for years, he bent and kissed each of them on the cheek, not air kisses, but real physical contact. 'You should have stayed in bed,' he said, in a doomed attempt at lightness. 'You both look awful.'

'There wasn't much point,' Matt replied. 'Neither of us has shut our eyes all night.' Abruptly, he leaned across the table and gripped Mark's hand. 'I really appreciate you doing this, Mark.'

Mark reddened. 'I *want* to, Dad. I just want to help.'

'Thanks. Rachel phoned. She'll be here in a couple of minutes.'

Mark shook his head ruefully. 'I'd rather be on my own. It's not as if I have to *do* anything. It's only a matter of riding with her, that's all.'

Matt smiled grimly. 'And making sure she doesn't get a smell of anything to drink!' He took Liz's hand, gripping it tight as a shiver ran through her. 'It'll be better with two of you. At least if you need to pee you won't have to chain her to a post.'

'If you want. But Jill hates Rachel.'

Matt smiled indulgently at Liz. 'Come on, Mark. How can she? They hardly know each other.'

Mark sat down and fiddled with a cereal bowl. 'She doesn't like the way she talks about *you*,' he blurted.

Matt and Liz exchanged hurried looks. Matt tried to laugh. 'Come on, Rachel doesn't do that.'

Mark's face was burning. 'She does. Jill says Rachel thinks you're guilty!'

As he spoke they heard the back door open and Rachel's heavy tread crossing the utility room. Matt stood up and embraced Mark. 'Make sure the ambulance driver takes it easy, son,' he said, in a voice creaking with emotion. 'There's a lot riding with you all.'

Mark worried at a thumbnail, already gnawed down to the quick since they had left the clinic a little before seven. The weather had played havoc with the traffic. He was cursing himself over and over, under his breath, for having agreed to the driver's suggestion that they take the M25 route around London. The traffic had been blocked solid in both directions for over an hour. They were never going to be at court before eleven.

Clinging to his grab handle as the driver swung between lanes in his effort to gain seconds, Mark threw another anxious glance at the nurse seated opposite him and from her to Jill.

She lay prone in the bunk, secured from the ambulance's wilder movements by straps around her legs and body. The pallor of her face had taken on a green tint. The sinews strained in her thin hands as she clutched the edge of the bunk. She was swearing softly to herself, the obscenities repeated in a pattern, over and over, like a spell.

'Jill, are you all right?' Mark touched her lightly on the arm. 'We won't be much longer.'

She groped for his fingers and closed her hand over his. It was trembling. 'No, I'm not all right.' The reediness in her voice had come as a shock to him. It was the voice of a woman three times her age. Beneath the thinness, though, there was a stubborn edge that reminded Mark of his father's mother, very old and frail, announcing her resolve not to die until her next birthday. 'To tell you the truth, Mark, I'm scared shitless.' Her fingers dug tighter into his hand, as though trying to still the trembling. 'Don't worry, though. I'm going to go through with it. I told your dad I'd help him, and I mean to do it.' She gave a short, coughing laugh. 'Ah shit, no, that isn't why I'm doing it. I'm doing it for me. For the pleasure of getting my own back on that bastard. Look at me, Mark.' She had pushed herself up onto one elbow and was jabbing a finger between her small, sagged breasts. 'Look at the state I'm in. How the guy fucked up my life. Can you imagine how *much* I've dreamed of having the chance to fuck him up, too? I trusted him, gave him everything, and he just . . . left me to rot. Literally to rot.' Abruptly she let herself fall back onto the bunk, her head turned away from him. He caught the glint of a tear as she turned. 'And the stupid thing is,' she said, her voice muffled by sobs that ran the length of her body, 'I still love him. I don't know what's going to happen when I hear his voice.'

He leaned closer, panic in his eyes, not noticing his fingers biting deep into her spare flesh. 'You *can't* let Dad down, Jill. Please.' He was sobbing himself now, frantic with anxiety. 'You *must* go through with it! It's my dad's whole life they're playing with. And Camilla's! Think about her. You can't let him get away with it a second time. You can't let Camilla turn out like . . .' He trailed away, tongue-tied, furious at himself.

Slowly, Jill turned her head to him, her sobbing subsiding. 'Like me?' she muttered hoarsely.

'That wasn't what I . . .' he stammered.

'Of course it was.' She smiled suddenly. 'And you're right. I *am* a fool. And he's a bastard. Don't worry. I won't let him screw your family the way he screwed mine.'

Larry was first out of the pick-up. There was a moment of total blackness as Chief Alvarez killed the lights and then a flashlamp slashed into life, picking out the ornate wrought-iron gates and white-painted wall. While the rest of the men clambered from the truck and shouldered tools, Alvarez jiggled a huge key in the corroded lock and the gates swung open.

Alvarez paused to study a piece of paper and then thrust it back into a pocket. With the men clustering close at their heels, they set off along one of the dirt paths between tombs that shone white in the lamplight, resembling toy palaces with their decorative ironwork, plastic vases and pious-faced plaster saints.

Abruptly, after eighty yards or so, the path petered out in an expanse of untended scrub. Alvarez advanced slowly now, playing the light onto a scattering of rough wooden crosses, half obscured among the vegetation. With a grunt, he halted by one of the crosses and pushed the sinewy grass aside with his boot, stooping to read the weathered plaque. Straightening, he turned and whispered a command to his men.

As they hurried to unfurl their tarpaulins Larry glanced at his watch and made a quick calculation. In Britain, it would be ten fifteen. Matt Stenner would just be stepping into the dock.

'And do you, personally, Doctor, believe in the validity of RMS? Do you in particular believe it plausible, or even possible, that a girl of eight could be repeatedly subjected by her father to sexual intercourse and then simply forget about it until years later?' Annie worked with conscious effort to inject conviction into her voice. She knew, along with Barnes, who sat with a patient half-smile on his face, and the judge, that the questioning was futile. She could have produced a hundred 'qualified' psychiatrists to answer no to those questions. It would not have made the slightest difference to the jury. By now they had heard so many supposed experts drawing totally different conclusions from the same facts that they must surely be discounting the lot of them. The case stood or fell by Camilla's diaries, and everyone in the room knew it. Annie was playing for time, and time was about to run out.

'No. I don't believe in the syndrome, for reasons I set out in my paper to the British Institute of Psychiatry in March 1995. In my view . . .'

Annie was no longer listening. The door of the public gallery had opened and closed. Frowning in an impression of concentration, she let her eyes wander to the public seats. Mark was shuffling along the row to join Liz. Seeing Annie look up, he broke into a grin and mimed wiping his brow. Annie turned away without acknowledging him and went on watching the witness mouth his theory, not hearing a word he said. When he at last fell silent she bowed. 'Thank you. No more questions.'

The moment the doctor had left the room, Annie rose to her feet again. 'Your Honour, we have one last witness. However, before bringing that witness to the stand, there is the matter, the subject of my application to Your Honour this morning, which I wonder if it would be possible to deal with now.'

The judge drew a long breath. 'The matter you mentioned you would like me to deal with in chambers, I suppose?'

'Yes, Your Honour.'

The judge grimaced, turning to Barnes. 'Mr Barnes? You're familiar with the substance of the defence's request?' Barnes nodded. 'And may I assume you have no objection to it?'

'Not to the matter being heard in chambers, Your Honour.' He grinned. 'No.'

Judge Davies glanced up at the clock. 'Members of the jury, I'm sure you've been concentrating hard on the very instructive testimony.' He was careful to allow no suggestion of irony to enter his voice. 'So I invite you to go and refresh yourselves with a cup of coffee. Please be back in your places in twenty minutes.'

Annie and Barnes entered the judge's room together. He was already drinking coffee, scrutinising the slip of paper Annie had passed to him that morning. He glanced up as they entered and waved a hand negligently at the two cups that stood with the coffee jug. 'Please help yourselves.' His eyes had already gone back to the paper. 'I don't have to tell you, Mrs Trevellyn, that this is a most unusual request,' he said, still without looking up.

'It applies to most unusual circumstances, Your Honour,' Annie replied flatly.

428

'Essentially you're making an application for the recall of Mr Letzer?'

Annie inclined her head. 'Yes.'

The judge cocked an eyebrow at Barnes. 'Any objection to that, Mr Barnes?'

'I object most strongly, Your Honour. With respect, I would submit that it would be wrong in principle. Any questions for the witness could have, and should have, been put at the time of his appearance. I feel it would be quite wrong to permit the defence's request.'

The judge looked enquiringly at Annie.

'The circumstances are, as I said, unusual, Your Honour. Our witness, who is absolutely vital to my client's case, was unable for medical reasons to be here before today.' As she spoke Annie produced a letter on the headed notepaper of the drying-out clinic. She had helped draft its carefully crafted text. 'As you can see, she has been very ill, and remains so. She is a very frail person, physically. She had to be brought to court this morning by ambulance.'

The judge grimaced. 'But, Mrs Trevellyn, is the defence really suggesting, in effect, that Letzer is an impostor, and that this witness will identify him as such, and as someone who had perpetrated the same deception on her?' The judge could barely keep the note of incredulity from his voice.

'Yes, Your Honour,' Annie responded simply.

'But your witness is to all intents and purposes blind. We have to rely entirely on her recognition of the voice?'

'They were lovers, Your Honour. We believe the witness's testimony would be admissible.'

'Your Honour,' Barnes intervened, 'I really must protest. What possible relevance can such testimony have in this case? We rely principally on the diaries together with Miss Stenner's own evidence. Mr Letzer's evidence is in any event not crucial to the prosecution's case. What possible point is there in having a debate as to whether he *sounds* like this woman's tormentor?'

Annie shook her head. 'With respect, to an outside observer Miss Stenner's sketches and notes are meaningless. The prosecution case relies heavily on Miss Stenner's *interpretation* of them. We contend that Letzer was instrumental in leading her to that interpretation, and to that extent his reliability is fundamental to the case.'

Davies took a long sip of his coffee, his eyes on Annie. 'Mrs Trevellyn,' he said slowly, 'as I see it, you need to have Mr Letzer back in the witness box before your new witness. Otherwise, you have the difficulty that I won't possibly be able to admit your witness's testimony as being relevant. I do think it would be helpful if you could offer the court some new evidence that would justify my granting your application. Evidence directly concerning Mr Letzer.'

'I *can* do that, Your Honour! Since Mr Letzer gave his testimony, further matters have come to light, in particular matters concerning a certain briefcase which the witness owns, an unusual model, similar to one owned by our witness's erstwhile lover. We would wish to call a private investigator who will produce testimony on that matter.' Annie licked her lips. 'I submit that justice cannot be served, Your Honour, in denying our application.'

Davies plucked at the flesh of his lower lip. 'Mr Barnes, I'm afraid if I refused and this case went to appeal, Mrs Trevellyn would have rather strong grounds, don't you agree?'

Barnes inclined his head. 'In all honesty, Your Honour, I have to agree with you.'

Davies looked at Annie, a faint smile on his lips. 'How do you suggest we proceed, Mrs Trevellyn? Presumably you don't wish your witness to be seen by Mr Letzer?'

'Ideally, no, Your Honour. I had thought that, given the exceptional circumstances, our witness might be seated in court, out of sight of the witness box, just next to the dock, for example, before Mr Letzer takes the stand.'

Davies stroked his chin and looked at Barnes, who shrugged. 'I don't see any objection to that. Where is the mysterious Mr Letzer? Is he still with us?'

'He was in the gallery just now, Your Honour. I would be grateful if, accepting that these are highly exceptional circumstances, he could be removed so that our witness might take her place unseen.'

The judge sighed, laying aside Annie's paper. He sat back in his chair, one arm sprawled on the desk, the other hanging loose, his fingers almost touching the floor. 'And what, Mrs Trevellyn, if your witness *doesn't* recognise Mr Letzer's voice?'

Annie shrugged and looked down at the floor before lifting her eyes and replying, very quietly, 'I think my client might be in very considerable difficulty, Your Honour.'

Twenty-Seven

Roy Erskine stepped out of the taxi and pushed money into the driver's hand. By the time the driver had eyed the money and begun to thank him, Erskine was already ten yards away, striding fast towards the steps of the court building. Pausing for only a moment to get his bearings, he hurried to the desk where two robed ushers stood laughing together. He drew an envelope from his pocket and handed it to one of the men. 'Can you get this to Annie Trevellyn, please? Court one. She's expecting it.'

Camilla watched uneasily as the frail, stooping woman, her eyes hidden by opaque sunglasses, picked her way carefully across the courtroom, the female usher's hand cupped under her elbow, guiding her to the tubular chair that had been placed beside the dock, below and behind the spot where Camilla's father sat. Reaching the chair, the woman turned with an awkward, spasmodic movement and lowered herself into it, hanging heavily on the usher's arm. After a brief, whispered exchange with the woman, the usher turned and strode quickly back to her place.

The judge gave the woman a slow, appraising look before saying, his eyes still on her, 'We'll have the witness back now, please.'

Camilla gripped the balustrade of the public gallery. With Stephen no longer at her side she felt sickeningly apprehensive and exposed. From the moment he had left, after a brief, whispered conversation with the usher, the desire to speak to her mother and Mark, sitting only a few yards from her, had grown almost unbearable, an overwhelming urge to let herself be drawn to them, to huddle with them against the world. She fought it off, focusing on the equally powerful sense that to succumb would somehow be disloyal to Stephen. She stole a glance at them and quickly turned away again, frowning. A new, eager light shone in their faces as they hunched over the rail, their eyes glued expectantly on the new witness. They held each other tightly by the hand. Mark was even smiling.

The whole room watched transfixed, sensing that something extraordinary was happening, as Letzer, led by the usher, made his way to the witness box. As he took his place his eyes went up to the gallery, seeking Camilla. Matt smiled grimly at the unease he read in the man's fleeting, aborted attempt at a grin.

'Mr Letzer, I remind you that you are still on oath,' the judge said neutrally.

'Yes, Your Honour.'

Matt frowned at the words. Strain had stretched the man's voice, raising the pitch, giving it a hoarse, unnatural timbre. His eyes continued to flicker constantly over Matt's head to the gallery, as though he were frantically trying to send a message to Camilla.

Matt glanced down at Jill, where she sat hidden from Letzer's view. She was slumped forward, her head buried deep in her hands. Beneath the thin fabric of her shirt the bony shoulders jerked and twitched as though an electric current were running through them.

Annie rose, smiling. 'Mr Letzer, we would be grateful if you would answer loudly and clearly, in your normal voice. Is that clear?'

Letzer shrugged and nodded. Again, he cast an uneasy glance up at Camilla.

'Answer the question, please!' Annie snapped the words, the affable smile evaporating.

'Yes.' He coughed. 'Yes. It's clear.'

'Good. Mr Letzer, do you own a briefcase?'

'Yes,' he said, warily.

'Can you tell us the colour, please?'

'It's a dark red. Burgundy, I guess you'd call it.'

'Thank you. And the make?'

Matt saw the Adam's apple bob in the man's throat. 'It's Gucci.'

'Can you tell us how long you've owned it?'

Annie felt excitement rising in her as Letzer shifted his feet, looked into the gallery, back at Annie, then into the gallery again. His face had drained of colour. He nibbled at a fingernail, then thrust his hand in his pocket and pulled it out again before saying, 'I don't know. Years.'

'How many years, precisely?'

The man shrugged, fidgeting. In the dock Matt moved involuntarily on his chair, his fists clenching in the effort to check his own rising jubilation. 'I'm not sure. It was a . . . ah . . . it was a present.' He cleared his throat, uneasy. 'Several years ago. Long before I came to England.'

'Is it the bag you took with you when you went to Mexico in 1991?'

Letzer flinched. Droplets gleamed on his forehead. 'I don't know what you . . .' Again, he looked up at Camilla. Abruptly, as though drawing on some inner force, his resistance stiffened. 'I don't know what you're talking about. I told you, I wasn't in Mexico then.'

'Really? Not in La Santa?'

'Your Honour, I really must object!' Barnes leaped to his feet. 'This witness was recalled for a specific purpose discussed with Your Honour and my friend. With respect, I feel it quite improper for my friend to

434

attempt to resume cross-examination of the witness. These questions could and should have been asked at his first appearance. Some of them were.'

Davies nodded. Sighing, he turned to the jury. 'Ladies and gentlemen of the jury, I'm afraid I shall have to ask you to return to your room for a few minutes.' He waited while the jury shuffled from their places and the door closed behind them before raising an eyebrow at Annie. 'Mrs Trevellyn?'

'Your Honour, while I appreciate my Learned Friend's concern, other matters which have a very direct bearing on my client's case have come to light since the witness previously took the stand. I hope Your Honour will agree that it is appropriate, in the interests of justice to my client, that I should use this opportunity to explore this particular avenue.'

The judge pursed his lips. 'I hear your objection, Mr Barnes. However, I think you must agree that *some* questions must be asked. As I see it, the direction of Mrs Trevellyn's questions will be irrelevant if the outcome of this appearance is as the prosecution might foresee. If, however, matters were to turn out differently then it seems to me these may be highly relevant matters. I think, Mr Barnes, that I shall have to overrule your objection.'

Annie watched the jury settle back into their places and then turned slowly to Letzer. 'La Santa, Mr Letzer. Does that place mean anything to you?'

He seemed to have used the break to get a new grip on his shaky composure. He shook his head. 'No,' he answered, looking directly at Annie now.

'You aren't familiar with the hotel Reina Isabella in that town then?'

'No.'

'Did you ever drive to that hotel one evening in your white MGB?'

He swayed, his eyes fixed on Annie like a seasick man keeping his eyes on the horizon. 'How could I, if I wasn't there?' The voice had risen in an angry, pleading whine.

'And so you never picked up a red-headed woman there who was holding your briefcase for you, the same distinctive briefcase you still use today?'

'No,' he said faintly. Then, louder, with the desperate emphasis of a man throwing caution to the wind, 'No. I don't know what you're talking about. I told you, I've only *been* to Mexico once in my life.'

Annie stepped closer, a finger raised accusingly. 'Let me put it to you, Mr Letzer, that the truth is that you previously practised in California under the name Lewis Hampton. You also advertised for business under the name Letzer, presumably already preparing a second identity, until the moment came for you to disappear.'

Barnes had sprung to his feet, an arm outstretched, outrage in his face. 'Your Honour, I object!'

'You embezzled money.' Annie had raised her voice, talking over Barnes's objection, ignoring him. 'You flew under an assumed name to New Mexico . . .'

'Your Honour! I really –'

A curt movement of Davies's hand cut Barnes short. With an intake of breath, he dropped reluctantly back into his seat.

'. . . where you rented a car, as Hampton, and drove to La Santa. La Santa is an out-of-the-way town on the Mexican coast with more than its share of drug traffickers and what as an American you might term hustlers. A place where the police would not investigate too strenuously when you faked your own death. Who really died in your place, Mr Letzer?'

Letzer reared away, clutching a hand to his head. 'Nobody. I never killed anybody.' He looked around him, wild-eyed. 'I would never . . . I could never *do* a thing like that. It's crazy.'

'Yet we shall be offering evidence from the local police that says a man did die in that crash, Mr Letzer. And I suggest to you that after the fake crash you collected your money, and your girlfriend, who had driven down in your car, and then . . . what *did* you do then? Take a boat across the Gulf back to America? And after a few years spending that poor woman's money, you started all over again, this time picking Camilla Stenner as your victim.'

He shook his head frantically. 'No. I love Camilla. I would never hurt her! I . . .'

A sob cut through the courtroom. Annie followed the judge's glance across to Jill. Still doubled over, she sobbed again, the sound louder now, an unmistakable note of hysteria in it. Letzer stared, too, his face still hot with emotion. In response to the judge's questioning look, Annie turned back to Letzer and gave him a serene smile. 'Thank you, Mr Letzer. No more questions.'

Matt watched, almost dizzy, hardly daring to think, as Letzer passed within feet of him, striding hard from the courtroom as though he felt the judge might change his mind and call him back yet again. As the door swung closed, Matt turned back to look at Annie, his palms slick with sweat. Her smile said it all. Everybody in the room had seen it. The man had been lying in his teeth.

'Jill Stanakis.'

The female usher took Jill by the arms and coaxed her to her feet. Shaking, her head bowed, Jill allowed herself to be led across the courtroom and made her way uncertainly into the box, the usher having almost to push her bodily up the steps.

From her seat Camilla studied the trembling woman. Her name had meant nothing to her. Cadaverous, pinched and mousy despite the smart clothes, she bore no resemblance to the smooth procession of doctors and psychiatrists Annie had so far called, with their confident bearing and brisk, well-rehearsed responses. Standing hunched in the box, she seemed small and cowed and broken, clutching the rail with one hand, the Bible swaying in the other as she repeated the oath in a tremulous croak.

As the sound of the American accent reached her, Camilla, without knowing why, felt apprehension begin to ooze through her, puddling like a liquid in the pit of her stomach. She sat further forward, frowning deeply. As she settled back to listen to the Stanakis woman, the sound of the door opening behind her brought her head swinging round. It was Naomi who entered. As their eyes met Camilla stifled a cry of surprise at the cruel, dismissive disdain she saw in Naomi's face. She had spoken against Matt, now her attitude to Camilla herself was unmistakably contempt. Confused and hurt, Camilla turned back to the drama below.

'Miss Stanakis,' Annie began, her voice seeming to reach Camilla as a far-off echo, 'thank you for coming, for travelling all the way from America. I know you've been unwell. Your story has been in the newspapers, hasn't it?' Annie turned to the jury as she spoke. In her hand she held two newspaper cuttings, one from the *Guardian*, the other from that morning's *Daily Mail*. She smiled inwardly. She could see a response in the eyes of at least half of the jury, who had either read them themselves or been told about them. By the end of the next adjournment those who had not read the articles would have heard every detail. Tara had finally earned her fees. 'Now, Miss Stanakis, as there may be some members of the jury who read neither the *Mail* nor the *Guardian*, could you begin, please, by telling the court how old you are?'

Jill ran her tongue several times over her lips, her head cocked towards Annie, her eyes invisible behind the sunglasses. Her mouth laboriously formed the words, 'Twenty-nine.'

Watching the jury with half an eye, Annie caught the delicate frisson of shock that ran through them. 'Thank you. Miss Stanakis, I wonder if I could begin by going back with you over certain events in your life. I would like to begin, if I may, with your teenage years, with your father in California.'

Slowly, never hurrying, often pausing for long periods to give Jill time to recover when emotion took hold of her, Annie coaxed her through her story. She began with the early teen years, the emotional fragility caused by her parents' constant fighting, her mother's sudden death. Painstakingly, letting Jill's brave, quavering answers do her job for her, Annie built up for the jury the picture of a young woman so emotionally battered that she had no defences left. Then, still leisurely, letting the picture gain force from emerging with tantalising slowness, she led her into the period after her mother's death, alone with her father, left to her own devices. At last she began to tease out similarities to Camilla's case, the depression, the anorexic bouts, the difficulties in relating to men.

'Miss Stanakis, did your father take any interest in your problems? Did he even *notice* them?'

Jill nodded, the most vigorous movement she had made since taking the stand. 'Of course! He was the one who insisted I go into therapy. He may not have been home much, he was still worried sick about me.'

'I see. So, despite his absences, you regarded him as a loving father, who cared deeply about you?'

'He *was* loving. And he did care, a hell of a lot more than it was in his nature to show.'

'Was that what your therapist encouraged you to think about him?'

'No.' The jury were on the edges of their seats, trying to catch her whispered answer.

'Perhaps you could speak a little louder for the jury. What, in broad terms, *did* he lead you to think about your father?'

Jill gulped. She swayed, gripping the rail to stop herself from falling. The judge leaned forward, concern in his face. 'The witness is obviously not very well. Perhaps she would like to sit down.' Jill nodded, manifestly trying to hold back tears. She sank heavily into the chair an usher hurried to place behind her knees.

Annie waited until she was listening before repeating the question.

Jill's mouth was open for some seconds before any sound emerged. 'He told me Dad had been screwing me.' Her voice was little more than a rustling in the rapt silence of the courtroom.

'You mean to tell this court that your therapist convinced you that your father had been making love to you? Committing incest?'

Jill nodded mutely, the tears running in rivulets down her furrowed cheeks.

'Miss Stanakis, before encountering your therapist, had there been any suspicion in your mind that such a thing had ever taken place?'

'No.'

'So, it must have been a shock to you, to say the least?'

'I was shell-shocked. Devastated.'

'Why was it that, with no other evidence, you believed such a thing about a father, whom you had thought, until then, had your best interests at heart?'

'Because I believed everything my therapist said. And I . . . he'd convinced me . . . I guess I'd convinced *myself* that I really did remember those things.' Her head jerked away from Annie, as though she were looking for an escape route. 'For Christ's sake, I was in love with him,' she rasped. 'Crazy in love.'

'And was he in love with you?'

Jill's laugh was the sound of dried beans rattling in a tin. 'He sure as hell *said* he was.' Deep loss mingled with the bitterness in her tone. 'Kept on saying it. Right up to the moment he ripped off every cent I inherited from Dad.'

Annie raised a restraining hand, watching the reaction that shimmered over the jurors' faces like wind on water. 'We'll come to that in due course. Can you tell us what happened after you became convinced of your father's supposed misbehaviour?'

Gradually, taking her time, Annie eased the story from Jill, lingering over the details, taking pains to frame her questions to give the jury the opportunity to reflect on the similarities between Jill's case and Camilla's; the way in which her therapist had influenced her to sue her father, despite her own misgivings, the man's use of hypnosis to enable her to elaborate on her 'memories'.

'How did your father respond to your starting legal action against him? Did he fight the case hard?'

Jill hung her head, almost disappearing behind the rim of the stand, her eyes screwed up behind the dark lenses. 'No,' she whispered, looking up again, her eyes streaming. 'He shot himself.'

Annie paused to let the effect of this settle on the jury, then asked, 'I'm sorry to press you on the matter, Miss Stanakis, but why do you think he did that? Shame?'

'He had nothing to be ashamed of.' She was crying

openly now, taking breath in strangling gulps. 'He just couldn't face it, being accused like that. Dad never touched me that way in his life!'

Annie moved a step closer. Everything in the way she moved expressed sympathy for the wretched woman. 'You say he never touched you? Do you have proof of that?'

'Of *course* I have proof. After he ... afterwards I checked out his credit card slips. He *couldn't* have done it, most of the time, anyway. He just wasn't *there*! The nights I was accusing him of ... those things, he was playing the tables in Las Vegas.'

'Miss Stanakis, you alluded earlier to an inheritance you had from your father. Would you be prepared to tell this court how much you received?'

'Sure. Give or take a hundred thousand dollars, three and a half million.'

Annie's soft voice sounded loud in the total silence that had fallen on the room. 'Over two million pounds sterling. Very similar to Miss Stenner's trust fund. You're a rich woman?'

Jill gave another dry laugh. 'I was. Like for about a month.'

'You no longer have the money?'

Jill shook her head. 'Lewis ripped me off. For all of it.'

'Lewis Hampton. Your therapist?'

'Yes.'

'He swindled you out of your money?'

'Every cent. He talked me into investing in a real estate deal. It was a scam. As soon as I handed over my cheque he disappeared. So did my money.'

'Did this Lewis Hampton tell you he was in love with you?'

'Did a day go by when he didn't?'

'Did you love him?'

442

'I was nuts about him.'

'Miss Stanakis, what is your opinion now as to this so-called therapist, Lewis Hampton's, true feelings for you?'

'Jesus, the man was stringing me along, of course.'

'To what purpose?'

'It's obvious, isn't it? First he suggested I sue Dad. Then, after Dad ... after he died, Lewis ripped off my inheritance. Like I told you, the moment I parted with my money, he disappeared, along with my three and a half million. The office closed down the same day. I checked out their scheme. The land they claimed they were going to build on belonged to some woman living in New York City. She had never even *heard* of them.'

'I see. Let's hope Miss Stenner receives sounder investment advice,' Annie murmured, as a smiling aside. 'Returning to your therapy, did this man, Hampton, ever use a particular expression to describe what happened to you, your suddenly remembering your father's supposed outrages?'

Jill cackled, a nerve-jangling, high-pitched sound. 'Oh, sure! All the time. RMS! Recovered Memory Syndrome! I was making medical history!'

'What is your view now, with hindsight, of the events you "remembered"?'

'They were garbage! Totally bogus! As bogus as Lewis Hampton's real estate schemes. Dad never touched me in his life.'

'Miss Stanakis, you are only partially sighted, aren't you?'

'You could put it like that. I can tell night from day, see shapes. That's about all.'

'Were you always afflicted in that way, or did something happen to you that damaged your sight?'

'Something happened,' she said bitterly. 'After Lewis left I started drinking –'

Annie interrupted. 'You didn't drink before he swindled you?'

'I never touched the stuff. I was completely lost, didn't know what I was doing. He turned me into a bum, a skid row alcoholic. I would drink anything. Still will,' she added, with a laugh like broken glass. 'Somebody sold me some shit. Home-made wine, he said. I never knew what it really was, though. I woke up in some drying-out ward with my sight shot.'

'Who do you blame for what happened?'

She covered her face with her hands, massaging her eyes, before looking up. 'Lewis, I guess,' she said, almost timidly.

'So, one way or another, Lewis Hampton has always been very much on your mind?'

'Obviously.'

'If he were to stand in front of you now you wouldn't recognise him, because you wouldn't be able to see him well enough?'

'Of course not.'

'And, anyway, in these days of plastic surgery, a person can so significantly change their appearance their own mother might not know them, can't they?'

Jill was trembling again, her hands leaping and twitching on the edge of the box. 'I wouldn't know about that. If I could see, I'd recognise him, for sure, whatever he had done.'

'Because everything about him has remained fixed so firmly in your mind?'

'Every detail of the bastard!'

'Among those details, can you recall whether he owned a briefcase? And can you tell us anything about it?'

Jill frowned. 'Well, yes, he did. It was weird really, because he was kind of, well, more or less a hippy in

444

the way he looked. You know – long hair, beard, jeans, that kind of look to him. But he had this real expensive-looking bag. Red leather. Gucci, I think it was, or Cartier, one of those names, anyway. I remember kidding him about his rich man's toy. It seemed so out of character.'

'Unless he had already started developing expensive tastes, knowing he was about to *be* rich,' Annie said tartly. 'Is there anything about him that would still, if he were placed in front of you today, enable you to identify him, unequivocally?'

Jill hung her head, fighting for control as the muscles in her face worked. She held her tiny, angular fists pressed hard against her mouth, gnawing at the knuckles. When she looked up, tears were trickling down once more from behind the dark glasses. 'Yes,' she breathed. The tremulousness in her voice rendered the word barely intelligible. 'Yes,' she repeated louder. She paused, still fighting to master the leaping, unstrung muscles of her face.

Annie let her gaze roam momentarily around the courtroom. Matt was on the edge of his seat, his big hands on the rail, his head thrust forward. Up in the public seats Liz and Mark sat with their shoulders pressed together, their arms tight around each other. At the opposite end of the gallery Camilla sat hunched against the parapet. Her head seemed to have sunk between the gaunt shoulders. She had guessed where Annie's questioning was leading. The knowledge, spreading in her like a cancer, had drained the life from her face. The enlarged eyes were cupped in deep pockets of shadow, the cheekbones thrusting at the skin above the papery cheeks. Behind them, Naomi sat serene as a Buddha, a knowing half-smile playing on her lips.

Jill cleared her throat with a hacking rasp. 'His voice.

I'd know his voice anywhere. For the rest of my life.'

Moving a step closer to the pathetic, quaking figure, Annie spoke gently. 'Miss Stanakis, only one question, and then I shall have nothing more for you. Did you recognise the voice of the witness who appeared immediately before yourself, using the name of Stephen Letzer?'

She flashed Matt a glance, unable to keep the smile of triumph from her lips. Matt was almost off his seat, craning forward, his eyes riveted on Jill. Above and behind him Camilla's face was deathly white as she stared up into Letzer's face.

She swivelled back to look at Jill. She had straightened, momentarily, throwing off the stoop. Anguish and relief jostled in her face. She held her hands clutched to the sides of her head, her fingers cupped over her ears, as though trying to block out an hallucination. Her upper body twisted rhythmically from side to side as she fought to find a voice amid the emotion.

Matt's shirt clung to him, drenched with perspiration. He could feel the presence of his family above and behind him as though they were pressing at his sides.

Jill lowered her hands to the edge of the stand, clinging to it, white-knuckled, as though otherwise she would fall. 'I've never heard that voice before in my life.'

Twenty-Eight

Larry stared down into the hole, watching the cords of muscle work under the sweating, coppery skin of the man's shoulders as he drove the pickaxe again into the parched earth. The man pitched to his knees, crying out in language Larry did not know as, with a soft splintering sound, the pickaxe plunged in up to the shaft. The man scrambled to his feet and pulled back, retching.

At a curt word from Alvarez, another of the men ground out his cigarette and snatched up a can of gasoline. He drenched two squares of rag and passed one to the man in the hole. Tying the other round his own face, he lowered himself warily into the hole. Carefully, pulling back frequently to gulp fresh air, the two men began scraping away the earth, exposing the rotting pine planks.

Annie came down the steps, unblinking and silent, walking with a quick, jerky stride. Her face had drained to a sickly pallor, her lips were clamped in a tight line. Roy Erskine walked at her side. Abruptly, she reached out and clung to his arm, surprising him with the weight she put on him. He studied her profile for a moment before glancing back at Matt. An instant later he turned quickly away again, a faint light of realisation in his eyes.

Matt and Rachel flanked the tottering Jill while behind them Mark had thrown a protective arm around Liz's shoulders and was scowling through stinging eyes at the smirking gawpers, his free hand clenched, only Liz's hoarse, whispered exhortations curbing his urge to lash out.

Matt stumbled on the wide steps, almost as unseeing as Jill, the sounds of the crowd no more than a formless roar. His head felt as though it were being crushed by a giant hand. When he spoke, his words sounded trivial and foolish in his own ears.

'Where's the ambulance? We'd better get her back inside, out of this.'

Jill bridled at the tightening of the nurse's grip. 'Fuck that, Matt,' she rasped with a quiet emphasis that brought surprise to his face, as though he had only just learned that she could speak. 'Don't talk about me as if I were a piece of shit.' Too exhausted to sustain her indignation, her voice quavered again. 'It *wasn't* him,' she rasped. 'I *would* have told them. It's the truth.'

Matt drew a long breath. 'Sure.' He looped his arm brusquely around her waist. 'The ambulance is over there.'

She reached down and snatched his arm away. 'Shit, no! I did what I could in there. What was I supposed to do? Lie for you? Look at me!' She held up a shaking hand. 'Do you have any *idea* what I've been going through? What it felt like to sit there, waiting to hear *his* voice? You're not shoving me back in that ambulance like I was some piece of baggage. I want a drink, for God's sake. That was the deal.'

Matt looked questioningly at Liz. She was indifferent, still too lost in her own desolation to care. He turned away, sighing noisily. 'Ah, fuck. You're right, that *was* the deal, wasn't it? None of it matters a shit any more, anyway.' Ignoring Rachel's pinch-mouthed protest, he began propelling Jill towards the wrought-iron gates that shut off the court precinct from the street.

Camilla had thought she was going to faint. For perhaps a minute after Jill had rasped out the words she sat slumped forward in her seat, unable to move, every physical and mental process paralysed. Then, abruptly, the black, corrosive cloud of fear that had settled on her during Jill's testimony evaporated, leaving her as the centre of an almost unbearable brightness. Elation took hold of her as she sprang to her feet and ran from the court, brushing past the last straggling spectators who had hung back to stare at her. She ran down the steps, overtaking the group that pressed around her family without glancing back.

She reached the hotel, dishevelled and frantic, light-headed at the sense of having doubted and of seeing her doubts swept aside, dizzy with the need to show Stephen that her love was stronger than it had ever been. She ran down the short corridor and upstairs to her room. Without pausing an instant to allow the pounding of her heart to subside, she flung open the door and ran headlong into his arms.

Dawn was breaking, dimming the flashlights. Larry and Alvarez watched, expressionless, as the two men carefully prised the leg bones from the soft mess of humus and wood splinters. They laid them, still trailing fronds of rotting cloth, on the ground at Alvarez's feet.

Crouching, Larry and Alvarez examined them in the light of Alvarez's lamp. Sighing, the two of them rose slowly to their feet. They were about to turn away when, on an afterthought, Larry went back to the pit and spoke to one of the men.

Pulling on the pair of work gloves Alvarez handed him, Larry took the skull the workman proffered and

449

turned it over in his hands, examining it. With a soft grunt, he held it out to Alvarez.

In the pale light Larry saw the Mexican's eyes narrow and then widen in surprise. '*Conyo tu madre!*' he breathed, not taking his eyes from the skull as Larry set it gently beside the two dirt-smeared shin-bones and dropped the gloves next to them.

Matt hurried Jill towards the hotel with Liz and Mark at their heels. As he reached the doors he glanced around for Annie. She was fifty yards behind them, coming on slowly, still hanging on Roy Erskine's arm. He hesitated a moment, and then, feeling Jill's impatience, pushed inside.

By the time Annie and Roy joined them at the bar both Matt and Jill were ordering refills. Jill grabbed the second brandy the moment the barman set it in front of her and downed half of it at a swallow. She was shaking continuously. 'It wasn't him, Matt. I swear it wasn't. I'd know the voice anywhere. I would have said if it had been. You believe that, don't you?' Matt shook his head slowly and nodded to the barman to take her glass. 'Forget it, Jill,' he said in a gentle murmur, his voice cracking with weariness. His face was sagging, all the fatigue of the long months of battle in it. 'You did your best.'

Annie ordered a tonic water and shook her head, pointing at the glass he held to his lips. 'It's not over yet, Matt.'

He felt a pang of emotion at seeing her eyes reddened and swollen. His hand gripped Liz's. 'You don't have to bother, Annie. I'm going down for a long time, and you know it.'

Annie looked at her watch, and then to Roy, unable to keep the desperation completely from her face. 'There's still Larry.'

Matt laughed sardonically. 'Sure. So, we have the chief of police of some dead-beat Mexican town, a wide spot in the cocaine trail, faxing to say a body in one of their graves isn't who they thought it was. If Jill had . . . if it had worked, okay, it would have been another nail in the prosecution's coffin. Now, though . . . how does it help?'

Annie's eyes flickered to Liz's, reading the fierce love and loyalty that burned amid the devastation, and then she turned quickly away, biting her lip hard. 'It'll help, Matt,' she managed to whisper.

Stephen Letzer drew away reluctantly, letting his arms slide from around Camilla until his hands rested lightly on her hips. The sheer happiness in the eyes that smiled up at him made him swallow. 'Darling, I have to leave you alone for a few minutes. There's something I've got to do.'

Camilla's iridescent eyes fogged as she caught the nervousness in him. 'What is it?' She drew herself closer to him. 'What could be more important at this moment than being here, with me?'

Very gently, his brow drawn into a deep frown, he disengaged. 'Fifteen minutes, darling. I promise I'll be back then.' Impulsively, he took her head in his hands and kissed her hard. 'Back for good.' Abruptly, he spun and strode to the door. 'Fifteen minutes, sweetheart. Promise me you'll wait here for me?'

Misgiving and mystification wreathed her face as she nodded and watched the door slam behind him.

The group at the bar had fallen into an uncomfortable silence, like mourners. Matt and Jill were still drinking with single-minded concentration, a litter of glasses in front of them. As he drank Matt never relinquished his grip on Liz's hand. The ringing of Roy's phone

451

broke the mood, bringing Annie's head up sharply. 'Larry?'

Roy spoke his name into the phone. He listened in silence for a moment, the skin of his brow beneath the sharp widow's peak furrowing.

'There's no doubt, at all? No sense in getting, I don't know, some X-rays, or something?' He listened again, his face unmoving. 'Okay, Larry. You did a great job.' He looked slowly around at them, his eyes alighting on Jill, waiting for her to lower her glass. 'The tibia was broken in two places.' He reached out and touched her shoulder. 'Sorry, Jill. The dead man *is* Hampton.'

For a moment Jill seemed to freeze. Her glass fell with a crash back onto the bar.

Roy looked dourly at Annie. 'One puzzling thing, though. He was supposed to have run into a tree, right? Well, according to Larry, his skull had a massive fracture just here.' He chopped two fingers at the back of his own head, just above the spine. 'Larry, and the local police are pretty sure he was murdered.'

A spasm shook Jill. She clasped her stomach, her face contorting. 'Someone get me to a bathroom. I'm going to throw up.'

Mark and Liz each grabbed Jill by the arm and half carried, half dragged her towards the washrooms.

Matt watched them go, still stunned by the news, until he was brought round by a cry from Liz, followed by the sound of Jill's distress. Snatching a cloth from behind the bar, he sprinted to help.

Jill had collapsed and now sat slumped against the corridor wall, her head between her knees, heaving onto the greasy carpet. As he kneeled beside Liz, pressing the cloth to Jill's mouth, the sound of a man's raised voice reached him over her retching.

Frowning, letting Liz take the cloth, he pushed himself slowly to his feet and took a few robotic steps

452

deeper into the corridor, stopping in front of a door.

'No, she isn't!' Letzer's voice shook as though he were on the edge of tears. 'She's *not* a flake. She's a sweet, wonderful, wounded girl. I'm sorry. I guess you've known for a while now but I just wanted to tell you, so there's no misunderstanding. I can't go through with it. I love her. I don't *care* about her money, or her family's money, or anybody's. I just want to be *with* her.'

The others, alerted by the commotion, were at Matt's side now, watching transfixed as the doorknob rattled. As it began turning, a screech, a harsh, animal sound of rage and loss, came from inside the room. In the same moment the crash of a glass shattering against the door made the listeners flinch. The door was thrown back on its hinges and Letzer emerged at a run, his eyes wild, his face and hair flecked with foam from what must have been in the glass.

Matt lowered a shoulder and stepped into his path. Twenty-five pounds heavier than Letzer, Matt sent the man slamming into the wall where he lolled gasping, his arms folded across his chest, his mouth working soundlessly. He did not look at Matt. Instead he turned with hunted eyes back to the open door.

'You can't do this to me. Not after all I've put into this, not for her, Steve. She's a . . . girl. She's not what you need.' They watched in blank astonishment as Naomi appeared in the doorway and stepped towards Letzer, her eyes wild, locks of hair dangling over her face. Oblivious to their presence, she stabbed a finger at his face. 'You can't turn your back on all I've done for you. What were you until you met me?' Her voice was rising again.

Jill, unnoticed, was dragging herself to her feet using the wall for support. Her mouth was agape, her brows knitted in concentration.

Naomi went on speaking, her voice lower now, pulsing with a new tone of controlled contempt. 'I *made* you, you son of a bitch. I put you together like a kid's toy. I –'

'It's her!' Jill's jagged shriek cut the air.

Naomi fell abruptly silent. A strange look, half panic, half defiance, seeped slowly into her face.

Matt stared from Naomi to Jill. 'Who? Who is she?'

'The Henderson woman! Bea Henderson! She's the one that fronted Lewis's real estate deal! She's the bitch that ripped me off!'

Without another word Jill launched herself forward, her hands crooked into claws, flailing for Naomi's face as they collided and stumbled heavily to the floor.

Before Matt could catch Jill's windmilling wrists and haul her off, writhing and screaming, Naomi was already bleeding from a row of deep claw marks on her jaw. He dragged Jill to her feet and shook her. 'Jill, for Christ's sake! Talk to us. What do you think you're doing?'

'Doing? I'm tearing the bitch's eyes out, the way I always said I would. She's the one who took my cheque. Three and a half million.' As she spoke she tried to launch herself again at Naomi. Matt grappled her back, surprised at her strength.

'But, Jill,' Annie said quietly, stepping forward, 'this is Naomi. Naomi Butler. She was helping Camilla before Letzer even came on the scene.'

'I don't know what her real name is. Could be anything. But I know *that* voice for sure.' Abruptly, her own voice rose to a scream. 'Police! Get the police here! I'm telling you, this woman's a thief!'

Matt took her by the shoulders and shook her like a doll. 'Jill! For Christ's sake calm down.' He waved a soothing hand at the panicked barman, who had come running. 'It's okay. We all need to talk.' He turned to Letzer, who was still rubbing his chest. 'This your room?'

Letzer flapped a hand at the open door. 'Help yourselves.' He turned towards the stairs.

Matt's fingers clamped around his arm, yanking him backwards, almost throwing him bodily through the door. 'You, too.'

'Leave him alone.' They all spun at the voice. Camilla looked down from the landing, an arm outstretched in protest. Moments later she had thrown herself down the stairs and into Letzer's arms. 'What's happening, Stephen? Come away from them.' She made to drag him away towards the stairs.

Letzer took a step to follow her and then, with a soft exclamation, he took her hand and drew her back. He shook his head at her imploring look. 'No, darling. There *are* some things that need to be brought into the open. We'd better all go in here.' He led the way into the room.

Naomi tossed her head, smoothing the loose strands of hair back into place. 'The hell with that. I don't have to listen to any more of this ... *crone's* ... delusions.' She swung away and began to stride off down the corridor. Mark stepped into her path, a head taller than she. She began to sidestep. 'Step out of my ...' Her words trailed off as she looked up into his eyes, saw him on the very edge of violence. The defiance draining from her face, she shrugged and walked ahead of him into the bedroom.

Letzer sat slumped in a brocade-covered armchair. With one hand he still massaged his chest. With the other he stroked the hair of Camilla who knelt at his feet, her head in his lap. 'There's a lot to tell, darling. The thing to remember is that I love you. You're the only one I've ever –'

455

Naomi's harsh laugh cut him short. 'Oh shit! Love her? *Her?*' Her lips were white with anger as she looked around the room, rolling her eyes. 'Jesus, it makes me sick to look at him! You just watch the bastard in six months from now when he's sucked her trust fund dry. Then you'll see what a lover he is, the little dick-head.'

'Shut up!' Letzer almost screamed the words. He cradled Camilla's head in his arms. 'Just because you've never been able to think of anything but money!'

Naomi laughed again, a short contemptuous bark. 'Me? Yeah, well, fuck you. You were happy enough to help spend it when it was there.' Her voice rose to a new pitch of vengeful fury. 'Now you think you've figured out a way to have it all for yourself. You –' She broke off abruptly, a hand to her mouth. 'Fuck, I really *am* going to puke.' She ran the three strides to the bathroom, slamming the door shut.

Matt, his mind clogged with anger and bewilderment, hardly saw her go. He stepped forward to stand over Letzer, a trembling finger pushed into his face, his other fist bunched. 'I think you'd better start telling us exactly what the fuck you two have been doing, hadn't you?'

Annie stepped hurriedly forward and bundled Matt aside into Liz's arms. 'Calm down, Matt. This is no time for man-to-man crap. We want to keep you out of prison if we can, not invent new ways to get you in there.' She turned to Letzer. 'Don't you think you owe it to Camilla to tell us what in heaven's name's been going on?'

Letzer struggled straighter in his chair. His tongue darted back and forth over his lips. He looked imploringly down at Camilla and then at the bathroom door before opening his mouth to speak. Words failed him.

In the silence as he tried again to find the words he wanted, the sound of running water sounded suddenly loud.

Matt and Liz stared at each other in a moment of mute horror, the memory of Camilla's attempted suicide coming simultaneously to their minds. Without a word, Matt turned the handle and, in the same movement, flung his weight hard against the door. The bolt tore free and he staggered into the room.

Water gushed from both taps into the bath. Automatically, he stooped to turn them off before looking around him. The meanly proportioned room was an afterthought, partitioned from the bedroom with cheap studwork. It offered no corner in which a person could hide. The casement window above the lavatory creaked back on its hinges. He crossed the room in a single stride and leaned out. The gravelled car park was deserted.

Letzer sat straight, an arm tightly around Camilla, as the words came in an unstoppable flood. He had encountered Bea Henderson, the woman they had known as Naomi, at a personal development workshop in California. She was some years older than he, and already respected in her field. Within weeks of meeting her he was completely besotted, even though he knew she was already in a relationship.

'With Lewis Hampton?'

Letzer shrugged. 'I never knew anything, except that he was a therapist. She was very secretive about him, always telling me she was about to ditch him, except the moment never seemed quite right. For a long time I thought she was using me, just to make him jealous or something. I really didn't think she was serious about me at all.'

'And you?' Matt was leaning against the dressing table.

Letzer looked apprehensively at Camilla. She was gazing at him, her eyes aglow. With a flickering smile, he went on speaking. 'Me? Christ, I was nuts about her. Eating out of her hand. She could be a very attractive woman. She listened, made you feel important.' Annie's gaze flickered to meet Matt's. He held it for a moment, his eyes veiled, before looking back at Letzer. 'What she said was kind of true, you know. I *was* pretty much of a bum until I met her. I was adrift, on my own. Didn't know what I wanted.' He glanced down at Camilla, his arm tightening around her. 'At first she really did straighten me out, more or less bullied me into doing those courses. Made damned sure I finished them, too. Looking back, I guess I owe her a lot.'

'You must be the only person on the planet,' Matt muttered.

Letzer shrugged. 'Yeah? Well, anyway, Bea ... Naomi, she's a pretty, well, *overwhelming* person. I wouldn't have thought I would have let anyone do it, but she did, she just strung me along for maybe a couple of years, always managing to convince me she was on the brink. Then, one day, in the middle of the afternoon, she phones me, out of nowhere. She's going down to Mexico with him and then she's going to dump him. Starts giving me instructions, how I've got to drive down there, meet her at her hotel. I mustn't tell anybody where I'm going, nor let anybody see me hanging around the dead-beat little town.'

Matt grimaced. 'And *you* didn't think it was strange? You didn't ask why if she wanted to leave the guy she didn't just pack a bag and move into your place?'

He hung his head, looking down at the floor between his feet. 'Well, Bea ... that was kind of her way. She

458

wasn't like ordinary women. She always had a ... a *drama* about her.' He glanced nervously at Camilla, plainly afraid of her response. 'The way she told it we just had to take off, start a new life. Suddenly, she couldn't bear to stay in San Diego a day longer. I was too happy to ask questions.' He kicked at the carpet with his toe and glanced at Jill from under his brows. 'Ah shit, I knew she was planning something, that she and the guy she was with had been hoping to come into some big money. I just assumed she had gotten her hands on her share.'

'You bet,' Jill spat.

'Yeah, well. Look, I didn't know anything about it.'

'You didn't know she was planning to take *his* share, too?' Annie asked. 'And that she was planning to kill him to get it?'

Letzer looked in panic from Annie to Camilla and back. '*Kill* him? You took the wind out of my sails in court when you told me he was dead. She'd never told me. I asked her about it just now. She told me it was an accident. They'd had an argument over her leaving. He'd started trying to knock her around. While they were wrestling he'd run the car into the only tree for forty miles. She jumped and ran for it. She said she didn't know he was dead, either, until you brought it up in court.'

He looked round, his eyes wide with dismay at Roy's breezy laugh. 'Somebody got knocked around, but it sure wasn't your girlfriend. My associate helped exhume his body this morning. Somebody had stove in his skull with a rock. That was *before* they set the car on fire and burned his body to a cinder.'

Letzer's face turned the colour of dough. 'Jesus!' he murmured, his face bereft. Camilla pulled his head down onto her chest, murmuring soothing words. 'I *saw* it.' He passed a hand over his eyes. 'The fire. As

I was driving into La Santa that night. I saw a wreck burning. The police and a fire tender were just arriving.' He closed his eyes. 'Oh Jesus.'

An eerie, keening sound rose as Jill slumped against the wall and crumpled slowly on to the floor. Tears burst abruptly from her closed eyes, the keening dissolving in huge sobs. 'Oh fuck! Oh fuck! I *loved* him,' she wailed between sobs. 'I still loved that man.'

Liz kneeled quickly at her side and cradled her head. 'How about her money?' she asked, her lips stiff with anger. 'Can she have that back, at least?'

Letzer shook his head, sinking his teeth into his lower lip. 'It's gone,' he mumbled.

Matt took a step towards him, making him cower. 'Gone?' He looked down at the pathetic figure hunched on the floor. 'Three and a half million dollars? There must be *something* left. You can't have pissed it *all* away!'

Letzer groaned. 'It was Bea. Her schemes. It just went. That's why she wanted to do it again. It took a while before I realised what was going on.'

'But you went along anyway?' Matt's voice was larded with contempt. Letzer stayed silent, burying his head deeper against Camilla. When Matt spoke again it was in a whisper. 'How come you chose *us*?'

Letzer stood up and took a few cramped paces around the room. 'You weren't targeted. You were just the first case that came to us that fitted.'

Matt shook his head. 'But one thing I don't understand. Naomi was recommended by some serious people. How come they had such faith in her if it was all just a scam?'

His laugh was half bitter, half admiring. 'I was as surprised as you are. She used to advertise in magazines. Not far out stuff – *Country Life*, *Harpers*, that kind of thing. She used to laugh at how easy it was, how many people there are out there just waiting for someone to take money off them to tell them why they aren't happier. Fortune-telling, cults, personal awareness, it's all part of it. It was through her work in the hospital that Bea had cottoned on to the fact that eating disorders often meant abuse. From there it was a short step to blackmail.' He shrugged. 'That was our first idea with you. It was only when she found out about Camilla's trust fund that she got more ambitious. Then, when she started to suspect there was something between Camilla and me she returned to the blackmail idea. She wanted to take the money and run.'

Matt sneered. 'But you wanted to hold out for the jackpot?'

Letzer's head came up sharply. He swallowed, composing his face. His hand tightened on Camilla's. He took a deep breath. 'Sorry. You don't seem to understand. Bea was *right* about Camilla. What she claims about her suppressing her memory of abuse is *true.*'

Matt stiffened as the door from the jury room swung open. He glanced up to the gallery where people were crowding back, jostling for seats. Liz was already in the front row, clinging to Mark's arm. She gave him an effortful smile, the twenty-four sleepless hours since Letzer's confession etched deep in her face.

On hearing Letzer's story Annie's instincts had been to ask Davies to throw the case out. Matt, though, had been adamant. Nothing less than an acquittal by the jury would do. He had insisted Letzer be recalled to the witness box, obliged to tell his story in front of the world. He had not counted, despite Annie's warnings, on the eloquence of Barnes's closing speech. The jury had retired with his words still ringing in their ears, imploring them to accept that, whatever the motives of some of the witnesses, Camilla's diaries alone provided adequate testimony to Matt's guilt.

He sat immobile, studying the faces of the jury as they filed back into court. The fat woman, her stringy-haired neighbour, all of these people had spent the last two weeks being shown into the most private areas of his life. And yet to him, they remained ciphers. His efforts to imagine personalities for them during the long, tedious hours of expert testimony had failed hopelessly. They had no more existence for him than waxworks. Some smiled or muttered to each other as they took their seats. None looked at him.

The hush in the courtroom was so deep that the click of the clock ticking up the minute sounded obscenely loud. Matt's mouth was parched.

'Members of the jury, have you reached your verdict?'

'Yes.' The foreman's eyes remained fixed on the usher.

'On the charge of unlawful sexual intercourse with a child, knowing her to be his daughter, do you find the defendant guilty or not guilty?'

Matt stared into space. The silence seemed to stretch out, as though the jury were taking pleasure in extending his agony. He could hear the throb of his own heart, feel the blood surge in his temples.

'Not guilty.'

Matt fell back into his chair, his head buried in his hands, not even hearing the foreman as he intoned the same words in response to each of the charges. He could neither think nor speak. Not even tears would come, no elation, no relief. It was as though, in their turmoil, his emotions had grid-locked, leaving only the emptiness of total exhaustion. Not guilty. Spoken in a drab monotone, the words pealed and echoed with the

462

head-splitting force of bells inside his skull, their sheer volume drowning out all thought.

He had no idea how much time had passed before he became aware of the hubbub of voices, of the court emptying around him, the tension draining away as though a balloon had been pierced. There was pressure on his arm. He looked up stupidly to see the dock officer looking down, smiling, urging him to his feet. He descended the steps from the dock as though he were in pitch darkness, unsteady, his legs numb, not feeling the solidity beneath them. Somebody touched his sleeve. He looked round into Annie's face.

He made to embrace her. She kept her arms folded over the heap of folders she carried in front of her, so that the embrace was tentative and one-sided. Her head lifted subtly as he kissed her, letting his lips brush her cheekbone. With his arms still awkwardly around her he looked deep into her eyes. What he saw in the depths froze his heart. From somewhere he summoned a smile. 'Thanks, Annie.'

She stepped back, the movement just enough to take her out of his arms. 'Congratulations. You got the acquittal.' She paused almost imperceptibly. 'You got exactly what you wanted, didn't you?' She swallowed. Her eyes were moistening. With a jerk of her head, she indicated the gallery. 'Your family is waiting.' Without another word, she turned and walked quickly from the court.

Twenty-Nine

A single leaf fell from the vine and seesawed its way through the gaping French windows to settle on the floor. Sitting at the library desk, plucking another handful of unsorted photographs from the drawer, Matt was shocked to see how the leaf was already vivid with red and gold veining. In another three weeks the whole vine would be bare again.

He sorted the photographs into piles. Every once in a while Liz would come silently to his shoulder and pick up those he set to his left and cross to the grate where, one by one, she would release them to flutter into the guttering fire. The desk and chair were the only two items of furniture left in the room, though the fitted bookcases were still full. Paler patches on the matting revealed where the deep leather chairs, the button-back sofa, the half-dozen nice mahogany pieces, and the faded oriental rugs had already been carried off to the van. From somewhere upstairs they could hear one of the removal men singing.

Liz picked up the fresh mound of rejects and flipped carelessly through them. An eyebrow flickered in surprise. 'These, too?' She extracted a few pictures and fanned them for him to see. They were of Annie, taken several years earlier, emerging from the pool. She was laughing at the camera, arms raised in salute, her hair pulled back from her face by the weight of water in it.

He looked up at her, a faint uncertainty in his eyes. 'Do you want to keep them?'

She shrugged. 'Annie might.'

'I wouldn't have thought so. But do what you want. Have you got the address of the flat?'

She gave him a lop-sided smile. 'Yes. I wonder how she's finding it, living in Prague. And William. It must be very strange for him.'

Matt spread his hands. 'From his letters he sounded happy enough. After all, could it be stranger than living here with Roger for a father?'

'What's Roger going to do? He surely won't want to stay in that huge house alone.'

Matt took her hand. 'I couldn't give a toss about Roger.'

'And Naomi? What do you suppose will happen to her?'

'God knows. Maybe the Mexicans will get around to charging her. Who cares? It's *our* future I care about.'

Liz smiled wistfully as he touched his lips to the back of her hand. She was struck again by the gauntness of his face, by how little weight he had regained since the trial. 'Matt, do we *have* to sell? This house has been so *good* for us. There are just so many memories here. Couldn't we just live in France but keep it, let it, if you like, but not sell. In case one day we want to come back?'

He did not answer at once. Instead, he stared through the open windows at the sloping lawn and the fields beyond. Every night since the trial he had woken at three in the morning, soaked in sweat, shivering with panic. Until dawn he would lie there, not daring to get up, not wanting to disturb Liz, to have to fend off her worried questions. It was more than he could face to share with her the unspeakable doubts that nagged unceasingly at him.

Since the trial he had discreetly researched Naomi's testimony. Everything she had claimed about perpetrators suppressing the memory of abuse was

465

absolutely true. He had not once used the back stairs, passing within sight of Camilla's room, without the memory of the diaries, with their dark, anguished images, bringing a sickening upsurge of self-doubt. The house had become a torture chamber.

He looked up slowly, shaking his head. 'I'll never be able to write another word in this house. Do you want to finish burning those?'

She hesitated a moment longer and then, nodding, turned to the hearth.

She was still letting the pictures trickle into the fire, taking care not to choke the flames, when the sound of a car in the courtyard made them jerk sharply around to face each other. They exchanged edgy, uncertain smiles. Liz sent the last photos spinning into the flames and, after one last tremor of hesitation, almost ran out into the hall.

Letzer was already out of the battered Volvo and running around to Camilla's side. He heaved at the door, yanking it open to allow her to climb out. He closed the door carefully, and turned to run to Camilla's side as she advanced warily towards the house.

Liz and Camilla broke ranks in almost the same instant, running to fall into each other's arms. For a full half-minute they stayed like that, neither of them uttering a coherent word. Camilla was the first to disengage, gradually unfurling her mother's arms from her neck and stepping back. She flipped a hand nervously at Letzer, who hung three yards behind her. 'I asked Stephen to come. I hope . . .' She trailed off, directing a quick, nervous glance at the house.

Liz stepped forward. 'Well, you're here,' she said, pointlessly. 'Let's go in.'

The silence hung heavily on them as they filed into the house. Rachel, whom the sound of the car had brought from her self-appointed task of supervising the removal men, leaned over the banisters to watch, purse-mouthed, as they filed into the library.

Camilla stopped just inside the door. Matt was standing by the fireplace, staring at the few yellow flames that licked among the flaky grey ash. A shadow passed behind her eyes as she took in the bare room. 'Hello.' She spoke barely loudly enough for it to carry.

Matt spun to face her, knowing his attempt to feign surprise was a transparent, clumsy charade. He stood for a moment tongue-tied, his mouth parched, his tongue like cloth. The 'Hello' he finally managed was a scorched croak. He shifted his balance, swept by the urge to run to her. Then, seeing her stiffen, he averted his eyes, waggling a foot awkwardly, shaking the intent from his muscles. His gaze falling on Letzer, at her shoulder, he moved his lips. The sound fell on his own ears somewhere between a grunt and a greeting. The ashes settled in the grate, sounding loud in the taut silence.

'The car not let you down?' He felt foolish, dismayed at his own banality.

Camilla fought back the urge to cry, hardly able to bear the spectacle of her father, who had for so long seemed so magnificent, so reduced. Letzer came to her rescue, moving to her side. He shrugged, his mouth twisting in a wry smile. 'Not so far. But then we've hardly been anywhere. We're both too busy studying.'

Matt nodded, too hard. 'Good. Great. And the flat? Not too cramped, after what, what you've both been used to?'

Camilla found Letzer's hand. 'It's not a flat, Daddy. It's a room. It's fine.' Her glance into Letzer's face sent a dart into Matt's heart. 'It's all we need.'

Matt nodded. His words came in a rush. 'Look, you know you don't have to . . . I know you might not want

. . . not from *us*, but there's the trust. For God's sake, you don't . . .'

He broke off, disconcerted by their silence. Then he ploughed on, pleading. 'At least get yourselves a decent *car*! It's starting to get foggy. Christ, I *hate* the idea of Camilla breaking down some night, slogging along the hard shoulder in the rain.' He choked up again as his words brought the moment flooding back with perfect clarity, the start of the nightmare, Camilla standing at the door, shivering in her saturated clothes, her hair plastered to her skull. 'It drives me crazy,' he whispered.

Letzer raised a hand and let it fall back to his side. 'Thanks again. But Camilla already told . . .' He paused, looking round at Liz, seeking for the word that would fit the new relationship. '. . . Liz . . . that we were okay. We can work it out just fine.'

From the doorway, behind them, Liz crooked a finger, beckoning to Matt. He nodded. 'Whatever suits you. Look, we were just going to take a walk around the grounds, for old times' sake. So you just take your own time.' He waved a hand vaguely around the room. 'There's just what's in here.' His eyes settled on Camilla. 'And your bedroom. The men just need an address,' he added, his voice thinning. He strode past them, taking Liz by the arm.

Camilla began browsing slowly along the bookshelves, examining the spines. Every so often, alighting on one that interested her, she would pull it out and peruse it briefly before placing it on a growing pile at her feet. For some time Stephen Letzer sat contentedly watching her, sitting propped against a wall, his legs out-stretched. At length, as the pile of books slowly grew, he rose and wandered to the desk where he began poking idly through the scattered photographs.

While Camilla went on selecting books he became engrossed in the photographs, entranced by this glimpse into Camilla's past.

The two of them concentrated utterly, the silence broken only by Rachel's appearances with coffee, or cakes, or on half a dozen other pretexts, or by Letzer occasionally calling for Camilla to identify the subjects of the photographs. Half an hour had passed before he held up a picture. 'Who's that?'

Camilla narrowed her eyes, moving closer until she was at his side, a hand on his shoulder. Reflexively, he took her fingers in his as she stared dreamily at the photograph. Outside a breeze stirred, rustling the vine leaves. The sound of a mower somewhere in the garden died abruptly. The voices of Matt and Liz drifted lazily into the room, along with the scent of the cut grass.

The photograph was of a man standing in the doorway to a log-built cabin, framed by a thick growth of honeysuckle and clematis trained over a trellis. A boy balanced precariously on the man's shoulders, holding on by tucking his feet into his armpits. The boy was laughing uproariously, his head entangled among the flowers. A young girl, her face half hidden in shadow, held the man by the hand. 'That's Mark, isn't it? And is that you?' She murmured something which he took to be yes. 'Where was it taken? Not here?'

'Mmm. Yes. That's the cottage.' Her voice had become distant, as though she were back in that long-ago summer.

'Who's that guy with you? Not your father?'

'No. That's Patrick.' She looked at his face, narrower than her father's, strong teeth glinting as he clenched his pipe, laughing around it for the camera. 'Uncle Patrick.'

'The one who died?'

'Yes. My husband. The one who left her the money.'

Rachel's voice made Letzer swivel. Rachel bent closer. She gulped loudly. 'He loved this house, you know.' She spoke to Letzer, the first time she had addressed him directly, as though it were a form of induction into the family. 'Absolutely doted on these two children. After . . . after I had my . . . problems, they were all he ever talked about. He couldn't do enough for them. They were a substitute family for him in a lot of ways.' She began to sob, her breath coming in great lumpy gasps. 'He was such a *lovely* man. So *unselfish*!' She fumbled in the pocket of her skirt for a tissue. 'He never . . . bothered . . . me, after my trouble.' She hurried from the room, sobbing brokenly.

Letzer looked up into Camilla's face, starting to grin. At the sight of her the grin dissolved.

All the colour had drained from her face. She was staring, transfixed, at the picture. Above Patrick's grinning mouth, his eyes were strangely still. Although Mark was laughing wildly, her own face was as unsmiling as a corpse's, her eyes not looking at the camera but cast to the ground.

'Camilla? What's the matter?' His eyes switched, disconcerted, from Camilla to the picture.

Camilla went on staring. In his free hand Patrick held a bulbous brandy glass. Even in the shadows it was possible to see that it was slopping to the brim. The familiar pipe was clenched in the gleaming smile. Remembered smells stirred in her, seemed to fill her being. She lifted her head. 'Daddy,' she called, in a chilling, strangled gasp. 'Daddy! Come here! Quickly!'

With Liz at his heels Matt raced through the open French window and stopped short, reaching instinctively for Liz's hand. Mark, who had been skulking in his room determined not to see Letzer, appeared, panting, in the hall doorway. Camilla had sunk to her

470

knees, still staring at the picture. Letzer crouched beside her, cupping her hand in his, repeating her name over and over, mopping the tears that poured down her face.

Matt stepped forward and plucked the picture from Camilla's unresisting fingers.

Realisation, when it came, struck him like a hammer. Panic seized him. He clutched a hand to his chest, staggering back to lean against the fireplace. Liz took a hesitant step towards him, looking from him to Camilla, uncertain who needed her most.

Matt was gasping, could hardly breathe. The memory seemed to be crushing his chest. It was five o'clock in the morning, already lightening, the dawn of a summer's day. Birdsong was already flooding through the wide open windows. Annie's stealthy departure had woken him. Lying there, in the dishevelled bed, still damp and fragrant from their lovemaking, he was roused by a noise downstairs. Thinking Annie had returned for something she had forgotten, already tumescent with renewed desire, he had crept down to surprise her. Instead of Annie, he had come upon Patrick, padding hurriedly across the hall to the terrace door, his dressing gown hanging loose.

Matt had been disappointed but not surprised. After Rachel's miscarriage she had not wanted to go on living in their own house, unable to stand the memory of the lovingly prepared nursery. They had been living in the guest cottage while they found somewhere else.

On seeing Matt, Patrick had seemed startled, mumbling incoherently about retrieving a book from the library, although he was empty-handed. He had staggered a little, and belched furtively. Matt had thought no more of it, beyond the sadness that came with the reminder that, since Rachel's disastrous miscarriage, and the loss of interest in sex that had followed it,

Patrick had been drunk more or less through the day. Without giving any further thought to it, Matt had made coffee and taken it up to drink in bed, returning by the back staircase, past the children's rooms.

He groaned aloud now, a harsh, anguished sound that made Liz exclaim fearfully and run to his side, as the remembered smells rushed in on him, filling his nostrils. The stink of tobacco and stale brandy.

A few months later, just long enough to have set up the trust, Patrick had driven off the quayside at Portsmouth, the car locked from the inside and two empty cognac bottles for company.

Matt pushed himself upright, shaking his head like a groggy fighter. Putting an arm round Liz's shoulders, he held the picture out in front of them. 'Patrick,' he mumbled. He gave a sudden mirthless laugh. 'Patrick! Oh shit! My brother!' He began to cry. With the tears coursing down his face he stepped past Liz and, stooping, lifted Camilla gently to her feet.

For a long instant they simply looked into each other's faces. Then, without a word, Camilla stepped forward and flung herself into Matt's arms.

As Liz, too, burst into tears, Mark ran across the room to throw himself into her arms. The two of them remained clamped together for some seconds before moving to join the others so that the four of them formed a tight knot, weeping and laughing together.

As the first release of emotion subsided, Matt slowly raised his head to find Stephen Letzer hovering apprehensively at his elbow. For a moment the two men eyed each other warily. Then, without a word, Matt reached out to take Letzer's hand. He hesitated a moment longer and then gave it a stiff, formal shake.

By the time their tears had almost ceased, Matt felt as though he were floating, enveloped in a delicious

sense of repose. The busy clack of Rachel's he...
she hurried from some distant part of the house pe...
trated his euphoria. After an enquiring look at Liz, an...
her brief nod, he stepped across to the fireplace and
dropped the photograph into the fire. It curled and
writhed in the heat. As Rachel appeared in the doorway, her face petulant and puzzled, it popped softly
into yellow flame.